Praise for *New York Times* bestselling author Nalini Singh

'Nalini Singh is a major new talent'
#1 *New York Times* bestselling author Christine Feehan

'Her books are gems, true treasures . . . that just get better and better'
Romance Reviews Today

'A writer that will no doubt shine for some time'
Romance Reader at Heart

'This book is a must even for those uninitiated in the paranormal genre. The story ends much too quickly, and the author's magical writing conjures up sensual images and intense emotions that linger long after the last word is read'
Romantic Times

'Sexy, crisp, hard-edged and intelligent, *Slave to Sensation* is a terrific book . . .'
Bookpage

Also by Nalini Singh

Psy-Changeling Series

Slave to Sensation

Visions of Heat

Caressed by Ice

Mine to Possess

Hostage to Pleasure

Branded by Fire

Blaze of Memory

Guild Hunter Series

Angels' Blood

Archangel's Kiss

NALINI SINGH

First published in Great Britain in 2010 by
Gollancz
An imprint of the Orion Publishing Group
Orion House, 5 Upper St Martin's Lane, London WC2H 9EA
An Hachette UK Company

1 3 5 7 9 10 8 6 4 2

A CIP catalogue record for this book is available
from the British Library

ISBN 978 0 575 09570 0

Printed in Great Britain by Clays Ltd, St Ives plc

www.nalinisingh.com

www.orionbooks.co.uk

CARESSED BY ICE

ARROWS

Mercury was a cult. That was what everyone said at the start. The Psy laughed at Catherine and Arif Adelaja's claims of being able to free their people from insanity and murderous fury.

To be Psy was to court the edges of madness.

It was accepted.

There was no cure.

But then Mercury produced two graduates of their early version of the Silence Protocol—the Adelajas' own twin sons. Tendaji and Naeem Adelaja were as cool as ice, their emotions holding nothing of anger or madness . . . for a while. The experiment eventually failed. The dark side of emotion rushed back into the Adelaja twins in an avalanche, and, sixteen years after being heralded as the harbingers of a new future, they committed suicide. Tendaji, the strong one, killed Naeem then himself. There was no doubt that it had been a mutual decision.

They left a note.

We are an abomination, a plague that will kill our people from within. Silence must never take root, must never infiltrate the PsyNet. Forgive us.

Their words were never heard, their terror never understood. Found by acolytes of Mercury, they were buried in a hidden grave, their deaths termed an accident. By then, Mercury had begun training a second generation, improving their technique, refining the tools with which to excise unwanted emotion from the heart and madness from the soul. The most important change was the quietest—this time, they had the cautious support of the leaders of their people, the Psy Council.

But they also needed support of another kind, the kind that would catch any other lapses and mistakes before they made it to the public domain . . . and to the ears of the still-skeptical Council. If the Councilors had found out about the continuing deaths, they would have pulled back. And the Adelajas could not bear the thought of their vision being consigned to the trash heap of history. Because, though shattered by the deaths of their twin sons, Catherine and Arif never lost faith in Silence. Neither did their eldest son—Zaid.

Zaid was a cardinal telepath with a furious ability in mental combat. He, too, had trained under Silence, but as a young adult, not a child. Still, he believed. The Protocol had given him peace from the demons of his mind and he wanted to spread that gift of peace, to quiet the torment of his people. So he began cleaning up the mistakes, wiping away those who broke under the experimental versions of Silence, burying their lives as efficiently as he buried their bodies.

Catherine called him her Martial Arrow.

Soon, Zaid recruited others like him. Others who believed. They were loners, unknown shadows, darker than the darkness, men and women whose sole aim was to eliminate anything that might threaten the successful realization of Catherine and Arif's lifelong dream.

Time passed. Years. Decades. Zaid Adelaja was washed from this Earth, but the torch of the Arrows continued to be handed from one acolyte to the next . . . until there was no more Mercury and the long-dead Adelajas were being hailed as visionaries.

The Silence Protocol was implemented in the year 1979.

The Psy Council was unanimous in its vote, the masses divided, but the majority in favor. Their people were killing each other and themselves with rage and inhumanity unseen in any of the other races. Silence seemed their only hope, their only solution for a lasting peace. But would they have taken that step had they read Tendaji and Naeem's last words? There is no one left who can answer that question.

As no one can answer why a protocol meant to bring peace also brought with it the coldest, most dangerous kind of violence—rumors of the Arrow Squad spawned on the heels of the implementation process, fed by the fear of minds going under Silence. It was said that those who protested too hard had a habit of simply disappearing.

Now, in the final months of the year 2079, the Arrows are a myth, a legend, their existence or nonexistence debated endlessly in the PsyNet. To the naysayers, the post-Silence Psy Council is a perfect creation, one that would never do anything as underhanded as create a secret squad to take care of its enemies.

But others know differently.

Others have seen the dark streaks of highly martial minds shooting through the Net, felt the cold chill of their psychic blades. But of course, these others cannot speak. Those who come into contact with the Arrow Squad rarely live to tell the tale.

The Arrows themselves do not heed the rumors, do not consider their secret army a death squad. No, they have remained true to their founding father. Their only loyalty is to the Silence Protocol and they are dedicated to its continuance.

Executions are sometimes unavoidable.

CHAPTER 1

A fist crashed into Judd's cheekbone. Focused on eliminating his opponent from the field, he barely noticed the impact, his own fist already swinging out. Tai tried to evade the blow at the last second but it was too late—the young wolf's jaw slammed together with a thick sound that spoke of damage on the inside.

But he wasn't down.

Baring teeth stained red from a cut on his top lip, he rushed at Judd, clearly aiming to use his heavier build as a battering ram to smash his adversary into the hard stone wall. Instead it was Tai who ended up with his back slammed against the stone, his mouth falling open as air punched out of his lungs in an uncontrollable blast.

Judd gripped the other male by the throat. "Killing you would mean nothing to me," he said, tightening his hold until Tai had to be having trouble breathing. "Would you like to die?" His tone was calm, his breathing modulated. It was a state of being that had nothing to do with feeling, because unlike the changeling across from him, Judd Lauren did not feel.

Tai's lips shaped into a curse, but all that materialized was an incomprehensible wheezing sound. To a casual observer it would have seemed that Judd had gained the advantage, but he didn't make the mistake of lowering his guard. So long as Tai hadn't conceded defeat, he remained dangerous. The other male proved that a second later by using the changeling ability to semishift—slicing up hands turned to claws.

Those sharp talons cut through leather-synth and flesh without effort, but Judd didn't give the boy a chance to cause him any real injury. Pressing down on a very specific pressure point in Tai's neck, he slammed his erstwhile opponent into unconsciousness. Only when the changeling was completely out did he release his hold. Tai slumped down into a seated position, head hanging over his chest.

"You're not supposed to use Psy powers," a husky female voice said from the doorway.

He had no need to turn to identify her but did so anyway. Extraordinary brown eyes in a fine-boned face topped by a choppily cut cap of blonde hair. Those eyes had been normal and that hair hadn't been short before Brenna had been abducted. By a killer. By a Psy.

"I don't need to use my abilities to deal with little boys."

Brenna walked to stand beside him, her head just reaching his breastbone. He had never realized how small she was until he'd seen her after the rescue. Lying in that bed, scarcely breathing, her energy had been contracted into a ball so tight, he hadn't been sure she was still alive. But her size meant nothing. Brenna Shane Kincaid, he had learned, had a will of pure, undiluted iron.

"That's the fourth time this week you've been in a fight." Her hand rose and he had to stop himself from jerking away. Touch was a changeling thing—the wolves indulged in it constantly and without thought. For a Psy it was an alien concept, something that could ultimately foster a dangerous loss of control. But Brenna had been broken by an evil spawned of his own race. If she needed touch, so be it.

Faint imprints of heat on his cheek. "You'll have a bruise. Come on, let me put something on it."

"Why aren't you with Sascha?" Another renegade Psy, but

a healer not a killer. Judd was the one who had blood on his hands. "I thought you had a session with her at eight p.m." It was now five past the hour.

Those stroking fingers slid to linger on his jaw before dropping off. Her lashes lifted. And revealed the change that had taken hold five days after her rescue. Eyes that had once been dark brown were now a mix he'd never seen on any sentient being—human, changeling, or Psy. Brenna's pupils were pure black, but surrounding those dots of night were bursts of arctic blue, vivid and spiking. They jagged out into the dark brown of the iris, giving her eyes a shattered look.

"It's over," she said.

"What is?" He heard Tai moan but ignored it. The boy was no threat—the only reason Judd had allowed him to land any of his punches was because he understood the way wolf society worked. Being beaten in a fight was bad, but not as bad as being beaten without putting up a solid resistance.

Tai's feelings made no difference to Judd. He had no intention of assimilating into the changeling world. But his niece and nephew, Marlee and Toby, also had to survive in the network of underground tunnels that was the SnowDancer den, and his enemies might become theirs. So he hadn't humiliated the boy by ending the fight before it began.

"Is he going to be alright?" Brenna asked, when Tai moaned a second time.

"Give him a minute or two."

Glancing back at him, she sucked in a breath. "You're bleeding!"

He stepped away before she could touch his shredded forearms. "It's nothing serious." And it wasn't. As a child he had been subjected to the most excruciating pain and then been taught to block it. A good Psy felt nothing. A good Arrow felt even less.

It made it so much easier to kill people.

"Tai went clawed." Brenna's face was furious as she glared down at the male slumped against the wall. "Wait till Hawke hears—"

"He won't hear. Because you won't tell him." Judd didn't

need protecting. If Hawke had known what Judd truly was, what he had done, what he had *become*, the SnowDancer alpha would have taken him out at their first meeting. "Explain your comment about Sascha."

Brenna scowled but didn't press him about the scratches on his arm. "No more healing sessions. I'm done."

He knew how badly she'd been brutalized. "You have to continue."

"No." A short, sharp, and very final word. "I don't want anyone in my head again. *Ever*. Sascha can't get in anyway."

"That makes no sense." Sascha had the rare gift of being able to speak as easily to changeling minds as to Psy. "You don't have the capacity to block her."

"I do now—something's changed."

Tai coughed to full wakefulness and they both turned to watch him as he used the wall to drag himself upright. Blinking several times after getting vertical, he lifted a hand to his cheek. "Christ, my face feels like a truck ran into it."

Brenna's eyes narrowed. "What the hell did you think you were doing?"

"I—"

"Save it. Why did you come after Judd?"

"Brenna, this is none of your concern." Judd could feel blood drying on his skin, the cells already clotting. "Tai and I have come to an understanding." He looked the other male in the eye.

Tai's jaw set, but he nodded. "We're square."

And their relative status in the pack's hierarchy had been clarified beyond any shadow of a doubt—if Judd's rank hadn't already been higher, he'd now be dominant to the wolf.

Shoving a hand through his hair, Tai turned to Brenna. "Can I talk to you about—"

"No." She cut him off with a wave of her hand. "I don't want to go with you to your college dance. You're too young and too idiotic."

Tai swallowed. "How did you know what I was going to say?"

"Maybe I'm Psy." A dark answer. "That's the rumor going around, isn't it?"

Streaks of red appeared on Tai's cheekbones. "I told them they were talking shit."

This was the first that Judd had heard of the clearly malicious attempt to cause Brenna emotional pain and it was the last thing he would have predicted. The wolves might make vicious enemies, but they were also fiercely protective of their own and had closed ranks around Brenna as soon as she'd been rescued.

He looked at Tai. "I think you should go."

The young wolf didn't argue, sliding past them as quickly as his legs would carry him.

"Do you know what makes it worse?" Brenna's question shifted his attention from the boy's retreating footsteps.

"What?"

"It's true." She turned the full power of that shattered blue-brown gaze on him. "I'm different. I see things with these damn eyes he gave me. Terrible things."

"They're simply echoes of what happened to you." A powerful sociopath had ripped open her mind, raped her on the most intimate of levels. That the experience had left her with psychic scars was unsurprising.

"That's what Sascha said. But the deaths I see—"

A scream ripped the moment into two.

They were both running before it ended. A hundred feet down a second tunnel, they were joined by Indigo and a couple of others. As they turned a corner, Andrew came tearing around it and clamped his hand on Brenna's upper arm, jerking his sister to a halt and raising his free hand at the same time. Everyone stopped.

"Indigo—there's a body." Andrew snapped out the words like bullets. "Northeast tunnel number six, alcove forty."

Brenna wrenched out of her brother's hold the second he finished and took off without warning. Having caught the unhidden blaze of her anger before she'd quickly masked it, Judd was the first to move after her. Indigo and a furious Andrew followed at his back. Most Psy would have been overtaken by now, but he was different, a difference that had predestined his life in the PsyNet.

Brenna was a streak in front of him, moving with impressive speed for someone who had been confined to a bed only months ago. She'd almost reached the number six tunnel when he caught up. "Stop," he ordered, his breathing not as ragged as it should have been. "You don't need to see this."

"Yes, I do," she said on a gasping breath.

Putting on a burst of speed, Andrew grabbed her from the back, linking his arms around her waist to lift her off her feet. "Bren, calm down."

Indigo raced past, a flash of long legs, dark hair streaming behind her.

In Andrew's grip, Brenna began to twist furiously enough to cause herself harm. Judd couldn't allow that. "She'll calm down if you set her free."

Brenna jerked to a stop, chest heaving and eyes surprised. Andrew wasn't so silent. "I'll take care of my sister, *Psy*." The last word was a curse.

"What, by locking me up?" Brenna asked in a razor-sharp tone. "I'm never going to be put in a box again, Drew, and I swear if you try, I'll claw my hands bloody getting out." It was a mercilessly graphic image, especially for anyone who had seen the condition she'd been in after they had first found her.

Behind her, Andrew paled, but his jaw remained set. "This is what's best for you."

"Perhaps it's not," Judd said, meeting Andrew's angry eyes without flinching. The SnowDancer soldier blamed all Psy for his sister's pain and Judd could guess at the line of emotion-driven logic that had led him to that conclusion. But those same emotions also blinded him. "She can't spend the rest of her life in chains."

"What the fuck would you know about anything?" Andrew snarled. "You don't even care about your own!"

"He knows a hell of a lot more than you!"

"Bren." Andrew's voice was a warning.

"Shut up, Drew. I'm not a baby anymore." Her voice held echoes of darker things, of evil witnessed and innocence lost.

"Did you ever stop to wonder what Judd did for me during the healing? Did you ever bother to find out what it cost him? No, of course not, because you know everything."

She took a jerky breath. "Well, guess what, you know nothing! You haven't been where I've been. You haven't even been close. *Let. Me. Go.*" The words were no longer enraged but calm. Normal for a Psy. *Not* for a wolf changeling. Especially not for Brenna. Judd's senses went on high alert.

Andrew shook his head. "I don't care what the hell you say, little sister, you don't need to see that."

"Then I'm sorry, Drew." Brenna slashed her claws across his arms a split second later, shocking her brother into letting her go. She was moving almost before her feet hit the ground.

"Jesus," Andrew whispered, staring after her. "I can't believe . . ." He looked down at his bloody forearms. "Brenna never hurts *anyone*."

"She's not the Brenna you knew anymore," Judd told the other male. "What Enrique did to her altered her on a fundamental level, in ways she herself doesn't understand." He took off after Brenna before Andrew could reply—he had to be beside her to deflect the fallout from this death. What he couldn't understand was why she was so determined to see it.

He caught up with her as she raced past a startled guard and into the small room off tunnel number six. She came to such a sudden halt that he almost slammed into her. Following her gaze, he saw the sprawled body of an unknown SnowDancer male on the floor. The victim's face and naked body bore considerable bruising, the skin splotched different colors by the damage. But Judd knew that that wasn't what held Brenna frozen.

It was the cuts.

The changeling had been sliced very carefully with a knife, none of the cuts fatal but the last. That one had severed the carotid artery. Which meant there was something wrong with this scene. "Where's the blood?" he asked Indigo, who was crouching on the other side of the body, a couple of her soldiers beside her.

The lieutenant scowled at seeing Brenna in the room but answered, "It's not a fresh kill. He was dumped here."

"Out-of-the-way room." One of the soldiers, a lanky male named Dieter, spoke up. "Easy to get to without being spotted if you know what you're doing—whoever did this was smart, probably chose the location beforehand."

Brenna sucked in a breath but didn't speak.

Indigo's scowl grew. "Get her the hell out of here."

Judd didn't follow orders well, but he agreed with this one. "Let's go," he said to the woman standing with her back to him.

"I saw this." A faint whisper.

Indigo stood, an odd look on her face. "What?"

Brenna began to tremble. "I saw this." The same reedy whisper. "I saw this." Louder. "I saw this!" A scream.

Judd had spent enough time with her to know that she would hate having lost control in front of everyone. She was a very proud wolf. So he did the only thing he could to slice through her hysteria. He moved to block her view of the body and then he used her emotions against her. It was a weapon the Psy had honed to perfection. "You're making a fool of yourself."

The icy cold words hit Brenna like a slap. *"Excuse me?"* She dropped the hand she'd raised to push him aside.

"Look behind you."

She remained stubbornly still. Hell would freeze over before she obeyed an order from him.

"Half the den is sniffing around," he told her. Pitiless. Psy. "Listening to you break down."

"I am not breaking down." She flushed at the realization of so many eyes on her. "Get out of my way." She didn't want to look at the body anymore—a body that had been mutilated with the same eerie precision Enrique had used on his victims—but pride wouldn't let her back down.

"You're being irrational." Judd didn't move. "This place is obviously having a negative impact on your emotional stability. Step back out." It was a definite command, his tone so close to alpha it set her teeth on edge.

"And if I don't?" She gladly embraced the anger he'd awakened—it gave her a new focus, a way to escape the nightmare memories triggered by this room.

Cool Psy eyes met hers, the male arrogance in them breathtaking. "Then I'll pick you up and move you myself."

At the response, exhilaration burst to life in her bloodstream, chasing away the last acrid tang of fear. Months of frustration—of watching her independence being buried under a wall of protection, of being told what was best for her, of having her rationality questioned at every turn, all that and more snowballed into this single instant. "Try it." A dare.

He stepped forward and her fingertips tingled, claws threatening to release. Oh yeah, she was definitely ready to tangle with Judd Lauren, Man of Ice, and the most beautiful male creature she had ever seen.

CHAPTER 2

"**Brenna**, what are you doing here?" The sharp question was bitten out in a familiar voice. Lara didn't wait for an answer. "Move aside, you're blocking the doorway."

Startled, Brenna did as ordered. The SnowDancer healer and one of her assistants slid past, portable medical kits in hand.

Judd moved when she did, continuing to obstruct her view of the body. "This room is getting crowded. Lara needs space to work."

"He's dead." Brenna knew she was being unreasonable, but she was sick of being pushed around. "She can hardly help him now."

"And what do you intend to achieve by remaining here?" A simple question that highlighted her ridiculous behavior with cool Psy precision.

Hands curling against the urge to strike out at this male who always seemed to catch her at her weakest, she turned and walked out. Packmates glanced at her curiously as she passed. More than one wore a look of judgment—poor Brenna had finally snapped. It was tempting to walk past without meeting their gazes, but she forced herself to do the opposite. She'd had her self-respect stolen from her once. She would not relinquish it ever again.

Several pairs of eyes shifted away at being caught staring, while others continued to watch her, unblinking. Had the circumstances been different, she would've taken their intransigence as a challenge, but today, she just wanted to get away from the overwhelming *dead* scent of the body. However, that urgency didn't blind her to the fact that even the boldest of them dropped their stares after looking past her shoulder.

"I don't need you to fight my battles," she said, after they cleared the crowd.

Judd moved to walk beside her, no longer a shadow at her back. "I wasn't aware I was doing so."

She had to concede he was probably telling the truth—most people in the den were simply too scared of Judd Lauren to want to draw his attention under any circumstances. "You saw the cuts." She could still smell the odor of death mingled with the metallic edge of blood. "They were just like *his*." The sharp gleam of a scalpel flickered in her mind. An image of spurting blood. Screams ringing against the walls of a cage.

"They weren't identical."

His cool response pulled her out of the nightmare chaos of memory. "Why do you sound so certain?"

"I'm Psy. I understand patterns."

Dressed in black and with those emotionless eyes, there was no doubt he was Psy. As for the rest . . . "Don't try to convince me that all Psy would've been able to process the details so quickly. You're different."

He didn't bother to confirm or deny. "That doesn't change the facts. The cuts on this victim—"

"Timothy," she interrupted, a rock in her throat. "His name was Timothy." She had known the fallen SnowDancer only in passing, but couldn't bear to have him being reduced to nothing more than a nameless victim. He'd had a life. A name.

Judd glanced at her, then gave a small nod. "Timothy was killed using the same type of method, but the details are different. The biggest being that he was male."

And Santano Enrique, the bastard who'd tortured Brenna and killed so many others, had taken exclusively women. Because he'd liked to do certain things, things that required a woman's— Brenna shoved the memories back into the locker inside her mind where she kept the darkest, filthiest pieces of what he had done to her. "You think someone's copying him?" The idea made her gorge rise. Even dead, the butcher's evil continued.

"Likely." Judd halted at a fork in the tunnels. "This isn't your fight. Leave the investigation to those who have experience in that area."

"Because I only have experience at being a *victim*?"

The metallic scent of blood rose from his shredded flesh as he folded his arms. "You're too blinded by your own emotions to do Timothy justice. This isn't about you."

She opened her mouth to tell him how wrong he was but shut it as quickly. Admitting the truth wasn't an option—it would sound insane, the ravings of a broken mind. "Go get your wounds tended," she said instead. "The smell of Psy blood isn't particularly appetizing." She was worried about how deep Tai had gouged him, but damn if she was going to admit that.

Judd didn't even blink at her insulting tone. "I'll escort you to your room."

"Try it and I'll claw out your eyes." Turning, she strode off, able to feel his gaze on her every step of the way until she turned the corner. It was tempting to collapse then, to release the mask of anger she wore like a shield, but she waited until she was safely back in her room before giving in. "I *did* see it," she told the walls, terrified.

The flesh parting under the blade, the blood pouring, the pallor of death, she'd seen it all. It had left her a trembling, shaken mess, but she'd found comfort in the fact that it had been nothing more than a nightmare.

Except now her nightmare had taken the ugliest of forms.

Judd ensured Brenna was in her quarters before he returned to the crime scene and spoke at length with Indigo.

Then he made his way to his own room. Once there, he stripped and showered to remove the dried blood on his arms. Brenna was right—the scent would only draw attention to him, given the changelings' acute sense of smell, and tonight, he needed to be invisible.

When he stepped out, he didn't bother to look in a mirror, simply thrust a hand through his hair and left it at that. A part of his mind noted that his hair was past regulation length. Another part dismissed the issue as irrelevant—he was no longer a member of the Psy race's most elite army. The Psy Council had sentenced his entire family—his brother, Walker; Walker's daughter, Marlee; and Sienna and Toby, the children of his dead sister, Kristine—to the living death of rehabilitation.

If they hadn't defected, they would have had their minds wiped clean, their brains destroyed until they weren't much more than walking vegetables. It had been a calculated gamble to come to the wolves. He and Walker had expected to die, but they had hoped for mercy for Toby and Marlee. Sienna, too old to be a child, too young to be an adult, had decided to take her chances with the wolves rather than face rehabilitation.

But the SnowDancers hadn't killed the adults on sight. As a result, he now lived in a world where his old life meant nothing. Getting dressed, he pulled on his pants, socks, and boots first. A man could defeat an opponent bare-chested; having bare feet was a far greater disadvantage. It was as he was pulling on a shirt that the expected message came through on his small silver phone. Leaving the shirt buttons undone, he read the encrypted words, translating them in his mind.

Target confirmed. Window: One week.

He deleted the message the second after reading it. His next act was to push up the long sleeves of his black shirt and wrap plain cotton bandages around his forearms—they would help mask the smell of rapidly regenerating skin. Brenna would have been very surprised to see how fast he healed.

His mind went over the murder scene one more time. He was certain they were dealing with a copycat. The cuts had been superficially similar to those made by Santano Enrique but nothing more. Where Enrique had taken pride in the precision with which he mutilated his victims' bodies, this killer had hacked rather than sliced. Indigo had also confirmed that no Psy scent had been found at the scene. The final deciding factor was that Santano Enrique was most definitely dead—Judd had witnessed the other Psy being torn to pieces by wolf and leopard claws.

There was no need for Brenna to worry that her tormentor had come back from the grave. Of course that was Psy logic at work and she was indisputably a changeling. More to the point, she didn't know that Judd been present at Enrique's execution and, by extension, her rescue. He had no intention of changing that. Because, while he might not be much good at predicting emotional reactions, he had learned enough about Brenna during the healing sessions—where he'd "lent" his psychic strength to Sascha as she worked to repair the fractures in Brenna's mind—to know she'd react negatively to the knowledge of his involvement.

I'm not a baby anymore.

No, she wasn't. And he wasn't her protector. He couldn't be—the closer he got to her, the more he could hurt her. Silence had been invented for those like him—the brutal killers and the viciously insane, those who had turned the world of the Psy into a blood-soaked hell so bad, Silence had become the better choice.

The second he broke conditioning, he became a loaded gun with no safety switch. That was why he was never going to do what Sascha had done and end the Silence in his mind. It was the only thing keeping the world safe from what he was . . . the only thing keeping Brenna safe.

Pulling on a black jacket identical to the one Tai had slashed, he slid the phone into his pocket. It was time to leave the den.

He had a bomb to build.

CHAPTER 3

Kaleb Krychek, cardinal Tk and the newest member of the Psy Council, terminated the call and leaned back in his chair, hands steepled in front of him. "Silver," he said, activating the intercom with a negligible use of his telekinetic abilities, "find all my files on the Liu family group."

"Yes, sir."

Knowing the task would take her several minutes, he mentally reviewed the call. Jen Liu, matriarch of the Liu Group, had made her thoughts clear.

"We have a mutually beneficial relationship," she'd said, green eyes unblinking. "I'm certain you would do nothing to jeopardize that. However, I'm not so certain of your colleagues on the Council. We're still paying for their last decision—Faith NightStar's prices have almost doubled as her family seeks to regain what it lost."

The NightStar Affair, as that particular political debacle was now called, had come about immediately prior to Kaleb's ascension to the Council. Faith NightStar, a powerful foreseer, had chosen to drop from the PsyNet and into the arms of one of the DarkRiver cats. Two Councilors had made the hasty decision to try and recapture her, putting her life at risk and alienating not only her family, the powerful NightStar Group, but also all the businesses who relied on Faith's predictions. Businesses such as the Liu Group.

Now, Kaleb stared thoughtfully at the transparent screen that had moments before held Jen Liu's face. The matriarch had been correct in her estimation of his loyalties. He valued the alliances he'd built up on his way to gaining a Council seat. Those alliances had been nurtured with cold-blooded precision—he had known that a Councilor who had the support of certain sectors of society would wield far more than his share of power. And Kaleb appreciated power. It was why he'd made Councilor at a bare twenty-seven years of age.

He tapped at the screen, switching it from communications to data mode, then pulled up files on the rest of the Council. Putting the bio files on one side, he accessed the ones on the NightStar Affair. Beside that, he left an empty space for the information Silver was collating.

Finally, he brought up a highly confidential file titled "Protocol I." Right now, all he had on that matter were suspicions, but that would change. The Liu issue would do for a first strike. He saw no need to draw blood . . . yet.

Kaleb was nothing if not patient. The same way a cobra is patient.

CHAPTER 4

One day after the murder, and countless hours of arguments with herself later, Brenna knew Judd was the only person she could ask, the only one who might possibly understand. And yet, he was also the worst, so cold that he sometimes appeared less human than a statue carved out of ice. Before being kidnapped, she'd gone to great lengths to avoid him, intrinsically disturbed by the inhuman chill of his personality.

Well aware her brothers would turn feral at the mere thought of her alone with Judd, she took every care to remain invisible as she tiptoed out of their family quarters after dinner and toward the section occupied by unmated soldiers. Judd lived alone, his brother, Walker, and the three minors having been relocated to the family section. The move had taken place four months after the Laurens first sought sanctuary with SnowDancer.

Surprisingly, it had been the pack's maternal females who had ordered Hawke to think about what it was doing to the Psy children to be isolated in the soldiers' area. Given how sensitive the females were to anything that might pose a danger to the cubs, Brenna would've expected them to demand distance—Marlee and Toby might be kids but they were very powerful kids.

Conversely, SnowDancer pups tended to play rough and could maul the Psy children without meaning to. But the maternal females had extended the invitation and Walker Lauren had accepted on behalf of his daughter, Marlee, and nephew, Toby. At seventeen, Toby's sister, Sienna, could no longer be classified as a child, but neither was she an adult. In this case, the headstrong teenager had chosen to stay with the children.

Leaving Judd alone.

As Judd was considered the most dangerous member of the Lauren family, his living quarters had never been in any question. He continued to be looked on with suspicion, though she knew he'd been integral to her rescue. While he hadn't been one of those who'd entered the pain-soaked room that had been her torture chamber—an omission for which she would always be grateful—he'd helped Sascha lay the psychic trap that had led to Enrique's capture. He'd proven his loyalty. But still he remained an outsider.

The unfairness of it rubbed at her sense of justice, but she couldn't blame her packmates for their feelings, not when Judd seemed determined to reinforce their attitude. The man was aloof to the point of rudeness.

Reaching his door, she knocked softly. "Hurry up." Though the corridor was currently deserted, she could near the sound of approaching footsteps. With her luck, it would be one of her overprotective brothers.

The door opened. "What—?"

She ducked under his arm and into the room. "Shut it before someone comes." For a second, she thought he would refuse, but then he pushed it closed.

Turning to stand with his back to the door, he folded his arms across a bare chest. "If your brothers find you here, they'll put you under lock and key."

She was suddenly hyperconscious of the scent of fresh male sweat and gleaming skin in a confined space. Terror spiked, but she squashed it almost before it arose, hiding it in that impregnable box in her mind. "Aren't you worried about what they'll do to you?" Despite the edge of fear, her fingertips tingled, wanting to touch this dangerous creature.

"I can take care of myself."

Of that she had no doubt. "So can I."

Judd's eyes, eyes the color of bitterest chocolate except for the flecks of gold in the irises, didn't shift their focus off her face. "What are you doing here, Brenna?"

She shook herself out of her fascination. "I need to talk to a Psy and you're it."

"What about Sascha?"

"She won't understand." Brenna both respected and liked Sascha Duncan, the Psy mind-healer who had mated with Lucas Hunter, alpha to the DarkRiver leopards. But . . . "She's too good, too gentle."

"It's a side effect of her abilities," Judd said in his usual icy tone.

It was a tone that infuriated the other males, but Brenna knew she wasn't the only female who wondered about thawing him out. Her claws pricked the insides of her skin as she was hit by a near-violent surge of inexplicable sensual hunger. She fought it—she wasn't stupid enough to think she could change him.

"Sascha feels the emotions of others," Judd continued. "If she harmed another being, it would rebound back on her."

"I know that." Fisting her hands, she turned on her heel and began to pace around the small room. His scent was everywhere, closing around her changeling senses in a dark and uncompromising masculine wave. "This is like a cell. Couldn't you put up a poster at least?" The size of the room was comparable to those of other unmated soldiers, but even the worst lone wolf made some changes to his living space.

In contrast, Judd's was stark in its emptiness, his bed the single piece of furniture, the sheet white, the blanket institutional gray. The only addition appeared to be a horizontal exercise bar fitted about a foot below the ceiling.

"I don't see the point." He leaned back against the door, the movement drawing her attention to a chest she knew was pure hard muscle. "Ask what you came to ask."

"I told you I'm seeing things. I saw that—that—" She couldn't bring herself to say it, to reawaken the nightmare.

Of course Judd didn't attempt to offer comfort. "I explained that they're likely nothing more than psychic echoes of the trauma you suffered at Enrique's hands."

"You're wrong. They're real."

"Tell me what you see."

"Bad, bad things," she whispered, hugging herself. "Death and blood and pain."

Judd's expression didn't alter. "Be more specific."

Sudden, blinding anger swamped the fear raised by the memories. "Sometimes you make me want to scream! Would it hurt you to try and appear a little human?"

He didn't respond.

"Walker's different."

"My brother is a telepath with a special affinity for young Psy minds. He was a teacher in the Net."

She took time to think that through, surprised he'd answered at all. "You're saying he already had the capacity to feel emotions before you defected?"

"We all have the capacity," Judd corrected. "The whole point of the conditioning under Silence is to cauterize that capacity—elimination is impossible."

She wondered what he saw in her face, because *she* saw only the most chilly calm on his. He stood unaffected by her anger, her fear . . . her pain. The realization caused an odd, hollow sensation in her stomach. "But you said Walker's different."

A nod sent several dark strands of hair falling across his forehead. "My brother's constant contact with children who hadn't yet finished the conditioning process, contact that continues with Toby and Marlee, means that he was always more susceptible to breaching Silence in the right environment."

"What about you?" It was a question she'd never before asked. "What did you do in the Net?"

She thought she saw his shoulders tighten. But when he replied, his tone was unchanged. "You don't need any more nightmares. Now, tell me what you see."

She stepped closer to the dangerous maleness of him.

"You'll have to talk about it someday." But she knew from his inflexible stance that it wasn't going to be today. So she gathered up her courage and opened that box of evil and death. "I saw Timothy's death in a dream. But . . . he didn't have a face then . . . just a smooth oval of bare skin where features should've been." She couldn't get the disturbing image out of her head. "I saw how he would die." A sharp blade cutting through muscle and fat to expose bloodred flesh.

Judd continued to watch her without blinking. "Could be simple transference—your mind's way of interpreting the images Enrique left in your brain."

It disgusted her that Enrique had gotten that far. Sascha had assured Brenna that she hadn't broken, that she'd kept the bastard from her innermost core, but it didn't feel like that. No, it felt like he'd crawled into the very essence of her being, violating every part of her from the inside out. And Sascha didn't know the worst of what the butcher had done . . . what she had submitted to—Brenna intended to take those secrets to the grave.

"Brenna."

Stomach churning, she raised her head. "Transference?"

His eyes were piercing, as if he were attempting to see through her skin. "You could be mistaking or merging an old or known image over a new one."

Because Enrique had liked to terrorize her by showing her recordings of his past kills. "No," she disagreed. "Even before I saw Tim's body, I could feel differences . . . in the cuts, in the evil." Enrique's favorite weapon had been a scalpel, used in conjunction with the telekinetic powers of his cardinal mind. Cardinals were the strongest grade of Psy, but Enrique had been a power even in that select company. "It's as if I'm being forced to watch someone else's fantasies." It was her ultimate fear—having her mind raped again, being shoved full of dark, nauseating thoughts nothing could wash away.

"You're a changeling, not a telepath." For a second, she thought she saw the gold flecks spark to life in the rich brown of his eyes. "There's more." Not a question.

She swallowed. "When I saw the murder in my dreams,

when I heard the screams, it—" Her nails cut into the fleshy pads of her palms.

"It what, Brenna?" His voice was almost gentle. Or maybe that was what she needed to hear.

"It excited me," she admitted, feeling dirty and wrong . . . a monster. "I *enjoyed* it." She had craved the agony of her victim, her blood fevered with sick excitement. "Every cut, every scream."

Judd's expression didn't change. "But only during the actual dream?"

She wanted to be held so badly, but Judd Lauren was about as likely to do that as he was to turn wolf. "It's like *he* left a piece of himself inside of me."

"Santano Enrique was a true sociopath. He didn't feel anything."

Her laugh sounded jagged to her own ears. "If you'd seen him as I did, you would never say that. He might have been cold, but he enjoyed what he did. And he infected me."

"Enrique didn't have that ability. Transferring mental viruses is a rare skill." He pushed off the door and walked to her. "Sascha found no trace of one in your mind and she'd know—her mother is the best viral transmitter in the Net."

"He did something!" she insisted. "These thoughts, these feelings, they're not mine." They couldn't be. Not if she wanted to remain sane.

"You shouldn't be seeing anything," he said, standing so close she could feel his body heat. Alarm and need mixed in raw confusion. "Your brain pathways function completely differently from those of a Psy."

She went to thrust a hand through her hair and stopped. Her waist-length mane was gone, another thing Enrique had stolen. "Do you think he changed that?"

Judd's muscles rippled as he uncrossed his arms. "It would seem to be the logical conclusion. If you let me scan your mind—"

"No."

He inclined his head in a small nod. "Fine. But that makes it much harder to diagnose the problem."

"I know. But no." No one would ever again crawl into her mind. For most victims, it was the last inviolate space. For her, it was a part that had been brutalized once and would never trust again. "Do you have any idea what it could be?"

"No." He reached out to touch her neck. "How did you get this bruise?"

Taken completely off guard, she found herself placing her hand over his. "A bruise? Maybe when I was sparring with Lucy." Brenna might not be a soldier, but she needed to be able to protect herself . . . now more than ever. Because the truth that no one knew, the secret she'd successfully concealed since the rescue, was that Enrique hadn't simply damaged her mind, he had destroyed her on a far more fundamental level, a level that threatened to obliterate her very identity. "Can you find out about my dreams?"

His hand was big under hers, his fingers long. She was exquisitely aware of every millimeter of skin-to-skin contact. Touch might be second nature to her race, but predatory changelings didn't let just anyone touch them. Only Pack, mates, and lovers had skin privileges. Judd fit none of those criteria. Yet she didn't push him off.

"I'll put out some feelers." He withdrew his hand, the roughness of his palm an unexpected shock. "But you have to accept that no answers may be forthcoming. You're unique—the only one of Enrique's experiments to have survived."

He watched *Brenna Kincaid leave Judd Lauren's room from the shadows. It was all he could do not to leap out and choke the life out of her right there and then. The bitch was supposed to die months ago, but she'd clawed her way back to life. And now she'd remembered something. Why else would she have pulled that scene with the body?*

The words that left his mouth were low and vicious.

He'd been close to panic in the days after her rescue, but thankfully, her memory had turned out to be full of holes. If those holes were filling up, he was in trouble. The kind of trouble that could lead to an execution—especially if she had that fucking Psy on her side. He should've betrayed the whole Lauren family the first chance he'd gotten, but he'd waited too long to use the information and now his greed had come back to haunt him.

It made no difference. He had no intention of being hunted down like a rabid dog. He stared at the pressure injector in his hand, the same one that had weakened Tim and made him such easy prey. It could be used on Brenna, too. The crazy-eyed whore was not going to mess up his life.

Judd kept his eye on Brenna until she reached the end of the long corridor and turned the corner to join the steady flow of people on the other side. His military-trained mind had picked up something in the air the second after he'd opened the door, but he could find no reason for the warning flag. Still, he didn't move until she was safe.

Then, closing the door, he glanced down at his hand, flexing and unflexing it in an effort to lose the imprint of heat burned into it the second he'd touched Brenna. It had been an utterly irrational action, prompted not by thought but by some buried instinct that had momentarily overridden his conditioning when he'd glimpsed the bruise marring her skin.

His phone beeped, reminding him he had a job to complete. He couldn't afford to be distracted from his goals by a changeling who looked to him to vanquish her nightmares. As if he were . . . good. What would Brenna say if he told her that he *was* the nightmare?

His phone beeped a second time. Picking it up, he switched off the alarm and went to wash off the sweat that coated his body. The tactile sensation of soft feminine skin continued to cling to his palm, but he knew it would disappear soon enough—the scent of death had a way of immersing everything in chilling frost.

And, Judd thought as he packed the surveillance equipment he'd need tonight, he was very good at causing death, had been since he was ten years of age. Tonight was a simple tracking job, but only days remained until the hit. The bombs were nearing completion. All he needed now was a window of time, of opportunity. Then blood would spread across his skin once more, a scarlet flower that told the true story of what he was.

CHAPTER 5

In the rich velvet night of the PsyNet, the door to an impenetrable vault slammed shut. A vast mental network that connected millions of Psy across the world, the Net housed their collective knowledge and was updated trillions of times a day as Psy uploaded data. It also allowed those of their race to meet at a moment's notice, no matter their physical location. Tonight, seven minds blazed into brightness in the darkest core of the Net, each appearing as a white star so cold, it threatened to cut.

The Psy Council was in session.

Kaleb was the first to speak. "What could you possibly have been thinking?" The question was directed at the dangerously powerful minds of Henry and Shoshanna Scott, married couple and fellow Councilors. "The Liu Group was not amused to find that their family archives had been hacked and several members' files tagged as 'at risk.' " They all knew the at risk label was one step away from a sentence of full rehabilitation.

"We are Council." Shoshanna spoke for both Scotts, something she seemed to be doing more and more. "We don't have to explain our actions to the populace."

Tatiana Rika-Smythe entered the conversation. "I assume you targeted other family groups as well. What was your purpose in placing the tags?"

"To monitor those who might be susceptible to breaking Silence."

"Rehabilitation takes care of that problem." Tatiana's voice held a ring of finality.

"If that's the case, then explain Sascha Duncan and Faith NightStar to me," Shoshanna said, referring to the two recent defectors from the Net. "Nikita? Sascha is your daughter after all."

"Two anomalies." Kaleb very deliberately backed Nikita. "Furthermore, it appears you were running unsanctioned searches long before those anomalies took place, so there can be no logical connection between the two."

"We saw those anomalies approaching, as the rest of you didn't." Shoshanna wasted none of the calculated Psy charm she pulled out for media appearances. "Have you heard the whispers in the Net? They're talking openly of rebellion."

"She's correct," Tatiana said, her allegiance unclear as always.

"I suggest we let them talk. To a certain extent." Kaleb directed his words to the entire Council. "Trying to stifle all dissent is what caused problems in the past. As the situation stands, we can keep an eye on the agitators . . . and take care of any problems before they have a chance to do any real damage."

"Be that as it may, that's not the issue at hand," Nikita pointed out. "I submit that the Scotts' findings be turned over to the Council. If they were acting as Councilors, then the information belongs to the Council. If they were acting on their own, they had no authority and the data should be seized in any case."

Kaleb was impressed by Nikita's neat trap, but said nothing to that effect. Shoshanna was already well on the way to becoming his enemy. But that wasn't what kept him silent—he wanted to see who would speak in the Scotts' favor, betraying a possible alliance.

"I'd be interested in seeing the data." Ming LeBon finally spoke. A master of mental combat, he was a Councilor no one but his most elite soldiers ever actually *saw*. Kaleb had been unable to find a single image of him—Ming was a true shadow.

"It may prove useful." Tatiana.

"Put it on the table and then we'll decide." Marshall, the most senior Councilor and their unofficial chair—by virtue of having survived longest as Council.

Three whose loyalties were unclear. Nikita and Shoshanna plainly stood on opposite sides of the line, and Henry was Shoshanna's.

"Unfortunately, that's impossible." Shoshanna's mental tone remained supremely confident. "It would require reentering each of the targeted files."

"Surely you kept a master log?" Marshall articulated what they were all thinking.

"Of course. However, that log was hacked ten hours ago. The data has been scrambled beyond recovery."

"Do you take us for rehabilitated idiots?" Nikita said, her psychic voice a razor. "No hacker in the Net is capable of circumventing a Councilor's security."

"It was a virus." Shoshanna refused to back down. "The proof is here." Something slammed into the empty "dark-space" inside the vault, a data file that vibrated with a broken viral signature.

Everyone but Nikita drew back. "It's safe," she pronounced a second later. "Not designed to spread through dark-space. Even if it were, all such viruses dissipate within a few inches at most. Dark-space is an inhospitable environment."

"For that we should be grateful. Otherwise the viral transmitters would've corrupted the entire Net by now," Shoshanna said, in a cool reference to Nikita's rumored abilities.

They took time to examine Shoshanna's evidence. It was compelling. The psychic file she'd presented should have been readable by their Psy minds, the streams of data clean and well ordered. But this data was tangled into a giant clump, distorted by twisted sparks of internal lightning that dissected and further destroyed as they watched.

"It's feeding on itself," Marshall murmured. "A cycle that constantly degrades."

"Undeniably an extraordinary piece of programming." Tatiana went even closer. "We need this individual working for us. I'd like to take on the task of tracking the perpetrator."

"Go ahead." Shoshanna "pushed" the file toward Tatiana. "You're unlikely to have much success. The hacker left no useful signature."

"The virus *is* the signature," Nikita pointed out. "Unless he was smart enough to mask it. This could fit into the pattern of disturbances attributed to the Ghost." She named the saboteur who had become a dangerous thorn in the Council's side.

"Possible," Kaleb said. "But there is another option—perhaps the Liu family decided to take the matter into their own hands after all."

"Whoever it was," Nikita said, "how much data did they siphon?"

"None. They inserted the virus and left. Nothing was removed."

"How certain are you of that?" Nikita again.

"Absolutely." Henry spoke for the first time.

"I assume you're aware you have to stop." Marshall. "With the ripples from the NightStar Affair still spreading, we can't run the risk of further alienating the most powerful of the family groups."

"Agreed." Shoshanna obviously knew when to cut and run. "However, while the majority of the details were destroyed, we have put together a list of ten individuals from memory. We intend to continue to monitor them . . . with the Council's permission."

"I see no problem with that, so long as you're discreet," Tatiana answered.

"Agreed. There is a further matter I wish to discuss." Shoshanna brought up another file, this one fairly thin in terms of data. "Brenna Shane Kincaid."

Kaleb recalled the name immediately. "Santano Enrique's last victim? What's your interest in her?"

"I assume you've all read the most recent report on what

we've been able to decipher of Enrique's notes?" Shoshanna waited until everyone had confirmed her supposition. "So you know it appears he might have achieved extraordinary things with her mind. We need to examine her."

"You know as well as I," Nikita interrupted, "that any attempt to remove Brenna Kincaid would be tantamount to a declaration of war against the SnowDancers."

"Don't want another mess in your backyard, Nikita?" Shoshanna's question was valid—both the recent renegades had come from Nikita's home region.

Nikita's mind remained undisturbed. "Not when the mess results from the mistakes of other Councilors." A cool response that reminded everyone of the Scotts' aborted attempt to capture Faith NightStar. "The girl is too well protected to be a viable target."

"Nikita is correct," Ming said unexpectedly. "Also, while Brenna Kincaid is interesting from a scientific standpoint, I'm sure none of us plan to duplicate the process."

"No." Tatiana. "The animals should remain animals. In any case, it may be that Enrique's alterations will close the issue for us."

"How so?" Marshall asked. "We can't chance the changelings discovering and attempting to utilize the process themselves."

"Her brain isn't built for what Enrique tried to do," Tatiana explained. "It may simply implode as a result of the internal pressure."

"And," Ming reminded them, "we've already set a plan in motion to take care of the changeling problem. I suggest we wait for that to bear fruit. Even if Brenna Kincaid's brain somehow survives the pressure, she'll be dead soon enough—along with the rest of her pack."

CHAPTER 6

It wasn't until the morning of the fifth day after the murder that Judd saw Brenna again. He was on his way to speak to Hawke when she walked into him from the opposite direction, destroying his decision to keep her at a distance—Brenna might look soft and harmless, but she had a way of turning his behavior treacherously unpredictable. Like now.

Catching her by her upper arms was reflex. Continuing to hold on afterward was a small but significant deviation from the Protocol. And he didn't care. "Where are—" He cut himself off when she lifted her face.

Her skin was drawn, her eyes almost sunken.

"Talk to me." An order.

Where she would've normally sharpened her claws on him for daring to give her one, today she shot a nervous glance over her shoulder before putting her fisted hands on his chest. "I was looking for you," she whispered, while he was still trying to assimilate the impact of her touch. "Drew and Riley haven't let me leave the apartment since after I returned from talking to you—someone saw us together. I only got out now by sheer luck."

Judd felt ice spread through his veins but it was a cold that burned. "I'll talk to them." No one was going to lock Brenna in again.

"Just take me outside, far enough away that they can't track my scent." A ragged plea. "Please get me out before I lose my mind."

"Follow me." Releasing his hold on her, he turned to lead her out. A feminine hand curved around his upper left arm, over the leather-synth of his jacket.

It if had been any other woman, he would've broken the contact and made very sure it wouldn't be repeated. But this wasn't another woman. "How far?" He asked because she'd become almost agoraphobic since the abduction—though she did sometimes venture a small distance beyond the den, she'd stopped attending college and never went for runs with her packmates.

"*Far.*" Her voice was resolute but her hand a vise around his arm.

He took her through several back tunnels to an exit that he knew was kept less well guarded than others because it opened directly into a garden in the White Zone. That zone was the closest section of the inner perimeter and was considered safe enough for pups to play in unattended. "Wait here while I check the area."

It took a few seconds for her to let go. "Sorry I'm—"

"If I had wanted an apology, I would have asked for it."

Her mouth snapped shut. "Where did you learn your charm—the gulag?"

"Something like that." He stepped out to find the garden empty. The pups had probably been herded inside when the sky grew heavy with the promise of more snow. Completing the visual scan, he did a telepathic one to confirm his findings. "It's clear."

Brenna emerged from the door with a confident expression, but the second she hit open air, her breathing went from smooth to rocky. He could sense her fear as if it were a physical wave smashing repeatedly into his body. Reaching back, he took her hand. Changelings craved touch. It centered them as much as it did the opposite to those of his race.

"Stay with me." Refusing to think about why he'd done something so alien to his nature, he pulled her through the garden and toward a narrow pathway. "Farther?"

"Yes." Her husky voice took on a hard edge. "I'm sick of being afraid. *He's* not going to win."

"You're too strong for that to ever be a possibility." After learning of what Enrique had done to her, Judd had expected Brenna's to be a shattered mind twisted through with madness. But not only had she survived, she was sane.

Her hand tightened on his. "Judd—"

Something brushed the edge of the telepathic scan he'd continued to run. "Quiet." He was conscious of Brenna's eyes on him as she stood close enough that her body heat reached him even through the enhanced insulation of his jacket. Consigning that knowledge to a dark corner of his mind, he refocused the scan. There were two soldiers walking in this direction, likely returning from a watch on the outer perimeter.

They wouldn't stop him, but he didn't intend to have his whereabouts tracked. That was why he'd worked out several discreet ways to ensure his frequent trips in and out of SnowDancer territory were never logged. However, if they saw Brenna, they would certainly try to hold her until they received instructions from either Andrew or Riley.

"Can you smudge their minds?" Brenna asked in a low whisper, pressing even closer to his body. "Make them look the other way?"

"Changeling minds are harder for us to influence than human." Strong Psy could kill changelings with a blast of sheer power but manipulating them was a different proposition. "There may be another option."

Sending out his senses again, he found six unshielded minds. Taking control was easy—young black bears didn't have much of a defense, especially this deep into hibernation. "Can you stay here by yourself for a few minutes?"

Skin pulled taut over her cheekbones as she nodded. "Go." Releasing his hand with notable reluctance, she backed up and moved behind a tree.

"I won't be long." He could see how close she was to panic, but to her credit, she only nodded when he gave the next order. "When you hear the guards begin to move, run southeast. No hesitation."

He headed toward the two men, making sure he was out of Brenna's line of sight before he blurred himself. Not even the other men in his highly specialized Arrow unit had possessed this ability. Most blurring, or "smudging" as Brenna had put it, occurred on the mental plane, with the Psy casting telepathic interference across the viewer's mind.

Judd was different. He could alter his own physical form. The skill was telekinetic rather than telepathic. Because Judd wasn't simply a strong telepath, nor was Tp his main ability, as was widely believed—as he'd gone to great lengths to make people believe. What would Brenna say if she realized he was an extremely powerful telekinetic—a Tk, the same designation as the killer who had tortured her in that blood-soaked room?

It was a question he'd never have answered, as he had no intention of telling Brenna the truth of what he was. Shifting his cells a fraction more out of sync with the world, he moved out past the two other men—when he blurred, changelings couldn't see him except as a shadow out of the corner of their eye. More importantly, they couldn't scent him either, a fact that supported his personal theory of how his ability worked.

A minute later, he sent the bears crashing through the forest on the right-hand side, and downwind, of the soldiers. The creatures made enough noise to distract them into changing direction. Settling his molecules back into sync, Judd deliberately crossed paths with the men—as if he were on his way back to the den.

"Anyone come past you?" Elias stopped, while his partner, Dieter, kept going.

"No."

Nodding, Elias took off after Dieter. Judd used the opportunity to lay a false trail all the way back to the den. Then, taking the time to hide Brenna's trail even as he hid his own, he headed southeast. He thrust some Tk through the air as he ran, muddying up and dispersing their scents so they couldn't be tracked that way either.

Brenna was fast. When he found her, she was well out of the White Zone, and in the central core of the inner perimeter—considered safe for adults but not children. There were sentries in this section, too, but they were stationed some distance away, on the border where the inner perimeter gave way to the outer. Around Judd and Brenna the forest was quiet, sound muffled by the thick blanket of snow. The trees were blue with it this far up in the Sierra, icicles hanging off the branches like transparent blades.

"Careful." He moved to cover her when she passed under a particularly lethal spike.

"What?" She looked up and behind herself, then shivered, shifting to lean her side against his chest. He froze, unmoving as the trees. His reaction didn't escape her notice. "I'm sorry, I know you don't like being touched. But I need it right now."

He'd come to expect bluntness from her. "You're not dressed for this weather." She wasn't wearing a coat, just jeans and a pink turtleneck, though her feet were encased in solid boots. He should have noted and remedied the lack before they left the den.

"I'm changeling. I don't feel the cold." Usually true, except that she was burrowing into his body, her hands raised between them as she turned slightly. One thigh pressed into his. "What about you?"

"I'm fine." He truly didn't feel the cold, but in his case, it had to do with his telekinetic abilities. "Take this." He shrugged off his jacket. It left him clad in a thin round-necked sweater as black as his jeans.

"I told you I d-d-don't feel the c-c-cold."

"Your lips are blue." He put the jacket around her shoulders. At the same instant, he extended his cold-deflecting Tk shield to cover her. The shield was created by reordering the air and dust particles to form a thin but highly impermeable—and invisible—wall.

She shuddered and began to push her arms into the sleeves. "You win. This is so warm."

Swimming in his jacket, she returned to her position against him. Neither of them spoke or moved for the next ten minutes. Brenna seemed content to simply gaze at the blue and white spread of the forest around them, but he was aware of every breath she took, every beat of her heart, every shift of her soft, warm body inside *his* jacket. The strength of that final thought sparked a warning in his brain that he chose to ignore.

Suddenly, the blinding light of the sun was reflecting off the snow and into his eyes. He glanced up to discover the clouds had dissipated while they stood in silence.

"Beautiful," Brenna sighed, hooking one arm into his, "but hard on the eyes. Come on. There's a lake this way. The area around it is a bit more shaded." Glinting off her cap of hair, the sun was a sharp knife that made him question what he was doing here. But he didn't stop walking until she did.

"There, see?" Looking out at the snow-covered surface of the small lake that during warmer months was painted with reflected images of mountains and trees, Brenna suddenly felt freer than she had in months. The fear that had trapped her inside the den was gone, crushed under the aching beauty of the wilderness she called home. All she'd needed was someone to walk with her this far.

Smiling, she looked up at the dark angel by her side. Dressed in black, with that hair and those eyes, there was no other way to describe him. "Thank you."

His lips were a beautiful shape, full enough to tempt but with a hard edge that made her stomach twist. Then he spoke and it was a brutal reminder that he wasn't simply a strong, sexy male. He was Psy. "Don't thank me. I've been unable to find any concrete answers for you in relation to the dream-visions. You need to talk to someone more knowledgeable—the dreams could be a sign of mental degradation."

She withdrew her arm from his and shoved both hands into the pockets of his jacket. The scent of him, powerful and intrinsically masculine, was intoxicating to her changeling senses, but she no longer wanted to be surrounded by it. "You think I'm losing my mind?" It was her secret fear, the monster under the bed, the cold chill down her spine.

"Psy don't dance around the facts. I meant exactly what I said."

God, but he sounded arrogant. "That's a load of bull." She scowled. "Your Council has double-talk down to a fine art."

Dark eyes with snow reflected in their depths turned to her. "They are not my Council and I am not their puppet." Icy enough to flay off her skin.

She winced. "Mental degradation? If that doesn't mean madness . . ."

"Enrique may have damaged parts of your organic brain tissue while running his psychic experiments, caused lesions or bruises." He watched her with the unblinking stare of a predator, as if gauging her strength. "He was a Tk and the use of telekinetic powers almost always has a physical effect. The autopsies of his other victims revealed them to have suffered major brain injuries."

Pictures. The butcher had shown her pictures of the others. "I remember."

"However, the likelihood of such damage is minimal. Sascha and Lara made sure to repair all organic tears before they began healing things on any other level."

Brenna bit her lower lip and took a deep, shaky breath. "Sascha said that that part should've taken longer, but that I was so determined to have my mind back, it was as if I *willed* the broken parts to heal." Almost as if she were Psy. "Maybe I rushed her."

"I called her after you spoke to me," he said, continuing to watch her with that hunter's gaze. "You did rush her, but not in the physical healing."

She wanted to smack him for his presumption, despite the fact that she'd asked for his help. "None of that changes the fact that Sascha doesn't have experience with this kind of thing." And the empath, who had the ability to sense and heal the darkest of emotional wounds, had already seen her broken and bloody too many times. No matter her kindness, Sascha reminded Brenna of things she'd rather forget.

"No. But Faith does." Judd folded his arms. "You need to talk to someone."

"I'm talking to you." Why, she couldn't rationally explain. He was cold and merciless, had all the charm of a feral wolf.

"I'll set up the meeting with Faith."

She gritted her teeth. "I'll do it. Vaughn doesn't like you, in case you hadn't noticed." She'd met both Faith and her mate, Vaughn, when the foreseer had come up to the den to accept a gift made for her by the nursery children, children who were alive because of a vision Faith had had. Without her warning, they would've lost several pups. "Not that you go out of your way to be friendly."

"That's irrelevant." Turning away, he looked out over the frozen vista. "Emotion is not one of my weaknesses."

Faith had just ended a short but disturbing conversation with Brenna Kincaid when Anthony Kyriakus, head of the NightStar Group—and her father—walked into the meeting room. Putting the phone in her pocket, she leaned into Vaughn, waiting for Anthony to speak.

"There's a Ghost in the Net." He circled to stand on the other side of the table.

It wasn't what she had wanted to hear, the child in her still hungry for things she knew Anthony might never be able to give her. Hurt was a dull ache in her body. Then Vaughn closed a hand over her nape and the sadness passed—she was loved, cherished, adored. "A ghost?" She sat and the men followed.

"No one knows the identity of this individual, but he or she is being credited with a number of insurgent activities." Anthony passed her a disc containing the names of companies that had requested a forecast since they last spoke—forecasts she provided under a subcontracting agreement with NightStar.

She put the disc to one side, more interested in this Ghost. "Is he one of us?" If there was one thing Faith and her father both agreed on, it was that they wanted their people freed from a Silence that was false—Anthony might be coldly Psy, but he was also the leader of a quiet revolution against the Council.

"There's no way to know. However, it is evident that the Ghost is part of the Council's superstructure—he or she has access to classified data, but hasn't acted on anything above a certain level. That could be because this individual doesn't have higher access, or because he—"

"—is being very careful not to do anything that might narrow the focus of inquiry as to his, or her, identity," Faith completed.

"Good strategy." The jaguar at her side finally spoke, his thumb continuing to stroke over her nape. "The Council's got to be pissed if this rebel is leaking classified data."

"Yes." Anthony turned back to Faith. "The Ghost was active while you were still part of the Net. Do you recall the explosion at Exogenesis Labs?"

"The place where they're theorizing about implants that might lower the percentage of *defects*?" She spit out the last word. It was the label the Council used to describe those who refused to buckle under the emotionless regime of the Silence Protocol. "They want to cut into developing brains and initiate Silence on an organic level."

Anthony didn't react to her open emotionalism. "The Exogenesis strike killed two of the lead scientists on the implant team and destroyed months of work."

"Your Ghost isn't afraid to kill."

Faith heard no judgment in Vaughn's tone—her cat had killed to protect the innocent. And children, the first victims of implantation should the procedure be put into practice, were the most innocent of all.

CHAPTER 7

"**It appears not.** The explosion was investigated by both Enforcement and the Council, but without active support from a majority of the populace."

"Why?" Vaughn asked, his body heat so seductive she found herself leaning ever closer to him, her hand on the hard muscle of his thigh. "Wouldn't this implant make the Psy even more efficient?"

Anthony nodded. "In a sense. But the dissidents argue that Protocol I, while ensuring universal compliance with Silence, would have the unavoidable side effect of linking our minds together. Not as the PsyNet does, but on a biological level."

Protocol I.

That it already had an official name was a bad sign. "They're talking about a true hive mind." Faith couldn't control the disgust that laced her words.

"Yes. It's nothing that appeals to those of us who prefer to run our enterprises free of interference. That would become impossible should the entire race begin to act as one entity." He picked up his organizer—the thin computer tablet ubiquitous among the Psy. "From the pattern of attacks, it appears the Ghost shares our goals, but without knowing his or her identity, we can't coordinate our efforts."

Vaughn leaned forward. "The more people who know a name, the higher the chance of exposure. I say let the Ghost do his—or her—thing, and ride the wave it generates."

"Your conclusion mirrors mine." His tone signaling the end of the topic, Anthony brought up something on his organizer. "BlueZ has been waiting for its latest prediction for a month. Can you move it to the top of your list?"

Faith picked up her own organizer. "I can try." She still hadn't cracked the secret of bringing on visions to order. It was beginning to appear that that was one thing the Council hadn't lied about—maybe there was no way to harness her gift that far.

Anthony moved on to another item on the agenda. Half an hour later, they were done and she was hugging him good-bye. He didn't return the gesture, but did pat her lower back once. Only a former inmate of Silence could have understood the incredible impact of that act. She had tears in her eyes when he pulled away and walked out the door.

Barker, a DarkRiver soldier, was waiting to escort him out of the pack's financial HQ. Located in downtown San Francisco, near the organized chaos of Chinatown, the building was both public and highly secure.

"Come here, Red." Vaughn dragged her into his arms, melting the lump in her throat with his rough brand of affection.

It scared her sometimes, the strength of what she felt for him. "He's important. The Ghost." She'd had a *knowing*, not a vision as such but a hint of how things might be.

That was when it hit her. A true vision. A split-second image of the future.

But this one had nothing to do with the Ghost. It was about Brenna. Death. The SnowDancer was surrounded by death, her hands drenched in blood. Whose blood? Faith didn't know but she could smell the raw-meat scent of it, the desperation, and the fear. Then it was gone—so fast she wasn't even left with an afterimage on her retinas, much less any of the disorientation that sometimes accompanied the flashes of foresight.

It had given her nothing concrete, nothing she could share with Brenna, but it did serve to back up her instincts about what the other woman had told her on the phone. Hugging Vaughn, she returned to the topic at hand. "Do you think I should contact the NetMind about the Ghost?" A sentience that was at home in networks of minds, the NetMind was the librarian and some believed, the policeman of the PsyNet. Faith, however, knew it to be so much more.

"This guy seems to be working fine alone. You sure you want to mess with that?"

"I should've known you'd take the side of the lone wolf," she teased, delighting in being able to do so.

He growled and she felt the vibration against her cheek. "Don't compare me to those damn feral things."

Tilting up her face, she smiled. "Damn wolves." It was an imprecation often muttered by DarkRiver cats.

"Too right." He kissed her. Hard. Fast. Vaughn.

"I'll take your advice—I don't want to inadvertently trigger something in the NetMind." Though the developing sentience was good, it wasn't completely free of the Council. "You know, I think the Ghost is going to be important to DarkRiver as well. Not now. But one day."

"A vision?"

She shook her head. "Not even a knowing, really, more of a—" The words wouldn't come.

"A gut feeling."

"*Yes.*" No wonder she'd been blocked—admitting to such a thing would've gotten her medicated in the PsyNet. "Oh, and, my darling cat, we're going up into SnowDancer territory tomorrow morning for a meeting."

"Who?" He fisted her hair in his hand, but she knew it was a gesture of affection.

"Brenna Kincaid." She decided not to mention that Judd Lauren would also be present. Vaughn had a decidedly negative reaction to the tall, dark, and very dangerous Psy. Judd . . . no, she saw nothing about him. Of all the people she had ever met, it was Judd who was the most opaque to her foresight. So dark. So brutally alone.

* * *

Twenty-four hours after she'd bowed to Judd's demands, Brenna still wasn't sure about meeting with Faith, but it was too late to back out. They got together in a small clearing about twenty minutes from the den. Despite her misgivings about this, Brenna had to admit the DarkRiver pair had picked a beautiful spot. The snow was soft underfoot and a frozen waterfall glimmered a few meters away, the ice glazed to an almost painful brightness by the midmorning sun. Faith's dark red hair appeared aflame against all that white.

Then there was no more distance between them. "Thank you for coming."

Faith smiled, but Judd spoke before the F-Psy could respond. "You chose a location extremely close to the den. Why not somewhere nearer your pack?"

Brenna had wondered about that, too. The cats might be their allies, but the two packs were not yet friends. And the males of predatory changeling species' were notoriously protective of their women—mates, daughters, and sisters. She should know. Drew and Riley were driving her to madness. It had reached the point where she knew something had to give. She just hoped they all survived the explosion.

But Faith seemed happy with her overprotective male. "Vaughn finds it amusing to get past your patrols without detection."

Vaughn looked unrepentant. "They're getting sloppy. Even with Red here stomping away, I had no trouble getting in." He grinned when his mate gave him a warning look.

Brenna felt something clutch in her stomach at the easy intimacy between the two, at the grin from a cat she'd never before seen smile. That was what she should be seeking—a sensual, affectionate changeling male. They didn't bother to hide their emotions, touched as easily as they breathed, laughed with their mates even if they didn't with anyone else.

The problem was that these days, only one man seemed to register on her feminine senses and he was a Psy who could give her nothing of what Vaughn gave Faith . . . even if he were interested. Which he clearly wasn't. Then why did she keep going to him, expecting him to fight her demons, to keep her *safe*?

"So"—Faith looked at her—"let's talk about your dreams."

They were nightmares, not dreams. "Do you think we could do it alone?"

Flickers of light came and went in Faith's cardinal eyes—white stars on black velvet. Sascha was a cardinal, too, but Faith's eyes were different from the other woman's, quieter, less open, touched with a stroke of darkness. Faith saw the future and her eyes said that that future wasn't always something good.

Glancing over her shoulder to her mate, Faith inclined her head in a gentle gesture. Brenna was fascinated by the Psy woman's interaction with a cat who had always struck her as wilder, more animal than most. Maybe she could learn something from Faith about managing unmanageable males.

Turning herself, she looked up at the profile of a man so lethally cold, she should have been too terrified to approach him. "Please."

Judd's hair lifted in the slight breeze and she had to curl her fingers to fight the temptation to touch. Because, rather than being crushed under the ice of his personality, her fascination with him continued to grow.

"I'll make sure no one gets to you." A promise so absolute, she felt it in her bones.

"Thank you."

His gaze flicked to Vaughn. "I'll take the south."

"I've got the north."

With that, the men were gone, shadows that blended into the trees ringing the clearing. Brenna waited until she could no longer scent Vaughn, trusting that he'd hold to the changeling code of honor and go out of earshot of normal conversation. "I don't know where to start," she found herself saying.

"You said you've been experiencing what might be called visions." Faith had a very clear voice, hauntingly so. "Tell me what you see and when it began."

Taking a deep breath, Brenna poured out the whole sordid

story, then asked, "Did he do something to my mind?" She stared down at the purity of the snow in an effort to make herself feel less dirty . . . less raped.

Faith's answer was to say, "Walk with me, Brenna." She took them on a slow stroll to the bottom of the waterfall. "Beautiful, isn't it?"

She looked up. "Yes." *Before*, she would've been the first to say that, to see the good out there. One day, she promised herself fiercely, she'd get back that lost part of her, the part that believed in joy.

Bending down, Faith picked up a smooth stone that had been stranded on the edge of the waterfall and rolled it between her fingers as she rose, her face set in thought. "I've never heard of a situation where a non-Psy was altered to have Psy abilities. But they do sound like visions of a sort." She dropped the stone back to earth and nodded as if reaching a decision. "I need to go into your mind."

"*No.*" An instinctive response, unadorned by civilized thought. "I'm sorry, but no."

"Never apologize for protecting yourself." Faith sounded furious. "I know what it's like to feel as if your mind is the only safe place."

"Except it isn't. Not anymore." That was what threatened to destroy her. How did she wash herself clean if the evil was lodged inside of her, becoming more a part of her with each passing hour? She dashed the incipient self-pity with sheer effort of will—it was a weakness she couldn't afford. "Can you still help?"

"I can try." Shoving her hands into the pockets of her coat, Faith blew out a breath. "Do you think you can access the part of your mind that the visions are coming from?"

"I don't know how." The truth was, she didn't want to go to that twisted place in her soul.

Faith's eyes held no judgment, only understanding. "I know it'll hurt, but I want you to attempt to relive the vision. At the same time, imagine shoving all that—thoughts, feelings, images—outward."

Brenna's gorge rose at the idea of returning to the malevolence, but she was no coward. She reached inward . . . and found it horrifyingly easy to awaken the memories, to feel the victim's fear and her own sadistic satisfaction. Stomach threatening to revolt, she thrust the emotions and images out of her mind with the desperation of a trapped creature. This evil wasn't her, couldn't be her. Because if it was, then she hadn't walked out sane from the butcher's torture chamber. She had walked out a nightmare.

"Enough."

Brenna clamped down on the repugnant stream of memory. "Did it work?" The snow was too bright. It hurt her eyes.

Faith was frowning when she replied, "I'm not that powerful a telepath, but I did catch bits and pieces—things you pushed outside your shields. All I can say is that it doesn't . . . taste like foresight."

"I can hear a 'but.' "

"There's something there that shouldn't be—not wrong by itself, but because you're changeling." The foreseer folded her arms around herself. "I hate the cold up here."

"I like it—the way the snow makes everything pure again." She regretted the words the second they were out. Faith's eyes were too intelligent, too knowledgeable. "Can you tell me anything more?"

Thankfully, the F-Psy took her lead. "I think Enrique succeeded in doing something to your brain itself."

At the echo of Judd's words, Brenna felt her nails cut into her palms. "Could he have caused irreversible damage?"

Night-sky eyes met hers. "I wish I could answer you with certainty, but I can't. I'm sorry, Brenna." She touched a hand fleetingly to Brenna's arm. "What I can say is that everything you've told me points to a psychic side effect, rather than an organic one. You were scanned at a human hospital, weren't you?"

She nodded. "Lara and Sascha wanted to make sure they'd caught everything." An M-Psy—gifted with the ability to see inside a body—could have done the same thing at less cost, but her pack didn't much trust any Psy hooked up to the PsyNet.

"Then I don't think you have to worry about brain damage—those scanning machines catch the tiniest tears and lesions. I should know. While in the Net, I was scanned on a regular basis."

The practical reminder grounded Brenna. She'd seen the scans herself, seen the lack of damage. "So what do you think he did?"

"Well, Enrique did say he experimented on changeling women. We read that as the justification of a madman, but perhaps it wasn't. Perhaps he succeeded with you."

"He still would've killed me." Enrique had been pleased with her, but only as you'd be pleased with a lab rat. It, too, was disposable. "Is there any way to find out what his goal was?" And whether he'd torn into her brain for reasons other than psychopathic pleasure.

"He has to have kept records." Faith sounded very sure. "I'll ask those I can, but it's almost certain that they're in the Council's hands by now."

In other words, utterly out of their reach. "If you had to guess, what would you say he was trying to achieve?"

"Let me think." Faith picked up a handful of snow and began to sift it through her fingers. Flakes caught on the dark green of her gloves. "Do you mind if I ask Sascha? I won't tell her details about the dreams—just what Enrique might've done to your mind."

Brenna looked at the waterfall rather than at Faith. "Ask."

Faith's eyes lost focus for a microsecond before brightening again. "Okay, I've got her." A pause. "Apparently," she said into the silence, "Enrique thought that changeling women were perfect because of their ability to bear emotion without breaking."

"Could he have been trying to create a hybrid?" Brenna scowled. "But that's stupid—he could have as easily spliced DNA, or gotten a changeling woman pregnant." But though he had violated her in so many ways, ways she still couldn't think about without her vision hazing over with the dark red of blood, he hadn't tried to impregnate her.

"Sascha agrees. So do I." The F-Psy dusted off her hands.

"From my own experience, I'd say it was more likely Enrique somehow ripped open a previously dormant section of your brain."

"A part that was probably meant to stay that way."

"Yes. What was done to you wasn't natural. But it was done."

"And I have to learn to live with it." The monster had stolen her right to choose.

"I'll give you what help I can. Sascha, too—she'll understand, you know." Faith's voice was gentle. "You don't have to worry that she'll judge you."

Brenna's throat burned with withheld tears. "How could she not? What I feel during those nightmares . . . it's twisted and *wrong*. And she's so good, so kind."

"Being an empath means she feels what you feel, including your pain and your horror. And she may be kind"—Faith smiled—"but she's assuredly not perfect. Ask her mate if you don't believe me. But that's a decision for you. As to our help, we'll do our best, but I'm not sure how much we can do."

"At least I know I'm not crazy." She tried to sound confident but the truth was, she wasn't sure. Maybe she was sane now, but what if the nightmare visions succeeded in changing that? It made her face heat up in raw panic, her heart stutter . . . and her eyes search for the cold comfort of a Psy lethal enough to vanquish all her demons. Her face flushed again, but this time, it wasn't fear that prompted it. "Can I ask you about something else?"

"Of course. Brenna . . ." Faith seemed momentarily lost for words, awkward. "I would call you a friend."

Before today, Brenna would have said that there were no two women further part. Faith was very composed, very *together*, while she was a mess. But now she realized that both of them knew what it was like to be forced to bear witness to things they'd rather not see. "I'd like that."

Faith's smile made her even more beautiful. "What did you want to ask me?"

"It's about—" She paused, knowing the second she asked this question, there would be no more hiding from the truth—that she'd gone to Judd for reasons other than his being Psy, reasons that had nothing to do with practicality and everything to do with how he made her feel as a woman. "You were conditioned not to feel."

"Yes. All Psy are."

"But you broke it. I heard it didn't take you that long after you met Vaughn."

Faith's nod was slow. "I think I know what you want to ask." The redhead's expression grew pensive. "Judd?"

Relieved at not having to articulate her complicated and confusing feelings for a man who had none, she nodded. "He's been out much longer than you, but he's completely shut in, completely Silent."

CHAPTER 8

"**The difference** between us is that both Sascha and I had our abilities turn on us in a sense. We had to embrace emotion or drown. I don't think that's the case with Judd."

You don't need any more nightmares.

"No." It hurt her to remember the bleak darkness in his eyes. "He was a soldier, I think."

Faith seemed about to say something, but then shook her head as if clearing the thought. "Aside from that, he's male."

Brenna had definitely noticed that fact. She'd never seen a man she wanted to stroke more than Judd. "You think that changes things?"

"If you'd asked me while I was part of the PsyNet, I would've said no, that we're all the same. Now"—she took a deep breath of the cold air—"I know that to be a lie. Men and women are fundamentally different. I don't think it was a coincidence that the first two to drop out of the Net because of emotion were female."

She understood the distinction at once. "Judd defected to protect the kids from rehabilitation, not because he felt things he shouldn't."

"Yes. But that in itself is a hopeful sign—that he did it to protect. If he—" Faith turned away. "I don't know if I should say this."

"Please. He won't talk." And a deep, unknown part of her flat out refused to do the sensible thing and walk away. She knew that a wolf male—able to give and accept the touch and affection she needed to be fully alive—would make her far happier. But it wasn't a wolf male she wanted.

Faith relented. "If Judd was who I think he was in the Net, I'm fairly certain he must have been offered a chance to escape the sentence of rehabilitation. That he didn't take it but embraced the likelihood of death to save the children . . . well, that says something about your Psy, doesn't it?"

Brenna had her own suspicions about who Judd had been in his other life, but she'd ask those questions to his face. "To reach that part of him—" She kicked at the snow, sending it sparking into the sunshine. "He's as stubborn as any wolf, and with the conditioning on top of that—"

"Would you like some advice?"

"Everything you have."

"Leave it." Faith's expression was solemn. "He's probably never going to break Silence—he's done and seen too much to chance feeling."

"No." She would not believe that. "It can be broken."

"It'll hurt. Both of you." The voice of experience. "And, Brenna, he's not the kind of man you need, to heal."

She gave a frustrated little cry. "Everyone thinks I should be wrapped up in cotton wool and babied—when I'm not being pitied, that is! But I'm no tame housecat. I never have been. What was done to me didn't alter that. I'm attracted to Judd's strength—give me a nice gentle puppy dog of a man and I'd drive him to tears within the hour."

Faith's lips curved upward, eyes crinkling at the corners. "Then I almost pity Judd." Leaning in, she whispered, "Make him uncomfortable. Don't take no for an answer. *Push.* Push him until he loses control. Remember, fire melts ice."

Brenna looked into those eerie night-sky eyes as Faith drew back. "Could be a dangerous game."

"You don't seem to be the kind of woman content with safe and easy."

"No." She also wasn't the kind of woman who gave up at the first obstacle. Judd might be categorically Psy, but she was a SnowDancer.

Almost eleven hours later, Judd found himself thinking of the way Brenna had watched him that morning as they made their way back to the den. Her gaze had been so intent, it had felt disconcertingly like a touch, no matter how impossible that was. However, the second they had actually entered the den, she'd left him and—

He shook his head in a futile attempt to wipe her from his mind. He had to concentrate. Thinking about Brenna had a dangerous way of derailing that. She was up to something, of that he was certain. Her expression had been—

Focus!

The church appeared on the other side of the street like an architectural specter, reminding him of who he was and what he did when darkness fell and people thought themselves safe in their beds. He wasn't so different from Enrique—death was his gift and the only thing he could offer Brenna. That thought finally cemented his focus. He extended his stride, concentrating on the yellow light spilling from the church's curved windows.

He had never decided whether the Ghost had chosen this as their meeting place out of perversity or hope. The church was small. It had been built after the Second Reformation half a century ago and was filled not with stained glass and candles, but leafy green plants and, in the daytime, bright sunshine. Tonight he entered to find it empty but for a solitary woman kneeling at the altar. He slid into a pew at the back, his eyes on the stars visible through the transparent dome of the roof. It made him remember what he'd given up when he'd left the PsyNet—the cool darkness, the icy flare of millions of minds.

"The young ones don't kneel, but the old grew up in the time of Rome." The voice was male and full of the same peace that soaked the walls of this building. It was the single thing this church had in common with the more ornate pre–Second Reformation churches—the sense of hushed reverence, a quiet that was so pervasive it was almost sound.

Judd glanced at the man who'd taken a seat beside him. "Father Perez."

Perez smiled, teeth flashing white against his teak skin. "That makes me sound like a candidate for the senior citizens' pension. I'm only twenty-nine." Wearing the winter uniform of a Second Reformation priest—loose white pants and shirt, the latter bearing a panel on the left side patterned with blue snowflakes, he looked even younger. It was the knowledge in his eyes that made him old.

Judd thought of him not as a priest, but as a fellow soldier. "It's your title."

"We've been working together for close to six years. Why won't you call me Xavier? Even our shy friend calls me by my given name."

Because using Father Perez's given name would be the first step on the road to friendship and Judd didn't want a friend. To do what he did, to be what he was, he had to retain his distance. From those who would be friends and the one woman who might be . . . more. "Did he give you something for me?"

A sigh. "No matter what you've done, Judd, judgment is not yours to make." Perez passed over a data crystal encased in protective plasglass. The crystals cost more than the ubiquitous discs, but they were more secure and held larger amounts of data.

Judd slid it into an inner pants pocket. "Thank you." He didn't need the data for tonight's operation, but he would for the next hit.

"The New Book says God does not wish to punish or harm us. God wishes us to learn and grow, to become better souls through the ages."

To believe that, he'd have to possess a soul. "What about true evil?" Judd asked, mind awash in memories of a blood-drenched room and a woman with bruises ringing her neck. "What does your book say about that?"

"That good men must fight the evil and that bad men will be judged in death."

Judd looked at the lone parishioner still kneeling at the altar. She was sobbing, the sound soft and almost apologetic. "Sometimes, evil needs to be judged in the moment, before it kills the good, destroys all light."

"Yes." Perez's eyes went to the woman. "That is why I sit with you."

"How do you balance the two halves of your self—the priest and the soldier?" *The light and the darkness*. It was not a question he should've asked, not a possibility he should've considered, but it was done and now he waited. Because he needed the answer.

"The same way you balance your todays and tomorrows. With hope and forgiveness." The other man rose. "I must comfort her. Only you can comfort yourself."

Judd watched Perez walk down the wide aisle and kneel to place his arm around the shoulders of the woman who wept. She turned into his embrace, finding succor. A simple act, but one that Judd was incapable of. He was a naked blade, his purpose—his gift—to kill. As a child, he'd been deemed unfit to live with others and relocated, brought up among the shadows. He had no business being in the SnowDancer den now that the rest of the family was safe, and absolutely no right to do what he'd been doing with Brenna.

And he had been actively *doing*, allowing her to get closer than he allowed any other being, coming perilously close to breaching Silence. That could not be permitted. Ever. Because while Brenna might see him as a man, the cold, hard truth was that he wasn't—he was an assassin. Trained. Honed.

And blooded.

***Remember,** fire melts ice.*

Brenna blushed at the memory of Faith's words and straightened her short black skirt. Teamed with a soft V-neck sweater in red, it was a perfectly acceptable outfit. Except that the sweater caressed her curves and the skirt shaped her bottom. Her hair still looked like hell, but the rest would do.

Drew scowled when she walked through the living room of the family quarters, but let her go without argument, probably guessing she was going to visit one of her girlfriends—especially since she'd deliberately hinted at that earlier. She knew she was procrastinating, but she had no time to bring up the topic of separate quarters right then. At least her brothers were no longer trying to confine her to quarters now that she'd shown she'd take off if they tried.

She got several slow male grins as she walked down the corridor and one outright request for a date. Though she had to refuse, the invitation bolstered her confidence—SnowDancer men could be incredibly charming when they put their minds to it. *Too bad I seem to have a fixation on the Man of Ice.*

It had taken her all day to work up the courage to follow Faith's advice. Frankly, part of her remained terrified that she wouldn't be able to handle anything sexual. It was the first time since the rescue that she'd even contemplated being with a man, the first time the idea hadn't made her break out in a cold sweat. Santano Enrique had tied her to a bed, kept her naked for his experiments, done other, sickening things . . . things she wanted to erase from her mind.

"Breathe." Reaching Judd's door, she unclenched her hands and rubbed them on her skirt before knocking. The memories she crushed into that locked box in her mind. She wasn't some *victim*, she thought, blood pounding a harsh drumbeat in her skull, she was an adult wolf in full sensual glory.

"Judd," she called sotto voce when the door remained closed. No response. Her nose backed up the fact that he was out—his scent was there but not as concentrated as it would have been had he been inside. "Brenna, you idiot." She wanted to kick herself. All this nerve-wracking preparation and she hadn't bothered to check if he was in. Now what?

Returning to her quarters—thank God neither of her brothers was still home—she put through a call to Judd's cell phone, expecting to find him elsewhere in the den. It didn't connect. "Turn it on," she muttered, then hung up.

Feeling a tad pathetic at being all dressed up with nowhere to go, she got undressed, crawled into her pj's and took out a book—a hardcover—Riley had given her for her birthday.

"Bloody expensive," he'd said, but there had been a grin in his eyes.

Her elder brother didn't smile like that anymore. She knew he blamed himself for not keeping her safe from Enrique, despite the fact that there was nothing he could have done. Riley had always been serious—ten years her senior, he'd pretty much raised both her and Drew, with the pack's help, after their parents died—but now he never so much as smiled. Drew put on a good front, but her wonderful, funny, smart middle brother was so angry.

Someone knocked on her door. "Bren, you back, too? Want some pizza?"

Tears pricked her eyes as she leaned against the metal bars of the headboard she'd fashioned using nineteenth-century patterns for inspiration. "What're you doing eating pizza at this hour, Andrew Liam Kincaid?" she said, forcing a smile.

Sure enough, Drew cracked open the door to throw her a grin. "I'm a growing boy."

"Well, I'm not, so don't tempt me." She opened the book. "Shoo."

"Your loss, baby sister." Sending her another grin, he pulled the door shut.

She squeezed her eyes closed and then took several deep breaths to think past the lump choking up her throat. But no matter how hard she concentrated, she was too emotionally torn up to focus on anything, much less the book in her hands. All she could think was that she needed Judd, needed him to hold her. She knew that to be a foolish, impossible wish, but the animal in her didn't care. Where was he? She tried calling him several more times, until finally, she could no longer fight the enveloping wings of sleep. What awaited her was anything but restful.

A jumble of sensory input, acrid fear on her tongue, a pulsating kind of panic. She'd made a mistake and now it had to be cleaned up—

Snatches of sound. A laughing child. Fear. Joy. Birthday cake—

He was so sexy, she wanted to—

Fear. A salty/wrong/bad scent. It was a mess. Had to be cleaned up—

Brenna moaned and turned onto her side. If someone had been in the room with her, they might've nudged her awake. But she was alone, and she was dreaming in inexplicable fragments, seeing broken snatches of thought. Her mind searched for an anchor and found the way blocked. It shouldn't have been.

A moment of clarity, of anger: *He shouldn't have done that!*

A second later, she was dreaming again.

Judd walked away as the first flames began to rise behind him, hands thrust into his pockets and head covered by the pulled-up hood of a black sweatshirt that turned him from Arrow to hoodlum. Even if he had been caught on surveillance equipment—highly unlikely, given his skills—his identity would be impossible to determine. To further muddy the waters, he'd gone to considerable trouble to ensure the blast bore no Psy fingerprint, using materials available to humans and changelings as well as Psy.

Alarms sounded behind him, followed by the hiss of sprinkler systems being deployed. That posed no threat. He'd designed the blast radius to take out a key section without reliance on the destructive powers of fire. Nothing inside that square should be salvageable if his explosives had functioned as they were meant to. And he had no doubts that they had—after all, he'd been trained by Councilor Ming LeBon himself.

CHAPTER 9

The guards didn't notice his telekinetically blurred body as he slid right past them and into the four a.m. darkness of the quiet street. The Council had made a cold calculation and located this lab in a suburban area, believing that here, among civilians, it would escape discovery and attack. They should've known better.

Fading into the shadows on the other side of the street, he checked the buildings on either side of the lab, ready to throw up a Tk shield to ensure their safety—because, unlike the Council, he didn't consider civilian casualties necessary collateral damage. His caution proved redundant. Not even a spark had escaped the confines of the target compound.

A perfect strike.

Lights began flicking on up and down the street as he watched. At the same instant, security personnel pounded out of the compound, searching for a trail that had gone cold the second after he'd walked out. It had taken them at least two minutes to respond. Sloppy. Whoever was running this op had become cocky after going undetected for over a year.

It was exactly the reaction Judd and the Ghost had planned on.

Satisfied, he took one last look at the rapidly dying flames and turned to cut through the middle-of-the-night black of a family's backyard. As he negotiated the garden and swingset, he found his eyes drawn to the still-dark window on the second floor. That room held a child, a small half-human, half-changeling boy with more energy than coordination. Judd had seen him several times during his trips to scout the area.

The child's presence had made the disguised lab across the road even more of an obscenity. Because what had been going on in that place was meant to destroy the minds and lives of children just like that boy. The room light finally came on as Judd scaled the back fence with grace even a cat might have envied, and landed in an even darker yard. No one was home here and wouldn't be for several days. He'd done his homework.

Deactivating the alarmed lock took him a quarter of a minute. Once inside, he stood with his back to the doorway, not going any farther. These people hadn't invited him in and he wouldn't violate their refuge. However, when he tried to relax his body and mind without falling asleep—a trick all soldiers learned early on—he found he couldn't. There was pressure on the back of his skull, a hard push he might've taken for an attempt to penetrate his shields had the pressure not seemed to come from *inside* his mind.

He rechecked his basic armor against psychic attack. No cracks. He was about to go deeper when the pressure simply halted. Unable to follow it any longer, he put the problem down to a lack of sleep and sent his mind into rest-and-repair mode. His concentration was so tightly focused, it was no wonder he missed the telltale signature in that mental push, a harbinger of something far more dangerous than any Psy weapon.

Three hours later, he left the house to blend seamlessly into the steady stream of early morning joggers and walkers. More than one changeling had pointed out that he looked Psy even when dressed otherwise, so he'd spent time watching young human and changeling males, and now affected their careless swagger. But it wasn't natural for him—he was a soldier, with a soldier's bearing, and that would never change.

He passed several Psy patrols without incident, aware they were illegally mind-scanning everyone who passed. What they would read off him were the fuzzy thoughts of a hungover human male. Meanwhile, he noted everything about them. Their black uniforms were indistinguishable from other units in the Psy forces, but for the small gold insignia on the left shoulder—two snakes twisted in combat.

He recognized it at once. These men were part of Ming LeBon's private army. Which meant that Councilor LeBon had been placed in charge of this little enterprise. Not what he would've expected, given Nikita Duncan's proximity to the area. Ming's home base, on the other hand, was in Europe.

Unless Ming had decided to relocate . . . perhaps to track down a rebel Arrow.

Judd still wasn't back when Brenna went to find him after waking from nightmare-laced dreams that had left her sweaty and gritty-eyed. "Where are you?" She wanted to cry, she was that desperate for him.

Cry?

The reaction was so unlike her, it slapped her fully awake. Frowning, she made a conscious effort to pull herself together. She wasn't one of those females who was constantly in heat. Though if she were, she knew who she would choose to rub up against. That hard soldier's body made her want to do all sorts of deliciously erotic things—she wondered if he had enough spare flesh on him to bite or if her teeth would slide off.

"Hello . . . Earth to Brenna Shane." Indigo's curious face came into her line of sight. "Why are you standing zoned out in the middle of the corridor?"

Brenna hoped her cheeks weren't as red as they felt. What was going on? Sure, she was attracted to Judd, but this raw sexual hunger was like nothing she'd ever before experienced. "Ah . . ." Her disrupted night had made her a bit slow. Wait, that was the answer. "I wanted to talk to you."

Indigo jerked a thumb over her shoulder. "Walk with me. I'm off to a morning session with Her Majesty."

"Who?"

"Sienna 'I'm a cardinal Psy and don't need combat training' Lauren. Damn juveniles. They all think they're invincible." Indigo scowled. "So what's up?"

"The murder," she said, wondering if Judd knew about his niece's recalcitrance. "Do you have any more information?"

Indigo's face closed over. "That's on a need-to-know basis and last time I looked, you weren't part of Security."

"I qualify." Brenna set her jaw. "Was it a Psy?"

To her surprise, Indigo responded without further argument. "Inconclusive. No distinctive scent, but we all know not every Psy gives off that metallic smell."

None of the Laurens did. Indigo didn't have to point out which one of the family had the skill to commit the crime. Heart chilling, Brenna gripped the lieutenant's arm. "You don't seriously think it could've been Judd. He wouldn't—"

"How well do you know him, Brenna?" Indigo shook her head. "The man's a fucking shadow. No, I don't think it was him—if it had been, we would have never found a body—but you're kidding yourself if you think he isn't capable of executing someone."

Brenna's gut was a huge knot. "Could it have been one of us?"

"You didn't hear this from me." Indigo's namesake eyes narrowed. "Hell, I don't know why I'm telling you—maybe to piss off your brothers. Why do you let them get away with that overprotective shit?"

She didn't want to go there today. "You were telling me about Timothy."

The other woman snorted. "Charming son of a bitch. Had a talent for sweet-talking his way into beds he shouldn't have been in."

"That's not a motive." Wolf changelings were highly sexual and single packmates often hopped beds. As for mated pairs, they didn't cheat. Ever. "If someone was mad over a stolen lover, they would've just challenged him to prove dominance." A fight but not to the death.

"Yeah, I think so too, but it's a lead. And that wasn't the only mess he got himself into. Timmy had indications of drug use. If he, for whatever reason, threatened to expose the piece-of-shit dealer and it was one of us . . . well, everyone knows Hawke's view on drugs."

Brenna nodded. "He would've sliced the bastard open." That one of her own pack could be evil enough to deal drugs staggered her. "It wasn't Jax, was it?" she asked with a fresh wave of horror. "He wasn't messed up." The Psy drug had a devastating effect on changeling bodies, leaving them trapped midshift. Death followed in days if not hours.

"No." Indigo gave a distasteful shiver. "Ruby Crush, street name, Rush."

A drug developed by a changeling piece of vermin and adapted to their physiology. "It boosts normal physical strength during the high, right?"

"As it scrambles the brain." Indigo shook her head. "Rush freaks turn into witless, giggling idiots. Tim had to have been very careful. No one ever saw him high." She glanced at her timepiece. "Got to go. Tell Judd I need to talk to him if you see him."

Brenna nodded, but hours passed and Judd didn't appear. Her frustration turned to worry, then jackknifed into anger. Where the hell was he and why couldn't he have called?

. . . You're kidding yourself if you think he isn't capable of executing someone.

. . . He's not the kind of man you need . . .

She tried to ignore the voices, but part of her listened. Part of her finally began to see.

Judd met the Ghost beneath Father Perez's church, having showered and changed in the small room Perez kept for situations like this. It wasn't yet noon, but it might as well have been midnight in the centuries-old crypt under the light-filled building.

"Why do you think some humans feel the need to inter their dead?" The voice came from the black pool where two corners met. "Changelings let their dead turn to dust."

Judd had neither the time nor the inclination to engage in a philosophical discussion. He wanted to return to the den and see if Brenna was okay. The talk with Faith had appeared to help her, but if she'd had more of those dreams, she could be in trouble. And he was the only one she trusted enough to come to for . . . comfort.

"Are there other labs?" he asked point-blank, well aware that his urgency to see Brenna was a minor breach of Silence, the first step on the road to temptation. He wouldn't touch her, he justified, simply make sure of her welfare.

"Of course, but the one you disabled this morning was the most important."

"Are you certain? With Ming involved, we could be looking at Europe."

"No, the Council would've preferred that—there's a problem with their head scientist, Ashaya Aleine, refusing to relocate."

"Must be something big if they haven't overridden her objections." No one stood against the Council without either an unimpeachable reason or an ace in the hole.

"I'm working on it—they've got a blackout around her. Everything's classified."

"Do you know her designation?"

"Gradient 9.9 M-Psy."

"Rare." Most Psy that powerful tended to cross the 0.1 boundary over into cardinal rank. Judd had always considered his own 9.9 Tk status an advantage. The telekinesis, when combined with his 9.4 ability in telepathy, made him far more of a threat than many a cardinal. Yet he didn't have the night-sky eyes that betrayed his power. When he tried *very* hard, he could even appear harmless. "How much damage did we do?" It might've only been a few hours, but data traveled fast in the Net.

"Unconfirmed reports state the prototype was destroyed. If that's true, it'll take them at least six months to reconstruct it. However, if we take Aleine out of the equation, we set them back years. She's the brains behind the entire project."

Judd had killed before. And he'd done so with clean efficiency. Not one of his hits had ever been labeled an execution, much less traced back to the Arrow Squad. "I'll need more data before I make that decision." He no longer trusted anyone when it came to this aspect of his abilities.

"I want to hold off in any case. We may end up needing the information in her head." A pause.

Judd's need to return to the den pushed at him to finish this and leave. "What?"

"I've heard rumors that Aleine might not be in full support of Protocol I."

That she was the scientist in charge of developing the implant nonetheless was no contradiction in terms—the Council had ways of ensuring cooperation. "What are the chances of turning her?"

"Slim to none. She's been in the Council substructure since she turned seventeen. Her entire family consists of a four-year-old son. Keenan Aleine lives off-site in an apartment in San Diego."

"With his father?" Psy bore children as part of fertilization contracts. Custody depended on the terms of the individual contract.

"No. The child is under Council protection. Lives in the same building as the Rika-Smythe family group."

"Convenient."

"That was my thought. I'll attempt to confirm."

Judd began to head for the exit. "Send me the data when you have it."

The SnowDancer tunnels were relatively quiet when he got back, but he ran into Indigo almost immediately. Suspicion was a hard edge in her eyes.

"Where were you the night Tim died?"

It was an unexpected question. Circumstances had led him to believe the SnowDancer lieutenant trusted him. Clearly, he'd been wrong. "Alone. In my quarters. And no, that can't be verified. Pity you don't have a Justice-Psy here willing to scan me."

"Oh, for crissakes, don't give me any shit." Indigo glared. "I've had it up to here with men and their attitudes. I had to ask, you know that." Then she was gone.

Not completely certain what had just taken place, Judd continued on to his rooms. Or that had been his intention. Halfway there, he realized he was heading to Brenna's instead and that his need to see her was no minor fault in the conditioning.

He stopped—he couldn't allow himself near her when he was this close to what could be a lethal edge. It took conscious effort to put himself back on the correct path. But he hadn't been inside his room five minutes when there was a knock on the door. He knew who it was. That knowledge didn't keep him from pulling the door open.

Brenna pushed past him and into the room, hands on her hips. There were dark shadows under her eyes, lines around the corners of her mouth.

"You had more dreams." He shut the door though his brain was sparking with all sorts of warning signals.

She blew out a breath between pursed lips. "Where have you been?" she asked instead of confirming his guess.

He wasn't accustomed to anyone waiting for him. The fact that she had, caused enough of a reaction that he folded his arms and leaned against the door. "None of your business."

"None of my—" She clenched her fists. "Would it have hurt you to leave your phone on?"

He'd been operating under full silence—the lab had had some incredibly complex intrusion detection systems. "It didn't occur to me that you'd attempt contact." It was the truth. He was used to walking alone, to surviving alone. It was a necessary adjunct of his particular ability. But Brenna had not only noticed his absence, she had worried.

His reaction to her intensified . . . enough to cause a mild pain response. Pain triggers were an integral part of Silence. Brutalize a child for something and he soon learned to stop doing it. Even if that meant shutting down his own emotions. That reminder, rather than the pain, was what made him say what he did. "You and I have no relationship that implies a commitment to constant availability."

Brenna's voice was harsh when she replied. "Don't you say that. We have something and don't you try to pretend it doesn't exist."

He unfolded his arms. "We have nothing." Because he could give her nothing, not even the comfort she so obviously needed. *The comfort she'd waited all night to find with him.* Rather than being there for her, he'd been out doing violence. "You're clinging to me because I helped you during the healing process. It's a normal psychological reaction."

"You are not like everyone says." She refused to drop her eyes. "I *see* you."

"You see what I choose to show you." He moved away from the door. "It'll be better for both of us if you speak to Faith or Sascha the next time you have a question. You appear to be getting too emotionally attached to me."

She actually growled at him, a low throaty sound that seemed incongruous coming from her slender throat. "If I was a violent woman, I'd claw you for that."

He held her gaze. "No matter how hard you push, I'll remain Psy. Silence is who I am." The Protocol had saved him from becoming a serial murderer by turning him into a sanctioned killer. Sometimes there were no good choices. "Go find a changeling to give you what you need. I can do without the disruptions."

CHAPTER 10

Striding across the room, she pulled open the door. "You know what, I think I will." With that, she was gone, striding down the corridor in tight jeans and a red sweater that drew male eyes to her body. It was only when one of those admiring males tripped over thin air that Judd realized he was using his Tk. He slammed the door shut before he could do any more damage.

A finely tuned spike of pain speared through his skull, signaling a detectable breach in his conditioning. He didn't want to fix it, didn't want to stop his descent into chaos. What he wanted was to hurt the men who'd dared look at her.

The thin line that snaked down the wall in front of him appeared as insubstantial as a pencil drawing, but it was a hairline fracture that could turn into a full break with a little more pressure. Just like his mind. He managed to control the unrestrained flow of telekinetic power before he caused the wall to collapse, but the rupture was enough to demonstrate exactly how close he was to a catastrophic loss of control. If he didn't fix the fault in his conditioning, it could mean death for hundreds in the den—adults, children . . . Brenna.

Sweat dripped down his spine as he backed up and sat on the edge of the bed to begin repairing the major flaws. The finer fractures that riddled the previously hard casing of Silence would have to wait until he was calmer. Right then, his concentration was shot. He could still smell Brenna's psychic scent in the air.

She was heat and woman, fear and courage, sensuality and laughter.

And she was not his.

If he tried to change that, he'd end up killing her. Because he wasn't anything as simple as a Tk. He was a Tk-Cell, a subdesignation so rare, it wasn't listed on any public record. After Silence, Tk-Cells had become the Council's dirty little secret, their most lethal assassins. Before Silence, before the imposition of *control,* those of his subdesignation had always ended up murderers, killing their wives and daughters first. It was as if their ability snapped out to strike at the only ones who might have pulled them back from the abyss.

Judd made his decision then and there. He had to leave the den before Brenna unknowingly set off his abilities. She had no idea of the horror she could unleash.

He wasn't an assassin by choice. He was one because he couldn't *be* anything else.

Judd found Hawke before dawn the next morning, having spent the previous afternoon and night sealing up the cracks in his conditioning—it was all that protected those around him from the killing rage of his ability. "I want out," he told the alpha. He wasn't used to asking for permission, would have just walked out had he been alone, but he wasn't. His unexplained disappearance would impact Walker, Sienna, and the kids' position in the den.

Hawke raised an eyebrow. "What does your family think about that decision?"

"They have nothing to do with it." A complete truth. "Walker's settled and able to steer them through any turbulence. I'm a disruptive influence." As the recent murder had shown, anytime things went badly wrong, eyes looked toward the Psy, toward him. "All of them have integrated into the pack to some extent." While he'd made every effort not to.

The SnowDancer alpha didn't look convinced. "Why now?"

Judd had already decided to tell *a* truth. It was simply not the one that mattered. "In the Net, I held a rank equal to those of your lieutenants. I knew that should we survive our defection, I'd lose that. It was a price I chose to pay." To save the children from the living death that was rehabilitation.

"So what's changed?"

"I didn't count on the fact that the enforced idleness, the effectual caging of my abilities, would have a consequence." Also true. Despite the covert work he'd been doing—both for the Ghost and to earn income for the family—the pressure was building. It was, he told himself, the reason why Brenna had been able to crack his shields with relatively little effort. He'd already been compromised. "Those idle psychic muscles need to be stretched or they'll begin to act without my conscious control."

"Like our beasts."

"Yes." He'd seen wolves go rogue, seen the damage they could do. "But worse."

"I'm not buying." Hawke leaned back against the dark wood of his desk, pale eyes more wolf than human. "I recognize control when I see it. And yours is precision-tuned."

No other option was feasible for his subdesignation. However, that wasn't something Hawke needed to know. "You've guessed at my position in the Net," he said instead. "I was who I was because my abilities lie in combat. Such aggressive abilities have to be utilized on a regular basis to ward off loss of control."

"How are you planning to do that?" No overt suspicion, but the implication was there.

For a fleeting second, Judd considered calling attention to the insult, but then stifled the reaction as irrelevant. To the wolves, he was an enemy, not a fellow soldier. "I have no intention of rejoining the PsyNet—it would mean death for my family should the Council realize we weren't executed when we walked into your territory. I can, however, blend in with the general populace and go freelance."

"As what?"

He met those cold wolf eyes. "As a man who cleans up certain kinds of messes, what else?" A brutal choice but one that would serve to keep his abilities in check.

"I can't let an assassin loose on the fucking public." Hawke shoved a hand through hair almost identical to the silver-gold color of his pelt in wolf form.

Judd didn't see the need to point out that he'd already been working for months without setting off alarms. The clients never saw him. He never met them. And he didn't kill for them. Not yet. "No wet work," he said. "I'd work in surveillance and protection in this state for the next three or four years."

Until Sienna became capable of taking over some of what he did to keep the LaurenNet functional, he couldn't go far. The familial Net linked him to his family and generated enough biofeedback to keep them all alive. No Psy could survive without that feedback. If he put distance between himself and the others, it would strain the already thin fabric of a network made up of only five minds, leaving more room for mistakes. "I won't practice my profession in your territory."

"What happens when Sienna grows up?" Hawke asked astutely.

"I'm considering mercenary work in the African states." In the deepest, darkest jungles where changelings held sway and where there were no Psy, no one who might possibly recognize him. And no woman with sunshine in her smile. He crushed that thought with merciless reality—the day Brenna *truly* saw him, the day she discovered the things he had done, he would lose her smile anyway.

"There is another option." Hawke's eyes were predator-still, watchful. "You could work as a SnowDancer soldier. That would allow you to use your abilities, correct?"

"Enough to blow off the most dangerous steam." The instant the words left his lips, Judd knew he should've lied. So why hadn't he? He looked inward and found his shields solid.

Yet something was making him behave in opposition to his own decision to leave the den. "However, it's not a viable option in my case. None of you trust me—it would be a farce."

"Trust has to be earned."

"Most changelings hate the Psy. SnowDancers go a step further." After having seen Enrique's handiwork, Judd couldn't argue with their reaction.

Hawke didn't dispute his analysis. "You helped get Brenna out—that's a good enough place to start. I want you doing soldier work."

It was the one response he hadn't factored into his plans. "I would have thought you'd throw a party at the thought of getting rid of me."

"The alpha in me says you could come in very handy."

Judd knew why Hawke wanted his abilities. It was the same reason the Psy Council had. A pet assassin was not something those in power wanted to lose. "If I decline?"

Hawke's eyes gleamed. "Then I withdraw safe harbor for Walker."

Only the adult. Not the children. It was more than the Council had offered and Judd had bathed in blood for them. "Fine." He silenced the part of him that questioned his easy capitulation. Walker had no need of his protection—his brother could save himself. "But I want the same autonomy as the rest of your soldiers." No more chains, no more cages.

"You have nothing to bargain with."

"I have my skills." It wasn't a threat. Not yet.

A low growl emanated from Hawke's throat, as if his beast had sensed the danger. But his voice, when it came, was calm. "Most men would've lost their temper by now. I sure as hell would've gone for the throat."

"I'm not most men." Sometimes, he wasn't even sure he was human, not a monster. "Of course, if I want revenge, I'll simply send Sienna your way." His niece could make Hawke lose his cool faster than any other man or woman in the den. "She's been in a particularly . . . interesting mood since you forced her to train with Indigo."

Hawke's face darkened. "Keep that damn brat away from

me—she's more trouble than a pack of rabid cats." He reached behind himself for a map. "I need a man to keep an eye on some stuff in the eastern quadrant."

Judd walked over to look at the large sheet of plaspaper as Hawke rolled it open across his desk. "Isolated area, no habitation within miles," he said, orienting himself. "Includes a segment of the outer perimeter." That perimeter was the den's first—if farthest—line of defense. That put his placement there in a new light. A test?

Hawke pointed to the border section. "We've had reports of people encroaching. Might be human or nonpredatory teenagers playing chicken, but we need to know if it's something more. No unnecessary contact. I need intelligence before we make a move.

"If it is kids, a good scare will make them mind their manners. If it's adults from a predatory species, they know the rules." That unauthorized access meant death. The SnowDancers weren't particularly forgiving and Judd had seen the bodies to prove it. It was why they had not only survived, but become the most powerful pack in California.

"Understood." Rusty sections of his mind stretched awake in anticipation.

"It's pretty damn lonely out there." Hawke glanced up. "You might not touch another person for weeks. I'll set you on a rotation—two weeks out, one week in. Most of my people in isolated areas do it that way."

"Touch is a changeling need." As important, apparently, as eating and breathing. He'd observed how aggressive they became without it. During Brenna's recovery, she'd often been surrounded by packmates.

What very few knew was that in the hardest sessions, the ones where she'd wanted no one in her pack to see her, but had needed the tactile contact, it was Judd who had held her. Oddly, she had granted him skin privileges—the right to touch—almost from the start. It had been the first time he'd had such sustained contact with another. She'd been soft. Warm. Trusting. And highly disturbing to his Psy senses.

"I'm designed to work alone." Nature's gift to him.

Hawke took him at his word. "There's an old cabin here." He indicated a spot close to the boundary that delineated the area into which the SnowDancers would accept no unauthorized entry. Their territory was so broad that it covered several regions where other species lived and worked, and they were more lenient about access in those sections, but the massive tract of heavily forested land stretching out in all directions from the den was sacrosanct. "It's fully equipped with comm equipment. You can use it as a base."

Judd left within the hour, having decided to cover the considerable distance on foot with the aid of his Tk abilities. It would both speed him up and serve the purpose of releasing some of the psychic energy built up in his system.

As he began running across the snow at a speed that would've shocked the wolves, he considered Brenna's probable reaction to his sudden departure. She was confident enough, had enough wolf arrogance that she'd be considerably annoyed if he wasn't there when she came looking. However, given that he was no longer her sole source of information about Psy-related material—and especially after what he'd told her to do yesterday, she might not even notice that he'd left.

His hands tightened on the straps of his pack. Rationalizing away the action as necessary to secure the light burden, he kicked up his speed until he was moving too fast to concentrate on anything but avoiding the obstacles in his path.

Brenna knew something was wrong the second she woke. She became convinced of it when Andrew gave her a big grin at breakfast. He'd been in a shitty mood ever since she'd returned from fighting with Judd yesterday, having found out exactly how much time she'd been spending with the man. They had had such a blazing row over it that she'd spent the rest of the day with Lucy and a couple of other female friends, disgusted with the whole male race in general. But now her brother was acting eerily cheerful.

"What did you do to him?" she asked without the least attempt at subtlety.

Andrew managed to look hurt, stopping with his coffee halfway to his lips. "Nothing. I can't believe you asked me that."

She'd been his sister too long to fall for the act. "Spill it or I'm going over there."

"Fine." Grinning, he started to drink his coffee with overt enjoyment.

Terrified that her brothers really *had* done something, she almost ran to Judd's room. Again, the scent was of emptiness. Heart thudding triple-time, she tried desperately to convince herself he'd just done one of his irritating disappearing acts.

"I set him on a watch."

Startled by that familiar voice, she swiveled to face Hawke. "Where?"

"Why is that any of your business?" Pale, pale blue eyes watched her without blinking.

She fisted her hands. "Don't," she whispered. "Don't play games with me." Hawke knew everything that went on in his domain.

"A year ago, you wouldn't have dared speak to me like that."

A year ago, she'd been someone else. "Things have changed."

"I can see that." He didn't sound as if he minded. "But your brothers can't. Drop this thing with Judd before you push them too far."

"You're my alpha, not my keeper. I already have two of those. Two too many."

He actually smiled—alphas respected spine. To demand unquestioning obedience was the sign of a bad leader. "Your Psy is in the eastern quadrant. I'll give you a map."

She hadn't really expected an answer—Hawke despised the Psy as much as her brothers did—but now that she had it, she pushed for even more. "Will you stop Drew and Riley from coming after me?"

"They'll try to trace you." Reaching out, he ran his knuckles over her cheek.

She allowed the touch, because Hawke was safe—as her brothers, despite their pigheadedness, were safe. "I remember, you know, I remember that you all came for me. That you held me when I woke." Riley, her tough, stoic older brother had had tears in his eyes. Drew had told her off, such love in every harsh word, and Hawke, he'd just touched her, let her scent Pack and know she was home. "I'll never forget, but I need to run free."

"I know, sweetheart." Dropping his hand, he gave her an inscrutable look. "I haven't told anyone else about Judd's location. You'll have maybe four days before your brothers track you down if you leave now and take one of the all-wheel drives. You'll have to shift and run the last part, but you should still beat him there. He's on foot."

The idea of running as a wolf made her want to break out in a cold sweat. She fought the reaction, which would be inexplicable to any other changeling. If Hawke sensed it, he wouldn't stop until he'd stripped her most shameful secret from her and it was something she wanted no one to know. "Four days?"

"The cats owe me a favor or two. I'll get Sascha to say you're with her. If I know your brothers, they'll give you three days before they decide to pay a friendly visit."

Smiling, she put her hands on his shoulders and reached up on tiptoe to kiss his cheek. *"Thank you."*

He held her to him. "You sure about this, Bren?"

"Yes."

CHAPTER 11

Returning to the family quarters with Hawke by her side, she sniffed past her smug brothers and packed a bag. When she came out of her room, Drew was scowling and Riley looked flat-out pissed.

"Don't even try to stop me," she said. "I need to be away from you two."

"We didn't do anything." Drew threw up his hands. "I don't think you should—"

"If you don't let me go today, I swear I'm moving back near the campus." To the hillside apartment she'd taken such pride in before Enrique had come into her life and turned her into a terrified little mouse too scared to leave the den. Well, no more!

Riley swore. "Those cats better take good care of you."

"Sascha won't let them do otherwise," Hawke said, slightly mollifying her siblings. "Come on, Bren. I'll walk you to the car." He shook his head when Drew and Riley tried to follow. Neither looked happy, but they obeyed.

Sighing, she went back and kissed them both. "I need to

become a wolf again." Truer than anyone knew. "I'll see you in a few days."

"Don't let any of those leopards sweet-talk you," Drew muttered, hugging her. "One scratch, one fucking scratch, and I'll rip out their guts."

"I'll be fine." When he finally let her go, she picked up her bag and made her escape. "I feel so guilty," she muttered when she was sure they were out of earshot.

"Don't." Hawke led her down to the garage level after a small detour to pick up the map. "You're a full-grown wolf, not a pup."

Stopping beside the forest-adapted vehicle, she threw her bag into the back. "Why haven't you gone overprotective on me, too?"

"I'm your alpha. My job is to make sure you're a healthy member of the pack, not a crippled one." Ruthless words, but Hawke had never been a man who cloaked the truth. "Go and do what you need to do to put the pieces back together."

She nodded and hugged him, understanding the deep caring that underlay words outsiders might've read as brutal. "I will." She would not let Enrique win. And she would not let Judd Lauren run from this . . . whatever it was.

Hours later, she emerged into the small yard in front of the cabin to find Judd waiting for her. Startled, she gasped. "How did you beat me here? I drove!"

His eyes flicked over her and she knew he'd noted everything in that single glance, including her lack of luggage. "You ran from the car in human form."

It was as if she'd been waiting for this moment, for this man, because she opened her mouth without any forethought and admitted the secret she'd gone to such great lengths to hide. "I can't go wolf." She hadn't meant to sound so shattered, but now a tear was streaking down her face and it was hot and wet and angry. "He broke me! That goddamn bastard broke me!" She turned and slammed her fisted hands against the trunk of a nearby tree. "He broke me!" Her bones vibrated from the impact as she brought her fists down for the second time.

"Stop." Male hands closed over her own from behind. "You'll injure yourself."

Lured by the touch, by the scent of him, she leaned back against his body. "I can't go wolf." It was a whisper this time, the anger washed away in that single pained outburst.

"I've seen you use your claws." His tone was icily Psy as always, but he'd curved his body protectively over hers.

The realization calmed her but not enough to stop her voice from trembling. "I can change in parts—claws, sometimes the teeth, but that's harder. My strength and speed haven't been affected. Same with my sense of smell and sight."

"Like Dorian."

"Yes." The DarkRiver leopard had been born lacking the ability to shift, but was, in all other ways, changeling. "But I wasn't born latent. *He* crippled me." Hawke's earlier words now took on new resonance. What would he say when he realized the extent of her impairment? "I'm damaged . . . maimed."

Judd didn't release her hands even when she dropped them to her sides, his touch firm and cool against the heat of her skin. "Have you told the healers about this? It may simply be that your body hasn't had enough time to fully recover from your injuries."

"I haven't told anyone."

Except him. Judd knew that should've made no difference, but it did. "Come. We'll talk inside." He tried to release her hands but she held on, her back pressing harder against his chest. He allowed her to prolong the contact. That was when the first warning signal flared in his brain, but there was no pain. Not yet. "What is it?"

"I'm scared." A tiny, shaken whisper. "It must be nice to not feel, to never be afraid."

"It's also a kind of crippling." Done by parents to their own children. "You don't want to be what I am." The idea of a cold, emotionless Brenna made him tighten his hold on her. A second warning sparked to life.

Pulling away her hands in a changeling-swift move, she twisted to put her arms around him. "Please."

There would be a price to pay. There always was. But Judd raised his arms and wrapped them around her smaller frame anyway, tucking her head under his chin. He could feel her trembling from the force of her tears. He wanted to halt those tears but didn't know how. So he did as she'd asked and held her, aware all the while of the building strain at the back of his head, the dull thud that announced an impending psychic backlash.

That backlash—the use of pain to coerce compliance—was called *dissonance*. Judd had found the term in an old and highly classified *Psy-Med Journal* article, an article he'd hacked into after figuring out something as a teenager—that Silence, at its simplest, was built on a foundation of reward and punishment. The larger the breach of conditioning, the stronger the pain.

The journal article had referenced a scientist named Pavlov's early experiments with dogs, as well as several later papers that expanded on his theory. Judd hadn't been able to access all those papers, but he had found enough to confirm his suspicions . . . and understand that his Council had trained him the same way you would a dog. Burn a dog enough times and he'll begin to fear fire. Shock a child with pain every time he laughs and he'll learn to never so much as smile. A dehumanizing equation but one Judd could not permit himself to break. No matter what the temptation.

"Brenna, you must stop," he said after several long minutes—her sobs had turned raw and painful. "Stop or you'll hurt yourself." He was holding her so tightly, he wondered that she could draw breath. But instead of complaint, her fingers clawed into his back, further strengthening the connection. "No more tears." His harsh order didn't have any effect. He'd never seen her so distraught. During the healing sessions, she'd been this angry, half-feral thing who'd refused to give in, refused to let Enrique win.

Finding the answer in that memory, he bent his head until his lips brushed her ear as he spoke. "You *will* defeat this as you've defeated every other thing he did to you. You are not crippled, not now, not ever." He'd kill anyone who implied otherwise. "You survived once and you'll keep spitting in his face by continuing to survive again and again."

Brenna found herself transfixed by those most unexpected of words. At first, Judd's voice had been a blur, but now it was a cool, clear anchor that hauled her out of her tears without compromise. That the words came from a Psy was not something she registered, only that they came from Judd, from the man who held her, his arms as unbreakable as steel bands.

She rubbed her cheek against the soft wool of his black turtleneck, able to hear the solid beat of his heart. "I'm sorry I fell apart on you." She'd been holding things together with sheer stubbornness for so long and when he'd touched her, breaking that ever-present barrier of Silent Psy reserve, it had all rushed out in an agonizing emotional torrent.

"It's understandable." Not the petting words a changeling man would've used, but they worked for her. She didn't need gentling. She needed what Judd had given her in those stark words whispered in her ear—the unflinching belief that she *would* get past this. "Do you want to go inside?" he now asked. "I can light the laz-fire."

She shook her head. "I'd rather walk out here for a bit. We could go get my pack."

"You're not staying." He released her and took a step back.

She rubbed her hands over her face, wondering exactly how much of a fright she looked—she was not a pretty crier. "Yes, I am."

Those dark brown eyes seemed to darken to pure black. "You have no reason to be out here. I can't do what I'm supposed to if I'm babysitting."

Her eyes felt swollen when she narrowed them. "Good try but you can't make me mad so I'll leave." She suddenly understood something else—the way he made enemies so that no one would even try to get close to him. "I can run the patrols with you."

"This is not up for discussion." A statement so arrogant, it reminded her of Hawke and her brothers. Great. Just great.

"I'm putting you in your vehicle and you're driving back to the den."

"Unless you're planning on using mind control, that's not going to happen." She was looking at him when she said that and saw something very dark and very dangerous awaken in those gold-flecked eyes.

"I'm fully capable of doing that." A warning, a threat.

Going with gut instinct, she placed her hand palm down on his chest. "To me?" He didn't speak and that was her answer. "Why do you allow me to cross barriers you don't allow anyone else?" Surely that meant he had feelings for her.

"Enrique was one of my own. And he hurt you."

"Guilt? That's why?" Her stomach dropped.

His fingers closed over her wrist, turning that sick sensation into something hungrier, more sensual. "I don't feel guilt. I don't feel anything." Surrounded by snow and ice, he was a man who appeared the blackest of shadows. Yet his hand was careful on her.

She smiled, confidence reassured. "I'm staying."

"I'm driving you back right now."

"I'll turn the car around the second you leave." Her skin tingled where he held it, his fingers strong, his own skin erotically rough. She wondered how that hand would feel stroking other, softer places. Heat uncurled deep inside her. "Why does my presence bother you so much if you don't feel?"

His hand tightened a fraction before setting her free. "Don't get in my way."

"I wouldn't dare." A complete lie. "Let's go get my things."

He jerked his head toward the cabin. "Go and start the lazfire. I'll bring your pack."

She was more than willing to let him walk off his temper. And the man had one, even if he wasn't willing to admit it. "The code's four-two-seven-zero." Because it was a pack vehicle, it wasn't keyed to any single individual's thumbprint. "See you when you get back."

He didn't leave until she was safely in the cabin. Watching him walk away, so tall and starkly alone against the snow, made her want to run outside and hug him. Just wrap her heat around him until her warmth melted his cold Psy armor. The problem was, Judd seemed determined to maintain that icy shield.

Shivering though the cabin was well insulated, she turned from the window and went to start the laz-fire. Unlike most clean-air devices, the LAZ energy source had been created not by changelings but by Psy. The reason? Laz technology saved energy and therefore money. The single thing changelings had done to adapt it was to add a holographic enhancer. It turned the efficient but colorless block of a portable laz generator into what appeared to be a perfectly real blaze, albeit one with zero chance of starting a forest fire.

Brenna checked that the generator was sitting in the correct place in the built-in fireplace before flicking it on. Flames burst into golden life, immediately lightening her mood. However, she didn't stay in front of the fire, going to stand at the window instead. Judd needed to know that he wasn't alone, that she was waiting for him.

Maybe he thought she was being disingenuous or that she didn't understand what he was trying to tell her. She understood. She just didn't accept it. Judd wasn't lost to Silence, no matter how much he wanted to be. She knew dominant males, had grown up around them, so she could guess what it must have cost him to stifle his pride and submit to his low rank in the SnowDancer hierarchy. But he'd taken the hit—to protect Marlee and Toby, and even Sienna.

He might think he was beyond redemption, but she knew otherwise.

His body appeared from the trees at that instant, her pack slung over one shoulder. Strong and confident, there was an arrogance to him that said he knew he was too dangerous for any of the forest inhabitants to mess with.

Smiling, she went to open the door. "Hey."

He dropped the pack inside the doorway. "I'm going to run a circuit. Close the door and stay inside until I get back."

She was about to tell him exactly what she thought of the way he was giving her orders when he turned and headed out.

She blinked.

The man was *fast*. Too fast for a Psy. Then again, she had a feeling Judd Lauren was no ordinary Psy. Kicking the door shut, she opened the pack to retrieve a small piece of malfunctioning comm equipment she'd promised to fix for Drew. Her brother might be infuriatingly overprotective, but he respected her tech skills.

It felt good to pick up her tools again, to feel the rush of mental stimulation as she began doing her kind of surgery.

Judd returned to the cabin after dark to find Brenna sitting on the floor by the laz-fire, tools and computronic parts set out neatly in front of her. She glanced up when he entered, but her smile was absentminded. "Gimme a few minutes, baby."

Baby?

Putting the use of the term of affection down to her preoccupied state, he hung up his jacket and took off his boots before going into the kitchen area. As he'd thought. She hadn't eaten. Pulling out two of the prepacked meals from the cooler, he put them in the cooking unit. He was trained to go without food for days if necessary, but Brenna needed to get some calories in her. Changelings burned energy faster than Psy. Added to that, she was still recovering from the damage Enrique had done to her body.

That done, he went to sit near the fire and watch her work. Two things became immediately clear. One, that Brenna loved what she did, and two, that she was very, *very* good at it. Not that that was anything unexpected. She was a qualified computronic tech and had been engaged in further study before a sociopath changed the course of her life.

The images came again—of her, bruised and battered, the blood on the walls, the sounds of tearing flesh. Enrique's screams. Everyone screamed at the end. Everyone.

Judd had watched the former Councilor being torn to shreds by claws and teeth and felt no sense of racial allegiance. Blood for blood. Eye for eye. Life for life. It was changeling justice and Santano Enrique had deserved nothing less.

Brenna suddenly smiled and it was a flash of light cutting through the grim darkness of memory. "Finished."

"Are you charging for that?" he asked, aware of the value of her work.

"Oh, it's for Drew."

"And what does your brother think of you being here?"

Color flooded her cheeks. "Um, he sort of might think that I'm with Sascha."

"Ashamed to be seen with a Psy?"

"You know," she said, scowl gathering, "I think Indigo's right about the size of men's brains."

Judd decided not to ask for clarification. "You need to eat." He fetched the meals.

For once, she didn't argue. Dinner passed in silence but one unlike any he'd ever before known. It was . . . easy. After they'd cleared away the plates, she pulled him back to the fire. "Sit." He obeyed, the sofa at his back. Following, she proceeded to tell him what Indigo had discovered about the murder victim.

"Rush is used primarily by changelings?" he asked, not familiar with the substance.

"Humans, too, but less so. Their bodies process things differently from ours." She stretched out her legs, the movement more like that of a cat than a wolf. "Ruby Crush was developed specifically for changelings, like Jax was for Psy."

"Jax isn't a recreational drug."

Brenna half turned to face his profile. "You mean it has a medicinal use?"

Medicinal. That was one way to put it. "In minute doses calibrated to precisely match the patient's weight and metabolism, it has the effect of both intensifying the strength and enhancing the endurance of natural Psy abilities."

She braced one elbow on the sofa. "Like an upper for the psychic mind?"

"Yes. But without the physical consequences suffered by street users. The effect fades over a set period and then you're back to a normal level of strength. No crash."

Brenna frowned. "You said physical. What about psychic?"

All at once, he understood why he'd told her, what he was about to confess. "They said there were none—the M-Psy in charge of dosing us."

"You took it?" A shocked whisper.

"I was an Arrow. An elite soldier." He had never before either confirmed or denied his rank. "We were the reason Jax was originally invented." So they could be better, faster, deadlier than anything else in the Net. "Taken in the correct dosage, it has none of the psychic side effects you see in the addicts." A slow loss of Psy powers followed by a quiet form of insanity and then death. Yet his people continued to use it. He'd heard it allowed feeling during the high, a chemically induced short circuit of the conditioning.

Scooting to sit in front of him, Brenna touched a trembling hand to his knee. It felt like a brand even through his clothing. "It terrifies me that you were exposed to it. Tell me about the effects the M-Psy didn't warn you about."

CHAPTER 12

He knew he should push off her hand. But he didn't. "It changed us while we were functioning under its influence, made us less human, more capable of killing. Perfect programmed soldiers who could still think with crystal-clear accuracy." Jax had altered the Arrows' view of right and wrong, made them incapable of seeing shades of gray.

"How long were you exposed to it, Judd?" She sounded frantic. "There could be long-term effects."

"A year," he told her, wondering why she wasn't running—he'd admitted to having blood on his hands. "I believe I'm safe. My brain didn't have a chance to reset permanently." As had happened with some senior Arrows. They truly *were* the darkness, lethal machines who followed the will of their handlers with unswerving dedication.

"Only a year." She rose up on her knees and leaned in close enough to grip his sweater. "How long were you an Arrow?"

He found he'd made a space for her between his raised knees. One more move and his hands would be on the soft curves of her hips. He fought the compulsion with the hard truths of memory. "From eighteen to twenty-six. Eight years."

But he'd been in training since the age of ten, since the day he'd first killed.

Brenna uncurled her hands from his chest and reached out to touch him lightly on the side of his jaw. He met her gaze, fascinated as always by the spiking explosion of arctic blue around the pupils. He'd never seen it as a scar, but as a symbol of her strength. Most people did not walk out sane after having their minds torn open.

"How?" she asked, dropping her hand to his collarbone. "How did you escape being administered with the drug after that first year?"

The dissonance had kicked in during that fleeting caress along his jaw, but the pain was slight. Easily manageable for a man trained not to break even under torture of the most inhuman kind. "I realized what it was doing to me seven months in." He had known his handlers would never agree to a simple request to halt the drug regime, not when Jax gave them a fully obedient and extremely lethal army.

"My abilities aren't common, not the specific subdesignation." Of which she could know nothing. The second she found out about his Tk, she'd classify him in the same group as Santano Enrique: *the cabal of murderers.* No matter what he'd decided about the need to force her to keep her distance, he didn't want Brenna seeing him that way. A jagged spike of pain speared through his skull—the dissonance had moved to stage two. "So there was no way for anyone to cross-check my statements about it."

She reached out to brush a lock of hair off his forehead and her skin felt so delicate, so different from his. "You lied."

"Yes. I began to deliberately make psychic mistakes while on Jax." Such as not applying enough pressure to cause death or the specific type of injury he'd been instructed to bring about. "Then I told them I was having dreams."

"Dreams?" Her forehead lined with concentration. "What's wrong with having dreams?"

"Psy don't dream." To dream was to be considered flawed. He'd begun dreaming as a child, but the dreams he had as an adult were not the ones he'd had then—before his ability had come to vicious life.

Brenna's hand clenched on his shoulder. "No freedom, even in sleep."

"No." He wanted to touch her hair, it looked so soft and silky. The dissonance became a fraction stronger, but it was nothing compared to what he'd undergone as a ten-year-old boy put into the custody of the squad's trainers. They'd placed modified electrodes on the most sensitive parts of his body, strapped him down, and proceeded to teach him the meaning of pain.

It had taken him only a week to learn to stop screaming, another five to stop blacking out. By his eleventh birthday, he could watch his arm being broken and not react. "My plan worked—they took me off Jax." They had also removed several others with related abilities. Interestingly, none of those men had ever asked to be put back on the drug.

"I can't tell you how happy it makes me to hear that."

He didn't respond, his attention caught by something else.

"You're staring," Brenna accused a minute later, a faint blush coloring her cheeks.

"I apologize." Her skin looked creamy and rich in the warm light from the laz-fire, her hair golden and her eyes—they appeared lit from within. "You're staring, too."

Her blush deepened. "I can't help it. You're so pretty, so perfect."

It wasn't the word he'd been expecting and he wasn't sure it was the one he wanted to hear. "Are you attracted to perfection?" He wasn't being vain. He'd been told during advanced training that he had a face of perfect symmetry, something that attracted humans and changelings alike, and could, therefore, be used to his advantage. He'd never followed that advice—it would have been one step too far into the abyss.

She laughed, the sound husky and intimate. "No, pretty doesn't do it for me. Otherwise Tai would have succeeded in reeling me in during high school."

He recalled the young wolf's face—a shock of straight

black hair, high cheekbones covered by healthy brown skin, slightly slanted blue-green eyes. The elements added up to a picture that Brenna's comment told him was attractive to females. *Pretty*. His hand curled into a fist on the carpet. "Then if you don't find me attractive, why are you staring?"

"I didn't say that." Brenna's voice had grown darker, hungrier. "If pretty was all you were, I wouldn't be so fascinated. You have dangerous eyes, a stubborn jaw, the body of a soldier, and the mind of a hunter. That, my darling Psy," she whispered, "makes you a gorgeous, sexy package I want to lick from head to toe."

Her confession was followed by silence so deep Judd could hear the whispers of the wind whipping around the cabin. Then her blush fired to red hot. "Oh, my God, I can't believe I actually said that out aloud."

Neither could he. The fact that she saw him as so sexually appealing was enough of a surprise to render him speechless. He was numb. Even the dissonance cut off—likely reading his reaction as one of complete unemotionality.

"Say something." Brenna's hand turned into a tight fist on his shoulder.

He found his voice through an act of intense willpower. "I'm not sure what to say."

"I don't usually say things like that to men." She scowled. "Are you sure you aren't using Psy powers on me?"

"I would never break that ethical law." His tone went cold at the implication.

She thumped his shoulder. "I was joking, you idiot." Blush having faded, her lips began to curve in a slow, teasing smile. "You don't know what to do with me, do you?"

Admitting that seemed like a bad idea. "If you were male, I'd simply throw you out with a few bruises. As you're not, I'm uncertain how to get rid of you."

"That's just mean." But she continued to smile. "Can I ask you something?"

At that instant, he was her personal Arrow. "Ask."

"Don't you want to—" She paused. "Actually, I don't think I'm that brave."

"Don't I want to what?"

"Forget I said anything." Rising to her feet, she ran a hand through her hair, sending the short strands spiking.

Still seated, he put a hand on her leg, on the sensitive skin behind her knee. A small touch but one that restarted the dissonance with a vengeance and froze Brenna. He knew why. According to his research on body language, the touch was an intimate one, something most females only allowed those they trusted. "Tell me."

Her expression was inscrutable when she glanced down. "You're Psy, figure it out. It's a logical progression." With that, she shook off his hand and walked toward the small kitchen area. "Do you want coffee?"

He changed position so he could watch her. "Alright." Coffee wasn't part of the Psy meal plan, but he'd become used to it since his defection. While waiting for Brenna to prepare the drink, he did as directed and worked through their conversation. It would've gone faster had he not kept getting distracted by the sight of her moving with feminine efficiency mere meters away. The sway of her hips was—"Don't I ever want to lick a woman all up?"

She squeaked, then swiveled to face him, bracing her hands on the counter behind her. "Not quite how I would've put it." Her tone was higher than normal. "But yeah."

"You," he said quietly, no longer able to lie. "You tempt me."

"Oh." Her breasts rose up as she took a deep, shuddering breath. "You've never let on."

Yes, he had. If she ever saw the way he watched her when she wasn't looking, she'd be in no doubt as to the strength of his unacceptable reaction to her. "Because it doesn't matter," he told her. "It changes nothing."

"Liar." She stared at him unblinking. "Other Psy don't feel desire."

"It's a major fracture in my conditioning," he acknowledged—to her and to himself. "A fracture I intend to repair." What he couldn't understand was why it had reappeared so quickly after the work he'd done to close it yesterday. He should've been immune to the sweet seduction of her body.

"Then what? You forget temptation?"

"Yes."

Eyes full of fire, she turned her back to him and continued with the coffee preparation. "You know that list about you? I should've added pigheaded to it."

Her anger fascinated him as much as every one of her other emotions. And admitting that brought him another hazardous step closer to the edge of a catastrophic breach. The dissonance spiked and this time he listened, because for him, the pain wasn't simply a warning to get his emotions under control, it was a warning to get his *ability* under control.

His power wasn't passive, wouldn't turn inward if he lost his white-fisted grip on it. No, it would go outward, would seek to tear flesh and crush fragile feminine bones. "Don't you ever wonder," he asked coldly, conscious that he was assassinating any chance he had with her, "if you're attracted to me because of what Enrique did?"

This time, she stopped what she was doing and stalked over to stare down at him. "What the hell is that supposed to mean?"

He rose to his feet. "He was Psy. So am I. He hurt you. Maybe you want to cancel out that experience with a positive one."

Her fists were bloodless skin over bone, her jaw set. "Unlike you, I don't think through every one of my actions. I behave according to my emotions."

He stood toe to toe with her, almost able to feel the psychic wave of her fury. "This time, that's not enough. You need to examine the reasons behind those emotions."

She blew out a frustrated breath. "And if I was looking for some kind of validation that not all Psy are evil monsters, would you be able to give it to me?"

"I can't give you emotional absolution." He might damage her even further. "I can't give you the kind of a relationship you need to heal."

"Heal? I'm not a damaged thing you have to put back together. I put myself back together!" She slammed her hand against her heart.

"But you haven't been in close contact with any male outside of your safe circle since the rescue." Except him. And under no circumstances could he have her.

"So you really meant what you said to me yesterday?" Her voice rose. "I should find myself a nice wolf and settle down?"

He fought off the rising incursions of dissonance, the razor blades sliding through his brain stem and traveling down his spine. "That would be rushing things."

"Oh, I see. You think I should fuck someone to get over my bad experience." The coarse words shotgunned from her lips like bullets. "No, wait, it's Psy men I'm apparently worried about. So maybe you're the one I should—"

"Don't say it." His fingers were gripping her chin though he had no memory of putting them there. *"Don't,"* he repeated when she opened her mouth.

She held his gaze. "Why? That's what you just tried to reduce us to."

"There is no 'us,' Brenna." There couldn't be, not if he wanted her to live the life she deserved. "For some reason, you're attracted to me. And yes," he said when it looked like she was going to respond with another burst of red-hot anger, "I'm tempted by you. But that means nothing."

"How can you say that?" She closed her hand over his wrist but didn't attempt to break his hold. "Look at yourself. You don't react like this to anyone else. Only me."

"I know. And if I keep reacting like this, I'll end up killing either you or another innocent." Releasing her chin, he stepped back.

"Kill someone?" Stunned incomprehension wiped away the red flush of her temper. "Why are you worried about that?"

Heading to the door, he grabbed his jacket and shoved on the boots he'd removed earlier. "Go to bed."

"Judd!" She stamped her foot. "Walking away isn't going to solve anything."

He pulled open the door and strode out into the cold. Small flakes of snow fell on his hair and the wind burned across his unprotected face, but he barely noticed, his mind still in the cabin.

Tonight, he'd come shockingly close to breaking Silence and *feeling* anger of the most violent kind. The anger of a Tk with his subset of powers wasn't normal in any sense—he'd found that out as a ten-year-old boy standing over another child's corpse.

Leaving Brenna might not fix anything, but it would keep her safe. From him. He'd known that should she say that last word, it would push him too far. He continued to feel the texture of her skin under his fingertips—warm, smooth, touchable. Gritting his teeth, he walked deeper into the winter-cloaked night, hoping the snow would chill the fire in what should have been the pure, unbroken ice of his heart.

Brenna threw her boot against the wall. "Men!" She considered running after Judd—she was fast even if she couldn't go wolf—but abandoned the idea in a fit of female fury. She was through with chasing him! He could chase after her for once.

Except that two hours later, he still hadn't made an appearance. "Fine," she said, turning over in the bed she'd appropriated. "I'll leave tomorrow if that's what he wants." How dare he say those things to her?

You need to examine the reasons behind those emotions.

His words wouldn't leave her alone, no matter how much she tried to forget them. Was that what she was doing—using Judd to get past her own fear? And she *was* afraid. Everyone thought she was so brave and strong because she'd survived with her sanity intact. It made her want to laugh, but with nothing even close to happiness. Because as she'd told Judd, and no matter what he'd said to the contrary, she was broken. Enrique had destroyed her spirit, made her suspicious and insular, where before she'd been easy to extend the hand of friendship, easy to smile, easy to see joy.

Today she faced the horror that he'd made her such a weak woman, she'd been ready to use another man to find her own courage. Something told her that Judd Lauren had been used quite enough. She didn't have to know the facts. She saw the truth in the shadows behind his eyes—he expected her to take what she needed and then leave.

She pulled the blanket up her body in a vain effort to warm the cold in her soul. "*No*. This isn't about Judd being Psy." It if had been, she would have gone to Walker. He was no less Psy and far more approachable. Or was that the attraction, another part of her asked—the fact that Judd was so damn dangerous, more than tough enough to take on her demons?

"So what if I'm attracted to him because of what happened?" She'd changed in her fight to survive the evil that had touched her, lost part of her innocence. But she'd also gained knowledge, learned who she was and what she could endure. The new woman she'd become found Judd Lauren fascinating.

Well, she had. Now she was too mad to care.

CHAPTER 13

Judd didn't return until he was confident Brenna would be fast asleep. He entered to find her cuddled up in front of the fire—in the middle of a camp bed she'd apparently dragged out of storage. She made a noise at the soft click of the door closing and he paused, waiting for her to wake up. But she continued to breathe in the rhythms of sleep.

Relaxing, he took off his jacket and quietly removed his boots and socks before going down on his haunches by the fire. Even his skull ached from the dampness caused by the snow—he'd deliberately not used his abilities to protect himself. But despite his need to regain control, he hadn't gone far from this woman who threatened him on a visceral level, unable to leave her alone in the darkness. So he'd stood watch and attempted, once again, to repair the most critical of the new flaws in the wall of Silence around his mind.

He wasn't a stupid man. He understood that Silence had been imposed on him, and was in no way natural. For most of his people, it was a violation of their freedom to choose. Protocol I, with its aspiration to cut into the Psy brain itself, would only further that violation. But notwithstanding all that, he also understood and accepted that for a small minority, Silence was a choice they would have made if given the option.

He was one of them.

For him, Silence was the answer to a prayer, a gift that allowed him to live a full life, not be caged behind bars or banished to complete isolation. His eyes fell on Brenna's slumbering form. No, he thought, he was wrong. His life wasn't full, not when he couldn't have her in it. But at least Silence allowed him to talk to her, to protect her, to be with her even if it was for mere fragments of time. Without the conditioning, he wouldn't have trusted himself within sight of her.

Unable to resist this chance to get even closer, he crossed the carpet and looked down at her. Under her lids, her eyes moved in the rapid movements that denoted deep sleep, perhaps a dream, but there was no sign of fear in either her face or her body. In other words, she was perfectly fine and didn't need him standing watch. He told himself to move, that this fascination he felt was exactly what he'd been trying to head off out in the snow.

Instead, his fingers curled as he fought the urge to reach out and test the fragile shadows thrown on her skin by her lashes. At that moment, Brenna gave a choked little cry, her skin suddenly marred by wrinkles that spoke of pain. Shivers followed, her whole body trembling despite the warmth of the laz-fire.

He knew what a changeling male would've done in this situation. It was the same thing his instincts were telling him to do, no matter that the action would undo any good the cold outside had done. The dissonance disagreed, shooting hot darts of pain into his eyes.

Then a sob caught in the back of her throat, making his decision for him.

Getting on the bed, he propped himself up on one elbow beside her and stroked his free hand over her hair in a gentle caress, excruciatingly aware that his body was a bare inch from hers. "Shh. Sleep. I'll keep you safe." It was a promise he'd give everything to honor.

Her trembling stopped after a few seconds and she closed

that one-inch gap to press into him. The heat of her seeped through her T-shirt, the blanket, and his sweater to burn his skin. Impossible. Yet with Brenna, it wasn't. When her hand rose out of the blanket to curl between their bodies, it was all he could do to keep from taking her into his arms.

Every warning beacon in his head flashed red. To expose himself to more contact would spell trouble for both of them. So he kept his distance—except for the fingers stroking through her hair—and watched her sleep.

Brenna knew she was dreaming. She also knew she couldn't try to wake. There was something she had to see, had to understand.

It was a true dream. Fractured, fragmented. But the strange thing was that it was black-and-white. She'd never dreamed in monochrome before. Her dreams were drenched in color, in scent. But this place was cold . . . metallic.

Power.

She had such power. And it was so finely controlled. One thought and the target's heart simply stopped beating. The man was dead before he hit the ground. She'd killed before. This one had been almost too easy.

For her people.

She did this for her people.

The cold water was cutting against her skin, but she had to wash away the blood. Blood no one else could see. Because she had executed an innocent. They'd—

Fragments of sound dampened by shadows of black and white, icy clawing fingers born of her own mind. A sense of danger closing in.

But no fear. No rage. No anger.

And that was when she knew.

This wasn't her dream.

Her heart began to race the second she opened her eyes. Until the moment she'd woken, it had been absolutely calm. Frighteningly controlled. She blinked several times to clear the images that continued to dance in front of her eyes, slowly becoming aware of the glow of the laz-fire in the hearth . . . and the fact that she was no longer alone in the bed.

Judd. His familiar scent calmed her panic before it could begin. Rising onto her elbow, she found him asleep on top of the sheets. One arm lay along the back of her pillow, while the other was braced over his forehead. He was still. Silent.

She couldn't even hear him breathe.

It scared her. "Wake up." She touched her fingers to the roughness of his cheek. It was the first time she'd seen him less than clean shaven. "You're having a nightmare."

His hand closed around her wrist with such unbelievable speed that she actually squeaked in surprise. He released her as quickly. "I apologize."

She put that same hand on his shoulder when it looked like he was planning to get up. "Stay." For a long moment filled only with the sound of her breathing, she didn't think he'd acquiesce, but then he gave a slight nod.

She didn't move her hand off his shoulder, hyperconscious of the muscle and strength beneath the black of his sweater. "Want to talk about it?"

"About what?" No tremor in his voice, nothing to betray the impact of a dream that would have terrified her had it been her own.

"Your nightmare." She knew what she'd seen even if she couldn't explain how.

"I told you, Psy don't dream."

Sighing, she snuggled impossibly closer, the wolf in her craving contact. It probably made Judd very uncomfortable, but he didn't make any move to break away. "Liar."

Judd felt his mind stop at that single affectionate word. He recognized affection, had been around changelings long enough to understand the import of such seemingly light-hearted comments. However, it had never occurred to him that he might one day be on the receiving end of this most sensual form of it. Especially from a woman who had been so angry with him bare hours ago. "A dangerous accusation." In the PsyNet, that would've been true. No one wanted to be indicted of having a flaw.

Brenna chuckled and tugged at the arm he'd placed across her pillow until she could rest her head on it. Her weight was slight, but he knew he wouldn't be moving before she did. "Promise I won't tell," she teased, breath whispering over the skin of his neck. "Your tough-as-nails image is safe with me."

It was difficult to focus with her curves pressed into him. He reached into the depths of his Arrow training and forced absolute restraint over his instincts. It was the only way he could allow himself this forbidden contact. "Why do you think I was dreaming?"

The atmosphere changed and though he wasn't looking at her, he picked up her distress from the sudden tenseness of her muscles. "Brenna?"

"I saw it."

The words hit him like bullets fired at close range. He knew what he'd been dreaming about—he always remembered the images he saw in sleep. "What did you see?"

"You killed someone." Said in a breathless whisper. "Then you discovered he didn't deserve to die."

Judd's brain shifted into automatic damage-control mode, spitting out option after option. At the top of the list was denial.

Never get into a situation where your status may become known.

If you are, however, trapped in such a situation, never admit anything.

Maintain control of your physical reactions if placed under duress and answer all accusations in the negative. Denial is key to protecting the squad.

Deny everything.

It was one of the very first things he'd been taught after being removed from his family and taken to the training facility. But he'd stopped running from the truth a long time ago. "It wasn't a dream but a memory." He braced himself against the horror, disgust, and rejection to come.

One of her hands rose to lie against his chest. "Why that man?"

He told her the truth—he would not defend himself with

hypocrisy and lies. "His name was on a list given to me by Ming LeBon."

"Councilor LeBon? The Arrows work for the Council?"

"No." That had never been their raison d'être. "The fact that the squad is currently under the direct command of LeBon arises from him being a senior Arrow himself, rather than his Council rank. Arrows are a force independent of politics and money. The man you saw me kill, however, was no threat to anyone but Ming. He had the unfortunate distinction of having cut into the Councilor's business interests."

"You weren't to know that. You trusted your leader." Her fingers spread on his chest, began to stroke. "It's what any soldier does."

"I was an assassin, Brenna," he said in a blunt repudiation of her attempt to find good in him. "I was given targets, told the preferred mode of death, and set a time limit. I never asked questions about who they were or what they'd done."

"Then how did you find out about the guy you were dreaming about?"

"A year into my work with the squad"—too late, far too late—"I did finally begin to ask those questions. The answers I received didn't ring true so I went searching." What he'd discovered had changed his identity from loyal soldier to cold-blooded murderer.

It was the second time in his life that his identity had been stolen from him. He had vowed that there wasn't going to be a third. "In the PsyNet, some segments of the populace call the Arrows a death squad, but we thought of ourselves as the first line of defense, protecting our people before they even knew they were in danger. Ming changed that, made us into bringers of death."

"Then you shouldn't blame yourself." Her voice was quiet, accepting. "You were—"

"Acting on orders?" he interrupted. "That's an excuse. I stopped making it the day I realized what I truly was."

Hand pressing down on his chest, she rose up on her elbow, eyes stormy. "Instead you're going to beat yourself up about it forever?"

"I'm Psy—I don't feel guilt."

A very unfeminine snort was his answer. "What do you call those nightmares?"

"You aren't seeing what I'm telling you," he said, staring into those extraordinary eyes. "I was the Council's pet assassin. There is nothing good or acceptable about that. Evil is the only applicable word." He paused. "This does clear up one thing."

"What?" Brenna asked, not yet finished with him.

"You have no need to worry that Enrique left some part of himself behind in you."

"Of course he did—otherwise I wouldn't be seeing your dreams."

"No, Brenna. You were afraid you were turning into a monster. But tonight, did you feel the same emotions you did when you saw the vision of Tim's death?"

Her eyes widened. "Oh." Dropping her head back down to his shoulder, she took several deep breaths. "I was seeing his dream, the person who killed Timothy, feeling *his* emotions as he thought about what he was going to do."

"Everything points to that conclusion."

Relief rushed through her like a flash flood. "I—" She shuddered.

"I know." Stark, unemotional words. More disturbingly, though he'd come to her last night, he didn't move to hold her as a changeling male would have done in the same situation. And she needed to be held.

But Judd wasn't changeling. He never would be.

CHAPTER 14

Kaleb read the précis of the report on his desk and looked up at his most senior aide. "You're sure there's been no error?"

"Yes, Councilor." Silver Mercant's eyes were an odd shade between gray and blue, and had apparently been the genesis of her given name. That extraneous fact was something Kaleb had made it his business to find out—he trusted no one near him he didn't know inside out.

"I rechecked every byte of data we were able to hack into and download. Unfortunately the facility was attacked before we broke the final encryptions," she said, "but we have enough to make a conclusive assessment. Someone has already authorized live trials of the Implant Protocol."

Kaleb leaned back in his chair and swiveled to stare out at the gray chill of Moscow. People hurried across the snow-flecked square, all walking as if they had somewhere to be—unsurprising, given the city's forty-year reign as one of the world's economic supercenters. "Were you able to determine who gave the order?" He turned back to Silver.

"Negative." Her eyes flicked to the window behind him. "It appears you have an engagement."

He'd already seen the trail laid by the approaching high-speed airjet. "We have ten minutes before my guest makes it down to this office. Tell me what else I need to know." This information could mean a change in his plans.

"The authorization came from very high up in the Council ranks. The individual or individuals were able to provide test subjects who either volunteered or were those who would not be missed—the notes are vague on that point."

An intentional oversight, Kaleb thought. No rational Psy would accede to having his or her brain implanted with a device that hadn't yet reached beta testing. He could almost guarantee there had been no volunteers.

"The data is fragmented," Silver continued, "but I'm ninety percent confident the test group is limited to ten members. They've already had one confirmed fatality."

"Find me that body." If not literally, then figuratively. A missing Psy who matched the description parameters.

"I'm already working on it." She glanced down at the flat screen of her organizer. "There are two other crucial factors. The first is that Ashaya Aleine appears to have solved the issue of Static."

Static, a term used to describe the buzz of background noise—the sound of millions of whispering Psy minds—produced during simulations to test the theory behind Protocol I. No Psy could function with that kind of mental distraction.

"The second factor?" A small light flashed on the surface of his fully computronic desk. The airjet had landed on the rooftop landing pad.

"It's common knowledge that Protocol I would never have worked as initially postulated because it would have reduced the entire population to one level. To use an analogy, we would have all become worker bees."

And a hive could not survive without a queen. "You're saying Aleine solved the problem of distinct but compatible implants for different segments of the populace?" Ensuring power remained in the hands of those who would use it to keep the Psy at the top of the food chain.

"Not completely," Silver clarified, "but she does appear to

have broken the implants into two categories—primary and secondary. Of the original participants in the trial, eight had secondary implants, two primary."

Two rulers. With possible total control over the other eight. Such influence would be the prerogative of those in power should Protocol I come to fruition. "See if you can get me any names." He had his suspicions, but what he needed was proof.

"Yes, Councilor." She gave a short nod and walked out.

Another light flashed on the gleaming black smoothness of his desk to indicate that his visitor had exited the glass hover-elevator and was heading toward his office. Touching a concealed panel under the desk, he initiated its secure mode. The desk turned opaque, hiding the computronics but continuing to record everything that went on in this room. Of course, he had no doubt that his visitor had come prepared for such an exigency.

A knock and then the door opened to reveal his administrative assistant, Lenik. "Sir, Councilor Duncan is here for your meeting." He shut the door as soon as she came through.

Walking around the desk, Kaleb went to meet her midway. "Nikita. It was good of you to come all this way."

Almond-shaped brown eyes looked into his, cool and certainly calculating. "As it appears we need to discuss certain discreet matters, it was the logical choice. Your offices aren't as closely watched as mine."

He had no need to ask for further explanation. The DarkRiver cats and their allies, the SnowDancer wolves, hadn't been shy about the fact that they were keeping tabs on Nikita. She was the only Councilor within easy reach of their territories since Tatiana's move to Australia two months ago. "Perhaps that will no longer be a problem in the near future." The Council had taken steps to eliminate the changeling issue.

Nikita shifted her head slightly and the light from the ceiling fixture bounced off the glossy black of her hair. "We will see. I'm not as convinced as the rest of the membership about the infallibility of the plan. Our data collection on the changelings has been allowed to lapse to a disgraceful level. We're making decisions based on outdated information."

Kaleb made a mental note to check her assertion. "The DarkRiver Project is still bearing good returns, I trust?" He was referring to the groundbreaking real estate deal between the Duncan Group and the leopard pack that controlled San Francisco and its surrounding areas.

"Yes," she confirmed. "Despite the annoyance the cats present in terms of Council business, they're good for my economic interests."

"A sharp distinction."

"Precisely. My profit margin will sustain major damage should the Council's plan succeed. But I'm sure you're well aware of that. It's why you asked me to meet you."

He gave a small nod. "I thought we might have a number of interests in common."

Nikita walked past him to the window, her composed business persona hiding a core of pure poison. "I thought you would ally with Shoshanna. She was responsible for your entry into the Council."

He came to stand beside her, hands in the pockets of his tailored suit. "On the contrary, Nikita. I alone was responsible for my ascension to the Council." He'd set his eye on the goal at age seven and never blinked. No one had been allowed to stand in his way. But then, all the Councilors had blood on their hands.

Nikita didn't dispute his claim. "Your jockeying for leadership is why Marshall has begun to back Shoshanna and Henry."

He watched pale winter light crawl over the square and saw in it another future, one he'd shape. "You're mistaken. I have no desire for the leadership. Leaders are the biggest targets and I haven't made it this far by courting visibility."

"Then you should tone down your aggressiveness during Council sessions, let Marshall know his position isn't in jeopardy."

"If he believes that, he's a fool." He gave her a skeptical look. "Henry and Shoshanna want to lead. Marshall would do better to ally himself with us."

"That still leaves Tatiana and Ming."

"From what I can see, Tatiana is the swing vote." The other

Councilor had made no alliances he'd been able to unearth. "However, we may have a situation with Ming."

"I'm listening."

He told her what Silver had discovered. "As the Councilor in charge of the Implant Protocol, he has to have full knowledge of the unsanctioned trials."

"This is unacceptable." Ice dripped off Nikita's every word. "You have proof?"

"Yes." Illegally obtained but legal now that it was in his hands. After all, he was a Councilor entitled to the information. "Several data files."

"It's much too early for live trials," Nikita continued. "The saboteurs will have their work done for them if the populace, and more importantly, the major families, refuse to support the Protocol because it appears dangerous."

He concurred. To succeed, Protocol I had to be proven safe—in terms of both Psy minds and their psychic abilities. "There has already been one fatality. If the news gets out . . ."

Nikita placed her arms behind her back. "It'll jeopardize the future of the entire operation. I assume you're working to track the ten involved?"

Kaleb nodded. "It's no use confronting Ming before we have more. We can't risk alienating him. If the Scotts seize majority control of the Council, it'll compromise a number of our interests."

"Agreed."

"There is another possibility," he said. "That the Scotts have inserted their influence into Ming's project without his knowledge—they've already shown a willingness to act without majority authorization."

"That would shift Ming's allegiance, or at least limit his support for their motions." Nikita seemed to come to a decision. "We'll discuss our next step when we have more data, unless you see a cogent reason for not waiting."

"There's no need to rush."

"I see a lot of changelings down there." She nodded at the square. "How's the racial situation in your town?"

Moscow was hardly a town, but he let it go. "Stable. The

local wolf pack is at present fighting for dominance against a well-established bear clan. As a result, they have no interest in Psy affairs. The humans pose no threat."

"They never do." Nikita dismissed the entire race with the flick of a hand. "Before Sascha dropped out of the Net, we learned that changeling packs aren't as isolated as previously believed—I'm now investigating how far that goes. Any indication your wolves might be linked to the SnowDancers?"

Kaleb shook his head. "BlackEdge has no connections outside the immediate region. They're too busy with petty local matters to think big."

"Let's hope they remain that way." Nikita started toward the door.

He fell into step beside her. "Leaving so soon?"

"I have a meeting in San Francisco in a few hours."

"The airjet should get you there in plenty of time." It was one of his, designed and built by a corporation of which he had majority control. "I'll keep you updated. I'm sure you have enough to handle in relation to the execution of the plan targeting DarkRiver and the SnowDancers." It was a very deliberate comment on his part.

As Nikita had made clear, she didn't support the Council's plan. However, she'd been placed in charge of it because Shoshanna had made a point of saying that as the mess was in Nikita's backyard, she should be the one to clean it up. Especially since her daughter was part of the problem.

Nikita gave him a chilly Psy smile. It meant nothing, of course. "If stage one of the plan works as expected, we should see a number of changeling fatalities within the next few hours."

CHAPTER 15

The morning after she'd witnessed Judd's dream, Brenna left the cabin for a walk. The air was fresh and crisp under the snow-heavy trees. Judd had already gone to check things at the boundary line, leaving her plenty of time to think.

You aren't seeing what I'm telling you.

Judd believed she was viewing him through rose-colored lenses, but he was wrong. She understood what he'd done, realized the darkness inside of him. But she'd also looked true evil in the face, had had the sliminess of it invade her mind. She knew categorically that Judd was not cut from the same cloth.

Not that his confession had come as a surprise. She'd sensed from the start that he was no angel. Still, he'd attracted her, the changeling heart of her sensing a strength in him that would complement and nurture her own. It had never scared her that—

Something made a sound to her left.

Freezing, she sniffed the air and felt her eyes widen. Her first instinct was to call out to Judd, but she had no idea of his exact location. Neither could she backtrack to the cabin—she'd walked a long way and was now cut off from both it and the weapons hidden inside. She couldn't even defend herself by going wolf.

Her stomach twisted, but she forced herself to think past the bitter taste of rage. If the intruders scented her, she was dead. Right then, she was downwind, a small advantage—she could probably take out two or three of them before they realized they were under attack. The trouble was, there were a lot more than three hyenas out there. And while hyena changelings were often cowards one-on-one, they wouldn't hesitate to go for a more dominant target if a pack of them found you alone and unprotected. She'd be torn to pieces in minutes.

Moving carefully to avoid betraying her position, she thanked the heavens for the firs that provided cover. Ordinarily, she would've gone up into those same trees, but that would trigger snowfall from the branches.

Snow!

Brenna, you idiot! It was a mental curse as she looked behind her and saw the solitary trail of footprints. She didn't have time to go back and erase them, but she made sure to cover her tracks from that point onward. Too late. Too slow. She was far too slow. She considered breaking out into a full run, but with so many of them, they would run her to ground before she reached safe harbor.

Brenna.

It wasn't exactly a sound in her head, not a spoken word in any way. She couldn't explain how she heard it, but she knew it was Judd. It "smelled" like him.

Still. Be still.

An illogical request, but she trusted him—and his abilities—too much not to realize he had to have a plan. She froze, even though the hyenas were getting perilously close.

Open.

She felt a push on her mind. Her mouth dried, her heart closed into a tight shell, and fear bloomed on her tongue. *No!* She didn't want anyone in her mind ever again.

Alright. But don't move. Trust me.

The hyenas were going to see her at any moment, but she obeyed his order. And when her skin seemed to *shift* over her skeleton, she tried not to panic. Then she felt her bones change shape in a way that wasn't anything similar to how they transformed during the shift from human to animal. It was too much. Her reactions were born from instinct, hard to control under normal conditions, impossible in a situation where she was already hovering an inch from panic. She would've fought then, disturbed the quiet and given herself away, but he set her free.

She hit the ground hard despite the thick layer of snow. Blinking away the strange disorientation that made it hard to focus, she got up, shook her head, and prepared to run . . . but found the landscape startlingly unfamiliar. She was no longer anywhere near the hyenas. Safe, she was safe. But Judd was nowhere to be seen.

"Where are you?" She scanned the area around her, but the snow lay unbroken. He hadn't passed through here. It took real effort for her to think past the wolf's need to go to Judd's aid, to help defend their territory, but she hunkered down to wait.

As things stood, Judd knew where she was and could find her more easily if she didn't move. It was common sense. That didn't make her any less scared for him. He was out there alone against a pack of hyenas—hyenas who should've been too terrified to come anywhere near SnowDancer land. Their boldness told her they were packing weapons more dangerous than simply claws and teeth. "Come on, Judd," she whispered. "Where are you?"

Judd was on the verge of flaming out—what he'd done with Brenna had taken a massive amount of energy. He briefly considered teleporting a gun from the cabin using what power remained, but realized the act would wipe him out and leave him a sitting duck. In human terms, he was running on fumes. An hour at most and he'd collapse on the psychic plane, his abilities useless for the next twenty-four hours or more. The physical collapse would hit a few hours after the psychic one.

If this had happened while he'd been uplinked to the

PsyNet, his psychic star would've flamed red for a few seconds just before he crashed, long enough for others to notice and use to their advantage. That was why Psy went to great lengths to avoid flameouts. It left them vulnerable—while their basic shields would hold, the more sophisticated protections tended to collapse, giving enemies a near defenseless victim.

Out here, however, even his family might not notice his condition. Because of the difficulty of keeping three immature minds from inadvertently dropping out of the LaurenNet and attempting to rejoin the PsyNet, they had been training Sienna, Marlee, and Toby to stay out of the LaurenNet as much as possible. It was a hard task—living on the psychic plane as well as the physical was natural for them. But their safety had to come first.

Having circled close to the intruders, he allowed his body to lean against a tree. While the physical collapse could be held off, it would sap his energy bit by bit, so he had to conserve it where he could. That collapse itself was nothing normal. Most Psy only flamed out on the psychic level. It was the nature of his abilities that altered things for him.

It makes you vulnerable. Ming LeBon's mental voice, the voice that had shaped so much of who Judd had become. *However, as it appears to be an unavoidable side effect of your abilities, I suggest you train your body to survive on the bare minimum of energy.*

Judd had been fourteen at the time and in thrall to his mentor. Ming possessed one of the strongest minds he had ever seen. The senior Arrow's ability in mental combat was unparalleled, but what set Ming apart from his peers was that he'd trained his body, too. He had a deadly facility in several human disciplines, including karate and the rare form known as katana.

The Way of the Sword.

Except that it used no blades but those created by skillful use of the body, honing men to a lethal edge. Judd had studied under Ming, then later under a human teacher, spending an entire year in the freezing chill of Old Sapporo. The abandoned Japanese city was so inhospitable, it was populated only by those who wanted to push their bodies to the limit, such as the disciples of katana. Though the highly offensive martial art—developed during the Japan-Korea war over half a century ago—could be used to kill, its worth to the Psy lay in the extreme mental and physical discipline it taught.

But even katana only went so far with a Tk on the edge of a flameout. Expanding his senses, he began to collect data. He wasn't changeling so it could've been difficult for him to identify the exact species, but some of the hyenas had shifted to their animal forms. There were twenty in the scan radius and many registered as carrying weapons. He needed a closer look at those weapons.

Making a quick decision, he moved closer, using what he'd learned in Old Sapporo to check the creeping shroud of exhaustion and keep his brain functioning. Once he'd positioned himself in the direct path of one of the hyenas in human form, he leaned against another tree and did the thing that only his subdesignation could. He blurred his body, becoming effectively invisible. It had been postulated that this aspect of his ability sprang from the same core as that of the F-Psy, that he was actually bending time.

Concentrate.

Wandering thought patterns were a sign of oncoming flameout. He managed to drag his mind back under control in the nick of time. A hyena male walked past, a weapon strapped to his back and another in his arms. Pinpoint migraines began to spark behind Judd's eyelids, but he maintained the "invisibility" until the invader was well out of range. Then he focused on getting out of the hot zone without leaving a trail.

The explosion came half an hour later.

Brenna heard the bang before she saw the smoke spiral up into the sky. The urge to head in that direction was so overwhelming that she had to grit her teeth to restrain it. Her family had not raised a stupid wolf. With the snow, the blaze wouldn't accelerate. Furthermore, the wood was treated to be flame-retardant *and* she had neither the firepower nor the backup to take on a whole pack of those damn scavengers.

But her frustration at being so helpless wasn't the worst of it—she was scared to death that they had gotten to Judd. Then he walked out of the forest. Racing to him, she put a hand on his arm. "What happened?" She took a second look. "Judd, your eyes!" They were pure black, no whites, no irises.

"They blew up part of the cabin," he said, ignoring her cry. "Given the noise, SnowDancer patrols are probably already heading this way."

"I know *that*!" Shock submerging under worry, she scanned his ashen face. "I want to know what happened to you!"

"I used too much power." Clipped words.

"When you got me out." It wasn't a question. All those weeks of healing with Sascha had taught her a few things about how Psy gifts functioned. "Because I wouldn't let you into my mind. I'm right, aren't I?"

"That's not an issue we have time to discuss." He jerked his head in the direction of the cabin, his eyes beginning to fade back to normal. "My tactical knowledge says the hyenas are long gone by now. We should head back there to meet whoever responds." He began moving.

She ran to catch up. "Are you going to be able to cope? Your eyes . . ."

He gave her a sideways glance so full of male arrogance, the wolf in her wanted to snarl. "Psy eyes do that when a large power expenditure is involved—I'm fully capable of making the necessary report."

"I should learn to keep my worry to myself where you're concerned," she muttered.

"That would be wise."

Scowling at his back, she decided to concentrate on something that didn't make her want to go clawed. "How did you get me out?"

"Teleportation."

Utter silence in her mind, the cold emptiness of angry fear. If he could teleport, that meant he was a telekinetic. A very strong Tk. Like *him*. The butcher. "When were you going to tell me?" Her heart felt like a block of ice.

"Never," he answered in a clipped tone. "You're not rational about Tk-Psy and your prejudice bleeds onto others."

She didn't quite understand what he was getting at, but she knew it wasn't complimentary. "This is between you and me, no one else."

He stopped and faced her, perfect Psy beauty and ruthless control. "No, Brenna. It's about you, your family, the entire den. You start hissing at me and they'll follow."

"Since when do you care what anyone thinks?"

"Since I realized that Marlee is beginning to exhibit signs of having at least some Tk in her skill set. It didn't show up in her initial tests but that occasionally happens with children who are very strong in another ability. But now it's rising to the surface."

Anger flashed to guilt, then back again. "She's a baby. No one in the den would go after a pup!" Her face burned at the idea, but at the same time, something else was trying to rise, information she couldn't quite grasp. All she knew was that it had something to do with the connection between Judd and Santano Enrique.

He folded his arms. "She's not going to stay a baby. If you poison the den against telekinetics, where's that going to leave her when she grows up?"

Her claws threatened to release and the rage washed away that ethereal piece of knowledge floating in her brain. "That's what you think of me? Well, fuck you!" Spinning away, she sprinted the rest of the way to the cabin fueled by red fury. It didn't improve her mood to realize that Judd kept pace. He was Psy—he shouldn't have been able to keep pace. But damn if she was going to ask him what he was doing to make himself changeling-fast. "The bottom-feeders are gone." Fragments of wood and glass lay scattered on the snow, the air thick with the astringent scent of explosive chemicals. But curiously, the cabin wasn't too badly damaged—the blast had only taken out one discrete section.

Going down on his haunches, Judd held out a hand. "Do you have a handkerchief?"

"Do I look like I have a handkerchief?"

"Any clean cloth will do."

"Wait." Skirting the debris, she went to a window.

"Don't enter," Judd warned. "We haven't checked it for explosives."

She gave him an evil look and, pushing up the window from the outside—after ensuring that it wasn't rigged to blow—reached in to pull open a drawer. The small kitchen towel was in her hand a second later. "Here."

"Thank you." Using the soft cloth, he picked up something she couldn't see.

"What is it?" she snapped more than said.

"A trigger. Unfortunately very generic."

"Maybe the techs can get something off it." SnowDancers made it their business to keep on top of new technology so they could beat the Psy at their own game. She used to help with the technical stuff . . . before.

"Oh," Judd murmured, "I think there's no maybe about it." He rose, the trigger in hand.

"You think it was planted?" She caught the scent of Pack in the wind. "Packmates incoming—they must've been in the area, to get here so fast."

"I sent Hawke a message this morning stating I'd detected signs of unauthorized access and suggesting it might be wise to inspect the border sections adjoining my watch."

Wolves began pouring out of the forest. She recognized Riley and Andrew. Shit.

CHAPTER 16

Brenna averted her eyes as her brothers shifted, having no desire to see them in the raw.

"I'm going to kill you" were the first words out of Andrew's mouth. "What the hell do you think you're doing with my sister?"

"Later." Hawke's authoritative voice.

Brenna looked up and found him standing across from Judd. He was dressed and in human form, having apparently run that way while the others had gone wolf. It was an indication of his strength, part of what made him alpha.

"You made good time," Judd commented to Hawke, then held out the trigger. "I have a feeling you'll find some prints on this. Convenient ones."

"You mean like this?" Riley's voice.

"What is it?" Brenna asked, still not looking. Of course she'd seen others naked after a shift—it was normal. But these were her brothers.

"A sweatshirt," Judd told her.

"A sweatshirt that smells like leopard." Riley again. "The whole area reeks of cat."

The silence that fell after his words was ominous. DarkRiver and SnowDancer had been business allies for over a decade but their alliance had turned into a blood bond mere months ago. Trust was a dicey thing.

Hawke's face was grim as he glanced at the damning piece of evidence. "If Lucas's people had been behind this, they would have done a better job of cleaning up. I can smell another signature below the leopard markers."

The others frowned and Brenna saw several pairs of eyes widen in puzzlement as they tried to sort through the scent layers to identify the vaguely "sweaty" taint of something that shouldn't have been there.

"It was a pack of hyenas," Brenna said into the quiet.

Everyone stared. Chief among their reaction was disbelief.

"Those scavengers?" Drew said at last. "You sure?"

Scowling, she rounded on him, keeping her eyes firmly above his neck. Her brother, like most changelings, was totally comfortable nude. It was her reaction that was unnatural. She knew that. She just didn't want to examine the reason why . . . was scared to discover what else Enrique had mutilated inside of her. "I didn't lose my nose during the abduction, only half my mind."

Andrew winced. "Christ, you're mean when you're pissed. But can you blame me? Hyenas don't go near anything that might bite back."

"We need to talk," Judd said to Hawke.

The alpha gave a sharp nod. "I want everyone except Riley, Drew, and Indigo to start running a search perimeter. Try to pick up the hyenas' trail. I'll make a few calls—we might get lucky if the eagles were in the area."

"Eagles?" Brenna looked up as if she might see some. "How many?"

"A small flight. They're here to attend a human wedding."

Clearly they'd made sure to ask permission from Hawke before setting foot or taking wing in the area under SnowDancer control. Otherwise, they would've been labeled enemies and taken out. A harsh law, but one that allowed stability in the agressive world of predatory changelings. Without it, the carnage that had been the eighteenth century's Territorial Wars would never have ended.

Hawke looked at his soldiers. "Go."

For a stunning few seconds, the world shimmered with a thousand brilliant colors as the soldiers shifted. Then wolves dashed off in all directions, their paws flying swift and silent over the snow. Brenna's entire body went immobile as she watched them move, so strong, so beautiful. Envy was a hateful buzz in her head, one that had the power to turn her bitter and full of spite—Enrique might not have killed her, but he'd succeeded in crippling her.

You are not crippled, not now, not ever.

The memory had her looking away from the sleek forms of her packmates to Judd. He was watching her, no hint of an apology in his features. Her earlier fury reignited, but Hawke spoke before she could let her temper get the better of her.

"Tell me what you found."

Judd responded with military precision. "They were carrying high-grade laser-powered weapons. None are readily available on the general market."

"Psy supplied?"

"High likelihood. They're produced by Psy companies."

Riley changed position and it caught her attention—her older brother didn't make random movements. It was Andrew who was the more physically impatient.

Hawke had also noted the action. "You have something to add?"

"For a race that dislikes using weapons," Riley commented, "the Psy sure seem to have some advanced ones."

"What makes you think the Psy have an aversion to weapons?" Judd asked, so eerily calm it made her want to shiver.

Riley stared hard enough to have sent lesser men cowering. "They've never used them to take us out."

"Only because such an open move would cause too big a ripple. It might destabilize the economy if people thought a Psy-changeling war was in the making." Judd's arctic tone was akin to the baring of fangs by a wolf. "That's why they prefer quieter, less detectable methods of removing changelings from the equation."

"Like setting us against the cats. Exactly how stupid do they think we are?" Hawke pulled a sleek black phone out of his back pocket and punched in a code. "Lucas," he said a second later. "We may have a situation." A short pause and then Hawke's face went preternaturally still.

Brenna stood in tense silence as her alpha listened to whatever it was the DarkRiver alpha was telling him, blindingly aware of the unsettling quiet of Judd by her side. A Tk. One of the same breed that had tortured her, broken her.

You're being stupid and childish, a part of her mind said. No, she wasn't, replied another part, one that had been bruised and bloodied.

"How bad?" Hawke asked, his savage tone snapping her back to the present. "Do I need to pull out my people?" Another pause. "Try hyena. I'll see you as soon as you can make it." He ended the call and returned the phone to his pocket.

"They were also hit," Judd guessed.

"Someone tried to snatch three cubs from a city kindergarten."

"Cubs hurt?" Indigo finally spoke.

Hawke shook his head. "It was in Chinatown, near their HQ. Kids went cat and roared their heads off. A teacher and several nearby shopkeepers got to them in seconds, but it was long enough for the attacker to blend into the streets and lose himself in the crowd. He also found the time to leave behind a piece of his clothing."

No one had to ask what scent had been embedded in that clothing.

"Cats have to be rabid—got to be some hotheads who aren't thinking straight," Riley said. "We going on alert?"

Hawke gave a negative shake of his head. "Lucas says he has the situation under control. He's contained the spread of information, and the juveniles who know have been told it looks like a Psy setup. He has them trying to track the attacker, which should keep them out of trouble."

"Not a bad result," Judd remarked. "Even a year ago, you would've shed some blood over this."

"Maybe, maybe not." Hawke's ice-blue eyes were almost silver in the bright daylight, beautiful in a way Brenna had never before noticed. He wasn't the kind of man who invited that sort of appreciation—he was too male, too hard. Exactly like Judd.

Soldier. Assassin. Tk.

"There's one more thing we have to consider." Judd glanced at the cabin and then back, something in his expression striking her as strange. "It might not have been the Psy. Others could have gained access to those weapons, humans and changelings included."

Andrew growled. "Trying to save your race, Psy? Who else would dare intrude on SnowDancer and DarkRiver territory?"

"What happens if you set up the dominant changelings in a region against the Psy?"

Riley understood first. "We wipe each other out, leaving the region open to takeover by a new dominant pack."

"Or a human conglomerate." As his expression had, Judd's voice sounded slightly *off* to her senses, but she couldn't put her finger on why. "The Psy Council ignores humans. Changelings don't, but you still see them as weaker. They're not. The Human Alliance has access to a massive amount of firepower and funds."

Hawke rubbed at his jaw. "If we track the hyenas, we'll have a starting point. You get anything else?"

"They knew where they were going—they'd done their reconnaissance and done it well enough to know the cabin was supposed to be empty."

"It doesn't add up." Riley's pragmatic nature asserted itself. "If their point was to start a turf war, why take out an isolated cabin?"

"First step." Judd's voice *was* different. Something was minutely off-kilter and it was rubbing her fur the wrong way. "A carefully planned and controlled escalation," he continued when no one interrupted. "Sooner or later, no matter what you or Lucas do, the packs are going to start sniping at each other."

"He's making sense." Andrew's acceptance was grudging, to say the least. "Stagger a series of small episodes and the bad blood builds up until, by the time the big one hits, we're not thinking enough to talk it down."

"I want those hyenas." Hawke turned to Riley. "The search here is yours. Drew, you and Indigo escort Brenna back to the den. I have to speak to Judd."

"I don't need babysitters," Brenna said through clenched teeth, able to feel the roughness of the wolf in her throat. "I'll can get back on my own."

"No." Hawke's tone was unbending, that of an alpha who expected instant obedience. "If they touch you, war *will* happen. You're a tactical weakness."

A mixture of fury and impotent rage coated her tongue. "That's a load of crock! Any one of the females or pups gets taken, it'll have the exact same impact."

"I'm not going to argue with you about this." Hawke jerked his head. *"Move."*

Brenna looked instinctively at Judd, knowing he was strong enough to take on Hawke. He returned her stare, impassive. "Hawke is right. Because of the abduction and rescue, you occupy a different status in the pack. You should return—the pack's coherence is necessary to support my family."

The betrayal crushed her but coming on top of what he'd said earlier, it also stoked her anger. "What else did I expect from one of the Psy?" It was a bitchy thing to say but she couldn't believe he'd turned on her like that—males were supposed to stick by their females, no matter what. It finally pounded home the truth she'd gone to such great lengths to ignore. Judd was incapable of any loyalty but the one he'd already given his family.

She turned to Indigo. "Let's go."

"Shift. It'll be faster."

Vicious anger raked its claws over her heart. "No." Let them think she was being a brat. "I'm running human." Suiting action to words, she took off, leaving behind both her packmates and the cold Psy male who had given her up without pause.

Judd watched Brenna until she was swallowed up by the winter-blue trees. Then he turned to the SnowDancer alpha. Hawke was watching him in turn, an inscrutable expression on his face. For a race notorious for their emotionality, the wolf was very good at keeping his feelings under wraps.

"There's not much more I can tell you aside from the exact make and models of the weapons I saw." He rattled off the numbers, but his attention was focused on the steady countdown of the timer in his mind. Five, four, three, two . . . flameout.

He was psychically blind.

It felt like losing a limb, losing all sense of identity. He was a psychic being, meant to occupy two planes. Now only one was open to him.

"Might help narrow things down," Hawke said and his voice sounded flat to Judd's altered senses. "Like you said, these weapons aren't exactly available at the corner store."

It was a struggle to focus when it felt like he was breathing through mud. "Even if you locate the supplier, be careful. If it was the Psy, they had to have known the hyenas were too inexperienced to pull this off smoothly. The operation might be a lot more complicated than it appears on the surface."

"I never take anything on face value." Hawke's eyes looked metallic to Judd's compromised senses, as if seeing things in technicolor depended on his psychic eye. "I need to talk to you about something else. What do you know about a Ghost in the Net?"

It was a question so unexpected, Judd went silent.

Hawke scowled. "Nothing?"

"He's a rogue." It had to be one of the women, he thought as he answered. Either Sascha or Faith still had contacts in the Net. "Not much is known about him, but he's anti-Council, from what I saw before I defected."

"Do you have any way to get more background on him?"

"No. He's in the PsyNet and I'm not," he lied without

compunction. Hawke might've taken them in but loyalty was another matter. The Ghost, on the other hand, had earned Judd's silence.

Wolf eyes looked at him with a predator's watchful attention. "You're not Psy any longer, Judd. Choose."

"I chose a long time ago." He held the alpha's gaze. "If I learn anything else, I'll let you know."

"While you're doing that, why don't you consider the decisions you need to make about where your loyalties lie."

Judd could no longer distinguish the color of Hawke's hair—the world had turned monochrome. But he held his ground. "Have you ever considered what I'd be if I wasn't Psy? There is no other available designation."

"You could be a SnowDancer."

CHAPTER 17

"**That's not** an available option for an adult Psy male. Your pack doesn't accept outsiders."

"Bullshit." Hawke snorted. "We accept human and outside-pack changeling mates all the time. It'd be a small pool if we didn't."

"There's a difference with Psy."

"Only if you create it. Marlee and Toby are already Snow-Dancer."

Hawke's words caused Judd to go motionless. "Don't make that statement unless you're willing to stand by it." To fight for the kids if Judd, Walker, and Sienna were somehow killed. "Everyone knows you despise the Psy."

"I'm not in the habit of saying things I don't mean." But he didn't deny Judd's accusation. "What happened between you and Bren?"

"None of your business." The answer came out so fast, he had no chance to censor it. *Instinct.* Something that could've gotten him rehabilitated in the PsyNet. Because what was instinct if not the harbinger of emotion?

"I'm her alpha." A command, an order.

Judd had never been very good at taking them. "As Brenna would say—you're not her keeper."

Hawke grunted. "You do realize Riley and Andrew will gut you where you stand if you so much as touch her."

"Also none of your business." Her brothers considered him an easy target. That was their mistake. "But I will ask you to keep her safe over the next day." Until he could take over the task himself.

"Going somewhere?"

Judd's vision was fraying at the edges, details lost to the encroaching darkness. "I'll be back in twenty-four hours."

Hawke didn't push for more, surprising given the tight rein he liked to keep on the Lauren family. "What do you think Bren would say if I told her you'd asked me to look out for her?"

"Most likely she'd show you her claws and say that she can take care of herself."

"She can. But I don't care what she thinks, she's not back to full strength yet." Hawke raised an eyebrow. "Want a piece of advice, one male to another?"

Judd waited.

"Wolf females get really, really, *really* pissed off when their males don't support them against others in public." A flashing smile. "You're going to have to grovel to get back in her good graces."

"Loyalty. I understand that." And he did.

Hawke angled his head. "One of the scouts is returning."

Judd didn't bother to waste words. He just walked around the cabin and jogged into the trees. He had three hours at most before the physical crash. Wanting to race through the forest, he nonetheless set a slow enough speed that he could keep an eye on his surroundings. Without his Psy senses, he wasn't human but less.

Psy were meant to be psychic. Removing that aspect of their makeup affected everything about them. His hearing was already compromised, sounds coming through as if blocked by a wall of water, while his sight was no longer as acute as it should have been. But it was enough to drive.

Reaching the vehicle Brenna had forgotten in her anger, he punched in the code, slid back the door, and entered. Given his destabilized state, he would have normally set it on automatic, but that was impossible in this territory. The roads were less than tracks in most areas, with none of the embedded computronic tags needed by the vehicle's navigation processor.

Falling back once more on the lessons he'd learned in the bleak emptiness of Old Sapporo, he arrowed his concentration to a fine point. He'd barely reached his destination when the physical crash hit full on. His mind blinked out—to all intents and purposes, he was now in an unbreakable coma.

Brenna pushed herself to the limit on the run back to the den and was exhausted by the time she returned. Peeling off from the other two, she headed toward her room. Unfortunately, since Andrew lived in the same family quarters, she couldn't get rid of him.

"That was some pace, Bren. Where did that come from?"

She spun around. "I don't know. I don't know where anything in my head or body comes from anymore. Even if you ask me a thousand times, I still won't know!"

"What's got your tail in a twist?" He scowled. "Your new boyfriend didn't kiss you right? Oh, I forgot. He's a fucking robot who doesn't know how to kiss."

Drew had always had the ability to push her buttons, but she was not in the mood for games today. She was mad, so damn mad. At Judd, at her brothers, at Hawke, at the whole bloody universe. "Maybe I'm not the one with the problem," she said, something mean and nasty inside of her taking over. "Why don't you find Madeline and get laid?" The pack's young females were all highly sexual, but Madeline was getting perilously close to crossing the line into slutty. "Maybe a good rut will get you off my back."

Drew's expression was pure thunder. "You're not too old for me to wash out your mouth with soap." Quiet, lethal, a reminder that her usually easygoing middle sibling was also a high-ranking soldier.

"Try it." It was almost a hiss.

Her brother blinked, visibly taken aback by the venom in her voice. She had always been the sweetest of the three of them, the one who could talk both Drew and Riley into almost anything. They'd babied her, protected her, loved her. But that didn't give them the right to stick their noses into her business. "You seem to have forgotten that I'm an adult female, not a juvenile," she said when he remained silent. "Touch me and I'll shred your face." Her voice was cold, cutting . . . mean.

"Jesus, Bren. Where the hell is that poison coming from?"

The taste of bile bloomed on her tongue as her mind recognized the horror. *This spiteful, violent woman isn't me*. Even when he pissed her off, even when he acted suffocatingly arrogant, she adored Drew. But if it wasn't her, then who else could it be? This wasn't a dream—she was fully conscious and spewing hatred.

It made her want to be sick.

Covering her mouth with her hand, she ran the rest of the way to her room and slammed the door shut. When Drew pounded for entrance, she told him to leave her alone.

"Damn it, Bren. You're in no shape to be alone. Come out, baby sister."

Tears filled her eyes at his unflinching affection. "Please, Drew. I need to think. Just let me think."

A small silence. "I'll always be here if you need me, you know that, right?"

"Yes. I know." But he couldn't help with what was happening to her mind. No one but a Psy could—except the Psy she'd given her trust to had turned on her.

She heard Drew's footsteps as he padded to his own room. The shower started a few minutes later. Suddenly feeling sweaty and dirty, she stripped off her own clothes with such haste she tore holes in them. It didn't matter. She had to wash off the filth, scrub away the stench of evil and that of her own ugliness.

The water smelled like rain, fresh and pure. After use, it would flow back out, purified by an amalgam of old-tech methods using natural cleansers and high-tech filters regulated by precision computronic processors. A perfect, peaceful cycle that stole nothing from the Earth and put no pollutants into it. So brilliant that even the Psy used it. Not because they cared about the Earth, but because this method was so cheap as to be laughable.

Scrubbing at her skin till it reddened, she tried to keep her mind full of such technical matters. As long as her brain was busy, she'd be safe from the putrid evil *he'd* planted inside of her, the rot eating away at her insides.

No, don't think of that. Think of the tech. So beautiful, so complex.

Before Enrique had kidnapped her, she'd been close to completing her certification as a Level 1 computronic technician. It was the highest of the ten available grades, requiring skill, intelligence, and something extra—the ability to innovate new systems, create new designs. It was unheard of for a twenty-year-old to tackle the certification, but she'd finished school at fifteen, the exams a cakewalk. Over the next five years, she'd steadily increased her tech rating from an initial 6, to 5, all the way down to 2. She would've been a Level 1 by now if he hadn't taken her.

Blood scented the air. Acrid. Iron-rich.

Blinking awake out of her semishocked state, she saw that she'd scrubbed so hard, she'd taken skin off her forearm. And still she felt dirty—she wanted to keep scrubbing, keep removing layers. The things the monster had done, the things he had forced her to witness, to remember, they dirtied her from the inside out, transforming her mind into a cesspool of malice, hatred, and the sickest of desire.

"No!" Turning off the water, she got out and dried herself. She would defeat the butcher. And she'd do it without the help of a Psy who'd not only lied to her, but had abandoned her when he should've stood by her.

Why? her brain asked. *Why did you expect him to stand by you?*

It infuriated her that she had no real answer to that question. Nothing but a burning anger that sprang from something in her that was miraculously untouched by evil.

You survived and you kept him from your mind. You didn't break.

Sascha had said those words to her the day she'd discovered Brenna in the grip of the killer's madness. Somehow, despite the agony of a hurt that had been everywhere inside of her, Brenna had managed to keep part of herself, a strong precious part, safe. And now that part knew Judd should've stood by her, though it couldn't explain why.

But if she had no answer to that question, she did have one to the issue of what she was going to do about her career. Dressing quickly, she went to the communication panel and put through a call to her old course supervisor.

He seemed delighted to see her. "Bren! You back up and about?"

"Yes, Dr. Shah. I wanted to talk to you about my Level 1 certification." Already her mood was lifting, her sense of self returning. "I'd like to continue the course."

His eyes widened owlishly behind the old-tech spectacles he insisted on wearing. "But didn't anyone tell you?"

"Tell me what?"

"You're already a Level 1."

She felt the anger return in a scalding wave. "I don't need or want special favors. I'll earn my certification." Pity would destroy her dream, completing what Enrique had begun.

Dr. Shah laughed. "The same stubborn Brenna I remember. My dear, you should know I'd never disrespect your abilities in such a way. Shame on you for thinking I would."

She frowned, anger replaced by bewilderment. "Then how can I possibly be certified? I never completed the final tests."

"Your long-term project—FAST." He said the acronym as one word. "I know you did further work on it after you gave me the draft, but I was impressed enough by that draft to submit it for review by the Computronic and Tech Professional Association."

Brenna's heart stuttered. Review by the association was the single sanctioned way to shortcut the requirements of the training program. But the association was tough with a capital *T*. In her five years of study, she had heard of only one other trainee who had successfully passed review. "Why didn't you tell me about the submission?"

"Well, while *I* was certain of the caliber of your work, I didn't want to get your hopes up in case some association idiot didn't have the brains to understand your genius." Dr. Shah's weathered face beamed. "But they did. So you're now Level 1.

"Since the college is still listed as your professional point of contact, I've got a stack of offers for you from the big conglomerates and research facilities. Would you like me to forward them as well as your certification code?"

She nodded, numb. The FAST project was an extremely lateral interpretation of her area of specialization—communication. It was also something she'd been working on since age sixteen. Her goal was to build a system that allowed real-time place-to-place transfer. In simple terms, *f*ast *a*nd *s*afe *t*eleportation for the masses.

It was pure theory at this stage, but she'd cracked a few of the initial problems. It would probably take her decades to turn theory into anything close to reality, but as a Level 1, she could get association grants as well as positions in companies that would fund her research. "Thank you," she said as the offers started downloading into her in-box.

"You're my prize pupil, but don't tell the others." He winked conspiratorially. "I expect you to keep me up-to-date with everything."

"Of course." Also a Level 1, he was her best technical sounding board. "Your views and opinions helped me get this far."

"We'll talk more later," he said. "Level 3 class to teach."

The first thing she did after the call ended was check her bank balance. Her eyes went huge. Before the abduction, she'd worked part-time at a SnowDancer lab—after Hawke had lured her back from a human competitor. Level 2 and 3 techs pulled great salaries, so her savings had been good. But now she saw that the college had refunded her course fees for the component she hadn't had to complete. She was flush and she was qualified at the top of her field.

The world was literally her oyster. And this den didn't have to be her prison.

It was two hours later—around nine at night—that she went looking for Judd "Damn" Lauren. She had things to say and he was going to listen. Ignoring the voice of reason, the one that said a Psy assassin was unlikely to be brought into line by her steaming temper, she stalked to his quarters. When that room proved empty, she made her way to the family apartment occupied by the rest of the Laurens.

She didn't get past the corridor outside the apartment. Little Marlee Lauren, her strawberry blonde hair in two pigtails and a smile on her lips, was bouncing a ball against the wall. Normal . . . if you overlooked the fact that she wasn't touching the ball.

Brenna's throat dried up at the same instant that the eight-year-old—a child whose calm bearing often had her being mistaken for older—realized she was being watched. Her ball fell out of rhythm, rolling to a stop at Brenna's feet. Heart thundering so hard she thought it might bruise against her ribs, Brenna went down to her haunches and picked it up, never taking her eyes off the little girl in denim overalls and a fluffy pink sweater. It was stupid, but she was scared of Marlee.

"Hi," she said, not rising. "This is a nice ball." She rolled the sparkly blue sphere back to Marlee, who grabbed it physically and held it to her chest.

"My uncle Judd gave it to me," the child volunteered, no Psy coldness in her face—Marlee and her cousin Toby had never finished the conditioning under Silence. To them, emotion was not an enemy but simply part of who they were. "He gave me a seesaw game, too, but that's really hard."

Both things to help train developing Tk powers, Brenna guessed. "Oh?" She tried to smile—Marlee was hardly capable of hurting her. But logic was no match for the nightmare of memory. "Actually, I was looking for your uncle. Have you seen him?"

Marlee shook her head, pigtails bouncing. "I could look in our secret Net but I'm not allowed. I could take a peek if you want." A soft whisper that asked for permission.

Something in Brenna tightened. "That's okay. I don't want to get you in trouble."

Marlee continued to stare at her with the pale green eyes she'd inherited from her father, Walker. "Why don't you like me?"

CHAPTER 18

The guileless question knocked all the air out of Brenna. Collapsing into a cross-legged position on the floor, she felt her face pale. Had Judd been right? Was she really such a bigot? "I think you're very sweet, Marlee."

"Then how come you don't like me? How come?" The stubbornness of her jawline was achingly familiar, apparently a Lauren family trait.

Brenna couldn't lie, not with Marlee's face demanding honesty. "You know how you can move the ball without touching it?"

Her pigtails bounced as Marlee nodded. "I'm a Tk. Only a little bit, though. I can't do it so good, not like Uncle Judd."

The reminder of Judd and what he'd kept from her was another punch to the chest. He'd had no right to do that. *Lying was not what should be between them.* And for that certainty, too, she had no concrete reason. "Yeah." She forced her fingers to uncurl. "A bad man who could do the same thing, a very strong telekinetic, he hurt me once. A lot. That's why sometimes, I get scared by other Tks."

"That's silly. Some of the wolves aren't nice to me, but I still like the others."

"Who's not nice to you?" She frowned, hackles rising. Wolf pups could get rough in play, but bullying wasn't tolerated under any circumstances.

"Some stupids." Marlee shrugged. "Uncle Hawke said since I'm little, I can hurt them if they try to hurt me."

Brenna knew that Judd, Walker, and Sienna had been banned from using their powers on SnowDancers. "Have you?"

"I used Tk to push Kiki down when she tried to bite me," Marlee volunteered, face mischievous. "She cried and tattled, but the teacher said it served her right."

Since wolf teeth could do considerable damage to weaker Psy physiology, Brenna had to agree. "I think so, too."

"I won't push you." Marlee dropped her ball and came to stand right in front of Brenna. "Don't be scared of me."

She nodded, tears thick in her throat. "Okay."

Smiling, Marlee leaned in and wrapped her arms tight around Brenna's neck. Shaking, Brenna held that small body to her own and let the tears roll down her face.

"It's okay, the bad man won't get you." Small pats on her back. "My daddy and Uncle Judd and even Sienna can scare him away."

It only made her cry harder. How could she have been afraid of this sweet, tenderhearted child for even a second? How? Was she that twisted, that badly damaged?

A movement.

She jerked up her head to discover Walker Lauren standing a few feet away. Unlike his daughter, Walker was quintessentially Psy, impassive, unemotional, cold. Yet there was a fierce protectiveness to him when he looked at Marlee.

Breaking the eye contact, Brenna hugged Marlee for several more seconds, soaking up her generous childish empathy. "Thank you," she said after they parted.

Small fingers began to wipe away her tears. "Want to play ball with me?"

Brenna looked at Walker. "If it's okay with your dad."

"Ten minutes," Walker said. "It's way past your bedtime."

Marlee heaved out a sigh so put-upon that Brenna found herself smiling. "Tell you what—I'll come by to play with you again sometime."

That satisfied Marlee and ten minutes later to the second, Brenna said good-bye and went to find Hawke. She ran into Riley instead. Her brother was happy to confirm that Judd hadn't returned to the den. "You shouldn't be sniffing around after him in the first place."

"Don't start. And I'm not sniffing at him." She was still mad over the way he'd abandoned her. Now he'd rubbed salt into the wound by not bothering to come back so she could flay the skin off his bones. That was how you fought. Disappearing was a sign of aggression and disinterest.

Fine. If that was how he wanted it, there were plenty more male fish in the sea.

She went prowling. It was time to get back in the game.

Judd woke to the smell of flowers and the sound of a soprano choir. He lay in bed and listened for several minutes as he checked his senses. All the mental and psychic channels were open and running at full strength. Satisfied, he swung his legs over the side and stood to begin going through a stretch routine designed to test every one of his muscle groups. The verdict was clear—he was fully functional.

Stripping off his briefs, he ducked into the tiny shower cubicle to his left. Once clean, he pulled on the pants and sweater he'd shucked before crashing yesterday. His jacket was in the car where he'd left it. When he opened the door and walked out into the hallway at the back of the church, he was struck by the crystal clarity of the choir.

The Psy had lost the ability to produce such tones after Silence, their voices too flat, too dead. But as his race didn't listen to music, that was considered no loss. Today, Judd knew that to be a lie—it was a loss, a great one. The fact he could understand both that truth and the beauty of what he heard was another warning sign, one he chose to ignore.

Father Perez emerged from another room down the hall. "Ah, you're awake." His expression was pensive. "You okay? Looked beat when you came in."

Judd had managed to make it behind the locked door of the spare room by the slimmest of margins. "I'm fine. Thank you for the bed." And for asking no questions.

"What are friends for?" Perez smiled. "How about a bite to eat? You've been out for"—he glanced at his watch—"close to twenty hours."

"I'll get—" He was about to say something else when a sense of urgency suddenly exploded to life in his brain. He had to get back—to Brenna. Before it was too late. "I have to go." With that, he ran past the priest and out.

The car was waiting in the attached indoor garage, fuel cells having recharged during his recovery. It was tempting to get in and take off without delay, but he spent ten careful minutes checking the car for tracking equipment. The SnowDancers were fanatical about keeping their den a secret—their tech arm had even perfected satellite-deflecting technology before the first spy satellite ever achieved stable orbit.

Judd agreed with their stance. Enemies couldn't target what they couldn't see. He'd do nothing to jeopardize the wolves' safety because that would jeopardize Brenna's safety. And that was unacceptable.

By the time he parked the car in the underground garage beneath the den, the warning in Judd's brain had gone critical. He began running full-tilt the second he hit the ground and made it to the Kincaid family quarters in less than a minute.

The door was open.

He entered to find Riley, Andrew, Hawke, and Greg—a wolf Judd knew to be both vicious and bigoted—standing in the living room. Greg was bleeding from several lacerations on his face and Andrew bore a number of cuts on his left forearm.

"Where is she?"

All four men looked up. Andrew bared his teeth. "Get the hell out! Your kind is the reason she's like this!"

Judd looked at Greg's face. "What did you do to her?" Ice spread through his veins, bringing the dark heart of him, the part that could kill without compunction, to the surface.

"Nothing!" Greg yelled. "That's what I keep trying to tell you all. I fucking did nothing to your little princess."

"Watch your mouth or I'll clock you myself," Hawke growled.

Greg raised his hands palms out. "Look, she isn't part of our regular crowd, but she spent the night hanging with me, Madeline, Quentin, Tilau, and Laine. We threw together some dinner and then chilled at my place. When the others left, she stuck around."

Judd was focusing very hard in an attempt to keep himself from killing Greg. He'd figured out that Brenna was behind the closed door at Riley's back. And she was in trouble. Despite the dissonance hammering at him, he could teleport himself across the space without problem. However, his instincts—that word again—told him to wait, that he needed the facts, needed to know what damage Greg had done.

"I thought she wanted to . . . you know." Greg shrugged. "But she left after an hour of talk and I gave it up."

"Just like that?" Andrew growled. "You're not known for your forgiving nature."

"I'm also not a moron. You and Riley would've eaten me alive if I'd done anything." The admission fit his personality. "And I thought she might be teasing to build up to the main event, like the females sometimes like to do."

The wolves didn't interrupt so Judd gathered that to be a truthful assertion. But he did not want to think about the "main event" and what might have taken place in that room less than fifteen feet from him.

"Then," Greg continued, "I got a call today inviting me here. I wasn't keen—I mean until she said you two were going to be out for hours."

"So you hurt her." Riley moved to grip Greg's neck in a bruising hold, his tone quiet. Deadly. "What did you do?"

Greg shoved at Riley's arm but couldn't break away. "She was wearing a robe, for crissakes!" he choked out. "What else was I supposed to think when she crooked a finger and told me to close the door?"

The image did something inside of Judd, broke one of the vital chains of control. He could suddenly feel Greg's heart as if it lay in his hand, the beat rapid and panicked. One hard squeeze and—

Hawke put an arm on Riley's, breaking Judd's line of sight. "He's telling the truth about the robe at least. Let him talk."

Riley didn't budge. "Did she say no? And don't you lie to me."

The chain slipped again. "Tell us or I smash your brain." He made the words matter-of-fact because they were. "You'll be lucky if you can feed yourself afterward." Moving up from the heart, he wrapped power around Greg's skull. And began to apply pressure.

Utter terror rolled through the other male's eyes. "Hawke, stop him!"

The alpha's gaze met Judd's. "Don't kill him yet. We need to know what happened."

Greg started speaking on the heels of that pronouncement. "I swear she didn't say no! I kissed her and went to put my hand on her shoulder. That was when she freaked. Clawed me before I could move. I didn't even push her, I was so busy trying to get out before she punctured my eyeballs or something."

Riley released Greg. He dropped to the floor, coughing. At the same instant, Hawke looked at Judd, the pale silver-blue of his eyes more wolf than human. "She won't let anyone near her, including Lara. Lara's gone to try and track down Sascha." White lines bracketed his mouth. "We'd force our way in but every time we try, she screams so damn hard we're afraid of damaging her."

Any more than she's already been damaged. Judd saw the unspoken judgment on all their agonized faces. His resolve firmed into granite. "I can pull her out."

Andrew made an angry move toward him, but Hawke pushed him back before Judd could. He wasn't going to play stupid games when Brenna's sanity was at stake. But he couldn't teleport in—seeing him use telekinesis would only enrage her.

"You sure?" Hawke shoved Andrew back a second time. "She was pissed with you to begin with."

Which was why she'd gone after this useless excuse for a male sniveling at their feet. But, a still clearheaded part of him pointed out, such an act of betrayal wasn't in Brenna's nature. It simply did not fit. "I have a better chance than any of you."

"Why? Because you're one of the psychopathic race that did this to her?" Andrew again, anger and frustrated protectiveness combined.

"I've walked in her darkness." It had been an unavoidable side effect of the healing process. He'd fed power to Sascha through a telepathic link, but that link had in turn fed him the horrifying agony of Brenna's memories. He'd thought the experience had had no impact. He'd been wrong. "I know what to say to bring her back."

No one got in his way after that. Before opening Brenna's door, he halted and turned to Greg. "You say a single word about any of this, you die." No room for negotiation.

Greg's eyes bulged. "I won't tell, I swear."

Turning, Judd put his hand on the knob, pushed it open, and stepped inside. She came at him in a silent hail of teeth and claws, slamming his body against the door and causing it to shut with a violent bang. He grabbed her wrists barely in time to save his eyes.

His hold made her fury go from red to molten. Restraints, he realized at once. Santano Enrique had used restraints on her. "Retract your claws and I'll let you go." He made his tone adamantine, so hard it was pure unbreakable metal.

Still eerily silent, she tried to use her legs to trip him up, but he was too fast, shifting his stance before she could get a lever. It made her shove forward in a rush of angry energy, the razor-sharp blades of her claws coming an inch closer before he stopped her. There was nothing sane looking back at him from the wild blue-brown of her fractured eyes. The Brenna he knew had retreated to a safe haven in her mind, the same place that had allowed her to survive Enrique. The rest of her was trapped in memories of brutalization.

Sascha could've taken those memories from her, but Brenna had been resolute—she wanted her scars. And as if to prove that those scars didn't weaken her, she'd recovered with such spirit that she'd turned herself into a miracle. But the very speed of her recovery had worried both Sascha and Lara. The two healers had been concerned about a possible relapse—but no one could've predicted this.

When she bared her teeth at him and began to twist and struggle, he knew she was going to hurt herself if he didn't stop her. Taking a chance, he released her wrists at the same time as he pinned her arms in a tight hug. Her claws scraped his sides, tearing his sweater and cutting through the upper layers of skin before he got her immobilized against his body. Her teeth clamped over his carotid artery. But she didn't bite through.

"Brenna, you will come back. If you don't, Enrique wins." He could feel the blood beginning to trickle down his sides, but it was Brenna's teeth that posed the real danger. He could disable her—if he was prepared to hurt her. He wasn't.

"He's winning right now," he told her. "Making you a whimpering, clawing mess everyone thinks is insane." Cruel words, but the only ones that would provoke her enough to snap her awake. "Is that who you are? A broken wolf? *What he made you?*"

Snarling, she released his carotid. "Shut up." Blind rage.

"Why? Everything I've said is true." He kept pushing where others would've stopped. "You have bloody claws, your face is feral and your clothes torn. You look like a woman who's jumped the ledge into madness."

She stamped on his boot with her bare foot. "I bet you learned your bedside manner the same place you learned your charm—the Council gulag."

He released her arms, able to hear the real Brenna in that biting statement. But she remained in place, face pressed to his chest. Chancing aggression, he put one hand on the back of her head in a gesture that was as instinctive as his knowledge of what to do and say to this changeling female. Another breach of the Protocol, another ice pick of pain through his cerebral cortex, but nothing dangerous enough to set off his murderous abilities. Not yet.

Brenna put a palm over his heartbeat. "I bled you."

"Surface lacerations. They'll heal."

"Too bad. You deserve to be clawed hard enough to bear scars." Callous words, but she was still tucked against his body.

The complexities of emotional interaction often eluded him but not with Brenna. Not here. Not now. "That would be a case of cutting off your nose to spite your face—you seem to have a distinct liking for my body as it is."

Her free arm went around his waist, the satin of her robe passing over his cuts like a cool breeze. "Maybe I like my men scratched up. Maybe I like to scratch them up."

"Is that why you chose Greg? Because he likes violence?" he asked, and suddenly realized that the chain that had broken inside him was nowhere close to being repaired.

"I figured if I was going to go bad, it might as well be in style." Her fingers dug slightly into his chest. "I wanted to make you notice."

Her honesty was unexpected. "You succeeded—I did."

"But you care about as much as you did before. Zilch." Liquid anger in every breath. "You strung me out to dry at the cabin!"

Now he understood exactly how powerful a rule he'd broken. "I almost killed Greg," he said. "In fact, I still have a connection to him. One thought and pieces of his skull will implode into his brain."

CHAPTER 19

Brenna went very, very quiet against him. "Pull back," she whispered. "Pull back."

"Does he matter so much to you?" He could taste the structural strength of Greg's skull, knew precisely how much pressure it would take to collapse it.

She snapped up her head, eyes frightened. "No. You're the only one who matters. You kill Greg and Hawke might have to execute you!"

He considered it. "He kissed you."

"He tried. Damn it, Judd. *Pull back!*" Giving a frustrated cry when he didn't reply, she stood on tiptoe and pressed a row of kisses along his jaw.

Soft. So unbearably soft. He'd never felt anything like it. "Now you've had ten times what he didn't come close to getting." Another kiss on his throat. "He matters nothing. So pull back or you're going back in my bad book."

"Was I out?" He broke the psychic thread that had kept him aware of Greg's physical status and position.

"Maybe." She nuzzled at his throat. "Did you let Greg go?"

"Yes." He slid his hand down to her nape. "He was in your

family's living area when I came in, but I'm guessing your brothers have gotten rid of him by now."

She dropped her forehead to his chest, letting him grip her nape in a hold most Psy would've read as threatening. "How do I face them?" There was deep humiliation in her voice. "Greg won't keep his mouth shut—everyone will know."

"He won't say a word. Trust me."

"But my brothers and Hawke. They know. I remember their faces when they came in before. They think I'm crazy."

"Then prove them wrong."

"What if they're not?" She sounded shaken, shocked. "I lost it, Judd. I really lost it."

"We'll talk about that later." They did have a problem to deal with and it had to be dealt with, not swept under the rug. "But first you're going to shower and get dressed so you can reassure your family." He spoke to her as he might to a new recruit, giving firm, short instructions. "Go on. I'll hold the fort." Releasing his grasp on her neck, he slid his hand down the curve of her back before lifting it away. A small indulgence. Worth the red-hot skewer of dissonance shoving through his spinal column.

She took a deep breath, then broke away. "You'll be here when I come out?"

He knew how much that question had to have cost this proud changeling. "Even Andrew couldn't move me."

Her lips quirked a little. "He's okay, you know. Just overprotective."

"I know." More than that, he understood.

Nodding, she turned and disappeared behind a door he assumed led to the bathroom. He leaned his back on the bedroom door—no one was getting through. He had made a promise and he would carry it through. Even as he thought that, vibrations traveled down his spine as someone banged on the door. "Brenna?"

"She'll be out soon." Judd shored up the barrier with Tk.

The bathroom door opened approximately ten minutes later. Brenna stood there wrapped in a fluffy blue towel that only just reached her upper thighs and seemed in precarious danger of falling off the rise of her breasts. "I forgot to take in a change of clothes." She blushed. "Didn't want to put that robe back on."

Since he found he had trouble enunciating words, Judd simply nodded. She walked shyly into the room and began to gather her clothing from the bureau. He caught a glimpse of pale yellow lace as she took things from a top drawer and ordered himself to look away. There was no reason for him to invade her privacy. "Would you like me to step outside?"

Brenna glanced over her shoulder, eyes huge. "Stay. You make me feel safe."

"Not what people usually feel around me."

She shrugged and he had to fight the urge to throw out some Tk and catch the towel he was sure was on the verge of being dislodged. "You don't usually cuddle people who are hysterical after a major freak-out."

Cuddle? It took considerable effort to force his mind back on track. "I said we'll talk about that later. Get dressed before your brothers decide to break down the door."

She turned back to her dresser and grabbed a pair of jeans and a blue sweater. Her legs were bare nearly all the way up and no matter how hard he tried not to look, he couldn't drag his attention from her. Her skin appeared as soft as her lips had felt, smooth and flushed pink from the heat of the shower.

A lightning bolt of dissonance shot through his spine, strong enough to cause spots in front of his eyes. Ironically, he managed it using the same tools he'd been given to handle interrogation under torture. He knew he was treading on thin ice—he'd come close to killing mindlessly today. That lack of discipline indicated severe degradation in critical components of his conditioning. Even knowing that, he couldn't stop his eyes from drinking in the sight of her, his body tightening in unfamiliar need.

Brenna spun around without warning, clothes clutched to her chest. Her breasts plumped over the top, drawing his eye. "I can feel you watching me."

"Impossible." That towel was going to unravel. If she moved her hands, it would fall. He decided he wouldn't use Tk to stop its descent after all.

She scowled. "Are you saying I'm not worth looking at?"

"I didn't mean to imply that." Was her skin that soft all over? That . . . biteable.

A second bolt shot through his spine, originating from his brain stem and traveling down. Designed to cripple an ordinary Psy. But he was an Arrow.

"You have that male look in your eyes."

In spite of the battle he was fighting to segregate the pain, it suddenly struck him that this might be distressing to her after her recent relapse. "I apologize. I didn't mean to make you uncomfortable."

Brenna wanted to laugh. "Why not?" She walked back to the bathroom, an extra sway to her hips. Damn but the man had some timing. There she'd been feeling about as attractive as a psychotic rat and then he'd looked at her like *that*.

As if he wanted to lick her straight up.

She shivered. Pure male heat, that's what she'd seen in those Psy eyes, raw and hungry and dominant. She pressed her thighs together at the images that assaulted her brain. He'd try to take over in bed, of that she had no doubt. He wouldn't let her pet him till . . . after. The man liked to be in control. Good thing she was no wilting violet.

"You're all talk, Brenna Shane," she muttered, dropping the towel and pulling on her panties over flesh sensitized from her thoughts alone. What would happen if he actually touched her there? She sucked in a breath, breasts rising. "A mess, that's what I am."

As today had made clear, she could flirt with the best of them, but getting down to business made her shatter into a thousand pieces. What she couldn't understand was why she'd gone after Greg in the first place—it was more bizarre behavior on her part. Sure, she'd been mad at Judd, but it wasn't like her to try to inspire jealousy by using another man. And Greg was in no way her type. Still, he hadn't deserved what she'd done.

Wincing, she wondered how bad a mess she'd made of his face. He'd hardly even touched his lips to hers when she'd felt the dark wave of violent insanity pour over her, thick and choking. The first few minutes after that were blacked out. All she could remember was seeing Greg backing off, hands pressed to a bleeding face. Just like her attempt at wreaking revenge, the disproportionate response made no sense.

Enrique had never kissed her. She'd been an animal to him, to be tortured and experimented on. A lab rat. It revolted her that the last time she'd been in wolf form, it had been in front of him. He'd somehow learned to force the change on her, humiliating her by taking what she most treasured and turning it into pain and a kind of psychic rape she had never imagined might exist. In the end, he'd torn her changeling heart right out of her.

"Brenna."

She started. "I'm coming." Shaking off the memories, she finished getting ready, then checked that her hair was okay. The short strands were another mark he'd left, one she hated seeing in the mirror.

Judd was standing almost on the doorstep and she nearly walked into him. It was all she could do not to hide in his arms. "I'm ready." She directed a bright smile his way.

He looked at her with the pure focus of a hunter. "You don't have to pretend for me."

She swallowed and let the smile fade. "For my brothers then. For Hawke. I broke their hearts once. I won't do it again." Seeing that angry pain in their eyes—the pain of men who hadn't been able to protect what they loved—devastated her. "Lie if you have to," she told Judd, "but don't let on how serious this was." She knew it had been very serious, a nightmare that had crushed her hope of normality.

"Alright. But you can't try to pretend that nothing happened." A command. "That'll only make them more concerned."

She decided to listen to him. "Okay." When he moved to open the bedroom door, she saw the jagged tears in the black wool of his sweater. "I'm sorry."

"I've told you, they're surface cuts. It'll likely calm your brothers to see that you drew Psy blood."

She laughed and that was when he opened the door. Andrew was arguing with Riley but froze the instant she exited the room, Judd's silent darkness at her back. Hawke was the first to move forward. "You look good, Bren."

"I feel good." She pressed her skin against his hand when he cupped her cheek.

Hawke's ice blue eyes looked over her head. "You brought her back."

"She had nothing to come back from." Absolute Psy calm as he lied for her. "You mistook a small setback for a complete degeneration."

Hawke scowled. "That was a hell of a lot more than a small setback."

"Bren," Drew interrupted, breaking Hawke's touch to pull her into his arms. His hug was crushing. "Greg swore he didn't touch you. Did he?"

She knew that if she said yes, Greg's life was forfeit. As it would have already been had she not stayed Judd's hand. Her Psy's reaction, on the other hand, was a different story altogether. That had been no act of emotionless Silence.

"Greg did nothing," she said. "He merely had the bad luck to be the first male I tried anything sexual with since the abduction."

Her brother released her. "I've never seen you like that."

"And you won't again." She didn't have any other explanation to give him and was hoping he wouldn't push. Then he opened his mouth.

But Judd beat him to it. "Sascha and I have been preparing for such a lapse, though we didn't believe it would occur so abruptly."

"What?" Walking closer, Riley tugged Brenna into the curve of his arm, turning her so she was no longer standing with her back to Judd.

"Your sister has a backbone of steel." Dark chocolate eyes met hers. "She refused to cry or release her emotions in any but the most restrained fashion during the healing."

"Building up the pressure," Brenna completed, moving from Riley's hold to stand beside Judd again. "I should've listened to Sascha." The healer had urged her to embrace and accept that she'd been hurt, raped in the most sadistic of fashions, her mind stripped and then filled with things that were not her own, her body tortured. But Brenna had simply wanted to move past it, to pick up the threads of her life as if they had never been snapped.

"You can listen to Sascha when she arrives," Hawke ordered. "She'll be here soon."

"No." It came out without thought. At the wary looks on their faces, she tempered her tone. "I need time to sort this out in my own head. Judd can help me if necessary."

"He's an assassin, not a healer." Riley's voice dropped close to a growl.

It wounded her that because of her, her generous, forgiving brothers had become so inflexible in their hatred of the Psy as a race. "Riley—"

"You'll see Sascha," he ordered.

"Enough." Judd's voice held an unmistakable tone of command. "Bullying her into seeing anyone won't help the situation."

Riley took an aggressive step forward. "We call this taking care of our own. You've done your bit, so get lost. No one wants you here."

Brenna felt her stomach drop. If Judd had been a changeling, those words would've been reason enough for a fight. A big one. And after having seen the look in his eyes when he'd spoken of executing Greg, she wasn't so sure about his control. Stepping back in what she hoped was an unobtrusive manner, she let the fingers of one hand brush over his thigh. The muscles were bunched, ready to attack.

"Brenna is perfectly capable of taking care of herself," he said. "If you want to help her, stop making her feel incapable at every turn."

She winced inwardly at that freezing tone. Oh, he was pissed, but covering it with a layer of Psy arrogance. "He's right." She looked at Riley, her hand flattening on Judd's thigh. Strong warm muscle. It hadn't relaxed even a fraction. "You two need to back off before you suffocate me. You, too," she said to Hawke.

White lines bracketed his mouth. "Until we figure out what the hyenas were up to, the rules still apply. You've become a symbol of changeling strength—if anyone succeeds in taking you out, it'll lead to blood. So stay in the den or within the inner perimeter."

It chafed but she nodded, deciding to fight one battle at a time. Right now, that involved keeping her brothers and Judd from tearing into each other. "But you have to send Drew back to San Diego and reassign Riley so he's not in the den so much."

Her brothers growled. Hawke raised a hand to cut them off. "That's family business. I need them here."

"Then I want a room at the other end of the den," she insisted, deriving strength from the dark angel at her back. "Or I swear I'm moving back to the city."

Andrew swore a blue streak. "Now you're being—"

"Don't." Judd's quiet menace.

Her middle sibling went motionless. "How do I know you're not . . ." His voice trailed off as she let out a choked cry, able to feel her face twisting into a mask of shock.

"That he's not what? Controlling me?" she asked, throat thick with hurt. "Is that what you think of me—that I have no spine unless a Psy is forcing it on me?"

"I didn't mean—"

"Then you shouldn't have said it!" She chose to turn the heartbreaking pain into anger. "I need you to stand by me, not chip away at my confidence. Do you know the only person in this room who's never made me feel inadequate? *Judd*."

Andrew sucked in a breath, as if he'd been punched. Riley was the one who answered. "You take these rooms. They're the most secure in terms of their location. We'll find bunks in the soldiers' section." He left without giving her a chance to respond, forcing Drew to go with him.

Hawke shot Judd a measuring glance. "I'm sending someone else to cover the cabin region for now."

"Understood."

Hawke left the next second.

Finally, she was alone. Except for the assassin at her back. "I need you to go, too."

The muscled thigh under her palm bunched. "I know what they don't."

She broke the intimate contact—though her body wanted to explore it, to roll the feel of his hard body around her—and turned. "I'll talk to Sascha soon. Promise."

Cool Psy eyes met hers. "I'll be in the den if you need me."

"Where did you go yesterday?" A tendril of remembered anger wormed its way to the surface.

"Somewhere safe."

She frowned. "The den is safe."

"Not for me." Not when he was unconscious and unable to defend himself. "At least a percentage of the population believes I killed Timothy."

"They'll get over it." She shifted her balance from one foot to the other, then back again before continuing. "I spoke to Marlee."

He waited.

"I'm sorry. I didn't know I was being such a bitch about Tk-Psy. I swear I didn't." She swallowed but didn't attempt to break eye contact. "There's so much in my head that doesn't make sense, like the way I went after Greg. I don't even like the guy."

Something dark in Judd reared its head at the mention of the other man. "See if Sascha and Faith have any new ideas about what might be happening. I'll do some digging on my own."

She thrust a hand through her hair. "I will. But the thing with Greg—"

"Don't say his name in my hearing ever again."

Brenna's mouth dropped open. "You're still furious." Her voice was a whisper.

She was wrong. If he'd been furious, blood would be soaking these walls, the smell of human tissue thick in the air. "Make those calls." He left before she could ask him any more questions. The answers might send her screaming.

* * *

Sascha turned to Lucas as they lay in bed, thinking over the call she'd received a few hours ago. "I'm worried about Brenna."

"I thought you said she was recovering." His arm came around her, urging her to sprawl over his chest.

"Pay attention." But she was where he'd wanted her.

A satisfied cat smile. "I am. Tell me about the wolf."

"I can't. Confidentiality."

His hand slipped over her naked bottom. "Bet I can make you talk."

"It's not playtime." She nipped at his chin though the urge to purr was strong.

He moved his hand to her lower back, his version of behaving. "Tell me."

"I don't know what to do." What Brenna had told her this evening—in particular the sudden changes in personality and behavior—was deeply troubling. "I'm worried I missed some of the damage in her psyche." Her mind-healing abilities were still new to her, having been suppressed by Silence for most of her life. A lot of it was instinctive, but Brenna's mind had been so badly torn apart. "Half the time, I didn't know what I was doing."

Lucas's arms tightened. "You brought her back. Don't second-guess yourself now."

"No," she disagreed. "She brought herself back. Her will, Lucas, it's like a steel flame, one that refuses to go out. Brenna should be dead right now."

"If she survived Enrique, then she can survive her own mind."

Sascha buried her face in the curve of Lucas's neck, breathing in his scent. "I'm not sure. Faith told me that most F-Psy in the PsyNet eventually go mad, and they're trained to deal with mental pressure. Brenna isn't."

Lucas's hand passed over her back, long soothing strokes from her neck down to the curve of her bottom and back. A panther's way of petting. "She might surprise you. She sure as hell surprised Hawke with her latest stunt—I had a chat with him about the hyena situation." His anger that someone had dared touch their cubs put a hard edge in his voice, but right then, there was also a touch of predatory amusement.

She knew it had to be caused by Hawke's apparent problems with Brenna—the two alphas hadn't really learned to play nice with each other yet. "What did she do?"

"She's hooked up with the damn Psy."

Sascha snapped up her head. "Judd? Brenna's with *Judd Lauren*?"

Her cat licked at her exposed neck. "You smell good."

Sascha tried to keep thinking. "But he's so cold."

"We changelings have ways of thawing out you Psy."

Sascha could hardly argue with her own body melting. But even as she gave in to her cat, a part of her worried. Something was very wrong with Brenna, and Judd Lauren's icy reserve might only exacerbate the problem—he couldn't give the changeling woman what she needed to heal herself. Touch. Warmth. Unwavering affection.

CHAPTER 20

Judd dreamed of killing again, of seeing his hands dipped in blood. Red. The blood was red in the otherwise monochrome landscape. That was when he realized he held Brenna's dying heart in his hands. It was beating, a pulsing accusation of what he'd done.

He wrenched himself awake, sending out a telepathic scan at the same instant. He found Brenna far faster than he should've been able to. She was safe. Asleep. But that was no longer an option for him. Getting up, he began doing pull-ups using the metal exercise bar bolted to the walls.

By the time the clock signaled dawn, he'd pushed himself to straining point. Judging that Brenna would be awake, he called her.

"What?" a sleepy voice answered.

"Did you talk to Sascha?"

She turned on the visual and he saw that her face was soft with sleep. It made the hunger in him twist, its claws raking down his insides—as if he had a beast within him, too. He'd spent hours last night restoring the fractures in his conditioning. It should be holding. But the second he saw her, he realized there was a major flaw he hadn't yet found, a hidden source of subversive emotion.

"Yes, sir, Judd, sir." A small smile. "She's coming up today to see me."

He heard the reluctance in her tone. "Do you—"

"No." Sharp. "I'll be fine alone. See you tonight?"

"I'll be in the den." Switching off the comm, he had a shower and then decided to work off his excess energy by checking in with Sienna. His eldest niece's abilities were developing at a rapid pace—if he and Walker didn't manage to teach her some control, there was going to be real trouble down the road. The problem was that, as with Judd, the telepathy everyone knew about was only her secondary talent. Her true strength was something so volatile, even Psy steered clear of those who had it.

Since Sienna was in an unusually cooperative mood, the session went well. He was returning from it midmorning—after a short detour—when a small naked body barreled into him in one of the main corridors. Steadying the boy with Tk, he looked down. The child lifted a finger to his lips. "Shh. I'm hiding." With that, he went behind Judd and scrambled into a small alcove. "Quickly!"

Not sure why he obeyed the order, Judd backed up to stand in front of the alcove, arms crossed. A flustered Lara came running around the corner a few seconds later. "Have you seen Ben? Four-year-old. Naked as a jaybird."

"How tall is he?" Judd asked in his most overbearing Psy manner.

Lara stared. "He's *four*. How tall do you think he is? Have you seen him or not?"

"Let me think . . . did you say he was naked?"

"He was about to be bathed. Slippery little monkey."

A giggle from behind Judd.

Lara's eyes widened and then her lips twitched. "So you haven't seen him?"

"Without a proper description, I can't be sure."

The healer was obviously trying not to laugh. "You shouldn't encourage him—he's incorrigible as it is."

Judd felt childish hands on his left calf and then Ben poked his head out. "I'm incorwigeable, did ya hear?"

Judd nodded. "I do believe you've been found. Why don't you go have your bath?"

"Come on, munchkin." Lara held out a hand.

Surprisingly strong baby arms and legs wrapped around Judd's leg. "No. I wanna stay with Uncle Judd."

Lara anticipated his question. "Ben spends a lot of time with Marlee."

"I spend a lot of time with Marlee," a small voice piped up.

Judd glanced down. "Are you sure he's wolf? Sounds more like a parrot to me."

Ben's face clouded. "Am so a wolf!" Letting go of Judd, the child shifted in a shower of multicolored sparks. Judd held his breath until a small wolf began trying to climb up his body. Ben's progress was hindered by the fact that he wasn't using his claws.

Bending, Judd picked him up and held him against his chest, unable to explain his own behavior. "He isn't clawed."

"Of course not," Lara said. "It's the first rule we teach them—no claws during play. Can you imagine the carnage otherwise?"

"Logical." The pup was batting at his chest, a warm live weight.

"That's why Tai is so embarrassed he went clawed."

Judd had already put the incident out of his mind. "We weren't playing. Claws were never an issue."

"Not for you. But they were for him." Lara blew out a breath between pursed lips. "He didn't mean to do it. He lost control like a child. I take it he hasn't apologized yet?"

"There's no need." Judd caught Ben as he slipped, holding the cub more firmly against him.

"Take my advice," the healer offered, "if the kid works up the guts to apologize, let him. It'll make him feel better."

"Alright."

"Ben." Lara's tone tried for harshness, but it was patent that she was charmed by her tiny charge. "Let's get going."

Ben's response was to growl and bury his head against Judd's chest.

"Do you want to spend the rest of the day in the Pen?"

Judd knew the Pen to be a fenced space inside the nursery bereft of toys. As a punishment, it seemed to work very well. It did this time, too. Ben wriggled and then shifted without warning. Reacting instinctively, Judd threw a Tk shield around the entire shimmer, keeping his hands exactly where they had been before the boy began to change.

Ben's weight hit his hands a split second later and the boy twisted to hold out his arms to the healer. "Do I gotta be clean?"

Taking him, Lara planted a smacking kiss on his cheek. "Yes, you do, my little escape artist." In her embrace, Ben giggled and turned his head for another kiss.

"Lara," Judd said when the healer turned to leave.

She raised an eyebrow.

"What would've happened if I'd moved and disrupted—" He didn't want to say the words in case they had a negative impact on the child.

"Don't worry." Lara stroked one hand over Ben's head as he laid it on her shoulder. "The process isn't that easily messed up. Otherwise the Psy would've taken advantage of the weakness by now." She seemed to have forgotten she was talking to one of the same race. "An extremely big disruption can cause errors in a shift. Most can be corrected—so long as it's not a major part of the brain that's compromised."

"But to shift near someone implies a relationship of trust."

Lara smiled. "I guess Marlee must like her uncle Judd a whole lot."

"Only she likes her dad more," Ben said in a stage whisper.

"Oh, well"—Lara winked—"second's not so bad. 'Bye, Judd."

Judd found himself raising his hand in response to the wave Ben gave him over her shoulder. He was still standing there trying to process the extraordinary encounter when D'Arn passed him.

The soldier stopped, then retraced his steps. "Let me guess—a woman or a pup."

"How did you know?"

"Not much else puts that look on a man's face." He grinned. "Me and a few of the others are going out to play some training war games. Want to come? Release the tension, you know—everyone's thinking about Tim. He was no prize, but he didn't deserve to be murdered. And now this thing with the hyenas."

"Any progress there?" If he'd thought the hyenas had targeted Brenna on purpose, he would've gone hunting himself. However—and though he could find no cogent reason for that suspicion—his instincts said that Timothy's murderer was the real threat. Even revisiting the scene this morning after speaking with Sienna hadn't clarified things. He had the unwelcome sense he was missing something.

"Some. We've got a bead on the bloody scavengers, but they don't need all of us today." D'Arn shook his head in a curiously canine gesture. "Anyway, you in?"

He nodded. Brenna was safe in the den and he had no surveillance work lined up. It might be that a hard physical workout was what he needed to clear up his brain so he could connect the dots he knew were there. "Rules?"

The other man began walking. "Human form. Drew's going to hand out laser badges. A hit with a laser rifle will register from anywhere on your body and list itself as a slight injury, a debilitating one, loss of eyesight—you get the drill." He pushed open a door.

"Teams?" Judd had played similar military games both in psychic and physical terms. An Arrow who wasn't a shadow didn't survive long.

"Two." He pushed through an exit. "Psy and human/changeling."

"Psy?" Judd asked as they made their way out of the White Zone.

"If you're not Psy, you have to hit the target in the back." He scowled. "Against all the rules of normal fighting, but if a Psy sees you coming during the game, you're automatically dead. No second chances."

Judd agreed—because while Psy couldn't manipulate changeling minds without massive effort, they could kill with a single focused blow. "You have human soldiers?" He had his Psy abilities to compensate for the changelings' advantages in terms of speed, sensory input, and physical strength. Humans, by that reckoning, had nothing. "People who have mated in?"

D'Arn shook his head. "Not all. Saul's ex-navy. He mated in. But Kieran was adopted as a child. Sing-Liu you've met."

Judd had never guessed that the small female with the flat eyes of a fellow assassin was human. She moved more like the DarkRiver cats. "Martial arts?"

"Nope. Our little China Doll likes knives." D'Arn had barely gotten the words out when a knife whistled incredibly close to his ear and thunked home in a tree. Instead of going on alert, D'Arn laughed and threw up his hands. "I was kidding, honey."

Sing-Liu materialized from their right. "One of these days," she threatened, striding over, "you're going to push me too far. And then I'll have to make you eat your words."

The SnowDancer male retrieved the knife he'd dodged and held it to his side. "Promise? Will it involve kinky things with rope and knives? Please?"

Judd wondered if D'Arn had a death wish. But then Sing-Liu laughed and kissed the soldier, eyes turning from assassin to pure seductive woman. Unexpected was not the word for it.

"Mated pair." The words came from Drew, who'd just walked up. "China Doll's a nickname. She doesn't mind—use it if you like."

"And get a knife in my back," Judd said, his Psy brain comparing D'Arn's behavior with Sing-Liu to his own with Brenna. It didn't take a genius to tell him he wasn't giving his wolf anything close to what she needed. "I think I'll pass."

"I had to try." Drew shrugged. "On to the games." His smile was distinctly savage.

Judd was more than ready, the tension in him wound to a fever pitch. "Let's play."

* * *

Brenna had been looking for Judd for twenty minutes without success. Sascha had just left after several hours of talk. The empath hadn't been able to give Brenna any answers but had convinced her that she didn't "smell" insane. Now she wanted to share her relief with Judd, wanted to tell him that the violent woman who'd shredded his skin yesterday had been an aberration . . . even if she didn't quite believe it herself.

"Lucy"—she stopped her friend in the corridor near Hawke's office—"you seen tall, dark, and silent?"

"Which one?" the other woman deadpanned. "Your one's playing war games with Andrew and some others."

Bren felt her face pale. "What?"

"Don't worry," Lucy called out as she headed off. "He's a big boy."

But Drew was *bloodthirsty*, especially with men who dared be involved with his baby sister. And after the way Judd had faced him down yesterday . . . "Calm, be calm," she told herself. "He's Psy. A very strong Psy." Oh, God. What if Judd killed Drew?

She thrust a hand through her hair. Inspiration struck. She could either go mad worrying or . . . Turning on her heel, she ran after Lucy. Her friend smiled and opened her mouth to speak.

Something crashed in Hawke's office. They both looked up as the door was wrenched open and Sienna Lauren came striding out. The door slammed shut after her, as if it had been kicked. The seventeen-year-old didn't see them—she was heading in the opposite direction, head down, fists clenched.

Lucy raised an eyebrow. "That one doesn't act Psy, does she?"

"No." Brenna thought about going after the clearly upset girl, but Sienna didn't know her and would probably not welcome the interference.

"Not like your one. That man is pure ice. Sexy ice but still ice."

Brenna had a moment's pause. "How do you know we're involved?"

Lucy's laugh was open and honest. "Did you hit your head or something, Bren? You smell like him, silly."

"Oh." But she shouldn't, not that deep. A scent layer only grew ingrained—unable to be washed off—between lovers. Something she'd never become with Judd if he got himself executed for killi— *Stop!* "Lucy, I need a favor. Can you get access to a vehicle?"

"Sure. So can you."

"Not without Riley finding out. Um, I'm kind of under den arrest." She was going to break the rules, but she wasn't going to be stupid about it.

"Riley's got some burr under his bonnet," Lucy muttered. "He chewed me out yesterday for nothing. I'll sneak you out and it'll be my pleasure. Where are we going?"

"Miss Leozandra's Beauty Parlor." Smack bang in the middle of Chinatown.

He was going *to take care of unfinished business this morning. The den grapevine had confirmed that the bitch was finally alone and unprotected. All he had to do was lure her to one of the dim corners of the garage.*

She'd come. If she had remembered his face, she would have squealed by now. It didn't matter. She had to die—he couldn't take the chance of her memory returning. They'd rip open his stomach and pull out his guts while he was still alive if they learned what he'd done. The drugs and Timothy's murder were nothing compared to his first crime.

He bit down the fear. She'd come. She trusted him. He was one of the good guys.

Once in the garage, he'd overdose her with the Rush already loaded into the pressure injector, shove her into the trunk of one of the Pack cars, and drive out. No one would ever figure out where she'd gone. Or they'd blame Judd Lauren. Yes, that would work. He'd make it look like Judd had killed her, maybe leave a knife coated with her blood in the Psy's room.

He smirked, fear buried under sick excitement.

His first surprise came when he got to her apartment. The door was covered with the cool, dangerous scent of the Psy she was undoubtedly fucking. He backed off without touching anything. The scent could be there because Judd had spent time inside, but he was certain the Psy had done something, set up some kind of weird psychic trap.

"Hey, you looking for Bren?" A smiling face, a packmate. "She's gone off with Lucy. Saw them leave."

"No." He couldn't have her finding out he'd been looking for her. It might serve to trigger her memory. "Drew actually."

"I heard something about war games."

"Thanks." His gut churned as he walked away. He could do nothing now, would have to wait until the grinning fool who'd interrupted him forgot he'd ever seen him outside that door. But he couldn't wait forever. Brenna might remember.

CHAPTER 21

To Brenna's surprise, they made it out of den territory without a problem. She crawled out of the backseat and asked Lucy to stop once they were no longer in any danger of being spotted by scouts. "I can take it from here."

"Sure?" A friendly question, nothing more.

"I need to *drive*."

"Have at it. I'll run back and pretend ignorance if Riley grills me."

Brenna returned her mischievous smile. "Thanks, Lucy."

"Anytime." She got out and Brenna moved into the driver's seat. Waving, she watched her friend disappear into the woods. Then she took a deep breath and the wheel. Her lips stretched into a huge smile. This felt like freedom.

The drive from the snow of the Sierra to the cold but dry bustle of San Francisco was spookily smooth. No traffic jams, no wolf sentries racing to stop her, no red lights. Perfection. She should've known it was too easy. After finding a vertical street park—her car being slotted up into the third level—she began the trek to the beauty parlor. Trouble struck less than a minute later.

A tall male with amber-gold hair materialized out of nowhere to lean on the wall in front of her. "I thought you were supposed to remain at the den."

"I don't believe this!" Folding her arms, she stared at the DarkRiver sentinel. "They snitched me out to the cats?" Who might be their allies, but were not yet friends. However, she trusted Vaughn. He'd come for her—she might've been unconscious at the time, but her wolf remembered. Vaughn was safe.

Of course, at this moment he didn't look particularly happy to see her. "The situation's volatile. Some of our people aren't feeling friendly."

"Oh." She'd failed to take that into account, an inexcusable mistake with what was going on. All she had wanted was to get out and fix this one thing she *could* fix, even if her mind was splintering into a thousand pieces. "I should go back, huh?" She couldn't hide her disappointment.

"What the hell—I'm around to provide personal bodyguard service." He gave her a look that could've come from either one of her brothers. "Where to?"

Wanting to hug him, she grinned. "Miss Leozandra's."

Brenna left close to sunset, after having been fed both a late lunch and an afternoon snack by Miss Leozandra's personal chef. She couldn't remember what she'd eaten, she was so excited with her shoulder-length look. The gen-synth extensions were flawless—even she couldn't tell where her hair ended and they began. And she had bangs!

Nothing could put a damper on her happiness, not even the knowledge that she'd been spotted returning by several sentries. Riley would know in minutes. She didn't care. Her joy increased with each exclamation that met her on the way to her quarters—the reaction was unanimously positive.

She didn't know who was more surprised when she turned the corner and found Judd leaning outside the door to her rooms. His face, of course, didn't betray anything, but she saw a flicker in his eyes, somehow knew she'd caught him unawares. As had he.

"You look fine." Disbelieving, she gave him the once-over. It was plain he'd showered and put on a fresh pair of black jeans and a black T-shirt. But the skin she could see was clear of bruises.

"Why shouldn't I be?"

"Because you were out in the forest with my brother." She unlocked the door and let him prowl in behind her, very aware that for all his determination to restrain his emotions, he'd come searching for her. He kicked the door shut as she fought to contain her joy.

"Hmm." Walking forward, he fingered a strand of her hair. "So soft."

She didn't say anything as he stroked the strands through his fingers over and over, as if attempting to figure out where the high-tech fibers joined her natural hair . . . or maybe he was simply indulging himself.

"Perfect." He let the strands slide away.

"Do you like it?" she found herself asking despite her better judgment.

"I already told you."

Perfect.

What she'd taken as a comment on the quality of the extensions had been about her. "Oh." Feeling a little shy, she nonetheless reached out and hugged him. He went stiff and she suddenly knew it wasn't a reaction to her touch. Pulling back, she began to push up his T-shirt. "Let me guess, broken ribs?"

"Brenna." He tried to stop her, but she swatted away his hand.

"Oh. My. God." The entire left side of his chest was black and blue. "Why aren't you taped up?"

"I don't need it."

She shoved down the T-shirt. "Fine. Be all macho about it." Then something else occurred to her. Her blood chilled. "Judd, what does Drew look like?"

"Worse."

"Is he dead?" she forced herself to ask.

"No."

Relief made her a little light-headed. "I thought you guys played with lasers."

"We made some new rules." It was obvious he wasn't going to tell her any more.

She threw up her hands. "You're not dead. Drew isn't dead. That's good enough for me." She turned to grab a couple of ice packs from the built-in cooler. "Sit."

"I said—"

"Sit."

He sprawled into a chair. When she wrapped the ice packs in a small towel and placed them against his ribs, he didn't protest. "What is it with men and testosterone?" she muttered, standing in the vee formed by his outstretched legs.

"I don't think you'd like us without it." He held the ice packs to his side by pinning them with his arm. "There was no need for this."

She was about to snap a comeback when she realized he'd come to her precisely because she'd fuss over him, no matter what he must've told himself to the contrary. Her throat tightened. "Humor me," she said, stroking his hair off his forehead. "You need a haircut." He'd always worn it very short, a sharp military cut.

"I'll razor it off tonight."

"Don't. I kind of like it this longer length." It brushed his nape, not too long but long enough to run her fingers through.

He looked up to meet her gaze. The moment stretched as she stroked the long front strands to the side. "I could just trim these bits that are getting in your eyes."

"All right."

The simple acceptance made her stomach drop, her protective walls collapse. "Are you up for a walk?" She didn't want to fight with Riley and it was certain that he was going to turn up soon to dress her down for her escape. She couldn't believe Judd hadn't said something already. But then again, he hadn't exactly behaved himself today, either.

He gave her the ice packs. "Wear a coat. It's already dark."

"What about you?" The defined strength of his forearms drew her eye. Her hunger to stroke him was almost painful. Why didn't he feel that same need?

"I'll get my jacket and meet you at the garden door."

Ten minutes later, they walked openly past the White Zone and into the inner perimeter—she hoped her brothers would get the hint.

Judd led her to a private spot before stopping. "Talk to me."

It didn't surprise her that he knew the real reason she'd asked him to come out here. She took a seat on a fallen log while Judd leaned his muscular form against a tree across from her, seeming to blend into the deep ebony of early evening in the Sierra.

"I'm messing up my family," she said, admitting the truth. "Drew and Riley—did you see their faces yesterday? They think they're losing me." To insanity.

"They're adults, they'll deal with it."

"Will they? Look at how they react every time I try to reclaim my independence." It was the flip side of their intensely loyal natures, a protectiveness that could destroy.

"They want to keep you safe."

She stared, incredulous. "You're taking their side?"

"In this one case, they're correct. You need to be protected from your own will." His voice was pure steel. "You could hurt yourself in your rush to fix things."

"Men!" It was a snarl as she got up and began to pace up and down beside the log. "You're supposed to support me, remember?"

"Only in public," he said with cool Psy logic. "If you want total obedience, get a dog."

She kicked snow in his direction. Caught by surprise, Judd deflected it with Tk. It just made her madder. "That's cheating."

"I wasn't aware this was a test." He remained unmoving as she strode over to stand in front of him, cheeks flushed red. Things went tight in his body, his skin stretching taut. Such passion in her, such anger. "You're beautiful," he said, disregarding the sudden spike of dissonance, the violent warning that he was too close to losing control of the horror that was his "gift."

She snorted. "I'm not that easily led."

Scowling, she turned to stride back to the log. His eyes found themselves drawn to the sway of her hips, to the lush bottom encased in tight jeans that showed off every defiant feminine curve. More sparks of pain, further warning signals. But that wasn't what made him raise his eyes to her face. It was her abrupt stillness.

He straightened, his senses flaring out. "The leopards." He knew their psychic signature now, could distinguish it from wolf.

"They're here." Her voice was a whisper. "And I don't think they're happy."

"Go back and get Hawke. I'll hold them."

Not arguing, she turned and took off at high speed. Judd moved in the direction where he'd sensed the DarkRiver leopards. They were waiting on the other side of a small clearing. Lucas, Sascha, Dorian, and Mercy. Mercy, Judd didn't know well, but he considered Dorian one of the most dangerous changelings in either pack—the DarkRiver male lacked the ability to change into leopard form, but that meant nothing. On the night of Brenna's rescue, Judd had seen the sentinel tear Enrique to pieces with his bare hands.

"You shouldn't be here." They'd broken the rules. The two packs had an alliance and had given each other the right to move freely in their territorial lands, but to come this close to the den with no prior notice was a sign of aggression.

Lucas waved Dorian and Mercy off when they made a move to cover him. But *he* went in front of his mate. Sascha scowled but didn't say anything.

"If we'd wanted war, we would've been in the den by now." The markings on Lucas's face—as if he'd been slashed by the claws of some great beast—were dark with blood. "We're here to talk."

"Then we wait." Judd took a position on the other side of the snowy clearing, marking an invisible line in the snow.

One that wasn't broken when Hawke and his lieutenants

arrived. Brenna, too, had returned. She took a position to his left while the others went to his right, flanking Hawke. The SnowDancer alpha took a step forward. "Lucas, this sure as hell better be something good."

Lucas mirrored Hawke's move, his face a mask of fury. "There was an attack on the DawnSky deer clan. They were butchered."

Hawke growled low in his throat. "How many dead?"

"Nine adults, three children." Lucas's markings became even more delineated. "Would've been more, but Faith had a partial vision and managed to get out a warning. Mercy and Dorian were close enough to intervene. Tamsyn and Nate are out there picking up the pieces."

Judd watched as Sascha slid her hand into her mate's, leaning against him but staying partly behind his back—giving comfort while not distracting him by becoming an open target. Lucas's fingers closed around Sascha's. "It was a planned slaughter. Six armed Psy against a herd of deer out for a graze."

Judd knew from living with the wolves that deer were one of the most peaceful of all changelings. They were also very weak in terms of physical strength. "Why?" he asked, though experience told him the presence of a Psy assassin probably infuriated the leopard alpha. "The Council always has a reason—they think five steps ahead."

Lucas's voice was close to a growl when he answered. "I went out to the site. There was a pretty slick attempt to mark the bodies as wolf kills—looks like they had weapons shaped to mimic claws. The bodies were shredded, but a very fine scent was somehow layered into two of the deer. Mercy and Dorian must've interrupted the murdering bastards before they could do the other bodies."

"If the deer had all died," Hawke said, a low growl in his tone, "no one would've been left to point fingers at the Psy. It would've been on us."

"Changing your reputation from powerful but fair, to that of indiscriminate killers." Judd glanced at the sentinels who stood behind Lucas. "Did you tag any of the Psy?"

Mercy looked at her alpha and answered only after his nod. "We saw them leaving but made the choice to help the injured rather than give chase. They hid their trail like experts and the deer are too traumatized to be of much help in terms of descriptions—they're schoolteachers and accountants, not soldiers."

"What about Faith, did she see anything?" Judd asked, knowing Faith's reputation as the strongest foreseer in or out of the Net.

Sascha shook her head. "She's taking this hard—she saw it after it began. Said she saw the consequences, not the act . . . saw a glimpse of a future drenched in bloodred."

There was an instant of total silence, then Dorian spoke, his rage more evident than the others'. "One of the kids thinks he saw an insignia on the left shoulder of their uniforms. Snakes. Kid's terrified of snakes, so he remembered."

"Now he's going to be phobic about them," Sascha said. Her tone was soft but her expression was full of anger.

Lucas turned to brush his lips over her hair. "Sascha wanted to stay with the survivors, but I figured we'd need a Psy perspective. Didn't know he'd be here." He nodded toward Judd and the act wasn't friendly. "Any ideas?"

"Some. Give me a minute." Death was his only talent after all. "I do know that the snake emblem belongs to Ming LeBon, but that simply confirms the Council link."

A fine-boned feminine hand slipped into his and he felt it in every cell of his body. He glanced down to find Brenna looking up and giving a small shake of her head. In that moment, time seemed to stop and he knew she was telling him that death was not all he was. He almost believed her. Except even at that second, he was aware of the monstrous thing inside of him. One moment of carelessness and it would crawl out to rain indiscriminate death on those around him. Men. Children. Women.

Hand remaining clasped to his, Brenna turned away, breaking the odd moment. "I'd like to help." Her words were directed at Sascha.

"I think you'd be very good with the young ones."

Because, Judd thought, Brenna knew what it was like to be helpless and breakable. He had vowed to ensure she'd never again suffer as she'd suffered in Enrique's hands, but the scars were already there and they had changed who she was.

"Judd?" Sascha's cardinal eyes turned to him. "I—"

"Yes," he said, before she could ask the question.

"I knew that. But I was going to ask how many hours you think you could give me."

When had Sascha gone from being uneasy around him to believing him "good"? "As many as you need." He couldn't heal traumatized minds as she could, but he could feed her extra power, a talent rare among Psy but which seemed to be paired with his little speciality. Some Psy abilities were like that—they came in sets.

"If Bren's going in, we need to ensure protection. There's already been one attempt to target her," Riley said.

"What are you talking about?" Brenna frowned.

Judd looked at the other man. "He's thinking we were wrong, that maybe the hyenas knew you were at the cabin."

CHAPTER 22

"How could they?" Brenna's brow furrowed.

Riley ignored her. "Judd can't help Sascha and keep an eye on security, too."

It was the first time either of Brenna's brothers had even obliquely acknowledged his skill at keeping Brenna safe. But Judd didn't take it at face value. Riley was a strategist, a man with cool focus, one who thought disturbingly like a Psy.

"She'll be fine—I've got the deer inside our perimeter, soldiers with them twenty-four/seven." Lucas shook his head. "But my gut says the Psy won't attack the same target twice."

Judd agreed. "They're using a scattergun approach to divide your resources and weaken you in specific areas, with a focus on eliminating those civilian or nonpredatory groups who might support you. It was a tactic used successfully by the Korean army during the Japan-Korea war."

Lucas narrowed his eyes. "Any idea what they might do next?"

"There have to have been more pieces. The deer hit is too large an escalation otherwise."

"If they've been taking out lone nonpredatory changelings,"

Hawke said, expression grim, "and laying the blame on us, we might not hear about it. The families of the victims would be too scared to confront us."

"Brewing resentment." Brenna's husky voice, changed forever by the nightmare. As if she had screamed so hard, something in her vocal cords had broken irreparably. "There's one thing I don't get, though," she continued. "I know I'm not a soldier, but we've all heard the Council's dead bodies stay buried."

"So why the half-assed job this time?" Lucas completed. "Two options. One, Faith was a wild card they didn't factor in."

"Or two," Judd said, "they've overstretched themselves by reaching into territory where they're the neophytes."

"What's your take?" Riley asked, still appearing calm in spite of what had taken place the last time they'd spoken.

Every one of Judd's guards snapped up—Riley was the kind of hunter who'd stalk before striking. "If I had to guess, I'd say they didn't forget Faith and likely chose the exact target without much prior planning."

"Why?" Dorian asked.

"Because if they had planned it down to the name of the group to be attacked, there would've been a higher chance of a foreseer picking it up."

Mercy scowled. "This seeing-the-future stuff makes my head hurt."

"It's more probable that instead of a specific target, they had the parameters of what they were looking for—a large, nonaggressive changeling group in a region not under direct watch by either SnowDancer or DarkRiver. Then they set up sentries and waited."

"The deer were just meat to them," Brenna said, outrage making her voice tremble. "Bugs to be squashed."

"Unfortunately Brenna is right. The deer were chess pieces."

Lucas shoved his free hand through his hair. "They messed up on the location—if they'd waited until the deer were deeper, Dorian and Mercy might not have made it in time."

Judd nodded. "Before the recent series of events, Psy and changeling concerns rarely collided. The Council's unaware of the nuances of life in the forests—the importance of scents and wind direction, the ranges leopard sentinels travel, a hundred small things that influence a successful raid."

"They're not going to remain that way," Hawke pointed out. "Each time they come in, they learn more."

Sascha made a sound of agreement. "And Psy are very good at collating data."

"This time, it won't be enough to simply track down and eliminate those personally responsible for the kills." Judd had seen how the changelings operated. An eye for an eye. Blood for blood. It was a law that worked with their system of honor. However, the Psy had no such honor. "You need to send a bigger message."

"He's right." Lucas looked at Hawke. "They've already figured out how to fake our scents. At least well enough to fool a casual observer. If they hit a man's family—he's not going to wait to make sure he's got the right scent. He'll go for your young in retaliation."

It was an ugly but clear description of the consequences of escalation. "You can't afford to go to full-scale war with the Council." Judd knew what the leaders of his people were capable of, the lines they'd cross. "It could be what they want—if you begin the aggression, then they're justified in using lethal force."

For several minutes the only sounds were of the wind whistling through the trees, and for Judd, the steady sound of Brenna's breathing. She was something he'd never expected and certainly didn't deserve. He could give her nothing of what she needed, but the dark heart of him was starting to understand that letting her go might not be an option.

She awakened something in him that was raw, desperate, and violent in a way that sprang not from anger but from passion. Sweat beaded down his spine as he fought the rising incursions of dissonance. It was stronger with each admission, each touch. And he didn't care. Part of him wanted to forget why the dissonance had been hooked so viciously into his psyche, forget what would happen if he snapped the threads of conditioning.

"Data," Hawke said, before Judd could give in to the madness. "The Psy love their computers. We hack their systems and destroy things, they're going to get the message."

You mess with our territory, we'll mess with yours.

Judd had always known that Hawke was one of the most highly intelligent predators he had ever met, but this was inspired even for him. Most alphas would've sought some form of bloody retribution—as had Hawke in the past—but for this particular game of chess, a lateral move was better, far better. "If you hit one of the major databases, such as the ones that feed data to the stock market, you disrupt things worldwide."

"Isn't most of the information backed up in the PsyNet?" Brenna asked. "I never really got why Psy like computers so much."

It was Sascha who answered. "The major factor is power. Because a lot of clerical jobs are held by low-Gradient Psy—people who don't have the psychic strength to access secure data vaults on a continual basis, it's inefficient to store day-to-day business records in the Net." When no one interrupted, she continued. "The other issue is that Psy have to do deals with the other races. Human and changelings both demand data they can access. If the systems go down, the Councilors' heads might explode. It really is a brilliant idea, Hawke."

The wolf flashed a smile. "Thank you, Sascha darling. Maybe you're with the wrong alpha, hmm?"

"I swear, Hawke." Lucas muttered, shifting so he was pinning Sascha to him with an arm around the front of her neck. "One of these days—"

The threat was cut off as Sascha twisted in his hold and kissed him. It was a short, affectionate act, yet Judd found himself transfixed by it. But it wasn't Lucas and Sascha he saw. When he looked down at the glossy strands of Brenna's hair, he could suddenly imagine what they'd feel like as they brushed over his skin in the most intimate of circumstances.

She looked up, eyes wide. *"Judd."* A low whisper meant for his ears alone.

He watched the rise of color flush her cheeks.

"Your timing sucks," she muttered, leaning deeper into him.

He absorbed the psychic impact of the touch, refusing to push her away. Contrary to her words, he thought his timing perfect. It was when they were alone and the fever started to rise that he became aware of the myriad ways in which he could hurt her, mutilate her. She called Enrique a butcher—she hadn't seen the things Judd had done as an Arrow.

"Do you have any hackers I can use?" Lucas asked, appearing mollified by his mate's kiss. "We've got the setup to run this in the second subbasement of our city HQ."

"How good are you at hiding your trail? The whole point is to not give them anything they can use against DarkRiver or SnowDancer." Judd forced his attention away from Brenna, from the unpalatable images of his past.

"They've never caught us yet." Lucas looked pleased as only a cat could. "Dorian's very good, but we need more hackers of his caliber if we're going to coordinate a big strike."

Hawke folded his arms. "We've got three who can stay under the radar and one who can do even better."

Beside him Brenna's body grew tense, muscles locking into place. Following her gaze, he saw it clash with Riley's. Her brother seemed to struggle with something for several seconds before giving a curt nod. "Bren's the best there is."

"I thought your degree was in computronics." It didn't please Judd that there was something he hadn't known about her. An emotional reaction. The sweat rolling down his spine felt like ice this time.

"My official degree." The mischief in her eyes was new. "Hawke says I have an unofficial one in creative systems programming." She laughed.

The sound, the intensity of her happiness, caused another mental chain to snap. The ends of his nerves seemed to *burn*, his spinal cord turning into a column of excruciating liquid fire—he was perilously close to a meltdown.

Acting before it was too late, he withdrew his hand from Brenna's . . . but didn't push away her body. "I'll run security on the hack team." He met Hawke's eyes. "When Brenna's there, so am I. I'll work with Sascha around that."

"Lucas, you have a problem with that?"

The DarkRiver male shook his head. "As long as there's no chance of you getting recognized." He scowled. "You look so fucking Psy, you might as well wear a holo-sign."

That his expression had fooled an alpha told Judd none of his internal struggles were showing. "I'll make certain my appearance isn't a cause for concern."

"There's one more thing." Lucas's markings darkened again. "The deer need to know they're safe. We track and hit the assassins first, a day or so before the computer strike so the Council thinks the blood was all we wanted. They might get complacent."

Judd looked at the DarkRiver alpha and understood that he'd made a promise to the deer to lessen their nightmares. It was how changeling society worked—the predators ran the show, but with it came responsibility. Unlike the Psy Council, the leopards and wolves took the safety and welfare of those under their leadership very seriously. Seriously enough to kill. Changeling justice, but as Lucas had pointed out, it would serve a dual purpose in this case.

And the Psy Council thought changelings stupid. That was their mistake.

Night had fallen during the meeting and it was well past dinner when they made it back to the den. He went with Brenna in spite of the increasing levels of dissonance—proximity in enclosed quarters would only worsen things. But the hunger in him, the raw painful thing that threatened to destroy him, wouldn't let him walk away.

"I'll throw something together in the kitchen," she said as they entered.

He remained in the living area, able to see her moving behind the kitchen counter. The second she turned her back, he took the chance to check the trap he'd placed on her door. Instinct and a need to protect had made him do it. There was something he wasn't seeing, some link his conscious mind hadn't yet forged, but his subconscious had, and it was adamant that she was in danger. Or maybe, he simply wanted her safe.

The trap itself wasn't psychic—he didn't have the ability

to tie his power to an object in that fashion. Instead, he'd created it using basic Arrow tech. The device was embedded in her old-fashioned doorknob, and it read the prints of anyone who entered. If the prints didn't belong to Brenna, Andrew, Riley, Hawke, or Judd, the device was programmed to send out an alert to his phone. And as Brenna had discovered, he could go from place to place in the blink of an eye. Teleportation weakened him, but a Tk of his particular subdesignation needed very little power to cause catastrophic damage.

He sat back, satisfied the device was functioning.

"Food's ready." Brenna walked out and his eyes drifted to the thrust of her breasts under her thin sweater. "Warmed-up leftovers okay with you?"

The hunger he wanted fed had nothing to do with food. "Yes."

Her smile was bright. "You're easy to please. Good, because I'm exhausted."

He slammed up desperate psychic blocks against visions of her in bed, warm, naked, and *his*. "Let's make it a quick meal." They were midway through it when his phone flashed. He glanced at the incoming code but put it down without reading the message.

"Who was that?"

The huskiness in her voice was like sandpaper across his straining flesh. "No one important."

Curiosity lit up her eyes, but then she shrugged and went back to her dinner. He scrutinized her for several seconds, as he'd never known Brenna to just give up, but she seemed genuinely tired. That made things easier. There were aspects of his life she didn't need to know about—the Council wouldn't hesitate to torture her if they thought she had information they wanted.

Her exhaustion was proven by the huge yawn she gave as they were finishing up. "I'm sorry, but I'm beat. Mind if we cut this even shorter?"

It was exactly the out he needed. "Of course not."

Yet he stood outside her door for long minutes. He was no changeling, but he could smell the feminine heat of her scent, almost taste the lushness of her, his psychic senses multiplying and intensifying the impact of the physical. His fingers curled at the remembered sensation of her skin against his. The compulsion to open the door, walk back in, and take the fatal step into sexual contact was so strong, he had his hand raised when his phone flashed again.

It was a blunt reminder of who and what he was. He didn't care. He'd crossed too many lines with Brenna to go back now. But he was dangerous to her in his current state. So he answered the call. "I'm on my way." Only then did he return to his rooms, gather what he needed, and walk silent and unnoticed out of the den.

His vehicle—separate from those owned by the SnowDancers—was hidden near one of the rutted tracks leading out of wolf territory. When he reached it, he found it undisturbed and in perfect condition. The engine started with an almost soundless purr.

A second later, he thought he saw a shadow in the forest. He sent his Tp senses in an outward scan, aware that his body and mind were both functioning at less than optimal levels. Someone could have followed him in the wake of his distraction with Brenna. However, the scan touched nothing but the open minds of forest creatures. Satisfied, he maneuvered the vehicle through the thick darkness of a cloudy night and onto the track.

The telepathic "knock" came when he'd almost reached his destination. *I'm here.* He eased the car into a single-level street parking slot and got out. *What's important enough to call a meeting in person?*

I wanted to talk to both of you, and the comm channels aren't secure at present—I'm working on getting some new encryption software to block any covert monitoring, the Ghost responded. *The Council's already begun eliminating the most vocal of the agitators.*

Judd smelled the biting freshness of oncoming rain as he cut through a children's park. *They knew the risk.* Crossing the road, he walked around the church and into the unlit backyard, home to a small graveyard for those who had chosen to lie under the sun rather than be interred in the crypts.

Father Perez sat on the back steps of the church and Judd

located the Ghost's dark shadow against a facing tree. "What did you find out?"

"I didn't see you arrive," the Ghost said. "Being out of the Psy-Net hasn't had any appreciable impact on you and your abilities."

Wrong, but it was an untruth that had tactical value. "I have to get back." Distance was simply turning up the notch on his need to be with Brenna, *to keep her safe*. There was a threat to her. His brain was fixated on the idea. But what he didn't know was whether the threat came from the outside . . . or from his own killing abilities.

The Ghost took the hint. "This data hasn't been confirmed yet, but it appears Ashaya Aleine may be forced to start her work from scratch."

"Why? The lab had to have backup files hidden away," Perez said.

"The recent loss of several of their top scientists negates the value of any such backups—they alone knew what their notes meant. Unfortunately Aleine's too well protected."

Perez sighed. "I was hoping you hadn't taken that route." His voice held sorrow. "You kill too easily."

The Ghost shifted in the darkness. "If I hadn't removed the scientists from the equation, all our work would have meant nothing. They would've begun implanting test subjects within the year. In a decade, we would have become a single hive mind."

"Not single," Judd said. "Psy wouldn't all be equal under Protocol I. There will be puppets and puppet masters." As an Arrow programmed to kill, Judd knew the truth of what happened when some were given absolute control over others. Power was the most rapacious of drugs.

"And so we spill more blood?" Perez asked. "Is that right?"

"I have no right to judge anyone else, Father." No matter what the Ghost had done, Judd knew he'd done worse. "Tell me what else you have—quickly."

By the time Judd left, the chill winter rain was coming down in a steady beat. He let it fall on him, let it wash away the death-soaked taste of this latest meeting. The dehumanizing cruelty that was the Implant Protocol was evil, but in fighting it, Judd knew that they, too, could become evil. The understanding came from some buried part of him, a part inextricably linked to what he *felt* for Brenna.

The thought further heightened his urgency to return to her. Speeding up his pace, he breathed in the scent of ozone and city. The street was deserted, the glow of the laz-lamps muted by the rain. Walking across, he stepped into the darkness of the park. As a child, he'd never once played in a place like this. His training runs had been supervised, his exercises regimented. Shaping him. Making him.

Pushing aside the memories, he traversed the park with long steady strides, heading for the car he'd left on the other side. He could run the new data crystal the Ghost had passed him in the car's system, but preferred to wait and do it on his personal organizer, which was double-firewalled against interference.

Movement! The warning shot through his head before he consciously realized what he was seeing. He twisted his body to lessen the damage as the large wolf slammed him to the ground. Air smashed out of his lungs and he had barely enough time to get up his arm before the wolf's fangs snapped down, going through skin and muscle to hit bone.

Cauterizing the pain, he shoved with enough Tk that the wolf released him, giving him a chance to get back on his feet. His arm hung by his side, useless until he could knit the nerve and muscle together. Bleeding from the arm and from deep gashes in his chest, he arrowed his abilities and forced power into his right fist. When the wolf launched himself a second time, he smashed his fist into the animal's windpipe. It went down but only for a second before slamming into his chest and bringing him to the ground once again.

Wolf jaws neared, their lethal intent clear—to crush his neck.

Judd had been trying not to kill, certain this was a SnowDancer—and which one. He hadn't forgotten Riley's calculating calm at the meeting today. But now he had no choice. He was bleeding too badly. Gathering everything he had, he prepared to punch into the changeling's mind. The wolf would be dead in about one second flat.

CHAPTER 23

"Judd!" The scream was so unexpected, he froze. So did the wolf. A second later, it jumped off his body and streaked off into the darkness. He could have reached out and destroyed it at that distance, but he held back. If that wolf was one of Brenna's brothers . . .

"Judd." Hands cradled his face as he sat up. Trembling fingers wiped raindrops from his skin. "My God! Your arm is shredded!"

"Brenna, what are you doing here?" He was already sending power down his arm, starting to knit the bone—the capability to heal himself was an adjunct of his Tk-Cell abilities.

"I can't believe you're giving me shit when you're bleeding to death!" She grabbed his uninjured arm, slung it around her shoulders, and pulled him to his feet. She was slight, so even with her changeling strength, it took considerable effort.

He'd lost more blood that he'd realized—his thinking was going fuzzy, causing him to fumble as he tried to fix the damage done to him. He should've killed his attacker in that split-second window between sound and hit, instead of trying to deflect. But then Brenna would've looked at him with hate in her eyes. Unacceptable.

"Come on, the car's not far." She put an arm around his waist. "Why didn't you teleport away when he attacked?"

"Requires concentration." He'd had no time to settle his thoughts into the right patterns. "I'll drive," he said as they reached the car.

She deactivated the lock by placing his thumb against it, then slid back the passenger door. "I thought you Psy were logical. You're in no condition to drive."

But he wanted to. Vaguely aware that that wasn't a rational desire, he let her half drop him into the passenger seat and close the door. Only when she was inside, too, did he start using all available power to minimize the injuries. Despite his erratic concentration, his arm was nearly back to functional, though it looked mauled. However, the blood loss was having a cumulative impact. He could hardly think, much less focus on fixing the holes in his torso. As a result, the gaping cuts continued to bleed.

"Lara's too far." Brenna started the car. "Hospital! There's one—"

"No."

When it looked as if she was going to ignore him, he grabbed her with his injured arm, shooting pain up his body. "I can't be DNA traced. The kids."

"Oh, God, I forgot." She wrapped something around his arm. "You're losing too much blood to wait till we get back to the den." It was already soaking through what he now realized was the damp wool of her coat. "Your chest, baby, your chest!"

He knew he needed help—the wolf had damaged a major artery or vein, he couldn't tell which at this point. He was able to keep the wounds from bleeding out but that was all. "Tamsyn's close. Coordinates." He managed to tell her the location of the DarkRiver healer's home before blackness descended.

Brenna brought the car to a screeching halt in front of a large ranch-style home about twenty minutes later. A scowling

DarkRiver male opened the door before she'd even gotten around the engine. She recognized him as Tamsyn's mate. "Help me!"

He ran to the passenger-side door. "Shit," he said when he saw Judd. "Move." Pushing her aside, he grabbed Judd's unconscious form and went to put him in a fireman's carry.

"No!" She slapped a hand on Nate's back, bare since he was dressed only in a pair of old jeans. "His chest—"

Nate looked down and seemed to notice what Judd's torn sweater and jacket had hidden. "Christ." Slinging Judd's arm around his neck, he half dragged, half carried the other man into the house. "Damn Psy's heavier than he looks."

She'd noticed that, too. Judd seemed to have a higher bone mass than most other Psy. But right at that moment, all she cared about was the fact that he was breathing. Following on Nate's heels, she barely remembered to close the door behind her.

"Put him on the table." A crisp feminine command. "Kit—go up and make sure the cubs don't come down."

"Sure." A tall auburn-haired teenager with sleepy eyes slipped past her.

"Chair." Judd's voice kicked her heart into hyperdrive. "Not table." A demand.

"He's as stubborn as the rest of you," Tamsyn muttered, belting her robe. "Put him in the chair before he collapses and makes a mess of my floor."

Brenna hovered as Nate obeyed Tamsyn's command. "Who did he piss off this time?" the leopard asked, as Judd dragged himself upright in the chair, eyes not fully focused.

"Honey, could you get me the stitch gun?" Tamsyn was already working with healer efficiency, cutting off the clothing on Judd's upper body.

Judd didn't make a sound or betray pain in any other way. But when his eyes met Brenna's, she was sure she saw worry in them. For her. Why? Not wanting to be in Tamsyn's way but needing to touch him, she waited until the healer had disposed of the clothing before going to stand at his uninjured side, one hand on his shoulder. His skin *burned.*

Startled, she bit back her gasp. Judd's skin had always felt slightly cooler than hers, as did Sascha's and Faith's. But tonight, he was an open flame. "Can I do anything to help?" she asked when he didn't push off her hand.

"Here." The healer handed her a damp cloth. "Gently wipe off the blood on his chest so I can see how deep the wounds are."

"Not that deep," Judd muttered, the words slurred but understandable.

"Be quiet." Tamsyn's tone was pure steel. "You could be a cat—bleeding to death but refusing to admit it."

Nate walked in at that moment with a small metal case. "Julian's still asleep. Roman woke, but Kit's got him occupied."

Nodding, Tamsyn began to clean the obvious blood off Judd's arm as Brenna did the same to his chest. At least he'd stopped dripping fresh blood; it was clotting faster than she would've believed possible even a few minutes ago.

"Changeling wolf claws and teeth, if I'm not mistaken," Tamsyn said, looking to Brenna for confirmation.

"Yes. In full wolf form." She didn't know if that made any difference, but it seemed to be the sort of thing a healer would want to know.

"That shouldn't be a problem, but I'll give him an antibiotic shot anyway. Judd, are you allergic to anything?"

Judd shook his head very slowly. "Antibiotic fine."

"Good thing we're not infectious," Nate said from his position leaning against the counter, "or you'd be going furry pretty damn soon."

Brenna jerked up her head, about to tell him to stop with the cracks, when she realized he was trying to distract Judd from what had to be excruciating pain. Not that you could tell from looking at him.

She'd grown up around hard men—Riley was a SnowDancer lieutenant and when Andrew wasn't babysitting her, he controlled the volatile San Diego sector for Hawke. Her father had been a soldier, too. But even her brothers would've winced at least once by now, and she knew for sure that they'd have sworn a blue streak and probably picked a fight with Nate to keep their minds off their mangled skin.

Not Judd. He was as unmoving as a statue.

Cleaning away the blood, she accidentally touched the raw edge of a wound. Her stomach clenched as if the hurt were her own. "I'm sorry, baby." Just because he showed nothing didn't mean it didn't hurt. Surely even Psy were incapable of shutting down their pain receptors.

His gaze never moved off her. The contact was intense in spite of the creeping fog in his eyes, but she held it, unable and unwilling to leave him to suffer in the cold loneliness of Psy Silence.

"I'm going to start stitching you up," Tamsyn said, breaking the heart-pounding connection. "Here comes the antiseptic."

Brenna had her hand on Judd's chest as she wiped away a final red streak and even so close, she didn't feel him flinch. That was beyond control—it was terrifying. What had Judd been through to gain such merciless command over his physical responses?

She saw Tamsyn pull out the stitch gun. "Wait! Aren't you going to anesthetize him?" Those snapping stitches *hurt*.

"Psy have odd reactions to drugs, anesthetics included. Sascha and Faith put themselves under." The healer met Judd's eyes. "Can you do that for me?"

He gave a small nod. "Yes." Closing his eyes, he went absolutely still. Brenna couldn't even hear him breathe.

Handing Nate the bloody towel, Brenna gripped Judd's hand and watched Tamsyn begin repairing muscle damage with a tiny internal-use stitch gun. "You're very good."

"I have a medical degree. Figured I might as well back up the healing gifts with good solid knowledge and equipment so I don't spend my healing energy unnecessarily." There was a darkness to the other woman's tone, as if she were remembering a time when her gifts hadn't been enough to save a life. "And you know how it is—we can assist each other with ideas and strategies, but changeling healers' gifts only really work well within our own animal species. I can't even get the gift to recognize Judd."

Brenna nodded. "What did you mean about the drugs?"

"Hmmm." She handed a slender metallic torch over to Brenna. "Shine that here so I can see what I'm doing."

Keeping one hand on Judd's, she did as asked. The beam delineated every tear, every shredded piece of flesh. Worry clawed through her veins, but she made sure her hand didn't shake.

"It's got something to do with their abilities and how energy is processed," Tamsyn said, picking up the thread of the conversation. "That's why Jax messes them up so bad."

Nate's explanation was blunter. "Drugs fuck with their powers. Sascha refuses to touch even beer or wine."

It put a whole new spin on what Judd had told her about Jax. "I didn't know that."

"Makes you wonder why they take Jax in the first place," Nate said. "Doesn't go with their need for control."

"Maybe they want to forget what they've become." Tamsyn's tone was sad. "Jax degrades memory, too."

Nate grunted. "Whatever the reason, it's still the weak ones who take it."

She understood. No matter what the race—changeling, human, or Psy—it was the weak, broken, or damaged members who succumbed. Brenna's lips tightened. Pain was no excuse for becoming an addict—she hadn't taken the easy way out and oh, how she'd wanted to. But the worst were the dealers, the scum who preyed on the vulnerable.

"So," Nate asked, "you know who did this?"

Her stomach curdled. "Can we talk about that afterward? I think Judd should be awake for it."

"Fair enough. I have to let Lucas and Hawke know you're here."

"Can you hold off for a few hours?" It would give Judd time to recover at least a little and she needed him at her back. If what she believed was true, then she couldn't do this alone.

The leopard male studied her for several seconds. "Give me a good reason."

Squeezing her eyes shut, she took a deep breath. The iron-rich scent of blood was overpowering to her senses. Her eyes snapped open. "Because I scented my family on Judd before the rain washed the markers away."

"Shit."

* * *

Judd returned to consciousness two hours after they'd arrived, his eyes looking a touch feverish but otherwise clear. Too clear, given the extent of his injuries.

"What, you gave yourself a psychic blood transfusion?" Tamsyn asked in a tart tone at odds with the concern on her face.

Judd flexed the hand of his bandaged arm, the thin white gauze appearing deceptively weak. "I need some food to replace the energy I lost." Not an answer.

Tamsyn scowled, but Brenna felt only warmth from her. Like Lara and Sascha, the DarkRiver healer was inherently gentle. "Why does everyone think they can get fed in my kitchen?"

Nate hugged his mate from behind, kissing the curve of her neck in open affection. "Because even Psy know you're a soft touch."

The other woman's scowl disappeared and she turned to steal a proper kiss from her mate. "Why do I put up with you?"

Nate murmured something so low that Brenna couldn't hear. Looking away from their easy intimacy, an intimacy which held hints of the deepest sensuality and love, she found Judd watching the pair. He glanced at her only after Tamsyn broke from Nate to walk toward the cooler. Dark chocolate eyes met hers. "That's what you should have."

His candor shook her . . . because it meant he'd accepted this thing between them, this beautiful, powerful thing. "Yeah? Well, maybe I want you instead." She didn't care that their relationship didn't fit into any established box, didn't care that her wolf didn't recognize him as her mate. "Just you."

"I made lasagna for dinner," Tamsyn called out. "That work for you?"

He continued to look at her, as if he'd drink her up with his eyes. "Anything is fine."

"Maybe I shouldn't waste my lasagna on you, then." Tamsyn grabbed a container from the cooling unit. "How about some cardboard instead?"

Brenna found herself amused in spite of the blood that continued to scent the air and the taut expectation that stretched between her and Judd. Lips twitching, she waited for his response.

"Cardboard has no nutritional value." Utterly toneless. "Lasagna would be a better choice."

Tamsyn threw up her hands. "I'd forgotten how bad you lot could be. Then again, Sascha was never as bad as you."

Something crashed upstairs.

Tamsyn didn't seem to notice, but then said, "Honey, could you go up and see if Kit's surviving our little darlings? Sounds like they're both up."

"He's fine." Nate didn't budge.

"I won't attack your mate," Judd said to the leopard. "I have no reason to."

Nate's response was a grunt. Brenna scowled. It was true that predatory males tended to be extraordinarily protective where their mates were concerned, but surely Judd had earned the cats' respect by now.

Fur ruffled, she was about to voice her feelings when Judd glanced at her and gave a slight shake of his head. "It is his home." His voice was pitched to reach her ears alone. "He has a mate and children to protect and I am an intruder."

"You helped get Sascha and Faith out of the Net. You've been their friend," she hissed, raging at the unfairness of it.

"No." Judd pulled his hand from hers. "I've always acted in my own best interest."

"That's not who you are." She refused to let him try to convince her otherwise.

His eyes fixed on hers, the gold flecks darkening to amber. "An assassin who looks after his own skin? That's exactly what I am, Brenna. I would rather die than harm you, but anyone else? I could kill them without blinking. It's what I was born to do."

* * *

Brenna knew she should be happy that Judd had admitted as much as he had about his feelings toward her, but she was still fuming over his intransigence on everything else when she walked into the living room at around seven the next morning. He was attempting to button a vivid blue shirt over his bandaged chest. Even injured, he was so beautifully built that her mouth went dry and her face flushed. The hunger was piercing, seducing her into moving forward.

"Let me." His arm had to be painful. And she couldn't begin to think about the wounds on his chest. If they had gone a little deeper . . .

"Brenna." He didn't halt her, but his tone held a dominant undertone she recognized all too well, having grown up with men who suffered from the same chauvinistic streak.

"I've never seen you in any color but black. Blue looks good on you." She buttoned the shirt over his bandages with tender care. The garment was a fraction loose, Judd's build more lightly muscular than Nate's. Her Psy was built for stealth and speed, his body a well-honed weapon . . . one she ached to stroke. The idea of running her hands over the smooth, powerful lines of his body made her fingers tremble.

One male hand closed over her wrist. "We have to discuss this before your brothers arrive."

Tears in her throat. "We've got time to have a cup of coffee."

"No, we don't. Nate made the calls long enough ago that they have to be close."

She knew the DarkRiver male had delayed as long as he could, but wished it had been forever. "Just one cup," she cajoled.

Tugging at her hand, he forced her to look up. "Why are you avoiding the subject?" The gold flecks in his eyes were sparking bright—it wasn't her imagination, they really were. Before she could ask him what that meant, there was a commotion out front and her brothers stormed into the living room followed by Nate and Lucas.

CHAPTER 24

Riley's face went hunting-still as he saw Judd's hand around her wrist. "I swear to God, if you don't stop touching her, I'll—"

"You'll what?" Brenna demanded, pulling away her hand but only so she could face Riley. "Finish off the job you started last night?"

"What the fuck are you talking about?" Andrew reached out as if to grab her and drag her to his side.

Judd was suddenly in front of her, having moved so fast she was left gasping. "I can't let you touch her in your current mood."

Looking around Judd, Brenna saw Drew's fingers curl into a fist. "She's my sister. It's one of you bastards that hurt her."

"Be that as it may, I'm not letting you near her until you get yourself under control." Judd's voice was cold, implacable, dangerous.

Growls sounded.

"Shut up!" Brenna yelled. "All of you!"

Her brothers looked at her, startled. The cats stayed on the edges of the room, probably not looking to interfere unless blood threatened to be spilled.

Judd glanced over his shoulder. *"Don't."* Pure male command.

"Don't you give her orders, Psy!" Drew again.

She'd had it. Pushing past Judd to stand in front of her middle sibling, she thumped a fist into his chest. "Do you know what he's warning me not to do? Accuse you or Riley of attacking him."

Her brother froze. "What?"

"Judd came in wolf-mauled," Nate drawled. "His chest's a mess and believe me, you don't want to see his arm."

"You think we did that?" The hurt on Riley's face was so raw it rocked her.

But she wasn't backing off. "You've threatened him over and over. And I smelled the scent of family."

Judd put a hand on her shoulder. "Enough, Brenna."

This time, she listened, unable to look at the pain on her brothers' faces. Turning, she buried her head against Judd's chest, forgetting about his injuries until the scent of torn flesh hit her. "I'm so—"

"Shh." Judd put his uninjured arm around her. The gesture had come about without conscious thought and now he found he couldn't let go, dissonance or not.

Meeting her brothers' gazes, he began to speak. "I initially had the same suspicions as Brenna, but I was wrong." He'd figured that out sometime in the early hours—it was what he'd wanted to discuss with her. "If you two were going to challenge me, you'd do it in broad daylight, not set up a sneak ambush."

Brenna went very quiet against him, one hand curled up gently against his chest.

Pain, such sweet pain to have her so close. Would she stay once she discovered the whole truth about him? The dark heart of him asked a harsher question—would he let her go? "Brenna knows that, too," he said, focusing on the here and now. "She's confused only because she smelled your scent at the scene. It shocked her. Which is probably what was intended."

Andrew shoved a hand through his hair. "Damn it, Bren. I didn't touch him. I can't believe you suspected me for a second."

Brenna turned her head but remained tucked under Judd's arm. "You haven't been acting like yourselves lately, either of you."

Riley swore, low and hard. "We almost lost you to a Psy murderer! I think the fact that we don't want you to shack up with one of that psychopathic race is understandable."

"Careful." A soft but lethal order from Lucas.

"Sascha is different," Riley said without turning. "*He's* not."

"I never thought you were a bigot." Brenna's words fell into a pool of heavy silence.

Judd found himself holding her tighter. He didn't need or want anyone to fight for him. That Brenna did, caused sensations inside of him he couldn't afford to embrace—especially given his injuries and the energy it took to fight the dissonance. But he had stopped doing what he should a long time ago.

Andrew met his eyes. "I didn't attack you. You'd be dead if I'd come after you."

Judd had had enough. "The sole reason I'm injured is because I was trying not to kill my attacker. If I hadn't held back, he'd have been dead before he touched me." He let them see the claws he'd kept hidden in an effort to assist his family's integration into SnowDancer.

But some wolves, he realized, would respect only unadorned strength. So long as Andrew and Riley thought him easy prey, they'd never allow him near their sister. He understood why—Brenna's man had to be able to protect her. It had nothing to do with Brenna's own abilities and everything to do with their need to keep her safe.

"Psy can't get into our minds," Andrew spit out.

Judd looked at the SnowDancer. "It's true that we can't manipulate you without major effort, but a blast of pure power at close range would destroy all of your higher brain functions, if it didn't turn your brains to liquid outright." He knew that from the darkest of personal experiences, one of the many nightmare images that haunted his sleep.

Of course, a Tk-Cell had other, quicker ways of killing. But he hadn't known that as a child and the changelings didn't need to know it now to grasp his point. "So if you ever do come after me, I suggest you follow your own rules of Psy/changeling combat and shoot me in the back." A split second's warning was all he needed to kill.

"Hell," Andrew said, his voice holding a new note of awareness. "We all get taught that during training, but when you just fought physically with the men who challenged you instead of doing something psychic, I figured it was Psy propaganda." He shrugged. "Does Hawke understand what you can do?"

"What?" Brenna demanded. "You're going to ask him to kick Judd out now?"

"That's not what I meant," her brother growled. "Stop being a brat."

"Don't talk to her that way." Judd had made his choice, found his loyalty.

Riley folded his arms. "There's one thing I don't get." His calm tone was so at odds with the tension-heavy air that everyone went quiet. The lieutenant raised an eyebrow. "But before we get to that, Bren, sweetie—you do realize Judd and Drew are exactly alike?"

Andrew stared at his brother. "What the fuck are you talking about?"

Judd was thinking the same thing. But Brenna laughed. Breaking his hold, she ran to hug Riley. "I'm sorry. I know you didn't have anything to do with the attack."

"What about me?" Andrew stroked a hand over her hair.

Brenna raised her head. "I'm undecided where you're concerned."

"You're getting mean in your old age." But he hugged her when she turned to him.

Watching them, Judd felt a heavy, dull pain in the region of his chest. The wounds, he concluded, that was all. Then Brenna pulled away from Drew to return to Judd's side and the pain intensified. "What don't you get?" he asked Riley.

"How Bren mistook our scent."

Judd nodded. "I agree. It has to be someone you trust enough to allow access to your belongings."

"Where he could've picked up things that carry enough of our scent to use as a mask." Andrew's claws sliced out. "The bastard has to be a soldier. We sweat buckets during training."

Lucas came to stand beside Riley. "Say the attacker had succeeded in killing you," he said to Judd, "what would that have done?"

"Caused a small amount of confusion." Judd had no illusions about his importance to the pack. "No large impact overall. We're the enemy—allowed there on sufferance."

Lucas looked thoughtful, his savagely marked face set in lines of concentration. "What if he'd targeted one of the Lauren children?"

Judd felt the black edge of his power gathering and had to force it back. "He'd be dead by now." It wasn't a threat, just fact.

"Damn straight." Andrew's voice was pure wolf. "Pups are pups, period. You go after one, you pin a big fat target on yourself. It would've set all the hunters on his trail."

"So," Riley picked up, "it looks like this probably wasn't about causing trouble in the pack or attacking the Laurens as a family. It was about Judd."

"That leaves a wide pool," Judd pointed out.

"Hell yeah, since you seem to go out of your way to piss off everyone you meet." Andrew was scowling. "But the hotheads would've gone for you up front. Sneak attack's not what's going to get them points in the den."

Judd agreed. "And there would be no reason for the planted scent if—" Something clicked in his Psy brain, the jigsaw pieces falling together in the lines of a perfect trap. "He wanted to isolate Brenna. Remove me, cut her off from you, and she becomes vulnerable."

Andrew's color faded. "Easier to take out."

Judd wrapped his arm around Brenna's shoulders again. She acquiesced without hesitation. It was an indication of deep-rooted trust. But the darkness in him no longer found that surprising, accepting it as his right. An irrevocable line had been crossed between yesterday and today. Brenna was *his*.

She blew out a breath, making her bangs dance. "Seriously, can you guys think past the overprotectiveness?" A very unfeminine snort. "Why would anyone have it in for me?"

Judd knew the answer, but it wasn't for public consumption.

"With the rain," Riley said when nobody else spoke, "there's no way to track him."

Brenna made a small movement. "I can think of one."

All five males looked at her.

"Okay, let's pretend I buy into your 'Brenna is the center of the universe' conspiracy theory"—she rolled her eyes—"there's one way to find out for sure." She shifted in Judd's embrace until his arm was around the front of her neck, while her back faced him, though she was very careful not to press against his injuries. "Act as though it worked—at least enough to separate me from you two."

Distracted by the soft curves of her body, he almost missed the import of her words. His blood heated, his heartbeat raced . . . and a wave of excruciating pain crawled over his mind in a malignant flood. He could handle the physical effects but couldn't control his Psy brain's need to shut down sections to save itself. The countdown had begun.

"Leave me," Brenna continued, "and go back to the den furious. Judd and I can camp out at the cabin—it's still livable."

"No." Andrew folded his arms.

"No more cages, Drew," she said quietly. "I love you, but no more. Until Enrique took me, you'd never have dreamed of trying to lock me up."

Shoving back the tide of dissonance, Judd looked up. "I'm more than capable of keeping her out of harm's way." None of the critical components of his mind had yet been compromised.

Brenna glanced over her shoulder and her expression wasn't happy. "I can keep myself safe. Just because a bastard got his hands on me once doesn't mean I'm helpless."

"The point is moot," Riley said. "Everyone knows we'd

never leave Bren alone in the cabin with you, even if that meant we had to drag her back screaming bloody murder."

Judd nodded. "We can run the same op from the den. It'll mean you three will have to act as if you've fallen out."

"I'm already alone in the family quarters," Brenna murmured, evidently seeing the truth in Riley's assertion "Fine. But I swear"—she scowled at Andrew—"you try to poke your nose into my life one more time and I won't be responsible for my actions."

Her brother grinned. "I knew you loved me."

Tamsyn wasn't happy about Judd taking off, but he wanted to return to *his* territory, land he knew with Arrow thoroughness after months of isolated exploring. Brenna wasn't convinced either, but she muttered something about stubborn, pigheaded males and pushed him into the passenger seat when he made a move to drive. Andrew and Riley had left several minutes earlier to lend weight to the idea that they had had a disagreement with their sister.

"I'll see you tomorrow at your HQ?" Brenna called out to Tamsyn from beside the car.

"I won't be there." Tamsyn made a face. "Computerspeak might as well be gibberish to me."

"I'll be dropping in," Nate added from the doorway, his eyes never leaving Judd. "See you there."

Judd gave a small nod, wondering if the cats would ever accept his presence as anything other than a threat. Likely not. That showed their intelligence—because he was a threat, a big one.

They'd begun to back down the long drive when he saw two little boys run out from behind Nate and Tamsyn. The DarkRiver male picked up the children and said something that made both his mate and the boys laugh. Judd looked away. That wasn't his life and it never would be. Yet even knowing that, Brenna had made her choice very clear.

And if she decided later that she wanted out?

The darkness, the badness in him, bared its teeth.

Tonight—maybe tonight—he could set her free. After that, she'd have to kill him to get away.

"Judd? Have you heard a word I've said?"

Forcing his mind back into rational patterns, he turned to her. "There's no doubt of it being a wolf now."

"What?" she asked, as she pulled out of the driveway and set the car on automatic hover-navigation, possible because the roads in this area were embedded with guidance chips. Hands freed, she slid the steering wheel away into its compartment and faced him. "Who are you talking about?"

"Timothy's murderer."

"What's that got to do with the attack on you?" She shook her head. "Anyway, both you and Indigo could be wrong. The Psy could have got in somehow."

He knew she needed a place of safety, needed to trust implicitly in her people. But she couldn't, not if she was to be on her guard. "You're reaching, Brenna. The body was found in the den, in an out-of-the-way location no Psy could know about."

"You guys can teleport over long distances," she insisted.

"Yes, but we have to have a solid mental image of our destination." He tapped a finger on the edge of his seat, a gesture that he caught almost as soon as it happened, but which he shouldn't have made in the first place. Psy did not fidget. "Even if one of my race *had* obtained that data, teleportation tends to leave us drained—the energy used is directly related to distance traveled. No evidence of a Psy presence was found within miles of the den."

"And"—a soft acceptance—"what was done to Tim had to involve a lot of power and strength. He didn't lie down and take it—there were bruises."

"I'd suggest it was a very physical struggle. Most Psy would have used mental means against a stronger changeling opponent." He made himself say the next words, though he knew it would only forge another point of similarity between him and Enrique. "Of course, using Tk to throw someone against a wall would also cause bruises."

Brenna's hand lifted to her neck and then dropped away,

her eyes losing focus. "He didn't do that by Tk," she whispered. "He used his hands to strangle me while he kept me immobile with his powers."

Another piece of the nightmare. "Brenna." It was a single word wrenched out of the most primitive part of him. The part that wanted to bathe in the dead Councilor's blood, unconcerned about the cost of such an extreme emotional reaction.

Brenna's eyes widened. Raising a hand, she brushed his hair gently off his forehead. "Why do I keep telling you things I swore I'd take to my grave?"

The contact shot electricity through his nerves. "Because you know I'll always be your shield against the nightmares."

Her face brightened. "Yes. You're tough enough to handle my demons." She took a shuddering breath and trailed her fingers down his cheek and along his jaw, but he felt the touch in far hungrier places. "So why are we talking about Tim instead of your attacker?"

Leashing his need was becoming harder and harder. "I think," he said even as his body urged him to do something other than talk, "Tim's death is why someone is trying to isolate you—statistically, it's the strongest reason for why you would become the target of another wolf. And I'm certain you were the target."

Her stroking fingers went motionless. "What possible reason could— The dreams." It was a gasp. "But how could he know I'd seen the kill in a dream?"

CHAPTER 25

"**It's not** a secret that you saw something. You screamed, 'I saw this!' when the body was found."

"Oh, my God." She slumped back in her seat. "The killer thinks I'm a witness and that I'll figure out who he is."

"Which means we have to track him down before he makes another attempt." Judd had promised Brenna safety and he would ensure it. Failure was not an option.

Brenna's expression shifted. "What will you do to him?"

"The same thing any other man would do." He dared her to stop him.

"I don't want you to go further into the darkness because of me."

"There's a difference between acting to protect someone and—" He cut himself off, suddenly realizing where he was headed.

"And what, Judd?"

He shook his head. "It's not relevant to the present situation."

"You're lying." A flat, angry accusation. "I can't believe you'd sit there and lie to my face after—" Jaw clenched, she turned away and pulled up the steering wheel, going manual again. "Fine. You keep your secrets."

It was almost a compulsion to push her, to demand she return her attention to him. And that was why he fought it. Because she didn't understand what she was asking for, what it would cost her. That thought stayed his hand as nothing else. But there was one thing he did need to know the answer to. He waited until they were almost to the den before bringing it up. "How did you know where I was last night?"

She threw him a glancing look. It was obvious she was still furious. "Driving that Psy brain crazy, isn't it?" Her smugness couldn't have been clearer.

"There was no tracker on the vehicle."

"Not when you checked." She maneuvered the car over the rough terrain with angry female confidence, having disengaged the hover-drive and shifted to tires. "I followed you out of the den and slapped a tracker under the chassis after you got in."

He remembered that shadow he'd seen. "I did a telepathic scan."

She shrugged. "Don't know how that works, but I didn't move out from under until you'd driven off. That reminds me—we'll have to send someone to pick up my car."

Judd knew why the scan hadn't located her. He'd made an elementary mistake and scanned the perimeter alone, rather than pushing outward in ever-increasing circles. To add insult to injury, he'd been so distracted last night that he'd allowed not one, but *two* pursuits. The wolf had to have followed him to the church, then lain in wait for his return.

Either he was getting careless or the more subtle effects of the dissonance—and of the battle between Silence and emotion in his brain—were already beginning to show. But that wasn't what concerned him the most. "I could've crushed you with the car."

"Not really." She sounded unworried. "You could only drive it in one direction."

"Brenna."

"You're just pissed because I managed to trail you out of

the den." She gave him a piercing look. "I knew something was up as soon as you got that call during dinner."

"How?" He didn't tell her to change direction when she headed for the underground garage. This vehicle had been seen by too many people in relation to him. He'd have to get a new one for his covert activities.

She brought the all-wheel drive to a halt inside the garage. "Not from your Ice Man expression. Somehow I . . ." Biting her lower lip, she shrugged. "I can't explain it. I just knew." Opening the car door, she came around as if to open his, but he'd already gotten out. She began to walk across the otherwise empty garage with him at her back. "If you rip open those stitches, don't come crying to me for sympathy."

"Noted." His eyes kept going to the sway of her hips, his control shot to hell. "You shouldn't have followed me."

"Why not?" She threw him an uncomplimentary look over her shoulder. "It's not like you're Mr. Communication."

"There are some things you don't need to know."

"Like what in the hell you were doing in a deserted park in the middle of the night?" She spun around to face him, arms folded. "You keep telling me you're an assassin and then you sneak out. Pretty easy equation, don't you think?"

He refused to listen to the voice that wanted to correct her. "Yes."

"Bull. Shit." With that very precise statement, she spun on her heel and toward the ramp leading up to the main den area. "If you'd been in a killing frame of mind," she threw back as she opened the door, "you'd have executed that wolf on sight."

He stood in the garage for several minutes after she'd gone, trying to think of an answer that would satisfy her. He couldn't, wouldn't, draw her into the gray world of the rebellion he had to fight. Stopping Protocol I was his attempt at finding redemption, if such a thing even existed for a man like him, but she had no need to pay for his crimes. He was her shield. Against the evil . . . and against his own nightmares.

Finally ready, he walked up and made his way to her rooms. She'd left the door open and he closed it behind himself. "Brenna."

She looked up from making coffee. "Don't lie to me, Judd. Keep your secrets, but don't lie to me." Quiet words but so passionate they felt like blows.

So he gave her no false answers. "I'd like some coffee, too."

She held his gaze for a long time, as if waiting for him to say something else. When he didn't, her spine went stiff and she turned her back to him. He had the violent urge to force her to face him, but fought it. Finally—and just in time—she was keeping her distance. Any longer and he knew he wouldn't have allowed her her freedom . . . even if she'd pleaded with him to let her go.

Even if she'd screamed.

CHAPTER 26

The bitch *had ruined his plans again. He'd been about to tear out the assassin's throat when she'd come racing out. He'd considered chancing it, but the fucking Psy had damaged something in his jaw with that single punch—he hadn't been certain he could maintain the killing hold. And if Brenna had seen him, she'd have known him. Now he had to lie low until the jaw healed. At least that wouldn't take long.*

It hadn't been a total loss, he consoled himself. Andrew and Riley were pissed. And he'd heard Brenna and the Psy fighting. It was obvious that the shine was wearing off whatever weird relationship they had. Forget about trying to isolate Brenna, all he had to do was wait until Judd Lauren left and she was alone in that big apartment.

She wouldn't put up much of a fight—Santano Enrique had fucked her over good. He decided he wouldn't kill her with an overdose after all. His fingers curled, imagining the slender width of her neck under his palms. He wanted to watch the life drain out of those witchy eyes of hers. Maybe, in the instant before she died, she'd remember the last time he'd had his hands around her throat.

CHAPTER 27

After a day full of silences and stilted conversation, Brenna came to stand beside him where he sat going over the files that had been in the data crystal the Ghost had given him. Hidden in his back pants pocket, it had somehow survived the ambush undamaged.

"Why are you still here?" she asked. "It's nine at night."

He closed the file and put down his organizer. "With your brothers being forced to keep their distance, your safety is in my hands."

He watched her face in the light thrown by the glow of the lamps she'd dimmed. Deceptively delicate-looking bones covered by creamy skin. Hair that shone gold and lashes that were a shade lighter, so long they appeared unreal.

She caught him staring. "Kiss me."

His undamaged hand fisted. "I told you—you can't get what you need from me."

"Liar." She leaned against the wall in front of him, small and curvy and determined. "You want me so much you're burning up with it."

"I don't feel lust."

If Brenna hadn't been so terrified of losing him to his own demons, she might have been put off by his seemingly intractable will. "That's a flat-out lie and you know it." He had so many secrets he wouldn't share, but she was determined to have this out at least. "You were practically eating me up with your eyes that day after my shower. I swear, if you deny it, I won't be responsible for my actions." And he'd break her heart.

He stood, the movement smooth, dangerous. "You don't understand what you're asking." Steely Psy focus, but she was certain she saw the gold flecks in his eyes spark.

Excitement licked along her skin. "I know there are pain controls in the conditioning," she began. "I called Faith today—"

"You think I'm scared of a little *pain*?" His voice had dropped a decibel, gone eerily darker. "You think I wouldn't risk my life to break the chains on my mind?"

She'd never seen him like this, his icy control morphing into what her animal senses told her was the most finely honed rage, so pure it dyed the air crimson. "Then what?" she dared to ask, walking until she stood only a few small footsteps away. "What has such a hold over you that you're willing to walk away from us?" From something more powerful and more real than anything she'd ever before felt

"I'm not anything like Faith," he said, a wall of stone in front of her. "My ability is nothing good." He thrust his hand into her hair with not the slightest warning, tugging back her head and exposing her throat. "My subdesignation doesn't exist on any chart but the one kept by the Arrow Squad."

Fear coated her tongue as she realized she had somehow succeeded in shattering a crucial part of his defensive shields—the question was, could she handle what she'd unleashed? "Tell me, Judd. I need to know." Because he was hers. Even here and now, her body hungered for him, his very darkness an aphrodisiac—because she was convinced he'd never harm her. Then he spoke and shattered every one of her cozy preconceptions.

"I could kill you during sex," he said, letting her straighten her head but not releasing her. "Stop your heartbeat, crush your windpipe, cut off the blood flow to your brain." The cold words hit her like gunshots at close range. "If not that, then perhaps I'd crack open your skull or your chest cavity. There are so many ways to kill with even a stray thought—of course it'd be less refined than when I've planned it out, but the end result would be the same. You in a body bag."

Everything chilled inside her. At that moment, she was almost ready to run. This man wasn't the Judd she knew. This man terrified her. "You can't manipulate changeling minds that way," she whispered, desperate to find a way out.

"You're not listening." His lips brushed her ear, but it was nothing erotic. "I don't have to influence your mind to kill. No telekinetic does. And I'm a very, very specialized Tk, subdesignation Cell. I can influence the physical structures of human, Psy, and changeling bodies," he said in her ear, the frost of death in his tone. "My control is fine enough that I can rearrange skin cells if I want to. You could say I'm the scalpel to Enrique's blunt object."

She would not cry—he had used the word *scalpel* on purpose. That had been Enrique's favorite weapon, the one he'd used to carve up his victims. The thought of Enrique nudged at a deeply hidden piece of knowledge in her brain, but she was concentrating too hard on Judd to pay attention.

"It's why you don't have scars," she blurted out, searching for something with which to ground herself. All soldiers had scars. But from the glimpses she'd had of Judd's body, she'd seen not the smallest mark, not counting the new injuries he'd suffered the previous night.

He drew back, his eyes going to her lower lip, which she'd caught between her teeth. It felt like he'd touched her . . . stroked her. Suddenly the fear transformed—into a passion that was so strong, it made her tremble. "The scars," she prompted, breathless.

"Getting rid of them was a training exercise to help foster control." His tone hadn't warmed up, but there was an inferno in his eyes. "Over time, my body seemed to learn the trick and now they disappear without conscious effort on my part."

Releasing her as precipitously as he'd grabbed her, he put several feet of distance between them.

She had so many questions buzzing around in her head but only one was important. "There has to be a way out." She wasn't going to lose him, her recent shock of terror be damned. "Stop trying to scare me and tell me how we get past this."

The gold flecks disappeared from Judd's eyes, the irises going pure black and merging into the pupils. She sucked in a breath but held her ground.

"When I was ten and not yet fully conditioned," he told her, "I had a spike of temper. It was directed at a boy who had taken the ball I was using to practice my Tk skills. He was dead before he hit the ground. The autopsy found that his brain had exploded from the inside out. His name was Paul, his ability was Medical, and he was eight years old."

"Oh, God, Judd." She went to embrace him, but he held up a hand to stop her.

"Your proximity tests my control and right now, it wouldn't take much to push me over the edge. One mistake and they'll be burying you tomorrow." A stark warning.

She could feel the unacknowledged pain in him as if it was her own. "You were a child, with a child's lack of control."

"And now I'm an adult with total control, but Silence is at the core of that control." The pure black of his eyes met hers, wouldn't let her look away. *"I will never choose to fully breach it."*

"I won't accept that." The trapped wolf in her bared its teeth at the very idea. "What did your subdesignation do before Silence?" Hope took root in her heart.

"They were either hermits, in jail, or dead." His blunt statement held the destructive force of hard truth, stifling all hope. "I've done my homework, Brenna." A cold Psy reprimand but those eyes . . . they spoke of passion and need. "Those who realized what they were early enough separated themselves from society and spent their lives ensuring they never came into contact with other sentient beings."

The inhuman loneliness of such a life shook her.

"The ones who weren't so lucky ended up killing by accident. However, because the nature of their abilities meant that all such killings took place during childhood, Tk-Cells weren't incarcerated but given training and a second chance." His eyes went even more black, something she wouldn't have believed possible a second ago.

"Some chose the hermit's way," he continued. "The remainder tried to lead normal lives but inevitably ended up taking another life in a flash of thoughtless rage—wife, neighbor, *child.* At which point, most of them chose to stop their own hearts. Those who didn't were locked into isolation cells for the rest of their natural lives, their minds chained so even the PsyNet was closed to them."

Brenna understood responsibility and punishment, but what Judd was describing was a kind of vicious cruelty. "How could they do that to—"

"We felt then, Brenna. The Psy felt everything. The imprisoned Tk-Cells *wanted* to suffer, wanted to spend eternity reliving the nightmare of killing what they most loved." Moving closer, he continued his relentless barrage. "There have never been very many of us—the scientists' favorite theory is that we occur by spontaneous mutation. That's the only explanation for our continued existence, given the fact that our genes are rarely passed on, especially under Silence. We don't make reproduction agreements. We don't father children. We don't *mate*."

She felt as if he'd slapped her. But instead of pain, her dominant emotion was anger. "So you're going to let fear drive you? You're choosing the isolation of Silence as your own personal cage! How can you do that to us?"

Those unearthly eyes were so close, she could see the reflection of her own furious expression in their depths. "I'd rather watch you take a lover than die at my hands."

She knew how much those words must've tortured him. Even now, the air was staining bloodred with anger. "And would you let that man live?" she whispered.

No response. That gave her hope even when hope seemed impossible. "Then we fight, Judd." She dared to place her hand gently on his chest. He flinched but didn't move away. "We fight until every avenue is closed and then we dig under the roadblocks. Because I am not walking away from us." Strong words, but she was shaking. He could destroy her with a few careless comments.

"You're the strongest, most determined woman I know." He played his fingers along the strands of her hair. "You'd make mincemeat out of a lesser man. It's a good thing you belong to me."

Relief almost collapsed her knees. "Not funny."

"I'm serious." Something very male moved over his face. "If you say yes now, I won't let you go if you decide I'm not what you want later on down the road. You say yes, you say yes forever. Be sure."

For a single taut second, she was afraid of the possession in that voice, the implacability in his eyes. Judd was no tame wolf who would do whatever she wanted. He was complicated and dominant and more than a little bad.

And he was hers, no matter that the mating bond didn't exist between them. She didn't need that validation. Not with her dark angel. "If I ever want freedom, I'll get it." Men like Judd needed to know their women had claws.

"Is that a threat?" Cool Psy arrogance as he drew close enough that her breasts brushed against him with each indrawn breath. His eyes faded back to normal.

She wanted to moan, having been deprived of his touch for too long. "How's your control?"

"Not good enough." The words were pure ice.

Most people would've read that as rejection, but Brenna knew it was a sign of exactly how much he felt for her. Heart in her throat, she pushed up his shirt to bare the ridged lines of an abdomen that made her mouth water. "I want to check your wounds."

"They're fine—I can move things inside my own body, shift blood, fix damage." But he unbuttoned the shirt and let it drop to the floor. The bandages joined it a second later.

Easy, so easy. Because he wanted this, too.

"You're healed." With her eyes, she traced every muscular

line, every inch of golden male skin. "Beautiful." It came out on a heated breath.

His chest muscles tightened. "Yes. No scars."

"Yes." But that wasn't why she'd called him beautiful. "Your body makes me want to do sweaty and hot and athletic things in bed. I want to kiss and lick and taste."

His biceps bulged as he fisted his hands. "Enough." Bending, he picked up his shirt. "I can't chance hurting you through an inadvertent activation of my abilities."

She reached out and tore it out of his hands. "I like looking at you half-naked. And if you can give me orders, you're still in control."

Heat flared in Judd's abdomen, accompanied by knife cuts of pain. She was pushing him on purpose and she knew just what to say to do it. *"Brenna."* A warning.

Her answer was a kiss pressed to the center of his chest. "Don't go all male on me. I might have an idea about how to get around your ability." She trailed her fingers over his bare skin, skin that was suddenly the most sensitive part of his body.

"I can't help being male." His erection was a pounding reminder of his sex. Of course the reaction was a breach of the Protocol, but he wanted more rather than less. Her body brushed his as she rubbed her lips over his skin and he had to bite off the harsh command for her to go lower.

Flicking out her tongue, she tasted him. "And what a sexy male you are. I could pet you all day." A sigh.

"Petting is a changeling desire." Except that he'd often wondered what it would be like to stroke her until she— Razors slicing across his brain. White stars in front of his eyes.

Her smile faded. "Judd. Your eyes—they flashed dark red for a second."

The color of blood, a visual reminder of what would happen to his brain if he continued on this road. "It's nothing. Tell me your idea."

Standing on tiptoe, she put the back of one hand against his forehead. "It's not my imagination. Your temperature is higher than normal."

It was a side effect of the amount of energy he was extending to block the dissonance, as well as speed up the healing process on his wounds—fast-tracked by Tamsyn's work, they had disappeared, but his body continued to repair minor tears on the inside. "Can you blame me?" he asked, instead of telling her the truth. "You're standing in front of me saying you want to pet me."

She laughed, a husky, sexy sound. Dropping her hand back onto his chest, she snapped her teeth at him. "I like to bite, too."

"Aren't you worried I might bite back?"

Wide eyes. "Oh, I hope you do."

Images cascaded through his fragmented shields. His teeth closing over the lush curve of her breast, the soft seduction of her inner thigh. The images were detailed, perfect—he'd had a long time to think about what he wanted to do. But even if he could survive it . . . "You're not ready." She'd pushed herself with Greg, hurt herself. He wouldn't do the same to her.

A scowl and then she did the unexpected—she leaned up and nipped at the side of his jaw with sharp little teeth. "How do you know? Maybe it was just the wrong man."

His hand clenched in her hair and he had no awareness of raising it. "I told you not to remind me of that incident."

Nails dug into his chest. "Then make me forget it."

Jealousy and possessiveness smashed through to become the dominating forces in his mind. He found his other hand was on her neck, curving to hold her. Gentle, his touch was gentle. He made sure of it, but she was most definitely in his power. Not that she seemed to mind, the smile on her lips pure invitation. Leaning in, he closed his teeth very deliberately over her lower lip.

CHAPTER 28

Her heartbeat accelerated under his touch as he released her lip. "Should I stop?"

"No." A whisper. "Kiss my neck, too. He never touched me there."

Stroking his hand down to rest below her shoulders, he bent to taste the skin of her neck. Soft, silky, quintessentially female. Her hand tunneled into his hair.

Pain and pleasure combined.

The dissonance was constant by this point. Broken shards of glass knifed through his cerebral cortex in an unrelenting cycle. But the pleasure . . . the pleasure was more. He'd never felt such incredible sensations. Then Brenna made a tiny, needy sound and the pleasure multiplied until he could hardly feel the pain.

Part of him knew this was dangerous. If he wasn't aware of the pain, if he didn't accept the warning and pull back, not only could his ability slip the leash, the dissonance might cause permanent damage to his neural tissues. But drowning in the rich taste of Brenna's sensuality, he didn't have the capacity to understand those perilous truths.

Kissing his way up her neck, he traced the line of her jaw

before returning to her lips. They were parted, her eyes closed. Accepting the invitation, he pressed his lips over hers. Flash-fire heat. Pure sexual need. His hand was on her neck again and he felt the jagged beat of her heart spike.

But she didn't pull away. In fact, she wrapped her arms around his neck and tensed. His body knew what she wanted though he'd never before touched her so intimately. Releasing her from his possessive hold, he caught her as she jumped to wrap her legs around his body. Holding on tight, he backed into a wall but didn't turn to press her against it. Because she was trembling. Scared.

He broke the kiss and, blinking past the blackness crawling at the edges of his vision, raised one hand to brush the hair off her face. "Why are you scared of physical contact?" She'd been raped on the mental plane. Of course there were physical repercussions—such a deep violation of the psyche was a nightmare most people couldn't imagine, much less endure. But he sensed there was something more to her fear.

Her lower lip trembled and a single tear formed at the corner of her eye. "He didn't just mess with my mind." It was a pained whisper.

He knew Enrique had hurt her body, cut her, beaten her but—"Sexual abuse?" Fury burned a cold fire in his veins.

"Not rape like we think of it," she said, fingers digging into his shoulders. "I mean, he did that to my mind—tore it open and forced me to see things I didn't want to see, put things in there that weren't my own thoughts, things that are still in there. I wash and I wash, but I can't get them out!"

"I know." He let her nuzzle her face into his neck, stroking his hand over her hair. "But he did other things." Acts she hadn't revealed during the healing sessions.

A jerky nod. "He—he liked to demonstrate his telekinetic control by forcing objects inside my body using only his Psy skills."

Red blazed in his mind and it wasn't pain. Gritting his teeth, he made himself stay silent and listen.

"I was so ashamed," she whispered, her cheek wet against his skin. "I was a wolf changeling—stronger, faster, desperate—and

I couldn't stop him. Sometimes he'd untie me but hold me down telekinetically so it'd be like I was holding myself down . . . like I was cooperating. Then he'd experiment with my pain thresholds. Mostly it was mental, but sometimes . . . sometimes he'd decide to see what my body could take."

"You have nothing to be ashamed of." How could she have even thought that? "Enrique was a cardinal Tk and a killer. He bears all the blame."

Her arms tightened. "I'm starting to believe in myself again, but anytime something sexual happens, I associate it with him. I can't seem to break the link though I know it's not right. I know not all men are like him, but . . ."

"What he did was about pain. This is about pleasure." Even a rebel Arrow knew that distinction.

Her tears stayed silent. Heartbreakingly so. "He made my body feel pleasure, messed with my mind until he controlled my responses and made me *enjoy* every humiliating, degrading thing he did." Shame layered her whispered words.

Judd wished Enrique weren't dead so he could torture the bastard. He'd keep him alive, make him suffer. You could cut off parts of a man without killing him for days, weeks if you were patient. "Enrique was a Tk," he repeated, "with only midlevel telepathy. He wanted to tear into your mind, but he never reached the inner core, the part that governs your emotions. He didn't have that ability. When he made your body respond, he did so by controlling your nerves."

Brenna had gone quiet, as if concentrating on his factual explanation.

"You were always aware of what was happening, weren't you?"

A warm breath against his neck. "It was like I could watch what he was doing to me but not stop it. I hated it, but my body did whatever he wanted."

"So there was no pleasure, only a physical response."

"Aren't they the same?" Raising her head, she looked him in the eye, the tears having left her gaze strangely clear.

"The order is wrong." He knew the logic, had been taught it as part of the conditioning process. When he saw her frown, he decided to prove his point. "If I told you I think you have the most beautiful body I've ever seen, would you feel pleasure?"

A blush colored her cheeks. "Do you mean that or are you making a hypothetical point?"

"I mean every word." She was soft and curvy and lushly female. Perfect.

"Of course that would make me happy." She brushed a kiss over his lips and it was so unexpected, he had to scramble to regather his thoughts.

"What if a stranger on a dark street said the same?"

"I'd get out of there as fast as my legs would carry me." She made a face. "You're saying pleasure is dictated by the heart and mind. I trust you, think you're sexy as hell, and so you pleasure me. Another man, while he might somehow be able to force my body to react, would give me no pleasure."

Every man had a limit. Judd figured he'd gone past his weeks ago. "The link must be present between a body and a free mind. Without that link, it's not pleasure but a facsimile so wrong it's pain."

She was silent for close to a minute. "I never thought about it like that, but you're right. It *was* pain. It tore me apart to have my body react against my will, hurt me so badly I had to curl up in my inner mind to survive. Sascha said it's the most basic of survival instincts, what sentient beings do when there's no other way out. Sometimes, they never return from the catatonic state."

Driven to the edge, but unwilling to chance hurting Brenna, he focused his rage into manipulating an inanimate object instead. The sofa raised off the floor behind her. "Yes," he said, hoping she wouldn't notice. "So embrace the pleasure you get from me. It's not tainted."

She smiled, slow and bright. "You're wonderful, you know that? All logic and reason but wonderful." A simple statement that meant everything. "And even more so because you've been holding me all this time without complaining. I'm no lightweight."

He debated whether to say it and decided for truth. "I'm a Tk. It costs me nothing to hold you."

Her face clouded over. "You're using telekinesis to hold me up?"

"Yes. It's who I am." It was time they dealt with that. "Look behind you."

Frowning, she glanced over her shoulder. Her mouth fell open. "You're making the sofa . . . and the table, float!" She turned back to him. "Why?"

"Too much power. I have to release it somehow."

She wriggled and he knew she wanted to be freed. He let her jump down, wondering what she'd do now. Able to rein in his most dangerous emotions now that she was no longer touching him, he brought the furniture back down to earth.

"Lift me," she ordered out of nowhere.

"Brenna—"

She took a couple of steps back to give him more room. "Do it, I want to feel your . . . energy, differentiate it from his." A stubborn look.

Judd had the sudden realization that if he ever saw fear of himself in Brenna's eyes, it would break him beyond redemption. "Hold still." He could do it while she was moving, but she might inadvertently hurt herself if she pushed forward at the wrong instant and redirected his kinetic energy.

Then he simply did it.

"Judd." Her eyes went wide as she found herself standing in midair, two feet off the floor.

"Should I put you down?" It cost him literally nothing to do this. In fact, it lessened the dissonance because of the discipline required to govern his Tk.

"No. Take me higher."

He obeyed. To his surprise she began to laugh. "It's like I'm flying." Curling up into a ball, she did a flip in the air, forcing him to concentrate even harder to compensate. At that instant, he was her personal Arrow, a slave who'd do this for as long as she wanted, just to hear her laugh.

"Do something else!" A grinning order as she returned to an upright position.

He began to press on her legs. After a second, she seemed to understand and cooperated as he took her horizontal. Now she really looked like she was flying. Her expression was both delighted and startled at the same time.

"Okay," she said soon after. "Enough. I don't want to wear you out."

"I'm fine," he said, obeying nonetheless. Because she'd asked. There could be no connection between his Tk and her lack of choice.

"Baby, I have plans for that hot bod of yours and for those plans to succeed, you'll need all your energy,"

He made sure her landing was soft. "Did my power scare you?"

"No." She sounded vaguely surprised. "I think it's because he never did anything like that. He was only interested in causing pain and humiliation, not playing."

Play. Another changeling concept. "Was that what we were doing?" He watched her cross the floor to him, graceful and deadly—Brenna Shane Kincaid could destroy him, and yet he offered no resistance when she put her hand on his chest.

"Your skin burns!" She scowled. "What's wrong? Don't give me any crap about it being nothing. Your irises are pure black again—the gold is gone and I can't even distinguish the pupils. No—wait." Her forehead wrinkled. "The irises aren't black—they're a deep shade of red!"

"It's not something you have to be concerned about."

She let out a low growl that sounded like it should've come from a much bigger creature. "I swear, you're going to drive me to grievous bodily harm one of these days."

He couldn't resist. Reaching out, he ran his finger over her cheek, along her jaw, and down her neck, closing his hand about her neck once more. Petting. Gentling. "Then you'd have to find another hot bod."

Her lips twitched and she raised her hand off his chest to close over the wrist of the arm holding her. "Very funny, but I'm not that easily distracted. Baby, please."

He was almost used to being called "baby" by her. "It's nothing you can change. Why should I burden you with it?"

"Because, my Psy darling"—she tugged off his hand and laced her fingers through it—"that's what lovers do. Share."

"We aren't lovers." He had to grasp every shred of reason available to him, because the touch of her hand against his was shoving emotion through him like a battering ram.

"Judd."

She was so stubborn she could have been Psy. But he was even more so—he'd learned not to give away anything even under the most extreme pressure. Which was why his decision to tell her made no sense. "Each time I break Silence, there's a feedback reaction; you know that."

She nodded, expression solemn. "What Faith said about the pain."

"It's called dissonance and it accumulates." Pain in his head, in his nerves, in his very bones. "I have to extend a certain amount of power to keep it contained."

Brenna jerked her hand from his without warning. "In realspeak, you hurt every time I touch you, every time we connect!"

He grabbed her hand again. "It's a programmed reaction, one I can handle."

When she tugged this time, he didn't allow her to get away.

"And that's another thing," she muttered, "how come you're so strong?" She didn't wait for an answer. "What happens if you try to dismantle the conditioning that causes the dissonance?"

"I can't afford to disengage that conditioning." An immutable fact. "I need the spikes of pain—they keep me from killing by telling me when I'm getting too close to an emotional reaction that might lead to the unintentional activation of my abilities."

"Okay, but why can't you get rid of the other parts of the Protocol—so you don't get hurt for feeling things below that unsafe level?" She bit her lower lip and gave him a guilty look through her lashes. "I asked Faith for help in getting you to break Silence."

A flare of red. "If you want to know something about me, come to me."

"I needed some advice!"

This time, it was Judd who pulled away. Walking to the other side of the room, he turned his back to her, bracing his palms on the wall. "There is no way to break Silence. Not for me. I refuse to become a danger to you or anyone else. This—tonight—is as far as I can go."

Brenna wanted to kick something. Instead, she went to stand behind him and, after a slight hesitation, put her hand on his muscled shoulder. His skin was a fever. It hurt her to know that her touch hurt him, but she also knew if she stopped touching him, she'd lose him to the talons of Silence. "Listen instead of doing the alpha male thing on me."

"Hierarchy is a changeling concept."

She wrapped her arms around his waist and pressed herself to his back. Then she bit him—a light graze over his naked back. He didn't growl as a wolf male might have, but what he did was just as dominant, just as deliciously sexy. She didn't want a puppy—she wanted a man with teeth. And Judd had plenty.

Looking over his shoulder, he gave her a dark glance. "Keep pushing and you might not like the result."

Something sizzled under her fingertips, a thousand tiny teasing bites. Delighted, she pressed a kiss over the skin she'd bitten. Judd looked away, pressing his hands harder on the wall in front of him. It had the effect of further defining the muscles in his back.

"What was that you did?"

"A controlled use of Tk." His voice was arctic in its extreme focus.

Dangerous, he was dangerous. Again her brain tried to tell her something important, but she was concentrating too hard on getting through to Judd. "Just listen, okay?" She kept going before he could interrupt. "I've been talking to Faith more than you know. She thinks that maybe Silence isn't all bad."

"The Protocol gives sociopaths free rein." Words that sliced with their brutal cold.

She shivered. "That almost felt like you cut me." The sensation had been of a knife passing close to her skin. It scared her—Santano Enrique had taunted her with his scalpels hour after hour. Sometimes he'd done more than simply taunt.

Judd turned to stone. "Stop touching me. I'm losing control."

There was something in his voice that made her obey. She unclasped herself from him and took a couple of steps back.

He didn't turn as he spoke. "I can cause telekinetic damage that looks like a cut, literally turn my will into a blade."

She swallowed at the image. "Okay."

"I didn't mean to hurt you," he said, every muscle on his back tight.

Her fear transformed into pure tenderness. God, the man was so hardheaded, so unwilling to see the truth. He'd likely kill himself before harming her and he thought he had to convince her of that? "I said it *almost* felt like you'd cut me. You didn't actually."

"So close, Brenna. Too close. You should be running, not trying to convince me to test my chains even more."

"That's exactly it," she said, fisting her hands in order to keep her distance. Touch was natural to her, the lack of it unbearable. Especially where Judd was concerned. "Maybe you can choose which parts of Silence you want. Where is it written that you have to accept or reject the entire Protocol? Faith says the skills she learned under Silence help her fight the cascades triggered by bad visions."

"What about Sascha?"

She breathed a sigh of relief—he was listening. "You know the answer. Silence was plain bad for her; it ran totally counter to her abilities. But not for Faith—"

He turned to face her at last. His expression stopped her in midsentence. "If Sascha exists, then it's logical I do."

"I don't understand." Her changeling instincts urged her to hold him to her with tactile contact. The need was so strong she had to physically force herself to pay attention.

"I'm her exact opposite." Judd crossed his arms over that beautiful chest that made her want to stroke. "She heals. I kill. Those are our gifts."

Anger burned through her sensuality but paradoxically stoked up the more profound hunger inside of her. Oh, how she wanted Judd Lauren. "Why do you insist on seeing yourself that way? You helped heal me, remember?" He'd "fed" Sascha his psychic strength, had often ended up totally drained, only to show up again the next day.

He waved off the reminder. "A lesser ability. My main one

can be used for little else but death. For me, Silence—all of it—is necessary. As long as I can discipline my emotions, I won't kill. Simple."

"I don't buy that."

"You've forgotten what happened to those like me pre-Silence."

"No, I haven't." The idea of her beautiful, loyal, and strong Judd spending his life alone or in a jail cell was her personal nightmare. "But they were the other extreme—no emotional control at all. I'm asking you to consider that there might be a middle way."

Something beeped, startling her into a slight jump. Judd took a sleek silver phone from his pocket and spoke a few terse words into it. All she really cared about were the last—"I'll be there as soon as I can."

She waited until he'd hung up to ask. "Where?"

"That was Indigo. They think they've tracked down one of the hyenas responsible for the cabin explosion." Picking it up off the floor, he pulled on his shirt. "They're holding him at the cabin."

"Why do they need you?" Her craving for touch, *his* touch, was a biting ache by now. Unable to resist, she closed the distance between them and began doing up the shirt buttons. "The soldiers question people all the time." If they got the wrong answers, they did more than just question. Brenna accepted the necessity of that—in their world, mercy was often taken as weakness. Which was why the SnowDancers made certain their public face was one of vicious strength.

Judd didn't push her away. "To scare him, what else?"

Finished with the shirt, she dropped her hands and looked up. "What's that supposed to mean?"

His eyes hadn't returned to normal. "Everyone in the pack has a position. You're a tech, Riley's a soldier, and Lara, a healer. Haven't you ever considered what I am?"

"A soldier like my brothers," she said, a painful knot forming in the pit of her stomach.

"The kind of soldier they call on when a mess needs to be cleaned up."

CHAPTER 29

"**Hawke wouldn't** use you like that." Wouldn't demand that price for the sanctuary Judd had sought for the children's sake.

"Hawke will do whatever it takes to keep the SnowDancers at the top of the food chain." A blunt answer. "But you're right—changelings don't much like to use assassins."

Attack from the front. It was a matter of pride. Of honor.

"But," he continued, frost chilling his voice, "there are a lot of things I can do without killing—or even leaving a bruise—in order to get someone to speak."

Brenna knew he expected that to send her running. But she'd grown up in a family of tough men. She wasn't some wide-eyed miss who didn't know the facts behind SnowDancer's power. "That doesn't scare me, Judd." Though she'd be lying if she said it didn't worry her—for him. What impact did it have on a man to be the darkest of enforcers?

"Good, because I told you—there's no going back." He turned toward the door.

"Bite me," she snapped, frustrated at his stubborn will, his refusal to even consider a way out of Silence. In the tense pause that followed, she finally listened long enough to her own instincts to understand something she'd known subconsciously since the day he'd told her about his telekinetic abilities. Frustration transformed into anger and it flowed through her like fire. "You know what really pisses me off?"

He paused with his hand on the doorknob. "I don't have time for games, Brenna."

"What really pisses me off," she continued as if he hadn't spoken, "is you daring to come across as so possessive and protective when you've been *lying* to me for months."

He went very still. "That's a dangerous insult."

"You're a Tk. Enrique was a Tk. You can throw men against walls and crush their bones. So could he. How am I doing so far?"

"Get to the point."

Her blood boiled at his icy response. "If strong Tk are so damn lethal, how did SnowDancer and DarkRiver men manage to execute Enrique without a single changeling fatality or major injury?" Striding to where he stood, she went toe-to-toe with him. "You were there the night they rescued me and executed that monster." She had complete faith in her pack's ability to deal with a murderous Psy, but Santano Enrique had been a cardinal Tk fighting for his life. "Weren't you?"

"What would it matter if I was?"

Her heart froze—she had wanted her sudden burst of insight to be nothing more than paranoia. "It matters because you didn't tell me! Why the hell not?"

His phone beeped again. They both ignored it.

"Because you didn't need to know." His jaw was as unyielding as stone. "It has no bearing on anything."

"The hell it doesn't." She thumped a fist against his chest, making him move back from the door. "It means you've been lying to me from day one! If you can lie about that, what else might you be lying about?"

He grabbed her wrist when she would've spun away. "You're acting extremely irrationally. This has nothing to do with what we were talking about."

She wrenched her hand from his hold, not wanting her

defenses falling victim to the raw heat of his touch. She was so damn hungry for him she could easily become his sensual slave. One, just *one* teasing stroke and she'd melt. Good thing Judd wasn't the stroking kind. "Guess what? Out of the PsyNet, this is called being furious. And, for your information, I'm planning on staying that way for a while." Wrenching open the door, she walked out and headed toward an exit.

She didn't give in to the shakes until she was hidden in the inner perimeter, surrounded by the thick dark of the forest. Placing a hand on the trunk of a tree, she tried to breathe evenly of the cold air, but it was all she could do to take in ragged gulps. Judd was right. Her reaction had been unreasonable on the surface, as if she were picking a meaningless fight. He didn't understand.

The fact of his keeping something from her because it might upset her, treating her like an invalid, was enough to make her mad. But that wasn't what devastated her—it was the realization that he'd seen her at her most broken, her most humiliated. She'd been tied spread-eagled on a bed in the butcher's personal torture chamber. Naked. Bleeding.

She didn't want Judd to have that image of her in his mind. He'd seen her during the healing sessions, but there, she'd been fighting back, proud of herself for surviving. But in Enrique's lair, she'd been close to giving in, close to having her will crushed. In the final hours before she withdrew wholly into her mind, she'd begged. If the butcher had promised to set her free, she would have crawled, would have cooperated with his sick games, would have licked his feet . . . anything to make the pain stop.

Tears streamed down her face for the second time that day, but these weren't quiet, silent tears. These hurt coming out and burned like acid on her skin. She bit her lips to keep from making loud noises. But the tears wouldn't stop. She was humiliated and hurt and angry and lonely, the emotions a caustic brew that made it impossible for her to draw a clear breath.

Hands on her shoulders.

They startled her enough that she allowed him to turn her

before lifting up her fists to keep distance between them. He hugged her to him anyway. "Shh. Don't."

It only made her cry harder. When his body curled protectively over hers and he rubbed his cheek against her hair, her heart almost broke. She knew the payment Silence must be demanding from him. And still he held her.

"Why?" She tried to push off his chest but he wouldn't let her. "Why?"

One of his hands rose to close over her nape in that dominant way she'd come to expect, a hold she allowed because she trusted. "I know how proud you are, how strong. That's how I see you and that's all that matters."

Her throat felt scraped raw. "Did you see me?" Splayed out on that bed, reduced to a *thing*, mind and body no longer connected.

"No."

"Don't lie to me again. I can't bear it."

"I didn't see you. Your brothers refused to let anyone near." But he'd gone into the room afterward. He'd seen where she'd been held, seen the restraints she'd bloodied in her attempts to get out, the instruments of torture Enrique had preferred over his Psy abilities.

Her tears had lessened, but she didn't stop crying altogether until several minutes later. If he never heard those broken cries again, it would be too soon. Her ensuing silence cut parts of him no one should have been able to reach. He wanted to force her to speak.

The blue flare around her eyes seemed to glow when she finally raised her head. "I made Drew and Sascha tell me the details of the rescue. They didn't mention you, aside from saying you'd provided a psychic distraction at a certain point in the trap."

"Sascha never knew about my involvement," he told her. "I was a last-minute addition when Hawke realized who they were dealing with. He figured it wouldn't hurt to have a Psy on board, especially a trained soldier. My job was to deal with any psychic offensive."

"Hawke trusted you?"

"No." Judd had no illusions about that. "But he knew I wouldn't do anything, not with the kids still back in the den." When she didn't respond, he continued. "I'm guessing Andrew didn't mention it because his memories of that day are confused at best. He was driven by pure anger. He might not even have seen me. I went in with the team to execute Enrique, while he and Riley peeled off to rescue you."

She'd been held in a large soundproofed room in Enrique's apartment, only meters from where her abductor slept. "Enrique was tired from the PsyNet battle with Sascha"—the other Psy had managed to weaken the former Councilor as well as confirm his identity as Brenna's abductor—"but he wasn't wiped out."

Judd had blocked Enrique's volley of objects as the wolves and cats swarmed in, unable to use his Tk-Cell abilities to stop Enrique's heart because his opponent had been too good at deflecting back Tk power. But then, so was Judd. While Enrique was focusing his efforts on Judd, erroneously judging him the biggest threat, the DarkRiver leopards and SnowDancer wolves had surrounded him.

The second they were in position, Judd had thrown everything he had at the other Tk, punching a hole in Enrique's physical shields. It was all the changelings needed. They'd torn him to pieces in a matter of minutes. Blood had sprayed the walls in a spurt of arterial red, a fitting coda to a killer's life. In the melee, no one had realized exactly what it was they had seen Judd do, leaving the secret of his Tk abilities intact.

Brenna's hand opened against his shirt. "You didn't see me."

"No." At least he could tell her that truth.

She nodded, as if accepting his explanation. "I'm glad."

He kissed the shell of her ear. "No more tears. Ever."

"Sorry, honeypie, but I'm wolf. We're temperamental—get used to it."

"Not that one. I'll accept darling and even baby," he said, *feeling* something unclench in his chest at hearing her sound like herself again, "but never honeypie."

"Babycakes?" She rubbed her face against his chest.

He took a page from Andrew's book. "Now you're just being mean."

She laughed and it was the best sound he'd heard in eternity.

He was late to the meeting with Indigo—further delayed by a call to let Riley know Brenna was alone—but he truly didn't give a damn. The only thing he cared about was that the captured hyena had once posed a danger to Brenna—his death warrant was already signed.

Indigo was waiting outside the undamaged section of the cabin, her breath frosting the past-midnight air. "Thought you'd never get here."

"Where is he?"

"Inside. Male from the PineWood pack—they control a tiny slice of Arizona." The high tail of her black hair swung as she jerked her head to indicate the door. "He's not talking. That's why I called you. Hyenas usually crack under pressure. They're scavengers, not predators."

Scavengers—those who preyed on the weak and helpless. If Brenna had fallen, the hyenas would have savaged her. His eyes flicked to the windows of the wooden structure behind Indigo, his senses searching for and finding the unfamiliar mental scent of the captive. The urge to crush his skull was overpowering, bad enough for the dissonance to warn him to pull back. He listened because the captive couldn't die. Not yet. "If they're cowards, what's given this one a spine?"

"He's more scared of someone else." Indigo's voice was not pleased. "And people usually start praying when they see me."

"You think it's the Council." They were the nightmare, the thing under the bed, the deepest darkness. And they knew how to wait. Much as a spider knows how to wait.

"Yeah—it can't be another pack." She rubbed her gloveless hands together. "If it were, he'd have sung like a canary by now."

"Is he blindfolded?" If, for no reason that he could foresee right now, Judd let the man live, he could not be allowed to become a threat to the family. Of course, given that Judd knew he wasn't rational where Brenna was concerned, the hyena's chances of walking out alive were close to nil.

Indigo nodded. "I put it on when I heard your vehicle."

"I'll make him talk."

Another nod and then Indigo led him into the cabin. The hyena sat on a chair in the center of the room, fear a damp sheen over his face. Seeing it, Judd glanced at Indigo. "You're right." No one that petrified would have held out for long otherwise, not with four wolves in the room—Indigo, D'Arn, Elias, and the knife thrower, Sing-Liu.

The hyena was thin with sallow skin. Black hair. A pathetic goatee in the same shade. The latter was a straggling attempt to hide a chin so weak, it was a wonder he hadn't wet himself. His eyes were covered by a strip of dark brown fabric but Judd didn't need to see them to know the panic skittering through the captive's bones.

Walking to stand behind the hyena, Judd placed a single finger against his temple. "Which part of your brain do you like the least?" He didn't need touch to work, but the theatrics helped. As did the mental push he applied, the one that must've felt like a slow-moving pincer around the man's head.

The hyena gasped but didn't speak.

"I'll destroy the part I choose, then," Judd said, making his voice metallically Psy. Despite his earlier thoughts about the threat to Brenna, he wasn't enjoying this. It was simply something to be done. Predators and scavengers respected only brute strength. The changelings weren't so different from the Psy in that regard.

The hyena's reaction was surprising. Tears leaked out from under the blindfold. "You weren't there!" he screamed. "You fucking weren't there!"

Judd stopped touching the man, his telepathic abilities sensing something odd. Backing up into the shadows at the edges of the room, he began working on the psychic level, aware of the physical conversation with the section of his mind functioning on that plane.

Indigo glanced at him. At his nod, she tugged down the

blindfold. "Don't look behind you" was her first order. "We weren't where, Kevin?" she prompted when the male didn't speak again. "You talk or I let him do what he's good at. I think you can guess what the result will be."

Yes, Judd thought, threaten him with the Psy bogeyman. But he was far more interested in something else he'd found in the hyena.

Indigo growled low in her throat. "Talk. Last warning."

"Parrish, our pack leader"—Kevin almost stumbled over his words in his effort to obey—"he said we had to do what the Psy said and they wouldn't touch us."

"Why?" Indigo folded her arms, looking down on the male. Judd recognized the move as a display of dominance. "Kevin, I asked you a question."

The hyena's swallow was audible. "Because otherwise they would wipe us out. They killed eight of our pups as a warning."

Indigo swore, arms unfolding. "Why the hell didn't you come to us?"

Judd knew that while the wolves wouldn't hesitate to destroy trespassers in their territory, they'd also help a weaker changeling group against an enemy that didn't follow the rules of engagement. One of the most important rules was: No targeting minors.

"We did!" Kevin's scream faded off to a whimper. "You wouldn't come."

"Who told you we wouldn't come?" Indigo had softened her voice and crouched down in front of Kevin. Not submission but a signal that he might come out of this alive.

Kevin took a deep, shaky breath. "Parrish. He went to Hawke and your alpha laughed in his face. Said the loss of our pups was good riddance to bad rubbish. Then the leopards said they wouldn't help us unless the wolves did!"

This time, Indigo's oath was considerably more blue. "That, I can tell you, is a complete lie. Hawke has a thing about pups, and the cats make their own decisions."

Kevin reacted violently to Indigo's statement, going so far as to make aggressive sounds in his throat. "It's not a lie!"

"Your pack leader sold you out." Indigo rose to her feet, rage a cold mask over her sharply defined features.

"No! He had no reason to."

"Yeah? Try delusions of grandeur. Maybe he thinks he's going to replace Hawke and Lucas."

Kevin stopped struggling. The silence lasted for several long seconds. "He said that that would be our revenge—to take your place."

"What were Parrish's orders?" Judd asked, near certain of the answer.

Kevin's whole body twitched, as if he'd forgotten the danger at his back. "To do what the Psy said."

"And what did the Psy say?" Indigo prompted.

CHAPTER 30

"**Weird stuff** about shields and lowering them." He sounded confused. "They hypnotized us to fix the ones who wouldn't."

"Give us a minute, Kevin." Raising his blindfold again, Indigo met Judd's gaze. He nodded toward the door.

Outside, the lieutenant leaned against the vehicle that had brought Judd to the cabin. "Mind control?" she asked, spine rigid.

He shook his head. "More like programming. Full mind control needs to be maintained by a constant link between the controlling Psy and the victim and that link sucks power."

Judd had never stepped over that line, but he'd been taught the technical aspects. He had no doubt that had he stayed in the Net, he would have ended up using that knowledge. Evil had a tendency to wear away at humanity. It was a truth the Ghost didn't yet see. "If you don't want that drain on your resources," he continued, "you can program someone to do certain things. The downside and upside compared to mind control are both the same—the victim cannot and will not deviate from the set plan. The hyenas wouldn't have turned back even if they'd been confronted by armed wolves."

"This is a mess." Indigo kicked up snow with her boot. "If they got to the hyenas, we don't know who else they might have influenced."

"Finding that out is your job." Judd began walking back to the cabin. "Mine is to clean Kevin's mind."

"Wait!" Indigo ran to his side. "We can use him as our eyes and ears."

He met her eyes. "No." That was on the other side of that line between humanity and the clawing darkness that constantly whispered at the corners of his mind. "I won't replace one kind of slavery with another."

Indigo's face blanched. "You make me feel like a monster."

Judd didn't answer, already to the door. Pushing it open, he walked inside. Kevin was in the same position as before, but his terror seemed to have whittled down to grim acceptance. He thought he was going to die.

Judd stood in front of the man. "I'm going to remove what they put in. The choices you make from then on will be your own."

The hyena's head snapped up, moving blindly in the direction of Judd's voice. "You're not going to kill me?"

"Not today." Judd went behind the male. *Lower shields,* he said telepathically. It was the first in a long list of commands the programmers could have used. But he had no need to go any further—Kevin's tough changeling shields disappeared as if by magic. The cruelty of whoever it was that had done this was beyond anything Judd had ever seen. They had left the changeling wide open to any Psy who knew or could guess the code words.

Once inside, Judd began to check the structure of the programming. The work was effortless—not only was he a strong telepath, he'd been trained in the very techniques that had been used on Kevin. Those skills told him that the binding was crude, done in haste. Clearly, the Council wasn't worried about failure. Then again, why should they be? While other Psy might be able to get into Kevin's mind, only a Psy with a very specific skill set could *undo* the original programming.

A few minutes later, he was about to reset the compromised neural pathways when he saw it. A Black Key. A tiny piece of psychic code that would kick in the second he began the reset. Kevin would die from a massive aneurysm in less than a minute.

He withdrew before carefully retracing his steps. Finally satisfied the Black Key was the single contingency, he spent ten minutes deactivating and removing it. Then he cleaned house. *Kevin.*

"Yes." The vocalization was distant—the hyena remained in the trance initiated by the code words.

Your mind is now free. As of this moment, you will not respond when asked to "lower shields." Do you understand?

"Yes."

Aware of the wolves looking on, bemused at what appeared to them to be a one-sided conversation, Judd checked for any further activation phrases then repeated his instruction several times to ensure comprehension before giving Kevin the order to wake with full memory of what had taken place.

The hyena immediately bent double, dry-retching. Judd looked at the nearest soldier. "Get a glass of water."

D'Arn obeyed without looking to Indigo. When the soldier returned and went to lower Kevin's blindfold, he glanced at Judd. Understanding, Judd stepped back into the shadows once more.

Indigo waited until the hyena was no longer shaking before asking him to tell them everything he knew.

Kevin was able to share details of three other planned attacks. To Judd's military mind, it was obvious that the PineWood leader had made no effort to keep a lid on the details. He'd known about, and relied, on the programming to ensure silence.

"I think there might be more." Kevin sounded broken, lost. "I'll see if I can find out anything."

Judd was no changeling but he understood why the hyena was so distraught. Hierarchy was important in changeling packs and that hierarchy relied on trust. What Parrish had done was obliterate Kevin's system for understanding how the world worked. It was the same psychological trauma that had destroyed so many young children at the dawn of Silence. The transitional children—those under seven years of age at the time of the Protocol's implementation—had been taught to devalue love, warmth, touch, everything that made them feel safe. More had died than survived.

"Don't put yourself in danger," Indigo told Kevin now. "With what you've given us, we can shut down this operation. How many in your pack?"

"A hundred but that includes the old and the very young." He coughed a couple of times. "There's about forty able-bodied. The Psy didn't bother to talk to the others."

"Not many." She looked over Kevin's head, toward Judd. "Can you handle it?" At Judd's nod, Indigo returned her attention to Kevin. "How stable is your pack?"

"Good. If you take out Parrish, Mahal or Lou-Ann can step in." His voice held acceptance of his leader's impending death. "I don't know if they're in on it."

"Don't worry about that, we'll figure it out." Indigo raised an eyebrow at Judd. "Could be they've all been brainwashed."

"It could." However, he considered it unlikely, given the crude nature of the programming. The Council hadn't spent too much time on this. "Who were the Psy who programmed you? Were they wearing uniforms?"

"No. Suits like the rest of them." Kevin didn't attempt to look over his shoulder. "I didn't see anyone who seemed really important. Nothing stands out."

Judd would have been surprised to hear otherwise. "Any names mentioned?"

"Not that I can—" The hyena paused. "Wait. I walked up on Parrish once while he was on the phone. He said he couldn't change things without Duncan's authorization."

Brenna felt unexpectedly fresh the morning after her emotional breakdown. It was as if the tears had released something toxic that had been brewing inside of her, setting her free. Added to that, Judd had messaged her to let her know he hadn't yet returned to the den. She grinned. The Man of Ice was learning.

Walking out of her apartment, she headed off to find

Hawke. She had work to do—she hadn't forgotten that Tim's killer might be gunning for her and she wasn't going to put a bull's-eye on her back, but neither was she going to let that piece of scum dictate her movements.

Hawke raised an eyebrow when she hunted him down in one of the workout rooms. "That look spells trouble." His entire upper body was drenched in sweat, but his breathing remained smooth. Healthy and muscled, he was quite beautiful in a very masculine way.

She was woman enough to appreciate him, but without wanting more. "I promised DarkRiver I'd help them hack into the Psy databases. Can you assign me an escort down to their headquarters?" Because she wasn't a soldier and she couldn't fight like one.

"They decided to set up special untraceable equipment for it." He picked up a towel and wiped off his face. "Should be ready by tomorrow. You want to go help Sascha instead?"

Brenna shook her head. "She said she doesn't need me till later. Right now, the deer are too traumatized to accept my presence."

"Makes sense. I've got a meeting that way tomorrow—you can hitch a ride with me," he said, slinging the towel around his neck. "I've already got SnowDancer guards sorted and DarkRiver has the whole place under watch, too."

"Trusting the cats, Hawke?" she teased.

He snorted. "Like I said, I'll have my own men there."

Relieved he hadn't stood in her way, she was about to head back to her room when Hawke's phone beeped. Since it was closer to her—on the floor with the sweatshirt he'd stripped off during training—she picked it up and handed it to him. It wasn't her intention to listen in, but he motioned for her to stay.

The conversation was short and ended with Hawke saying, "You've tracked down the pack?" A pause filled with the most lethal anger. "Then do it today. We don't know what else they might have been programmed to do."

"Do what?" Brenna asked after he'd hung up.

"Judd's not going to get back till after dark," he said instead of answering. "He asked me to keep an eye on you."

She concentrated on the first part of his response. "What does he do for you, Hawke?" Her heart was a block of cold stone in her chest.

His face went dangerously neutral. "I don't know if I like your tone of voice." It was a reminder of who he was.

But she knew her status, too. "I'm not a juvenile to be slapped down." She faced off with him, eye to eye. "Answer my question. What do you ask from Judd in exchange for giving sanctuary to the kids?"

His pale eyes iced over. "Judd is a fully trained Psy assassin with experience in covert wet work. I'd be a fool if I didn't utilize his skills."

She choked back a cry. "How can you ask that of him?" An alpha looked after his own. He didn't destroy them. But maybe Hawke didn't consider the Laurens his own. After all, and for reasons she'd never known, he hated the Psy as much as her brothers did.

His face gentled, an unexpected softening of harsh masculine lines. Closing the distance between them, he cupped her cheek. "He is who and what he is, Brenna. If you want something different, you shouldn't be with him."

"He's the only one I want to be with."

"Then accept his beast like you do your own."

Hawke's words wouldn't leave her alone as she went through the day. It was disturbing to think that she might be asking Judd to change when she professed to want him for himself. "But asking him to break Silence is different," she muttered to herself as she scanned the details of another of the job offers Dr. Shah had forwarded her.

If Judd didn't dismantle the conditioning, he'd continue to hurt each time they touched, each time he felt anything for her. How could a relationship survive under that kind of pressure? "No, Brenna, be honest." She sighed and went to the next offer. While everything she'd thought so far was true, there was another truth—she wanted Judd to hold her, to offer her affection . . . to love her. A selfish need.

What if accepting his beast meant denying the needs of her own?

It made her head ache, especially when she added in the fact that her beast didn't recognize Judd as her mate. The mating bond was conspicuous in its absence. "Enough." Thinking herself to a standstill was not going to help matters. And if she didn't stop thinking about Judd, she'd start to speculate about what it was he was doing today.

Covert wet work.

Her stomach turned. If he came to her with hands dipped in blood, would she accept him? Her fingers trembled. She had no easy answers to that question and that shook her. Taking a deep breath, she forced herself to pay attention to the next offer on the list. It was from a corporation named Sierra Tech.

She knew a lot about ST—SnowDancer was the majority shareholder, at sixty percent. DarkRiver held twenty and a human conglomerate named Dekell the other twenty. ST was offering her a great package and her wolf would prefer to work for the pack. Not that all ST employees were wolves. It was considered a plum company to work for by scientists and techs across the globe. The only reason ST had no Psy employees was that it competed directly with several Council-backed labs.

Sierra Tech went to the top of her list, but she hadn't made her decision. Her current frame of mind didn't exactly lend itself to the task. Even when she finished looking over the offers and moved on to repair some small comm malfunctions for packmates, her mind remained chaotic. Lunch and dinner came and went, but she had no answer to her own uncomfortable question.

Would she hold Judd if he came to her after utilizing his skills as an assassin?

She went to bed mentally exhausted but woke after only a few hours of disrupted sleep . . . because she could smell Judd's scent in her quarters. Getting out of bed still half-asleep, she saw it was four a.m. She walked out wearing the satin slip she used as her nightgown, her feet bare.

"Judd?" For a second, she couldn't locate him. Then her night vision kicked in and she found him seated in an armchair close to the coffee table.

He was watching her, his entire body motionless. It didn't strike her that she should be afraid or even wary. Yawning, she walked over and sat on his lap, curling her body into the armchair. His arms came around her without hesitation, one hand curving around her shoulders, the other sliding to close over the bare skin of her upper thigh.

The sensual contact brought her to full wakefulness. Wrapping her arms around his neck, she nuzzled at his throat. "Are you okay?"

His hand shifted to slide between her thighs, surprising a shocked feminine sound out of her. "Judd? Baby?" Something was wrong. With a changeling male, she would've let her body soothe him, used touch to connect. But Judd was Psy . . . and hers. At that moment, she knew the answer to the question that had tormented her all day—she would hold him, *accept him*, no matter what.

That was what mates did.

She didn't care if there was no bond—no one was going to tell her she wasn't meant to be with this man. "What do you want?" she asked, but he remained silent. Deciding to let instinct guide her, she softened for him.

His other hand tangled in her hair, tilting her head back in a sharp move. She went rather than resist. A woman who loved a dominant male had to know when to bend . . . and when to bite. His lips crushed hers, his hand squeezing her inner thigh. Moaning into the kiss, she opened her mouth. He didn't wait for any more permission, ravaging her with a sensual fury that had her trying to press even closer.

Her body craved Judd. She had no desire to back off, perhaps because she hadn't had time to be afraid, or perhaps because she could feel the hunger inside of him, a hunger only she could assuage.

He bit at her lower lip. She bit back.

His back muscles were rock hard under her palms as she splayed her hands and luxuriated in the unrestrained masculine heat of him. "No," she protested when he broke the kiss to run his lips down her jaw and over her neck. She tugged at his hair. He nipped at her neck in reprimand. Something *melted* between her legs and when he stroked his hand farther north, she wanted to urge him to go faster.

He cupped her. Strong. Bold. Possessive.

She felt her claws threaten to release, sparks shooting behind her tightly closed eyes. And then he began to massage her like that, while her body simultaneously tried to get closer and writhe away. Her slip rode up and her bottom came in contact with the hard ridge of his erection.

A whisper of fear fluttered in her belly.

But her panties were gone, torn off her and oh God he was touching her skin to skin and his fingers were rubbing at the entrance to her body and— Crying out, she orgasmed with an almost painful clamping of internal muscles long unused. She buried her face in his neck and he held her there with his hand on her nape as he coaxed more and more pleasure out of her body.

The scent of him coated her tongue until she licked at him, taking the salt/ice/man scent inside. Slowly, the orgasm turned into a buzz of sensual heat, leaving her sated. Murmuring her pleasure, she relaxed back into her earlier curled-up position and opened her eyes. At first, she didn't realize what it was she was seeing. Why were there pieces of wood everywhere? And did her kitchen bench look lopsided?

Judd's teeth clamped down on her shoulder, as if he knew he no longer had her undivided attention. She jerked up. "Judd. Judd!" She tugged at his hair.

His answer was an explosion of tiny telekinetic bites in very sensitive places. Her entire body arched as pleasure short-circuited her nerve endings. In the corner of her eye, she saw the kitchen bench collapse, giving one final groan of creaking distress. And then all she could hear were her own gasping breaths.

By the time she came back down this time, she was lying crosswise in his lap, her slip puddled around her waist, the straps snapped. Judd wasn't touching her exposed flesh, just looking at her breasts with hunger that was close to madness.

Giving a sob, she placed her arms tight around him once more, eyes wide as she watched the violence over his shoulder. "Stop. Please, baby, stop." Small pieces of broken furniture circled the room in a savage storm. "Judd, darling."

CHAPTER 31

His entire body shuddered. "Brenna." It was a raw sound stripped of his usual control.

"Yes." She hugged him harder, her breasts crushed against the cool softness of his leather-synth jacket. "I'm here."

"Did I hurt you?"

Hurt her? "You pleasured me." The exquisite heat of it continued to spiral through her.

He withdrew his hand from between her legs and she had to fight her moan. "Baby, the furniture . . ." The pieces hadn't stopped flying.

One of his arms remained clamped around her back as he raised his head. "Critical breach." He was beginning to sound close to normal. "Power sent outward instead of focusing on you."

"You didn't hurt me," she repeated. "Even out of control, you didn't hurt me."

"Not this time." The broken pieces of furniture began to settle on the floor.

She pulled back, wanting to meet his eyes. They were dark, devoid of those sparks of gold. "What happened?" He was never going to believe he wouldn't hurt her—she'd have to rely on time to fix that. "Talk to me." Brushing the hair off his forehead with one hand, she pulled up her slip with the other.

His eyes fell to where she clutched the slippery material above the curve of her breasts. "You need to get dressed first."

She might have argued with him if the ruins of the bench hadn't chosen that instant to compact with a groan, sending up dust she could taste. "I'll be quick." Wriggling off his lap, she blushed. "You're still—"

"Go."

She went. Sometimes, discretion really was the better part of valor. Dropping the slip and pulling on a pair of sweats and a T-shirt took maybe two minutes. She ran back out. "Oh!"

Judd had turned on the light and already cleaned up most of the mess using his telekinetic abilities. As she watched, the last broken pieces settled down into a neat pile by the door. "I'll replace everything."

"I'm not worried about that." Walking over, she fought the urge to touch him. He was all coiled muscle and intensity. Dark. Dangerous.

Take him as he is.

Her spine straightened. "Now tell me what happened."

His tone was flat as he told her about the PineWood pack. "We went in, cleaned out their den. A number of them were compromised—I had to undo the programming."

Relieved he hadn't been forced into using his more covert skills, she blew out a breath. "There's no need for you to beat yourself up about that. You did something good."

"It's not that." A bead of sweat rolled down his temple and she remembered the pain. The dissonance. But before she could speak, he told her the rest. "What our contact didn't know was that the Psy had attempted to place commands on immature minds, too."

"Children?" Her voice shook. "They tried to do that to babies?" She wanted to bury her head in the sand and not hear the rest of what he had to say—she'd almost died after having her mind raped. And children were so much weaker. "How many?"

"One died before we reached their den." His cheekbones stood out like blades against his skin. "I was able to remove the programming on the others but two are damaged. Their brains couldn't handle the pressure and battered themselves bloody trying to get out."

"Oh, Judd." She could feel his hurt inside herself. "There was nothing you could have done."

Another bead of sweat, the only indicator of the amount of pain he had to be in. "There was no reason for them to mess with the children's minds. *No reason.* They were too young and weak to provide assistance in the plot. It was done as a message."

The most visceral kind of fury exploded in her. "They've crossed the line. But"—she stared him in the eye—"you haven't."

"I know."

Startled, she snapped her mouth shut. "Then why . . . ?" She waved her arms at the ruin of her living room and kitchen.

"Don't you recognize rage when you see it?"

"Oh." She wasn't sure what to say to that blunt admission. "You've broken Silence?" Something in her said it couldn't be that easy.

His next words proved it. "If I had, you wouldn't have been able to bring me back." His eyes traced over her body and though she was demurely covered, she felt her nipples peak, her thighs press together. "I can still taste you on my lips."

She put a hand on the wall to steady herself, certain her knees were about to buckle. "You pushed your anger into sex." Burning it up without causing harm to living creatures.

"It wasn't planned." He couldn't seem to take his eyes off her lips. "I was about to leave your home when you walked out. I should have never come here in the first place."

"I didn't mind." Heat in the air, so thick she could almost touch it. Her eyes dropped to his erection, hard and heavy against his jeans. She wanted to feel him in her hands, to experience more of the animal passion he'd shown her tonight.

Something smashed to the floor, jolting her out of the erotic fantasy. Her eyes widened as she realized he'd thumped the armchair—one of the few undamaged pieces of furniture in the room—hard onto the floor.

"I need to leave." He pulled out a phone, skin stretched tight over his features.

It made her wonder if he was as tightly stretched in other places.

"Brenna."

"Why not?" She met his gaze. Stubborn. Needy. Changeling to his Psy. "I don't care if you destroy the whole apartment."

His hand clenched on the slim width of the phone. "As the state of this room shows, I'm no longer listening to the dissonance. It's not keeping me in check. All it would take to kill you would be one mistake in the heat of passion. *One.*"

The taut restraint in his voice cut her. "Judd, I need you." They had to find a way past this. She was so hungry she was almost to the point where she wanted to cry. "I need your touch and I need to touch you in return."

A crack appeared in the casing of the phone in his hand. "Where's your comm console? I'll call someone to stand watch—you're not safe from Timothy's assailant."

"No." She thrust a hand through her hair, fingers shaking with need such as she'd never before felt. Yes, changelings craved touch. But this was something so primal it was a claw inside of her. "I'm awake. I'll stay that way. I'll call you if anything happens."

"Somebody is trying to hurt you." Something not wholly on the side of the angels moved at the back of his eyes.

She had already decided she wasn't going to run from what he was, but that didn't mean she was going to submit to his every wish. "I don't need a babysitter if I'm wide-awake." She swallowed. "Go. Looking at you makes me *want.*"

For a timeless second, it appeared he wouldn't listen. Then he turned on his heel and left even as she reached out to touch the odd glint of dark red she thought she saw at the side of his face. "Oh, God." She fought the urge to collapse, to rage at the unfairness of it all. Instead, she pushed up her sleeves, found the vacuum-bot, switched it to manual, and began to clean up the dust Judd hadn't manage to corral.

Judd touched the wetness near his jaw and brought his fingers up in front of him. Pale red stained his fingers. His first guess was that he'd been cut by a piece of flying debris but when he moved to the mirror over the sink, he discovered his mistake.

The blood had leaked from his ear.

Extreme dissonance.

His body was literally fighting itself, the conditioning and its attendant pain controls slamming up against the emotions he shouldn't have been feeling. He wiped away the blood and did an internal check. The rupture had already healed over, his body having automatically utilized the same technique as the one that made his scars disappear.

But he knew it couldn't keep up with what was happening inside him. Sooner rather than later, he'd have to shut down every facet of emotion, every glimmer of passion. Because otherwise, his brain would look exactly like those of the hyena children he'd seen.

Bloody. Battered. Irrevocably broken.

Several hours after her cleaning frenzy, Brenna found herself bad-tempered from lack of sleep, lack of touch, and a sensual need that refused to quit. It probably wasn't the best of times for her to be charting a hack, but she'd made a promise. So here she was with Dorian in the second subbasement of DarkRiver's business HQ.

The blond sentinel had growled at her several times, but she'd just snarled back.

"You're going about it ass-backwards," he said for the fourth time in an hour.

Brenna's eyes narrowed. "The whole plan is to sneak in, not stampede so loudly that everyone from the Psy Council to your uncle in Poughkeepsie can hear us."

"Where the hell is Poughkeepsie anyway?" Dorian pushed into her personal space, standing with his hand on her chair as he leaned over her shoulder to look at the screen.

Brenna was itching for a fight after the frustrated night she'd had. But there was something she had to talk to Dorian about. "Can I ask you a question?"

"What?" He scowled, tapping at her screen and threatening to shift the pathway she'd mapped out. "You should've gone—"

"Dorian."

Her tone must've gotten through to him because he swung around to take a seat in the chair beside her, swiveling so he faced her profile. "What is it, kid?"

He was the only one she let get away with calling her that—she had guessed that Dorian, who had lost his sister to Enrique, saw her as another baby sister. It was the reason he acted so bossy with her. That was more than okay with her, because while Dorian was hard to read, if he was anything like Drew and Riley, then his sister's murder had to have devastated him, tearing into the protectiveness at his core.

"First, Judd knows but that's all. Don't tell anyone else, okay?"

His surfer-blue eyes were piercing. "I can't make that promise until I know if it'll affect either of our packs."

"It won't." Glancing over her shoulder to double-check that no one was listening, she turned back to the DarkRiver sentinel and simply asked what she needed to know. "How do you deal with not being able to change into animal form?"

Dorian's face reflected surprise. "Most people dance around that. Like they're afraid of hurting me." His voice said that that was a ridiculous worry.

"Please tell me." She held his gaze. "Please, Dorian."

Realization dawned. "Oh, damn, sweetheart. That bastard messed you up, didn't he?" Reaching out, he stroked a hand over her hair. "How bad?"

The gentleness brought tears to her eyes. "I can use my teeth and claws, but I can't shift fully. No loss of strength, speed, or flexibility."

Dorian dropped his hand to lie on the back of her chair. "I

grew up latent—I never had anything to lose." His tone was matter-of-fact. "But you're different. Are you sure it's permanent?"

"I don't know anything. But I want to prepare myself for the worst-case scenario." That way, her heart couldn't break all over again.

"Alright." Dorian's handsome features settled into decisive lines. "The first thing you have to do is stop feeling sorry for yourself."

She swallowed but didn't defend her emotions. This was why she had asked him. Dorian might see her as a sister, but he was the kind of brother who'd give it to her straight.

"You survived," he said, "and you aren't a basket case. You should be fucking proud of yourself. He tried to cripple you, but he didn't succeed."

"No. But he stole something precious from me . . . he stole my wolf."

The depth of pain in those words stopped Judd in his tracks. He'd raced down here after discovering Brenna's absence from the den, ready to face the consequences of last night's critical breach. But he wasn't prepared for this. For a Brenna with trembling hands and a whisper of a voice.

Moving soundlessly out of the doorway, he leaned his back against the wall and hoped they were too distracted to scent him. He knew he should leave, should allow her privacy. But he couldn't. Brenna should've asked Dorian's opinion while Judd was with her—but she hadn't. Because Judd was Psy and couldn't give her comfort.

Not only had he never truly understood the staggering depth of her loss at not being able to shift, he'd left her in the early morning hours when she had needed him so desperately. How could he blame her for going to another man for succor? Yet he did.

"Enrique stole a lot from you." Dorian's voice cut through the air. "But you can get some of that back."

"How?"

"Build on your strengths, Brenna. Become so damn good at those things that no one dares to hold the other against you."

Good advice, Judd thought, his fingers curling into fists.

"Okay. Okay." Brenna sounded as if she was putting that will of hers to good use.

"Anytime you need me, just call. Alright, kid?"

Judd's fists were so tight, he was in danger of fracturing his own bones. He understood why Brenna had needed to talk to Dorian. He even understood that the leopard saw Brenna as a young sister, not a potential lover. None of that made any difference. Judd wanted to be the one she turned to when in need.

Ice picks of pain shoved through his skull, dissonance so vicious it nearly shut down his consciousness. The countdown was getting inexorably closer to the end. Uncurling his fingers with sheer force of will, he watched the blood rush back in. Last night had made it clear that he'd already crossed too many lines, broken too many rules. Soon, it would be too late to draw back.

"Thank you, Dorian."

No, he would not pull back. Brenna was *his*. His to pleasure. And his to comfort. Squaring his shoulders, he stepped into the doorway.

CHAPTER 32

Dorian and Brenna both looked up. He'd expected surprise and perhaps fluster, but Brenna's face reflected an expression he could define only as relief. Getting up off her chair, she pressed her body into his, burying her face against his chest. "You need to hold me."

He could follow orders, especially when they were given in a familiar female voice hiding a tremor. Raising his arms, he wrapped them around her body. She didn't seem to mind being crushed, her own arms holding on tighter.

Dorian's eyes met his over the top of her head. The leopard had an inscrutable look on his face. But when Judd inclined his head in thanks, Dorian returned the gesture.

After escorting Brenna back to the den sometime around three in the afternoon, Judd left to help Sascha with the deer. Brenna had decided to stay behind because she had a viral problem to figure out, but her torn loyalties were obvious.

"Your work is important," he told her. "We need to strike at the Council's heart."

"I know." She flashed a smile. "But thanks for saying it anyway."

He left her hunched over her personal computer and spent the rest of the day feeding Sascha power. When it became clear he wouldn't make it back to the den before dawn the next day, he rang Riley. "Keep an eye on her. The stalker's been quiet, but he's out there."

Riley made a sound of agreement. "She's not going to like it."

"Do you care?"

"I care about keeping her alive." A pause. "I'm checking out the soldiers."

"Any indication who it might be?"

"Not yet." Riley's tone held both frustration and pure focus. "Do what you have to do to help DawnSky. I'll take care of Bren."

Judd ended the call, his mind on the killer and the concordant threat to Brenna. It made him even more determined to return to the den as soon as possible. However, because of the number of victims, he didn't make it back until after eight the next morning. He was tired but not drained—because Sascha was having to work very slowly, the draw on his psychic strength had been steady but not intense.

Many of the DawnSky children were close to catatonic. Several had seen their parents being torn up. One young boy had been trapped under the body of his dying mother; another had tried to protect his siblings, only to get his chest carved open. He'd survived, his mind strong. Others . . . others were broken. The healing process was going to be a long one, but Judd had pledged himself to it.

That thought in mind, he headed to his room to wash up before going to Brenna. Not seeing her wasn't an option. He made it to her apartment a few minutes after nine. But when he entered her quarters—she'd keyed him in—he found not Brenna, but a note pinned to the new kitchen bench she had put together using a thick plank and precise towers of synthetic bricks. Smart.

The note was short and very Brenna. *Left before dawn to*

go use my other degree. Have bodyguards so don't worry. Be back when the work's done. Get some sleep. Bren.

Putting the piece of paper in his pocket, he called through to DarkRiver HQ to confirm. It was Clay who answered. "She's in the basement with Dorian. Andrew's with her. Riley's gone to keep watch on the healers doing the physical nursing."

So much for the siblings keeping their distance from each other. Given their closeness, he'd known it would be difficult. "Thanks." Hanging up, he used telekinesis to get rid of the debris by the door, teleporting it discreetly into one of the large recyclers kept in a corner of the underground garage.

That done, he decided to bow to Brenna's order and catch some sleep. The less sleep he had, the worse his mental degradation would get. But he'd only been asleep for three hours when he woke. Something was wrong. Parts of his brain he'd never seen active were sparking in awareness. And those sparks tasted like Brenna . . . and terror.

He called Clay. "Where is she?"

"She left close to two hours ago. She was riding with her brothers."

Two hours wasn't enough time to return to the den unless they'd floored the accelerator. "Why did they leave?"

"Something about an urgent call. Everything okay?"

"Yes." He hung up, still convinced something was wrong. If the call had been urgent enough to pull Brenna away from something so important, they would have pushed their vehicle to the limit and arrived by now. He tried to call Brenna's cell phone, but no one picked up.

Get outside the walls.

It was a command from that newly awakened section of his brain. He listened. The second he exited the den, those firing sparks turned into a firestorm. It was as though he could feel Brenna screaming. Shutting down everything else, he concentrated on following that odd psychic echo. The instant he had a link—an inexplicable link—he began running. He found them twenty minutes from the den, no car in sight.

Road likely blocked in some way they couldn't clear. Forced them to proceed on foot. Ambush.

Cool Arrow calculations in a dark corner of his mind as he took in the scene: Andrew lay on the ground, Riley and Brenna on their knees on either side of him. It was immediately clear that the fallen SnowDancer wasn't breathing. His pulse was also absent when Judd placed his fingers against the other man's throat—not surprising, given the size of the hole in his chest.

Brenna shook, looking to him with eyes gone wild with grief. *"Judd."* The clothing on the right side of her body was dirtied with muddy slush, her face slightly scratched.

Standing, Brenna's head reached just over Andrew's heart. Putting together the visible facts—Andrew's wound, the dirt on her—Judd reconstructed the scene in milliseconds. The bullet had been aimed for Brenna's head. Andrew had sensed danger at the last moment and shoved aside his sister. He'd saved her life, but hadn't been fast enough to dodge the bullet himself.

He saw Riley doing CPR and knew that that wouldn't be enough. Andrew's heart was obviously shattered, the sniper's bullet having hit it at the exact spot to cause maximum damage. He couldn't feel an exit wound, which meant the bullet had to be lodged within the mangled flesh. Judd touched Brenna's cheek in a fleeting caress, his mind going at a hundred miles an hour. "Stop, Riley."

Riley raised a face strained white. "We have to keep going."

Judd put a hand on the other man's shoulder. "His heart is damaged. I need to fix it." He had never done anything like this, never even considered that he could. His job was to stop hearts, not repair them. But he knew the finest details of how the organ functioned—to destroy you had to know how things worked. "Breathe for him but don't touch his heart."

Riley didn't argue. "Do it."

The first thing Judd did was send a Tk shock to Andrew's shattered heart, starting it again, hopefully in time to keep his brain alive. As Riley bent to blow breath into his brother's lungs, Judd used Tk to keep that heartbeat going. Then he began picturing what needed to happen to the destroyed cells for Andrew's heart to beat on its own.

He'd have to reconstruct the damaged section from the cellular level up, putting the SnowDancer's heart back together like the most intricate of jigsaw puzzles. The problem was, some of the pieces were missing or too damaged to function. New pieces would have to be created from somewhere. Judd wasn't an M-Psy, but he could *move* things, make them change shape . . . smooth over scars by manipulating the cells. A child's trick given new purpose.

At no point during the operation did he stop thinking. He had to be absolutely correct about the precise degree of each and every cellular movement. One mistake and Andrew's heart would not beat after Judd stopped making it beat. That was an outcome Judd couldn't accept . . . because it wouldn't be only Andrew's heart that would break.

A slender hand clasped his shoulder at some stage and he knew it was Brenna. Her touch should have destabilized him, but it did the opposite. It anchored him. An abnormal reaction he'd have to consider later, when his mind had room for thoughts other than the methodical repair of a heart that had been blown to pieces.

"Jesus," Hawke whispered from beside Brenna, so many hours later that the light was starting to fade. The alpha and several others had arrived soon after Judd—she'd somehow gathered enough calm to call the den using Riley's phone. Hers lay forgotten in the car.

She knew what had caused Hawke's surprise. They could literally see Drew's skin *shifting*. At first, it had seemed an illusion, but then she'd realized her brother's horrific wound was disappearing second by slow second. Four hours into it, something metallic had pushed up out of the wound. The bullet.

Fingers trembling, Brenna had taken it as soon as it rolled free and handed it to Hawke, who'd wrapped it in a piece of cloth torn from the shirt he wore under his jacket. That had been an hour ago. Judd hadn't spoken or looked away from what he was doing the entire five-hour stretch, Riley had kept breathing for Drew, and Brenna had held on to Judd, instinct telling her it was the right thing to do.

Judd suddenly lifted his hands from Andrew's chest. "Riley, move." His voice was rough, holding the rust of disuse.

Riley broke contact and a bare instant later, Drew's body jerked as if an electric shock had passed through it. Brenna gritted her teeth, knowing that Judd had just tried to restart her brother's heart after stopping whatever it was he'd been doing to keep it going. But there was so much blood on Drew's chest! Her hand clenched on Judd's shoulder. He reached up to touch her fingers for a second, staining them dark red. "His heart is beating on its own. He's breathing."

Disbelieving, she came close enough to touch Drew's neck. His pulse beat strong and powerful. Shaking, she pulled out and used the edge of her own shirt to wipe away the blood. "Please." Please let him be safe.

Riley was the first to see it. "It's gone."

Then she saw it with her own eyes. The wound had ceased to exist. Under the blood, Drew's skin was pink and tender but it was unbroken. She turned to the man by her side. "Judd, oh, my God."

He didn't seem to be able to focus on her. His eyes had gone black at the start then slid back to normal near the end. Now, they were close to dazed. Worried, she pulled back from Drew. "Baby, what's wrong?" Putting her hands on his cheeks before she realized she had blood on them, she leaned close. "Judd, speak to me."

"Flameout." A single word and then his eyes went pure black again, the whites disappearing as before. Except this darkness held tinges of bloodred. It terrified her. She expected him to fall unconscious but he shook his head. "One hour."

"One hour." She remembered his disappearance after he'd teleported her during the hyena situation and made the connection. He had to be in a safe place within the hour. "Okay, okay."

Andrew coughed at that second and she switched her attention back to him, aware of Judd doing the same. After a few more coughs, her brother's lashes lifted to display familiar blue eyes. "What the hell happened?"

Sobbing, she kissed his cheek. He struggled to raise his arms to hold her but didn't seem to have the strength. "Hey, sweetheart. Come on."

"You lost a lot of blood." Judd's voice. "Full recovery will take time."

She broke away from Drew to hug Judd. "Hold on," she whispered in his ear, knowing he wouldn't want to display weakness in front of the others. "Can you walk?"

A small nod, but she didn't really believe him, not with the way his face was losing color. This was worse than at the cabin. She got to her feet. "Let's get them both inside."

Her comment snapped everyone to attention. Within seconds, Drew was loaded onto a stretcher someone had had the foresight to fetch, and Riley and Tai were carrying him off to the den. Lara hovered anxiously at his side. Dismissing the other men, Hawke went down on his haunches, threw Judd's arm around his shoulders, and dragged him upright.

"To my room," Brenna directed.

Hawke didn't argue and not much later, Judd was in the bedroom. He supported himself, one hand on the wall. "No assistance."

Hawke looked to Brenna. "Is he serious? I'll have Lara in here as soon as she checks Drew out."

"No," Judd said again.

She wanted him in bed. "He's still conscious and able to make a decision," she said to Hawke. "Let him recover in peace and he'll be fine." If not, she would get the medics herself.

Hawke scowled. "If you need anything, holler." He glanced at Judd. "What you did today—I've never seen anything like that. I didn't think it was possible. Get some rest and then we'll talk." He left.

Brenna was the only one who heard Judd's reply. "According to my trainers, it isn't." He swayed on his feet.

She rushed to hold him up. "In bed. Now."

"I need to shower."

About to say absolutely not, she realized he was covered in sweat and blood. It would hardly make for a restful sleep. Helping him into the cubicle, she began to tug at his clothes. He stopped her with a hand on her wrist. "No."

She was ready to push him off when she saw the look on his face. Pure male pride. "Fine." She sighed. "But if I don't hear from you in five minutes, I'm coming in."

Walking out, she kept every one of her senses on high alert as she turned down the bed and whipped up a high-energy drink from a mix Drew often used. The shower turned off after exactly four minutes.

By the time she got back into the bedroom, Judd was asleep. Putting down the drink, she brushed damp hair off his forehead, the tenderness in her heart overwhelming. "God, I love you." She kissed his temple and for a second it felt like something in him responded. But he was out cold.

Shaking her head, she got up and began to pick up the clothes he'd left crumpled on the floor in what struck her as a very uncharacteristic bit of messiness.

Ironically, Drew was up and around before Judd. He came knocking twelve hours later, just after she'd finished breakfast—a bit of a misnomer, as she hadn't actually slept, too worried about Judd. He was in such a deep sleep, she kept checking to see if he was breathing. "How are you feeling?"

"Fantastic for a guy who apparently had half his chest blown off."

She was careful when she hugged him, aware the repaired wound had to hurt. "Drew, you stood in front of that bullet for me." It had happened so fast she still couldn't sort out the sequence in her head.

He laughed. "I meant to push you in front of it. Damn."

"Idiot." Sniffling, she broke the hug. "I love you."

"That's what baby sisters are for." He opened his fist to reveal the bullet she'd picked off his chest. "Do you know the name of this little piece of evil?"

Her gut roiled at the sight of that twisted piece of metal. "No."

"ShrapnelX. Illegal as hell." His expression was pure fury. "It's meant to spread into five sharp points on impact and claw its way through anything it touches." He put it into a pocket. "Which makes me a walking miracle. I'm told it's thanks to your boyfriend."

"So he's my boyfriend now?" A very important concession.

He scowled. "Don't rub it in. Lara says I'm missing some flesh from lower down in my chest and that's just what we can see—it's like he moved bits to fill in the gaps."

"He did." She'd seen it happen in front of her eyes. "Will you be lopsided?" She was trying very hard not to cry. A world without Drew to fight with was unimaginable.

He hugged her anyway. "Nah. It'll fill back out." A pause. "Probably." His arms tightened. "So, where is he?"

"Sleeping," she said against his chest. "And no, I'm not waking him—he's exhausted. I'm so glad you're okay."

He crushed her to him. "Hell, I'm not going anywhere. Need to stick around to make sure he treats you right."

"He will." She smiled and leaned back enough that she could look up at him. "Don't judge him by his Ice Man persona. He's different."

"No, he's not, sweetheart," Andrew said. "I think Judd's the same as any wolf in the den—he simply hides his animal better."

Coming from a changeling, being called an animal was the highest of compliments.

CHAPTER 33

Judd woke to the realization of a warm female body curved into his, her back to his chest. He hadn't put on anything before crashing and Brenna was only wearing what felt like a thin slip that had pushed up during sleep to bare her legs all the way to the top. One of his arms was being used as a pillow, while the hand of his other lay on the smoothness of her upper thigh. Their legs were tangled, one of his pushed between hers.

Skin-to-skin contact all over. But not so much as a hint of dissonance.

He checked his shields and found them secure. His power reserves were another matter altogether. He was tapped out. When he glanced at the time laser-projected onto the facing wall, the color a deep green, he realized why. Despite the darkness, it was just after noon—Brenna had likely turned off the simulated daylight. He'd slept for seventeen hours at most and his psychic abilities needed close to twenty-four to regenerate. However, physically, he felt fine. It didn't make sense, but he wasn't complaining.

Feeling very alive and very male, he moved his hand over

Brenna's thigh. She murmured and heat spiked in his gut. He waited for the pain response to kick in and punish him for breaking conditioning. It never came. His hand clenched on her.

"Judd." A sleepy complaint.

He gentled his touch. "Sorry." Kissing the curve of her neck, he waited for the pain again. Nothing. "It's tied to my abilities." Of course. That was why the dissonance had been so extreme, why he'd started to bleed. *Because that was how his Tk worked—by applying pressure.*

"What is?" She sounded half-asleep.

"The dissonance." They'd used his own abilities to punish him. It made perfect sense—linking his abilities negatively with emotion reinforced the need to repudiate that emotion, which, in turn, kept his telekinesis from getting out of control.

But now he was wiped out, which meant that while the dissonance controls still *existed,* there was nothing for them to draw power from. More importantly, until his abilities regenerated, he was no danger to Brenna. He could touch her, taste her, love her. He was hard before the thought ended.

Moving his hand up her thigh, he felt the lace edge of her panties, so delicate under his fingers, but not as delicate as her skin. Sliding a finger under that edge, he ran it down to brush her curls.

"Judd!" A gasp to full wakefulness. "What are you doing?"

"Touching you."

Her head shifted on his arm. "Oh." A whisper. "Doesn't it hurt you?"

"No." Spreading his fingers, he cupped her as he had once before.

She squeaked out a cry. "Baby, you heard of foreplay?"

He might even have smiled had he known how to do it. "I'm just getting started." The heat of her burned his skin. "I've had a really long time to plan."

"P-plan?" She coughed as if to clear her throat. "What do you mean—plan?"

He pulled his hand out of her panties to run his finger along the waistband, pushing up his thigh at the same time to rub more intimately against her. His erection throbbed at the proximity. "I thought I should be prepared if the opportunity to touch you without danger ever came to pass."

Her stomach muscles contracted under his palm. "Is it a detailed plan?"

"Very." He breathed in the scent at the curve of her neck, then kissed.

She shuddered and tried to turn but he only allowed her halfway, keeping their lower bodies intertwined. Then he braced himself on one elbow and simply looked at her. This close, the darkness was no barrier to his visual mapping of her features. Her eyes glowed a little, especially the flare of blue around the pupils.

It fascinated him. "Beautiful."

She reached up to tangle her hand in his hair. "Let me turn properly."

He pushed his thigh higher, pressing into the damp heat of her. Her gasp was both startled and inviting. He moved his thigh back and forth a couple of times. Her eyes fluttered shut. "Tease." It was a husky accusation.

"On the contrary. I intend to deliver." He tugged her hand from his hair and nudged her back into her previous position, spooning his body around her.

She made a displeased sound. "I can't touch you this way."

"I know." They called him the Man of Ice, but where Brenna was concerned, he was anything but. If she stroked him, he wouldn't be able to complete even a tenth of his plan. And for a man who'd been hungry as long as he had, a quick bite held no appeal. He wanted to linger, to gorge, to indulge. With that thought in mind, he ran his hand back under her slip and over the warm silk of her skin. "Is your skin this soft all over?"

Her heart thudded under his touch as he went higher. "Some places are even softer."

"Now who's the tease?" He ran his thumb along the underside of one breast.

Her hand clenched on his forearm. Kissing the side of her neck once more, he repeated the stroking caress but went higher. Again. Higher. He could feel her holding her breath as he lingered just below her nipple.

"Judd, please."

He flicked his finger across the tightly furled bud. She cried out and asked for more. He didn't give it to her. Instead he retreated to draw a slow circle low on her navel.

"I'm going to kill you."

He chuckled and it was a sound he'd never before heard come from his own throat. "Patience is a virtue."

She seemed about to reply but then he began retracing his prior journey, his goal her neglected breast. She went quiet.

Anticipation lingered in the air and he was so sensitive to its touch he could almost taste it. Her skin flushed with heat, her breathing jagged. And when he touched her breast, the rhythm of her heart turned into a staccato drumbeat. This time, he didn't flick her nipple but closed his hand over the firm, hot rise of her flesh. "Your breasts make me want to bite."

She arched into his hold, her hand squeezing his arm. "Do it." A dare. An invitation.

"Not yet." That would accelerate something he was determined to draw out forever. "I want to savor my first bite."

Her claws nicked his skin. "No more playing."

He bit her neck in response, making her tremble and withdraw her claws. "So impatient." Not giving her any warning, he slipped his hand down and under the waistband of her panties again. Spearing through her curls, he pressed his thumb on her clitoris at the same time as he used his fingers to tease the damp entrance to her body.

She gave a startled cry and then her body went taut. Liquid heat covered his fingers, scenting the air with a sharp wildness. He continued to stroke her as she shuddered several times before her body went soft and sated. Even then he didn't stop, indulging his need to pet her with long, easy movements as she lay quiescent.

When she finally attempted to turn, he withdrew his thigh and let her, but kept his fingers where they were. She nuzzled at his throat, ran her fingers over his chest. It was no longer an odd feeling for him to be touched by her, but the sexual context changed the tone of the caresses, gave them a different weight. He liked the result.

"Where did you learn all this?" she murmured. "You're a virgin."

He almost halted. "I suppose you're right, technically speaking." Sex had effectively been wiped out by Silence. Oh, his race had continued practicing it for the sake of procreation—until technology had made that unnecessary—but it had become a mechanical, passionless act. In the present time, normal Psy considered sex an impractical and worthless "animal" exercise. His brethren didn't value the beauty of bonding with another being on such an intimate level.

Brenna was kissing a line across his chest. "Technically speaking?"

"I'm very good at research—some might say I was obsessed with this particular topic." He slid his fingers up and out to rest his hand on her abdomen once again.

She ran her teeth over his skin. "Exactly what kind of research did you do?"

"An Arrow never divulges his sources." Using the hand under her head to tangle in her hair, he kept her in place as he claimed a deep kiss. She responded with pleasure but below that was a strange tension that he knew she probably wasn't aware of.

Scars from the abduction.

They'd take time to heal. He didn't allow himself to think ahead to the moment when he'd enter her body. That would be the most difficult part, connected so profoundly were the sensations with the nightmare. "Do you want to be on top?" he asked against her mouth, recalling her lack of fear when she'd straddled him in the armchair.

"Will that interfere with your master plan?" She smiled and he felt rather than saw it. Her hand began to slide south.

He pushed it back up. "There is a degree of flexibility built into the plan. But you don't get to touch me yet."

A sensual feminine laugh. "I'm okay, baby." Her hands

gripped the sides of his waist. "I'll let you know when I need something other than what you're doing."

So she *was* aware of her anxiety, unsurprising really, given her will. "Don't scratch too hard."

Another laugh. "I'm not the dangerous one in this bed. You're driving me crazy, you know that."

"Good. My research tells me that that is my job as your lover. I hear predatory changeling women are tough critics."

"Believe me, you have nothing to worry about." She licked at the skin of his neck.

Breaking the contact, he fit his body over hers, alert to her reaction. She didn't withdraw, so he braced himself on one arm and brought the hand of the other up to close over her satin-covered breast. She sucked in a breath. And when he nudged at her with the painful hardness of his erection, she didn't hesitate to wrap her legs around him. "Kiss?"

He fulfilled her request, already addicted to the taste of her. His male instincts bucked at the reins, wanting to go quicker, deeper, but he held fast, helped by the very skills that usually kept him coldly distant. As they kissed, he massaged her breast, testing what made her moan, what made her wriggle. Brenna, he discovered, liked it when he was firm in his touch. Soft caresses just made her complain with feminine impatience.

He was very, very glad for his lover's preference. He knew he could do gentle—he had the control for it—but tonight he wanted to love her with everything in him. "Off," he ordered, pushing up her slip. The plan had called for this to come later, but he hadn't factored in the seduction of this particular woman so lush and welcoming beneath him.

She raised her arms and he pushed the material over her breasts with every intention of pulling it over her head . . . but found himself unable to move any farther. The mounds of her breasts thrust upward in pure temptation, the nipples hard and tight. He wanted to see them properly. Not thinking, he tried to use Tk to flick on a lamp but, of course, nothing happened.

Reaching across, he manually turned on the small light integrated into the headboard. It emitted a warm, almost hazy, glow. Brenna gasped but didn't say anything, letting him devour her with his eyes. Her nipples were a dark strawberry color, the upper curves of her breasts creamy . . . but for a scatter of freckles that taunted his analytical Psy mind with their wild abandon.

"Judd?"

The thick desire in her voice was the last straw. Dipping his head, he sucked one tight bud into his mouth. Her hands gripped his hair as her body twisted under him as if to escape. But when he released the nipple to switch his focus to the other, she protested.

The sensations inside him were pure chaos. Fire and need and erotic heat. But blending into that dark male passion was something gentler, an emotion that didn't dull the jagged edges of his hunger but which made him aware of Brenna's reactions on an almost subconscious level. *Tenderness*. It was a strange feeling. So raw, so powerful, and yet it engendered the most intense care.

He let her nipple slide out of his mouth. She pulled him back, but he was more interested in running his gaze over the sheen of wetness on her breasts, wetness he had caused. A surge of possessiveness gripped him by the throat. Yes, she was most definitely his. Spurred to see more of her exotic female body, so unashamedly curvy, so different from his, he dragged the bunched-up slip up over her head and threw it aside.

"Keep them there," he ordered when she would've lowered her raised arms.

She curled her fingers around the bars in the headboard, her eyes watching him with unconcealed interest. The position left her entire upper body exposed to his gaze and he took blatant advantage. Leaning in, he blew a breath across her nipples. Her body rose and fell in a sweet, soft wave and she held on tighter to the thin metal rods.

"It's time for my bite," he warned.

"Oh, God."

The desire in that groan made his erection pound in time with his heartbeat. "Which side should I start on?"

Swallowing, she licked her lower lip. "Your choice."

He cupped her left breast, shaped, stroked. And then he did what he'd threatened—he closed his teeth over one luscious side and pressed just hard enough to have her bucking under him. A long taste later, he did the same to her other breast. "Mmm," he murmured, raising his head. "I think I'll have seconds." And he did.

Her chest fell up and down in ragged bursts. "Baby, are all your plans so detailed and slow?"

"Why?" He nipped at the underside of one breast.

She shivered. "Because I think you might give me a pleasure-induced stroke at the rate you're going."

Running his hands along her rib cage and to the dip of her waist, he kissed his way down the valley of her breasts and over her stomach. "Sometimes," he said, "I'll probably just pick you up, thrust you against a wall, and drive into you so hard, you'll scream." He used two fingers to pinch her clitoris in a firm grip as the last word left his mouth.

She exploded, her body arching so fiercely she lifted off the bed. Releasing the pearl of flesh that could cause such exquisite pleasure, he rose to kiss her neck as she shook with the aftereffects of her orgasm.

A feminine hand clenched in his hair. "You did that on purpose." Husky, pleasured.

"What?" He began tracing a return path down her body.

"The image of you driving into me and then the touch." She didn't stop him when he began to lay kisses along the waistband of her panties. "Your way of proving the mind-body connection."

He looked up with an internal scowl that he was sure had made it to his face. "You're supposed to be too sated to think." Or worry.

She chuckled. "My gorgeous, sexy Judd, at this point my brains are pure mush." She reached down to push sweat-damp strands of hair off his forehead. "But I know tenderness when I feel it."

He moved and his shadowed jaw brushed over her skin. She made a feminine sound of pleasure. "I don't think it's possible to come three times in one session."

Shifting further down, he rubbed his cheek along her thigh. "I love a challenge."

"And I love what you said about pounding me into a wall until I scream." A sensual confession. "When are you going to follow through?"

His erection seemed to get impossibly bigger, the blood vessels expanding to stretch his skin to bursting point. "Stop talking."

"Why?"

"You're derailing the plan."

She put one leg over his shoulder as he lay cradled so close to the core of her. "I think it's my turn anyway. I wanna touch."

He bit at the inside of that shapely thigh. "No."

She flinched but it wasn't the bad kind. "No fair." Her foot rubbed at his back.

He realized he'd have to move to get rid of her panties. "Are you particularly attached to these?" He fingered the lace around the crease where her thigh curved against the most intimate part of her.

"Wh-what?" Her hands dropped from his head to dig into the sheets.

He filed away her responsiveness when touched in that particular area. "I'll take that as a no." Gripping hold of the front, he tore the fragile fabric off her body. The scraps fell away like mist.

She made a shocked sound, then went completely still, as if conscious of how open she'd become to him. Sliding a hand up the inside of her thigh, he looked up, glad for the light that let him see the emotion flickering over her face. "Can I bite you here, too?"

CHAPTER 34

Her eyes went huge but it seemed to take her a few seconds to get the words out. "How"—she swallowed—"how do you know you'll even like the taste?"

His changeling was playing with him. And tonight, he could play back. "Good point. Let me do a taste test." Holding her gaze, he stroked a finger through her liquid heat, barely entering her body before withdrawing. Then he lifted that finger and sucked it into his mouth, aware of Brenna's body flushing around him.

When he withdrew the finger, she said, "So?" A very sexual question.

He answered by dipping his head and using his mouth on her. Her cry was husky, arousing. The heel of her foot pressed hard into his back as she twisted. When her other leg came up over his shoulder, he spread her open with the fingers of one hand and continued to taste. Taste as only a man who'd been starved could taste. With everything in him, with absolute concentration and utter focus.

* * *

Brenna was trying to breathe, but it wasn't working very well, her air coming in broken pants. Judd was—oh, Lord, he was destroying her with pleasure. For a man who had never done this before, he was blindingly good. It made her very curious as to just what kind of research he'd been doing.

He nipped at her with his teeth.

She whimpered and ordered herself to find some shred of control at the same time. Otherwise Judd's arrogance would become impossible. Except that he was doing the most exquisite things to her with that clever mouth and control seemed a foreign concept.

His finger touched her entrance, circled, teased. But he didn't push in. Then he did it again. And again. And again. By the time he did begin to slide that teasing finger inside of her, she was so crazy with anticipation that the spike of fear her mind associated with an invasion of her body was buried under an avalanche of sensation.

"You're too tight," he said, sounding completely and deliciously dominant.

She squeezed her inner muscles around his finger in retaliation. "Tight," she managed to say, "is considered good."

He began moving that finger in and out. "Not when you're so tight, I might cause you pain."

It was getting impossible to have a coherent thought but she tried. "Judd, baby, do it before I lose what's left of my mind." She'd felt the rigid length of him against her, knew how much he wanted her. All that hot, hard flesh . . . "I want you inside me."

"You need a little more foreplay."

"I take it back!" she cried. "Foreplay sucks!" Why had she not realized that Judd's icy control, when melted, would translate into endless patience in bed?

"I disagree." Then he was kissing her again, tasting her most intimate flesh as if it were a delicacy he'd waited a lifetime to savor. The dark red of desire washed across her mind and when she surrendered, it was to the depths of her being.

* * *

Judd felt Brenna's surrender within his mind, as if he were reading her innermost thoughts with some heretofore unknown sense. Raising his head, he pushed out of her hold, kissed his way up her body, and braced himself with one arm on the bed, the hand of his other still between her thighs.

When he kissed her, she threw her arms around his neck and gave him everything he asked for. And when he went to push a second finger into her, she didn't protest, only breaking the kiss on a gasp and moving one hand to clench on his biceps. He spoke with his lips against hers. "Brenna?"

Her eyes fluttered open, bright and extraordinarily beautiful. "Come inside me now. I need you."

The simple request shot his plan to hell. "I'm afraid of hurting you." Not physically but mentally, psychically.

She pushed at his shoulders. "I want to switch."

Understanding, he withdrew his fingers on her moan and moved off her onto his back. Ceding control was difficult for him but he trusted Brenna on a level he'd never before trusted anyone. When she sat up to straddle him, he was stunned speechless at the proud female beauty of her. He luxuriated in the feeling, conscious that he'd have to retreat as soon as his power regenerated.

Reaching down, she closed slender fingers around the painful length of his erection. He gritted his teeth and fisted his hands around the bars in the headboard but didn't take his eyes off her. The play of emotions over her face was pure seduction. Pleasure, surprise, hunger.

"You're right," she whispered, examining his engorged flesh with those bright eyes. "I'm going to feel every inch of you going in." She shifted to put her body in the right spot, then used her hand to guide the tip of him into her before letting go.

He stopped breathing for a few seconds as the pleasure traveled from the apex of his erection down the length of his body. Until that moment, he'd never realized the mind-blowing sensitivity of that bundle of nerves—how could his people have given up this incredible rush of sensation? When he opened eyes he hadn't been aware of closing, he found Brenna on her knees above him, her head tipped back.

"Look at me."

She obeyed with a shudder that vibrated through him, reaching out her hands at the same time. He raised his own and clasped them to hers. Pushing against his hold, she began to lower her body, accepting him centimeter by slow centimeter. Their eyes never broke contact and the intimacy was so intense, Judd knew that had the dissonance been functioning, it would have killed him.

She stopped suddenly, chest heaving. "You're stretching me so tight, I can't bear it." Then she groaned and moved again. "Sweet mercy."

He was close to begging for mercy himself, burned by the scalding heat of her, thrown into a sensory inferno more acute than anything he had ever before felt. His hands tightened on hers, but she didn't complain. Instead, taking a deep breath, she squeezed her fingers around his and bore down on his erection, taking him inside to the hilt.

Pure sexual pleasure/pain.

His back bowed as he fought to remain conscious under the overload. For an Arrow trained to resist sensation at all costs, feeling this much was akin to being thrown into the most dangerous of flames.

It was Brenna's touch that brought him back from the edge—she surrounded him, a seductive mix of grace, female demand, and hunger. Opening his eyes, he found her sitting stock still. "What's wrong?" His voice was scraped raw, as if he'd been screaming.

"I'm getting used to you." Her eyes came closer as she leaned in, stretching out his arms until his hands lay beside his head. "You"—she brushed her lips over his—"fill me up."

He groaned, straining not to rise up and take command. That she'd accepted the intrusion of his body was more than enough. This time. Because he was very definitely repeating this, no matter what he had to do to cause another flameout.

Brenna kissed him again and this time it was wild and furious and wet. "Move in me," she whispered. Releasing his hands, she placed her own, palms down, on his chest.

He was incapable of speech so he just put his hands on her

hips and began lifting and lowering her in rhythm with the movements of his own body. All his research had disappeared from his brain—what guided him was age-old instinct and an unrelenting tenderness toward his lover.

At first he kept it slow, letting her become accustomed to him as he drowned in the maddening ecstasy of her touch. Then she began to urge a faster rhythm and he responded by slamming into her, raising his body as she lowered hers. Crying out, she dug her fingers into his chest and rode him, wild and uninhibited.

When she made a frustrated sound, he caught her and flipped her to her back. She didn't protest, twining her legs around his waist. Reaching down, he rubbed at the hard bud of her clitoris as he took over the driving rhythm, pounding them both into a pleasure that seemed impossible. Somewhere along the way, he lost the ability to think.

Brenna's legs were jelly. "I don't think I can move," she mumbled into Judd's neck, where her face was currently buried.

His response was a grunt. His hand stroked her bottom once before falling away—as if he didn't have the energy to do more.

She ran her fingers over his chest, nuzzled at his pulse, and took the scent of him into her lungs. She already smelled of him, but from today, the scent would be inside her very pores. It made her feel possessed, protected, adored. It was good to belong to him, even if he did have a tendency toward dominance.

"Once more."

She was sure she was having an aural hallucination. "You did not just say 'once more.' "

"Before the Tk comes back."

She shook her head. "You're crazy." After that loving, he'd be lucky if she moved anytime this century. "Good thing I like crazy."

"One hour. Nap. Then again."

Despite her exhaustion, she found the femaleness in her reacting to the determination in his tone. "You are so sexy."

"I know."

It made her smile. "Yeah?"

"This beautiful changeling keeps telling me." His hand closed over the back of her nape. "Now sleep."

She did. Exactly one hour later, she woke to the touch of male fingers and lips, her body relaxing in the most sensual way. They danced more languidly this time, and Judd let her cuddle and pet him as much as she wanted.

His muscles were hard and warm under her fingertips, his skin holding the flavor of salt and man. It made her deeply happy to be so intimately connected to him. "I want to do this every day for the rest of my life."

His eyes were sparks of gold in the darkness. "Yes."

But he had to leave her when the Tk regenerated. "Brenna—"

"Shh." She shook her head, aching to cross the divide between them. "I'll see you tomorrow morning." It was obvious he didn't want to go. Equally obvious to her heightened knowledge of him was the pain—the dissonance—he refused to betray. "Tomorrow morning, baby."

He finally left after several more minutes of persuasion on her part. Only then did she lie back against the pillow and let the tears come. Was this all they'd ever have—stolen moments when Judd was stripped of a crucial part of his psyche? It seemed so hopeless. She might've cried into the night, but exhaustion took her under after a few minutes, and when she woke, hope reawakened with her.

"I made love to Judd Lauren," she whispered, amazed. Even a month ago, that would have seemed a fool's dream. "Then I guess I'm a fool." Smiling, she pushed off the bed, showered, and grabbed a bite to eat. Afterward, knowing it wouldn't do any good for Judd to be trapped in the confines of an apartment stamped with the psychic echoes of their loving, she headed toward one of the specialized tech chambers to do some work.

Judd found her halfway to her destination. "Don't you need to be at DarkRiver?"

No words of romance, but his eyes held such dark fire that even as her body thrilled to life, she worried. "Judd, you have to pull back or the dissonance will punish you."

"Never thought I'd hear you say that." The intensity of his gaze didn't change.

Shaking her head at his stubbornness, she answered his question. "I've done most of my bit in terms of programming—Dorian will give me a call if he needs anything."

Her words cut through the sensual resonance still vibrating through Judd's whole body, reminding him of something very important. "Why did you leave DarkRiver yesterday? Who called?"

Brenna paled. "It was an ambush. That bastard could've killed Drew! It was only because Riley gave chase and scared him off that he didn't keep shooting."

He wanted to hold her, but couldn't chance bodily contact, not with the memory of their intimacy so fresh. His hand fisted. "Do you know the identity of the caller?"

"The message was passed on by DarkRiver's main receptionist." She thrust a hand through her hair. "It came in through their general line. We should have known something was wrong, but we weren't thinking because the message said that there had been a Psy attack on the pups and several were dead."

"Riley didn't call back to confirm?" It was standard operating procedure in most tactical and military units.

She winced. "I think he was too angry . . . and the shooter counted on that."

Emotion as a weakness—it was what he'd always been taught. "Considering the import of the message, why didn't the cats know?" Clay, as a sentinel, would certainly have been informed by the receptionist.

"The message was in the code Pack soldiers use," she revealed. "It said that this time there was incontrovertible proof of DarkRiver being involved. God, we were stupid!"

"Not necessarily. If it was in code, then Riley was correct

to assume it came from a legitimate source. Even if he had called back, the shooter may have been prepared to intercept."

Smart. But in his cleverness, Timothy's killer might have made a fatal mistake. "How many people know that code?"

"I have no idea."

"I'll ask Riley. Can you trace the call itself?"

"I'll see if Dorian can hook into DarkRiver's comm system, but if the shooter used one of the public phones in the den . . ." She shrugged. "How can we have bred such evil? I can't imagine it, and yet it's true." She sounded angry and sad at the same time. "Here's my stop—I'll probably be inside the chamber for hours. See you for dinner?"

He knew she was deliberately putting distance between them, too perceptive not to understand the devastating impact it had had on him to experience the fury of their intimacy after feeling nothing for most of his life. "Yes. How secure is this room?"

She showed him the security system. "All sorts of tech work goes on in these rooms so they're close to impregnable, more to protect the public than us, but once I go in and lock the door, no one can override the lock. Don't worry—I have no intention of making this easy for that piece of scum."

Satisfied, he left to find Riley. "How many men and women know that code?" he asked the lieutenant.

"About a hundred." Riley's voice was a growl. "Forty of them were on scheduled watches in other areas at the time of the shooting. That gives me sixty to work through."

It was still a large number. "We need to detail their movements over the period of the attack."

"Yeah, except most of the soldiers are single and wolf-independent. It's going to take time and this psycho's starting to lose it—using that code was stupidity on his part." Riley didn't have to add that stupid or not, the killer was hunting Brenna in earnest now.

Judd continued to have the feeling he was missing something, but no matter how long he thought about it, he couldn't fathom an answer. "Do you want my assistance?"

Riley paused. "No. I can't justify you trying to break open

loyal men's and women's minds over one bastard." But he looked as though he wanted to consent. "You keep Bren safe and I'll track him down."

Judd had no intention of following that order—not when their quarry was a threat to Brenna—but he simply nodded. Leaving Riley, he made another call. "I can't come down today," he told Sascha. "I apologize."

"Don't worry—I was thinking of suggesting that anyway," she said, to his surprise. "We did so much yesterday—the deer need time to recover. This kind of healing is slow going."

Hanging up after discussing when she might need him again, Judd returned to his room. Though the hunt for the killer occupied a considerable portion of his brain—as he purposefully approached the problem from a different angle from Riley so as not to duplicate their efforts—there was something else he had to think about.

Reaching up, he began using the exercise bar to do chin-ups. The repetitive act helped focus his mind as it multitasked. One thing was certain—he refused to never again experience the intimacy of being with Brenna. It wasn't the sex, though that had been the most amazing experience of his life. It was the way he'd made her laugh, made her smile, made her complain and then cuddle. All because she'd felt safe, reassured by the strength of their emotional connection.

He would not steal that feeling from her. And he most definitely was not going to surrender her to another male who could give her what she needed. The idea made him want to break something. However, regardless of what he'd considered in the heat of passion, he couldn't keep forcing flameouts in order to protect her from his Tk-Cell. Which left him with a choice and a question he'd rejected earlier—how to disable the Silence Protocol, in particular the dissonance, without unleashing the killing rage of his gift.

His phone beeped. Dropping down from the bar, he picked it up. "Judd."

"It's Hawke. Can you meet me by the waterfall?"

He realized the alpha probably wanted to ask him about the deprogramming he'd done with the PineWood hyenas. "I'm on my way." The walk to the exit brought him into contact with several changelings. That wasn't unusual. What was unusual was the response his presence elicited. Smiles, waves, shouted hellos and even slaps on the back when he didn't move away fast enough.

He'd almost reached his goal when Indigo stopped him. "I've got something you'll want to hear."

CHAPTER 35

She drew him into the shadow of a nearby alcove. "One of Tim's friends got back from out of town today and found a message on his home comm—left the night Tim died. Tim said he had some info he wanted to pass on to Hawke through a trusted source. Confirms he was about to rat the dealer out."

It wasn't much, but it was another piece of data to feed into the continuously running psychic program in Judd's head. "Did you manage to track down any other confirmed users?"

"Yeah," she said. "But they know shit—this guy is smart, never showed them his face. Coward. If not for you, we'd be mourning Drew today. I'm going to enjoy ripping out the killer's throat when we find him." A grim smile later, she was gone.

Judd appreciated Indigo keeping him updated, but he wondered at her motives. Notwithstanding anything he'd done, he remained outside the SnowDancer hierarchy and the wolves trusted no one who wasn't their own. But there wasn't any room in his head for that unimportant issue right now.

Exiting the den, he made his way through the icy cold of the piercing winter's day to the frozen edge of the waterfall.

Hawke was already standing there, arms folded. At his feet sat two wolves. From their size and attitude, Judd could tell they weren't changelings. It wasn't the first time he'd seen the SnowDancer alpha surrounded by the wild wolves who roamed some of the same range as the changelings. He'd even heard it rumored that the creatures considered Hawke their alpha, too—something more likely to be true than not. Hawke was so close to his animal that at times, it wasn't clear who or *what* was looking out of those pale eyes.

The wolves watched Judd approach, but didn't make any aggressive sounds or movements. "You're late," Hawke said.

"I was delayed by a number of the pack."

Hawke nodded. "After what you did for Drew, I think they want to throw a damn parade in your honor."

"I hope you put a stop to that idea."

"I don't know—maybe it would finally put your niece into a good mood."

So that was what this meeting was about. "What's Sienna done now?"

His late sister's seventeen-year-old was walking a very thin line. She'd been almost fully conditioned when they'd defected, which had left her in a difficult position, even more so because of the problems that came with age in relation to her abilities. But overshadowing that was the fact that she seemed to have made it her new purpose in life to annoy Hawke in as many and as varied ways as possible.

"She's convinced some of the juveniles she can read their thoughts and that I'm paying her to do exactly that." Hawke was scowling, but there was amusement in his eyes. "I've got confessions coming out my ears."

"I'll talk to her." Walker had taken charge of the two younger kids—his daughter, Marlee, of course, and their nephew, Toby. It had been natural for Judd to do the same with Sienna—he could help her in ways Walker couldn't. Of course, his niece didn't think she needed an adult keeper.

Hawke waved a hand. "Don't worry about it. I'll deal with her."

In the first few months following their defection, Judd

would've nixed that idea. But after having witnessed the way Hawke handled the wolf juveniles, he knew that while Sienna might get her hide stripped on the sharp edge of his tongue, she wouldn't come to any real harm. "Then why did you ask to meet?"

"You." A harsh response that made the wolves growl. "You're a problem."

"So much for the parade." He paused. "Does the pack know the details of what I did?"

Hawke shook his head in an immediate negative. "They think you somehow deflected the bullet. We've been helping that rumor along."

"Good." That meant his newfound skill remained a tactical advantage. "Then what's the problem?" If the alpha tried to separate him from Brenna, he'd have a fight on his hands. A bloody one.

"You're causing havoc in the pack. What's your fight count to date?"

"Do you want the exact number?" Judd had been facing off challengers since the day he walked into the den.

Hawke snorted. "I know the number. I also know you've won every single one of those fights." He went down on his haunches to pet the wolves. They growled and butted their heads against his touch before loping off into the woods. Hawke stood back up. "Which leaves me with a powerful male in my pack who stands outside the pack structure."

He recalled Indigo's recent behavior as well as certain other acts. "Some of your people have already begun treating me as if I have status."

"Yeah. They figure they'll just wear you down."

"Wear me down to what?"

"Joining the pack fully or getting the hell out." A blunt choice. "I can't have a strong lone wolf in my territory."

"You want to give me an official rank." Everyone in the pack had one. Status could be changed in one of two ways—through a physical fight or by the utilization of a complex system of skill sets and respect he didn't completely understand. However, he'd been in SnowDancer long enough to guess at some of it—Lara's status was apparently the same as Indigo's, while the elderly librarian, Dalton, had Hawke's ear anytime he cared to speak.

"Yes."

"I had rank once." As an Arrow. One of the elite. "What I realized is that blind trust in any hierarchy is idiocy." He'd been nineteen when he'd understood how ruthlessly he'd been betrayed and used.

"We're not Psy." Hawke scowled. "Do you see Indigo or Riley bowing and scraping to me?"

That was also true—the predatory changelings held their leaders to tough standards. He'd seen a grim example of that in Parrish's execution. Not one of the hyena pack had asked for mercy for their leader. The ritual death had, in fact, been administered by the incoming alpha. Bloody justice but justice nonetheless.

It was a system of checks and balances that had been denied to the Psy populace for over a century. "Even if you make me a soldier, I'm unlikely to obey your every order."

"If I'd wanted mute obedience, I'd have found a pack of sheep." Hawke's response was almost a snarl. "You in or not?"

He would never walk away from Brenna. Or from his loyalty to his family. "Yes." He was prepared to accept a lower rank than he had held in the PsyNet, though it chafed. Pride. An emotional weakness, but he'd never claimed to be perfect. It was his race's goal of icy perfection that had stolen their humanity.

Hawke grinned. "You should've asked what rank you'd be assigned before you accepted. Too late now."

"I assumed low- to midlevel soldier." And Psy did not make baseless assumptions.

"I go through this whole song and dance telling you you're too fucking strong to be left to roam and you think I'm going to give you a rank that'll confuse the hell out of the pack?" Walking forward, the alpha slashed out with his claws, the move so fast that Judd didn't have time to react. It would've been logical to blast out with Tk power, but his martially trained mind processed Hawke's body language and came to the conclusion that he wasn't under attack. Reaching up, he felt four thin lines on his neck. Surface cuts but enough to color his fingers.

Hawke slashed his own palm and let it drip to the snow. Acting on instinct, Judd spread his bloody hand and caught a drop of Hawke's blood. It burned hot, as if it carried fire. Something snapped tight inside of him, but when he looked into the psychic plane of the LaurenNet, he found no new connection.

The burning sensation lingered even after he dropped his hand. "What was that?"

"The completion of a blood bond." Hawke closed his hand into a fist, stemming the flow of blood. "You're now a SnowDancer lieutenant."

Judd looked down at the snow stained pink and then back to those pale eyes. "You despise the Psy." He didn't know the reason for that hatred, but he knew it existed.

"To hate you all without reason would make me a bigot." Hawke's mouth twisted. "And I prefer not to think of myself that way." There was something deeper in the alpha's voice, layers of emotion Judd couldn't read.

"Is it Sascha?" Hawke had a distinct liking for Lucas's mate.

A smile wiped the grim expression off his face. "She did kind of throw my opinions about Psy sideways, but—" He shook his head, as if halting himself before he said too much. "I trust those who've proven their loyalty. You've done that over and over—being warm and cuddly isn't a requirement. Welcome to the pack."

Judd went down to clean off the blood with snow, somehow knowing the result could not be so easily wiped out. Hawke was doing the same. The wolf's cut had already clotted. While Judd's healing was a result of his Tk-Cell abilities, Hawke's was thanks to changeling strength. Alpha changeling strength.

"So," Judd said, "what do lieutenants do?"

"A hell of a lot of work." Hawke's grin was a touch evil.

"Guess the holiday's over." The dissonance spiked in tune with his sense of belonging, his pride, and his thoughts of a woman with eyes of shattered blue.

Brenna gasped the second she opened the tech chamber door. "Hawke blooded you!" Giving an excited shriek, she jumped into his arms, legs wrapping around his waist.

He caught her reflexively. "Careful. My abilities have regenerated."

"I thought—" She shrugged. "I thought the time apart might have helped dampen the feelings from last night."

"You're right." He saw no need to mention that the dissonance was no longer strengthening at a steady pace—it was getting exponentially worse. At no time during the day had it halted altogether. Nonessential parts of his brain were already compromised.

She rubbed her nose against his in playful affection. "So you're a lieutenant now."

"Does that make a difference to you?" He was genuinely curious.

"Baby, I knew you were bossy the first day I saw you. This just confirms it." She nipped at his lower lip. "The only difference is that I'm happy for you. You and I were always going to be."

"Destiny?"

"You'd better believe it. So what are we going to do to make it happen?" Her expression shifted without warning and she dropped off him, breaking all contact. "Your eyes . . . the pain, it's worse than before, isn't it?"

"It—"

She held up a hand before he could tell her it didn't matter. "It's not nothing, not when I can see blood spots in the whites of your eyes." Her voice trembled for a second before she got it under control. "How bad?"

He couldn't lie to her. "At the current rate, it'll soon cause permanent damage to my brain." A hard, rough form of rehabilitation, apt to leave him a vegetable.

CHAPTER 36

In the darkest core of the PsyNet, the pure black walls of the Council chambers streamed with data, endless silver columns too fast for the eye to see but legible to the psychic mind.

"We've lost control of PineWood," Nikita said. "Parrish—the alpha—is dead, and someone's not only deprogrammed the rest of the pack, he or she has armed the hyenas' minds against further interference. Trained personnel may be able to break those blocks, but it will take considerable effort. It's not worth our time."

"Sascha?" Shoshanna asked.

"No." Nikita was certain of that. "She doesn't have the necessary skill set."

"Neither does Faith NightStar," Marshall pointed out.

"Which leaves us with an unknown." Kaleb, who'd been uncharacteristically quiet to that point. "If I'm not mistaken, programming and deprogramming skills are taught exclusively to certain branches of our armed forces."

"Correct." Ming's icy blaze. "It has to be one of the elite soldiers."

"Someone outside the Net?" Nikita knew full well that, contrary to what the masses believed, there were some Psy who were not hooked into the PsyNet. Not renegades like her daughter, but those who had never uplinked at all . . . because they had another option. The existence of the "Forgotten" was one of the Council's many dirty secrets.

"Not necessarily," Kaleb said. "I think it's becoming obvious we have a serious internal threat."

"The Ghost." Marshall's star went a cold, cold white.

"He has to be operating with an associate or associates," Nikita added. "One Psy can't be so skilled in both psychic and physical warfare. The lab explosions were very precise, involving a high degree of technical knowledge—wholly dissimilar to the expertise required to siphon data from secure PsyNet databases."

"Then there are the assassinations." Tatiana spoke up. "We've lost several top scientists."

"I'm checking my databases for possible renegades." Ming was silent for a minute. "Over the past ten years, we've lost one Arrow and seven soldiers with the requisite skills—in circumstances that made recovery of their bodies impossible."

"Who was the Arrow?" Tatiana again.

"Judd Lauren."

Nikita recalled the case. "I think we can safely cross him off the list. The entire Lauren family has been dead for over a year."

"Is that certain?" Marshall asked. "We never found bodies."

Nikita knew the wolves. "The SnowDancers don't leave bodies to find. I can't see them giving sanctuary to any Psy and particularly not a Psy of Judd Lauren's abilities. He would have been a clear threat—their rule is to kill first and ask questions of the corpses."

"Talking of the wolves," Shoshanna said, "Brenna Kincaid is still listed on the Tech Association database as an active Level 1, which means she's alive."

"Give it more time—they'll be killing each other soon enough." Tatiana's cool tone. "Ming, what about the other seven soldiers you lost?"

"I'll trace them," Ming said. "But I agree with Councilor Krychek—certain other recent events would seem to suggest an internal problem."

"What's happening with the chat room situation?" Tatiana asked.

Marshall highlighted a file from the scrolling streams of data. "Henry is in charge of that particular issue."

But it was Shoshanna who answered. "We've taken care of it. Those who were openly discussing incendiary matters have been counseled to cease and desist."

Nikita wondered if "counseled" was a euphemism for the mildest form of rehabilitation, which left most of the higher brain functions intact while deleting large sections of memory. She had to admit it was a good choice. They couldn't afford an unseemly number of disappearances after the recent rash of murders caused by anchors who'd escaped their handlers. "That leaves the ones operating below the radar."

"I have the NetMind searching," Kaleb said, referring to the unique sentience that lived in and made order out of the chaos of the PsyNet.

"That brings up another issue," Marshall said. "The NetMind has been getting very erratic of late. It's only recently reported back on possible signs of a serial killer who may have been operating undetected for years."

They had all noticed it. The NetMind's recordings were more fragmented than before, and there were gaps filled with dark spaces, a low buzz of background noise—almost an echo—that none of their best minds could filter out.

"This is a theory unbacked by any research," Kaleb said into the silence, "but I believe the NetMind may be passing through a period of adolescence. If so, that adolescence is likely to last decades, if not centuries. We have no concrete idea of its age or the speed at which it matures."

Shoshanna spoke on the heels of his pronouncement. "Given that the research of over a century has not yet managed to uncover the NetMind's inner workings, I would say it's safe to assume this issue will have no easy answer."

"I agree." Marshall. "We have to initiate other options to

find the identity of the second tier of discontents. Ming, do you have people we can use?"

"My forces are currently heavily involved in relocating the Implant Lab. Because of the sabotage risk, we're moving it to a hidden location in the cornfields of Nebraska."

"As I recall, wasn't Aleine resistant to the idea of a move?" Nikita had met the head researcher. The woman had a will comparable to any Councilor's.

"That issue has been resolved."

Nikita wondered what leverage Ming had used—it had to have been very persuasive. "But if that's the case, why not move her to a location out of the United States?" Some of the eastern European sites were far better suited to clandestine research.

"Zie Zen," Ming said. "He's the biological father of Ashaya Aleine's only child. They have a joint parenting agreement and he wishes his coparent to remain in the country, as she's training the boy in certain unusual aspects of his abilities."

Nikita was well aware of who Zie Zen was, having run across the powerful businessman more than once as they vied for the same contracts. "We can't afford to obstruct business—not after the Faith NightStar fiasco." She directed her words at the Scotts, the two who had caused the whole mess.

But it was Tatiana who spoke. "How secure is the new location?"

"Extremely," Ming responded. "No one in the lab knows where they're being moved and once they arrive, they'll be under a communications blackout, except for monitored calls with their family or business groups once a week. Their PsyNet access will be policed at all times—setting up the tracers is what's taking up so many of my forces. As for Council staff, only the bare minimum know the new location. The short list is one hundred. If we have a leak, we'll know where to start looking."

"Did you check for changeling threats?" Kaleb's question was one Nikita had been considering asking. "The secrecy could be for nothing if they locate us."

"There is no strong pack or family unit in the vicinity."

"And," Tatiana added, "changelings don't much care what

we do so long as it doesn't affect them. I believe we must concentrate on the threat from within."

Ming's star flared. "Agreed. There is no risk of an outside strike on the new lab."

"Let's hope your confidence is justified." Shoshanna.

Nikita wanted to say something about what she and Kaleb suspected, if only to put an end to the other Councilor's arrogance. But the time wasn't yet right—they were still gathering evidence. However, they could certainly start the process.

She waited until the Council session had ended before asking Ming for a private meet. Kaleb had left her to fire the first volley. That implied no relationship of trust—she didn't trust anyone and neither did he. But he might make a useful ally. If he proved an enemy . . . well, deaths could be made to look like accidents.

Ming followed her into the Duncan family vault. "Nikita, what can I do for you?"

"Ming, I didn't want to bring this up in open session in case there was a good reason you wanted it kept secret from a certain other faction"—sow the seeds slowly—"but why didn't you tell us about the live trial of the Implant Protocol?"

"Your intelligence is faulty. There have been no live trials."

"I have confidence in my source," Nikita said. "Apparently there are ten participants. One fatality to date." She showed him the data file and watched as he downloaded it into his mind.

When Ming next spoke, the ice of his mind could have cut diamonds. "Thank you for bringing this to my attention. I intend to find out who authorized this and order an immediate reversal. The process isn't refined enough for such testing."

She believed his rebuttal. As the Councilor in charge of their armed forces, Ming had no tolerance for deviations from the chain of command. "That was my evaluation as well." She left it at that. Let Ming make his own conclusions, determine his own enemies. Arrows, even former Arrows, were very good at killing. It was their reason for being.

CHAPTER 37

Midnight the day of his entry into SnowDancer's hierarchy, Judd stood in the back of Perez's church, behind the curtains that usually hid the choir prior to their entrance. Tonight there was no choir, no light, just him and a man who might well be another Arrow.

The Ghost spoke from the depths of the shadows he seemed to court. "I wasn't sure you would respond to my message."

Judd leaned against the wall. "Why not?"

"I was wrong in my earlier assessment—you've changed, been influenced by the world outside the PsyNet."

"My stand on Protocol I will never change." It was an abomination, a desecration that could not be permitted.

"No conflicting loyalties?"

"Not yet." But if it came to that, he had already made his choice. Her name was Brenna and she was his heartbeat. "I would suggest you agree to let me disclose some of what we know to those who now share my life. They're your allies." And he would not lie—or keep needed information—from those who trusted him.

"My allies? Not yours?" The Ghost's voice was measured, cold, Psy.

"They're my people now." He might be a fallen Arrow, but he was also a SnowDancer lieutenant.

"So, do your people care about the Psy?" The Ghost didn't ask who those people were, keeping to their unspoken code. You could not betray what you did not know.

"They care about the stability of this world. The Psy have the capacity to destroy it if they carry on in their current path." Like it or not, the Psy were the most powerful race on the planet. In the past, they had been conscious of the effects of their decisions on the other races. No longer. "No one needs to know where my information comes from."

"We're a team, Judd. I'll bow to your judgment."

"What did you want to discuss?"

"The Implant Lab is in the process of being relocated. Details." He threw across a data crystal. "The data is sensitive. From what I've been able to confirm, it appears that only a small percentage of the Council superstructure knows its exact location."

Which meant that if they acted on it, the Ghost's anonymity could be compromised. "Were you able to confirm the damage done by our last hit?"

"Yes. There's no question—they've been set back, almost to square one."

"So we can hold off acting against the new lab. Leaks happen."

The Ghost paused. "There are rumors of a live trial in progress. If true, it means there are surviving copies of the experimental implants."

Judd's mind rejected the idea of unique individuals being turned into automatons. "I was under the impression the implants weren't that advanced."

"All of my intelligence says the same. My measured guess is that somebody acted precipitously and the implants will take care of themselves—I wouldn't be surprised if they've already begun to fail."

"Keep me updated. If necessary, I can make the destruction

of the new lab look like an unfortunate accident." It would require more planning and the cooperation of the pack, but it could be done.

A nod from the Ghost. "Do you ever wish to return to who you were?"

An unusual question, but the answer was easy. "No."

Brenna was in bed when he came to her quarters. Moving on silent feet, he paused to check that the security device on her door was functioning at an optimal level. He wouldn't rest easy until the killer had been caught—he'd already discarded twenty of Riley's original sixty suspects using pure logic, but his instincts told him he was close to running out of time.

Brenna opened her eyes when he entered her room. "You're back." She smiled sleepily at him from her nest in the blankets.

He sat on the edge. "I need to tell you something."

"I'm here." She scooted closer, but didn't touch.

He knew the distance had to tear at her changeling need for contact and the maleness in him raged against that—he was supposed to give her what she needed, not cause her pain. "I want to tell you where I go," he said, giving her another kind of intimacy, "and what I do when I disappear from the den." He began at the beginning—the fateful meeting on the PsyNet, a meeting he was sure had been engineered by the Ghost. But the other Psy had only found him because Judd had wished to be found.

"He'd been watching me, seen my subtle insubordination. I met Father Xavier Perez a year later." In a bar where he'd gone for data and Perez had gone to get blind drunk. But those were the priest's secrets. They had nothing to do with their work.

"Kindred souls." She was even closer, as if she couldn't stay away.

Neither could he, despite the fact that he could sense the cascade of fine blood vessels bursting and being repaired instantaneously inside his skull. His Tk-Cell abilities were keeping up with the damage. Just. "We, all three of us, want to protect the Psy from the biggest threat since Silence." Though Xavier Perez's motive remained a mystery, the man's loyalty was unquestionable. "Protocol I will lead to the destruction of the young—their minds will be cut into, their individual identities destroyed."

Brenna's hand curled around his, separated only by the blanket. He felt her warmth. It wasn't enough. He was starving for her, a clawing, almost animal hunger inside him.

"Judd—I smell blood." She jerked upright and reached to switch on a lamp.

He stopped her with his other hand. "It's just a nosebleed."

A small silence, then she pulled away from him. *"No."* A pained whisper. "It'll kill you if we don't stop being together."

He wiped away the blood with the sleeve of his turtleneck, able to tell it was dark and rich. "There is another option, as you once said. I have to disable the Protocol." And somehow keep from turning into an inadvertent murderer.

CHAPTER 38

The first body was found twenty-four hours after the Council meeting. The young male—who turned out to have been an inmate at a pre–Rehabilitation Center prior to his early and unexpected release—had died of massive neurological trauma.

Kaleb put down the report and turned to look at Nikita, who was staring out at the city of San Francisco. They were in the office area of her private penthouse, safe from prying eyes. "They're tying up the loose ends."

Nikita shook her head. "The autopsy showed a localized implosion in the segment of his brain that would have held the implant. It failed and destroyed itself in the process."

Kaleb wasn't so certain. "The timing's too convenient."

"Yes. There is that."

"Either way, it appears the problem is being buried."

"It doesn't matter." Nikita's voice was low, measured. "Ming has to have his suspicions if not outright proof. He'll withdraw his support of any further propositions on the part of the Scotts."

"Do you think they were foolish enough to have themselves implanted?"

"If the implants are indeed failing, we'll know the answer soon enough."

Kaleb nodded, looking out at the morning sun glittering off the water that edged this city. He couldn't help comparing it to his landlocked home. Two very disparate cities, but power felt the same whether here or there.

CHAPTER 39

Brenna's heart was a twisted knot of pain and fury when she ran into Hawke the next day. Damn the Council for putting that poison into Judd's brain. Touch and emotion were the cornerstone of who she was, but they were toxic to him. He'd left early this morning, saying he had to consider how to break the chains of Silence without becoming a danger to her or anyone else, but she was no longer sure that that was the right thing to do—what if the attempt proved lethal?

Hawke frowned when he saw her. "What's the matter?"

A sense of pure strength, unvarnished dominance, came over her. It didn't feel like her—as her previous episodes hadn't felt like her. Shaking off her panic that the madness was returning, she said, "Nothing."

"Come on, darling, you doing okay?" A rough question.

She put her arms around him. "I need a hug." He immediately gave her what she wanted. She sniffed, knowing this was a side of Hawke the soldier males and females never saw. "Can I ask you something?"

He rubbed a hand over her back. "Go on."

"Why haven't you taken a mate?"

He went still around her. "Where did that come from?"

"The subject of mating's been on my mind," she said truthfully. "I got to thinking what a good mate you'd make, but only for a woman tough enough to take you on." He was an alpha wolf and he could get brutal, but she somehow knew he'd never harm a hair on his mate's head. Just like her fallen Arrow.

"You know mating isn't that simple."

She knew. The same way she knew that something was "missing" between her and Judd, something important. Yet he was *hers*. She refused to believe he wasn't her mate. "Lots of people take permanent partners when they don't find a mate by a certain age." Mating was a magical, wonderful thing, but fulfilling relationships could be had aside from it.

Hawke chuckled. "I'm only thirty-two, not quite in my dotage."

She snarled softly. "That's not what I meant and you know it. I hear the women talking, you know. They say you don't even attempt to form long-term relationships, that as soon as anyone tries to get even a little possessive, you move on."

"Should I tell you this is none of your business?"

She hugged him harder. "It is, too." As her alpha, he belonged to her as much as the pack belonged to him. "I want you to be happy and I don't think you are." Maybe because she was hurting so badly herself. The idea of a life without Judd was a nightmare.

Hawke didn't respond for a long time. "She was two years old when we met. I was seven. I knew she was my best friend straight away. As I got older, I also knew she would grow up to become my mate."

Brenna didn't want him to continue, a horrible feeling in the pit of her stomach—she knew what had happened to SnowDancer two decades ago, the bloodshed, the loss. She held on to Hawke, held on hard, trying to anchor him with the bonds of Pack.

"She fit me in a way no one else ever will. And she died when she was five and I was ten."

A single tear rolled down her face. She wished anything that she could turn back time and save that life, because mating was a one-shot deal. Though Hawke had been too young for the bond to actually materialize, he *had* found the woman who was meant for him. That didn't happen twice. "I'm so sorry."

"I've learned to live with it." He nuzzled the top of her head with his chin. "But you don't have to. If you've mated with Judd, you won't get any shit from me."

She couldn't admit to him that she felt only a dull emptiness where the mating bond should've been. It wasn't fair—she loved Judd. Why didn't her wolf recognize him as her mate? Taking a deep breath, she pulled out of Hawke's hold. "I won't tell anyone."

He used a thumb to wipe the tear off her face. "I don't even know why I told you." He sounded bemused. "You're dangerous."

She choked out a laugh. "No. I just have the bad habit of caring for men who can't seem to care for themselves."

"Speaking of the damn Psy, where is he? I need him to sit in on a meeting."

"He's somewhere close," she said, knowing her dark angel was watching over her. "Can I ask what the meeting's about?"

"The cats think they have something on the Psy who hit DawnSky. The hyena leader knew nothing about it—it was a fully Psy raid." His voice had dropped, become lethal in its quietness. "Goddamn bastards killed children."

"I hope you rip out their guts while they're still breathing."

Hawke's grin was feral. "That's why I like you, Bren. You're more wolf than girl."

He shouldn't have *used the code. He'd been overconfident. Now Riley was questioning all his top men. Sooner or later, they were going to figure out that he hadn't been where he was supposed to have been the day Andrew got shot.*

It didn't matter. As long as Brenna wasn't around to point the finger, they'd never be able to prove that he'd done anything more than break watch without authorization.

No more fucking around. Today, he finished it.

CHAPTER 40

Judd took his position against the wall in the meeting room, impatient to get this over with so he could return to Brenna. Of course he wouldn't approach her, but he could keep an eye on her from a distance. His well-honed instincts were screaming at him by now, telling him that danger was only a heartbeat away.

If he could, he'd lock her in for safety. But that would kill her as surely as murder.

I'm never going to be put in a box again . . .

No, he couldn't do that to her.

"We're live," Indigo said as the huge comm screen at one end of the room came on. Lucas appeared on-screen, flanked by Dorian and Mercy, much as Indigo and Judd flanked Hawke.

The leopard alpha met Judd's eyes, raised an eyebrow, then turned to Hawke. "So you finally did something about him. About bloody time."

Judd shifted to bring Lucas's attention back to him. "I'd say we came to a mutual understanding."

It wasn't Lucas who spoke next but Dorian. "So how does a Psy lieutenant hunt?"

He met the leopard's bright blue gaze. "Very quietly."

"So do snipers." Dorian's expression was calculating. "We should talk."

"I might need a sparring partner." If he succeeded in breaking Silence, physical contact in another arena might serve to blunt the truly dark aspect of his abilities around Brenna. Because no matter what happened, he was what he was. Killing was built into his genes.

"Karate?" Those completely human-seeming eyes brightened in interest.

"Katana."

"Hot damn. Let's do it."

Lucas coughed. "If you two have stopped flirting, we have business to discuss."

Indigo grinned but stayed silent. Mercy wasn't so reticent. "So that's what it takes to get into Dorian's pants. I'll let the sentinel-chasers know." Her packmate's growl only widened her smirk.

Hawke nodded at Lucas. "You got something?"

"We think we've tracked down the assassins who hit DawnSky."

All amusement faded from the air. Judd looked at Lucas. "Are you certain? I told you that uniform is worn by every member of the Psy force under Ming LeBon's command."

"That's the problem," Lucas conceded. "We've narrowed it down to a specific squad, but there are fifty of them. Six Psy were spotted during the attack."

Dorian shrugged, no mercy in his face. "You know my opinion—gut them all."

"We do that, it's a declaration of war." Lucas's tone said he wouldn't mind going head-to-head with the Psy. "But that's what they want—it'll give them an excuse to come down hard on all changeling groups in the area. A pinpoint hit will deliver our message far more accurately."

Judd knew Lucas was right. "I may be able to get you the data."

Everyone looked at him.

"I have contacts in the Net." He let that sink in, let them judge his loyalties. "Not everyone is happy with how the Council is running things."

Hawke glanced at him, then gave a small nod. A concession of trust. "Backup plan," the alpha said to Lucas, "we take out the exact number of Psy who attacked the deer."

"That'll make the point with a little less finesse, but yeah, it could work." Lucas tapped his finger on the dark wood of the table he sat at. "I've been thinking about their tactics—trying to turn the packs against each other."

"So have I," Hawke said. "They have to have used it before, and successfully, to try the game on us."

Lucas's facial markings went white against his skin. "Doesn't say much about our intelligence if we can be worked so easily."

"We weren't. But weaker packs would be."

"You're too divided," Judd broke in. "It's the first lesson Psy soldiers learn. Don't try to take out changelings—get them to take out each other."

Someone growled and Judd wasn't sure that that primal sound hadn't come from one of the feminine throats. He remembered how Brenna growled at him when he got her mad. Her wolf side fascinated him—he liked seeing her claws.

"Let me guess," Hawke said, "before, the Council kept their interference minimal in this region because SnowDancer and DarkRiver kept each other in check."

Judd nodded. "Yes. And if the computer attack doesn't succeed in warning them off, they'll keep picking away at you and your nonpredatory allies—until your power base is eroded to the point of nonexistence. Then they'll launch a quiet offensive to install Council-friendly packs in place of your former allies."

His last words had the effect of a bomb. Questions came at him from every angle until he raised a palm for silence. "Yes," he said. "There are packs that have made agreements with the Council for money, land, or simply immunity from Psy strikes."

"So even if we set up some sort of chain of communication to prevent the Psy from starting another territorial war"—Hawke's face was wolf-sharp—"we have no way of knowing who's snitching to the Council?"

"I'd operate on the assumption that everything you say is being reported back."

"That can be turned to our advantage," Lucas pointed out.

Hawke nodded. "After we run this next op, we need to talk about how to fix our lines of communication—packs can't remain isolated from each other anymore. Not if we're going to survive the Psy Council."

The meeting broke up soon afterward and Judd immediately contacted the Ghost. Because he didn't want to leave the den, he took the chance of sending a coded message asking for a call on a secure line. The Ghost responded within seconds. "This call should be untraceable, but we can't talk for long."

"Understood." Judd laid out the situation with the deer and the Psy without mentioning either DarkRiver or SnowDancer. Just as he didn't know the Ghost's identity, the Ghost had no knowledge of where Judd went after he left the church.

"You need the names of the exact officers?"

"Can you get them?"

"I'll have to break into a secure PsyNet database, but that shouldn't pose a problem unless the information has been highly classified. I assume you don't want to talk to these men?"

Judd didn't answer because no answer was needed.

"My goal is to help my people," the Ghost said in the chill tone of a Psy fully enmeshed in Silence, "not sell them out. I may be a revolutionary, but I am not a traitor."

"To fight an evil that butchers innocent women and children isn't treason."

"I agree—at least in this situation. Killing those deer was akin to taking out the most helpless civilians in a war no one knows is taking place."

"Case by case? Fine. Your conscience will tell you where to go."

"I have no conscience, Judd." The Ghost's voice dropped. "I've got so much blood staining these hands nothing will ever wash it away."

"The future might surprise you." It sure as hell had shocked him. "And if you don't have a conscience, why did you become a revolutionary?"

"Perhaps I want to grab power for myself."

"No." Of that he was certain. "You do it because you see what the Council is turning the Psy into and you know it isn't right. We were the greatest of races once upon a time, the true—and just—leaders of the world."

"Do you think we can have that back again?"

"No." The world had changed, the humans and changelings gaining in strength with the passage of time. "But we can become something even better. We can become free."

Brenna was fixing some kind of a small computronic device when he found her in her quarters. "Judd," she said, putting down her tools. "You can't be here. The dissonance—"

He interrupted her panicked words. "I need to ask you something important."

"What could be more important than your life?" She sounded close to tears.

"*Your* life. If you die, I don't know if I'd stay sane." A simple truth.

Her hands trembled as she lifted them to push back her hair. "Ask your question."

"The ferocity with which the shooter is stalking you argues for a deeper motive than the fact that he thinks you'll remember something about Tim's death." Finally, he knew he was on the right path. "You know something else he's scared you'll reveal."

"Tim's death has to be it. It would mean a death sentence for him."

"But, Brenna, he *knows* you didn't see anything." He leaned forward but caught himself before he touched her. Even so, he felt the start of a nosebleed. He managed to stop it with Tk, but it wouldn't last. "He planned Tim's death to the letter, made sure there was no trace evidence, no trail, and no eyewitnesses. He knows he didn't betray himself."

"Maybe he's crazy. Like you!" Her nostrils flared. "Do you think I can't smell you bleeding?"

He focused on the first part of her statement. "He's acting with too much logic to be crazy. Think, Brenna, what else could you know?"

"Nothing!" She threw up her hands. "I was in healing for months, then I was being babysat by Drew and Riley. And you, come to think of it. I'm still being overprotected!"

Judd felt ice crawl down his spine as his brain made the connection that had been eluding it for days. "The day of Tim's murder was when you started acting out—not following orders, behaving aggressively."

"I was behaving normally," she retorted.

"Yes." He met her eyes. "For the first time since your abduction, you behaved as someone fully healed would behave."

Brenna frowned. "Judd, you're going to have to spell it out for me before you bleed to death on my floor." Despite the sharp words, her worry for him was a wound in her eyes.

"Brenna, what happened the day Enrique kidnapped you?"

"Why are you asking me that?" she snapped. "You know I don't remember."

"Why not? You remember everything else." Every cut, every blow, every hurt.

"Shock." She hugged herself. "That's what the healers said."

"Your pack found evidence of an unknown van in the area at the time."

"Enrique must've knocked me out somehow." Her frown reminded him that they'd gone over this topic many times. "I'd never get into a van with a stranger."

"No, you wouldn't."

"Then, why—" Horror bloomed on her face. "No," she whispered, rocking back and forth. "No, you're wrong."

Judd wanted to be wrong if it would wipe that look off Brenna's face. He'd been blinded by her loyalty to the pack when they'd first broached this topic and even now had not even a shred of evidence to support his theory, but he had instinct. The details of the kidnapping were the one thing Brenna, *and only Brenna*, knew about.

It made far more sense than her being targeted because of the statement she'd made about Tim's murder. She'd been openly shaken at the time, and a smart wolf could have talked his way around anything she claimed to have seen. But with her gone, no one would ever be able to prove what Judd now suspected—that a fellow wolf, a packmate, had sold her out to Santano Enrique . . . to be butchered like so much meat.

CHAPTER 41

Nikita uploaded the data crystal she'd received that morning onto a computer in her penthouse suite. The crystal held a file she'd paid a premium amount to acquire. Her contact had considered it little enough compensation for putting his life, and his sanity, on the line. Nikita had had to agree. Kaleb's little gift—it was rumored he had the ability to cause permanent insanity—made even the most experienced of them reconsider.

The file finished loading. It was several pages long and stamped with the seal of the training facility where Kaleb had been placed at age three, when he'd first begun exhibiting his considerable telekinetic strength. As was usual, the juvenile files had been sealed at Kaleb's majority, which was why she'd had such trouble getting them . . . and why she hadn't known the name of Kaleb's trainer: Santano Enrique.

Filing away that unexpected piece of data, she scrolled down. She soon began to notice odd gaps in the record. There was a continuous accounting of his progress up to age seven years, four months, but the next entry didn't appear until age seven years, seven months. What had Kaleb been doing in the intervening three months? Again and again, the pattern repeated itself. The gaps were highly irregular. Training logs were meant to be kept strictly up-to-date.

She restarted from the beginning and immediately noticed a second pattern hidden in the first. Each gap in the log appeared one week to the day after Kaleb had had a personal training session with Enrique. With any other trainer, it would've been a cause for concern, but not a major problem overall.

However, Santano Enrique had been no ordinary cardinal. He'd been an exceptionally high-functioning sociopath, one of the small minority whose aberrant brain patterns had been given free license by Silence. Enrique had escaped all the procedures set in place to detect such anomalous minds and become Council. Now it appeared that Kaleb had been far more than merely Enrique's student. He'd been his protégé.

The NetMind's recent slew of fragmented reports, especially in relation to the unknown serial killer, took on a new implication in light of this information. The last time they had had such problems, the NetMind had been under Enrique's control.

Returning to the file, she saw that Kaleb's power arc had also been unusual. Most cardinals followed a steady and predictable progression from ungoverned and unreliable to total control. Her daughter, Sascha, of course, had been a different story. It would have been far easier for Nikita to terminate the fetus as soon as the in vitro psychic tests showed the near-certain presence of the E designation. It was, in fact, what the Council had ordered in the early years of Silence. The ability of E-Psy to heal emotional wounds had been considered redundant in a race that had no emotion.

A decade later, they had discovered the Correlation Concept—a direct if not scientifically provable relationship between the number of latent E-Psy and the overall stability of the populace. In simple terms, the fewer the E-Psy, the more cases of sociopathy and insanity. Now E-Psy were brought to full term and forced to contain their abilities under several undocumented layers of conditioning. That was what had led to Sascha's irregular development.

Nothing like that could account for the nature of Kaleb's psychic growth. At ten years of age, he'd been as focused as an adult. His concentration hadn't lapsed during the occasionally problematic period of adolescence, but evidenced a sharp decline at age sixteen. That would have been a cause for severe concern, except that Kaleb had stabilized within the month. Despite considerable testing, the M-Psy had been unable to find any evidence of psychic or physical trauma that could account for his relapse. In the end it had been noted down as a delayed adolescent reaction.

Nikita had reason to disagree with that diagnosis. Closing Kaleb's file, she pulled up another. It had been opened after the Council became aware of Enrique's sociopathic history. They were using all of their resources to make a list of past murders that may have been committed by the now-dead Councilor—in case he'd left behind evidence aside from any possessed by the changelings. Loose ends had to be stifled before they spoke.

She scanned the list they had to date and found it at once. A changeling female—a swan—had disappeared seven days before Kaleb's logged decline. And the decline had begun approximately twenty-four hours after Kaleb returned from one of those unexplained absences, likely times when he'd been with Enrique.

Not a protégé. An accomplice.

This could become a problematic issue if Kaleb ever lost control of his murderous appetites. Until then, she'd continue working with him. Every one of the Councilors was a killer in some form. Kaleb simply did his killing in a less sanctioned way.

CHAPTER 42

An hour after he'd been forced to leave a distraught Brenna—she'd thrown him out when his nose started bleeding openly—Judd received the encrypted message from the Ghost. A simple list. Six names.

He called Brenna, audio only. The sight of tears on her face was disturbing to his senses. "I'm leaving my watch outside your door. Riley's sending a replacement." He'd already spoken to her brother about his suspicions and the other man was pulling together duty and leave rosters from the time of Brenna's abduction. The data would help narrow their suspect base, but Judd's sense of urgency said it wouldn't be fast enough.

"I hope the bastard does try for me again—I want to flay him alive." There were no tears, only a lacing of the most unadulterated anger.

"Be careful of everyone." Riley had set tasks far from the den for those on their short list of suspects, but the killer could always sneak back in. It was also possible that he'd gained unauthorized access to the classified code and wasn't a soldier at all.

"I will. Has the bleeding stopped?"

"Yes," he said and ended the call. Not technically a lie. His nose wasn't bleeding anymore, but other things inside him were.

D'Arn soon arrived to take over the watch and Judd left to deliver the names to Hawke. He was almost there when he saw Sienna limping out of a training room. She had a bruise on her cheek and her lip was promising to swell. A few months ago, he'd have discovered the name of the perpetrator and taken care of it. That was before Hawke—with Judd and Walker's cooperation—had thrown Sienna into a training program designed to turn her from "tame housecat" to wolf. "Did you try to take on Indigo again?"

Sienna's jaw became an obstinate line. "She keeps making me do exercises over and over. I wanted a bout."

"And look where it got you." Indigo walked out of the same room. Dressed in loose black pants and a gray T-shirt, she didn't have so much as a hair out of place. "Good for me, though—helped work out the frustration from the crap I'm wading through."

He knew she was referring to the drug situation, which she was now focusing on as Riley took over the murder investigation. "That bad?"

"Not if you compare it to the outside world, but I can't believe how *any* of that poison got in here in the first place. We're a goddamn pack. We look out for one another, get our strength from pack loyalty, not—" She glanced at Sienna's interested expression. "I'll fill you in later."

Judd waited until the lieutenant had left before speaking. "Why don't you follow Indigo's training advice?"

Those night-sky eyes flashed. "They treat me like I'm a pup! I'm a cardinal who could kill them with one psychic hit and they expect me to do physical exercises more suitable for a child!"

He let her blow off steam—for some reason, Sienna's conditioning had begun to fail almost immediately upon defection. That was going to become a severe problem, because her abilities were as lethal as she believed. Maybe more so.

"You're no longer in the psychic world," he told her, hardening his tone. "And the fact that this is a physical issue is an excuse. You have the same difficulty following orders in psychic training."

Her eyes narrowed. "Maybe because you treat me like a child, too."

"Why do you think that is, Sienna?" He folded his arms—this was important. Family was important. It formed the basis of Pack. Brenna wouldn't thank him if he neglected his responsibilities in this arena, no matter his need to return to her. "You're a cardinal, you should be able to work that out."

A sullen silence. He didn't understand what was going on with his niece—she was the most unpredictable of the three minors in the Lauren family. It made no sense, not when she'd been arctic in her emotionlessness in the Net, enough so that she had already begun receiving placement offers. One overture had come from Ming LeBon himself.

"Building blocks," he said when she maintained that obdurate silence. "Without a strong base, you'll crumble the first time you meet someone smart enough to work out your lack of a foundation."

She swallowed and looked him in the eye. "I'm seventeen now. Why won't anyone treat me like it? The wolves get treated better!"

"It's not discrimination and you know it. It's the fact that you can't follow orders, and right now, you can't even defend yourself without killing someone."

"You're not so good at following orders either!"

He waited.

"I'm not an idiot," she muttered. "I know you were an Arrow and I know Arrows are too valuable to be sentenced to rehabilitation."

Her tone dared him to disagree, reminding him of another strong-willed female. "And?" He had to identify what she knew before he answered.

"They must've had some plan for you to escape rehabilitation." She squared her slender shoulders. "A new identity, something!"

"The sentence was for everyone in the Lauren family," he said, accepting that she deserved to be treated as an adult at least in this. To do anything else would disrespect her intelligence and spirit.

"Why?" she interrupted before he could answer. "I know my mother committed suicide and we had some incidents of instability in the family, but why sentence us all?"

Yes, she was smart. "We're very strong as a group, Sienna. Before Kristine's death, we had three cardinals." That didn't count his, Walker's, or Marlee's considerable powers. "We threatened someone powerful enough to get us wiped out."

"I figured . . ." She looked up. "And you?"

"My name was removed from the family register at age ten." The age at which he'd first killed. "My birth certificate doesn't exist, nor do any medical records aside from those in the squad files." Including a DNA profile that would send up a classified red flag if he was ever typed. "As far as the general Net is concerned, I don't exist." No Arrow did. "There was no need for a new identity. I wasn't considered a Lauren."

Her eyes widened. "Then why defect?" she whispered. "You walked into what should have been certain death."

Looking into that bruised, confused face, he decided to tell her the truth. Because Sienna's abilities, while very different from his own, sprang from the same dark core. "There is a line that, once crossed, can never be uncrossed." He reached out to touch her hair. The dark red strands were soft under his fingertips. It was the first time he'd ever touched her in anything other than training.

"If I had let you all die while I remained safe, it would've pushed me over that line." Because they'd been under his care. He might have been wiped from the official records, but he'd always existed to Walker, Sienna, Marlee, Toby . . . and Kristine. She'd been his sister and mother to this powerful girl. But unlike her tenacious, headstrong daughter, Kristine had broken irrevocably under Silence.

Sienna's face turned heartbreakingly fragile. She gave a tiny jerk forward before stopping. And because of Brenna, he understood. Ignoring the damage it might cause, he tugged her into the enclosure of his arms. She was frozen for a long time and then he was sure she cried. As he held her, he felt things, his shielding close to nil. Warmth, affection . . . the protective love of a brother for his lost sister's child. Sienna looked so much like Kristine, but until this moment, he hadn't acknowledged the pain that caused him. The dissonance was an excruciating symphony of spiked hammers in his head.

"Does it hurt?" he asked, suddenly aware that that might explain some of Sienna's behavior. She had martial talents like him, and unlike either Faith or Sascha. From everything he knew about how the other two women had broken Silence, he was almost certain that martial minds were conditioned in a unique way—particularly when it came to the strength of the dissonance. "The fragmentation of Silence, does it hurt?"

A slow nod. "I can't be like before, but it's as though my mind wants to force me." Her voice was muffled against his chest, but he heard the incredible pain in it.

It put the final seal on the decision he'd made in the predawn darkness after leaving Brenna, devastatingly aware that he couldn't give her what she needed to feel safe and happy. It broke something in him to fail her that way. "I'll figure out a way to undo the pain protocols."

"You know we can't." A whisper. "You and I . . . we need the pain to remind us to keep it under control."

It.

Their different but equally destructive abilities. "Maybe we can make new rules for a new life."

"What if it doesn't work?" she whispered. "What if we hurt people?"

Images of bloodied and twisted bodies cascaded through his mind. "We won't." He only hoped he would be able to keep his promise . . . and that Brenna wouldn't pay the ultimate price for choosing to give her heart to a rebel Arrow.

CHAPTER 43

He was sweating. *It had taken him two hours to return to the den after Riley had sent him on some bogus training exercise. After Brenna was dead, he'd return to where he was supposed to be without anyone being the wiser. The perfect alibi.*

He glanced at his watch and then at Brenna's door. D'Arn was leaning against the wall, but the killer didn't make the mistake of assuming the other soldier wasn't aware of everything going on around him. Sights, sounds, smells. It was why he'd chosen this hiding spot, in the wrong direction for the air currents to carry his scent.

All he needed was three seconds with that bitch who just wouldn't die.

He glanced at his watch again, knowing he'd never get a better chance. The Psy was gone and if D'Arn fell for the distraction, Brenna would be alone for at least one crucial minute. More than enough time to take care of business. Another glance at his watch.

Five, four, three, two . . . one.

D'Arn jerked to a standing alert as the alarm blared through the den. Coded for sound, this one screamed that something had happened in the nursery, something bad enough to require the declaration of a full emergency.

The killer smiled. He had placed the crude bomb to maximize chaos—by collapsing the entrance to the nursery—but had tried to ensure none of the pups would be hurt. He wasn't a monster.

D'Arn started to run in the direction of the nursery, then hesitated. Brenna's door opened. "Go!" she yelled. "I'm right behind you. I'm part of the comm team."

The killer knew that, had seen the emergency roster. Brenna would now zip back inside to grab her emergency communications equipment before racing to the command center to direct operations inside the den.

"Move!" She slammed her door, but the killer knew she wouldn't have stopped to lock it. If she had, he'd get her as she walked out, her concentration elsewhere.

D'Arn took off at a run, his instinct to protect the young overwhelming everything else. It was what the killer had counted on. The Psy were right—emotions made changelings weak, open to manipulation.

He stepped out as D'Arn disappeared around the corner. He had a very short window of opportunity—too bad he wouldn't be able to choke the life out of her as he'd planned. He palmed the pressure injector full of one hundred percent Rush and reached for the doorknob. It turned without resistance.

One more second and it would be good-bye, Brenna Shane Kincaid.

CHAPTER 44

Judd was running full-tilt to the nursery, Hawke at his side, when his phone began to beep in an intense, irregular pattern.

It was linked to the alarm on Brenna's door.

Screeching to a stop, he used every trick he had to focus despite the number of bodies moving past him. One second. Two. Too damn slow. *There*. He teleported out. Brenna's door was closed. He pulled it off using Tk and sent the wide piece of plascrete smashing into the corridor, nearly mowing down another SnowDancer soldier.

Brenna was on the floor, bleeding from cuts on her lip and cheek. He went to pick up her attacker and throw him into the wall, but she shook her head slightly. He froze. The man whirled to face Judd, but he never got the chance to speak. Brenna swept out a leg and smashed him to the ground before jumping on his back and swiping her claws down hard enough to reveal flashes of bone.

The killer screamed.

Judd put him in a telekinetic choke hold. "You don't have the right to scream."

Brenna looked up as the man gurgled, desperate to breathe. "You were right—he was there." A feral snarl as she held him down. "He was the reason I got into that van. He offered me a ride." Gripping her attacker's hair, she jerked back his head. "Let the bastard speak."

Judd released his hold, aware of others arriving at the scene. "I can tear his mind open, download everything he knows. Of course, he'll be a drooling mess by the end."

Brenna's captive coughed and tried to speak. "No. I'll talk."

Brenna jerked his hair harder. "So *talk*, Dieter."

There was no mercy in her and Judd approved. This man had used his position to prey on those who trusted him. Judd remembered him squatting beside Timothy's dead body, pretending to help, telling them how perfect the room was if you wanted to surreptitiously dispose of a body, how the killer had to be someone smart.

"I met him a few months before you got taken," he coughed out, "Santano Enrique."

Someone hissed in the doorway, sounding more cat than wolf.

Brenna dug her claws into his shoulder, scraping bone. Dieter's scream was high and shrill, rising above the shriek of the emergency alarm, but she kept him conscious. "Did you give me up to him?"

"Yes." Dieter coughed up blood and Judd realized he was crushing the man's internal organs. He forced himself to pull back. This was Brenna's fight.

"Why?" Betrayal laced her voice. "You were my brothers' friend. You were Pack."

"It was a straight business deal. He gave me Rush at a real low price. Made me rich." Dieter didn't try for Brenna's sympathy, as if he knew he'd get none. "All he wanted was a favor now and then."

"Like picking me up on the way to class," Brenna whispered, tone raw. "Like telling me I was needed at the den. Did he come back from the grave and ask you to shoot Andrew, too?" Her next move was so fast, Judd almost missed it. She smashed Dieter's face to the floor, hard enough to cause unconsciousness but not death. The alarm cut off at that same instant.

Getting up, she wiped the blood off her mouth with the back of her hand. "Elias, Sing-Liu," she said to the two soldiers who'd stopped in the doorway, "take him to the lockup."

Judd blocked the doorway. "I'll take him."

Brenna growled. "You'll kill him. We need to know what he fed Enrique."

"I can get that." Judd could almost taste the man's death on his lips.

"His execution belongs to Tim's family." She stepped around the body to face him. "Tim died. I didn't."

Blood for life. Life for life. Changeling justice.

But Judd wasn't changeling. Dieter's heart pulsed in his psychic hold. Just one— Brenna gripped the front of his shirt. *"Stop."*

He stared at her. "No." His mind recognized killing, was drawn to the taste of it.

She kissed him, bit down hard on his lower lip. Dissonance crashed into him, combining with the sensory pleasure, the iron-rich taste of blood, and the hunger for violence. It scrambled his pathways for an instant. That instant was enough. When she drew back, he was still homicidal, but he could think past it. "You're right. We need to know what he knows. I'll take him."

This time, she didn't try to stop him as he hauled the changeling over his shoulder and strode out, Elias by his side. The other man kept growling low in his throat until Judd dumped Dieter in the lockup and secured the door. "Does he need a healer?" Judd wanted him very alive for the questioning.

Elias's eyes were flat. "He needs to be dead, but I'll call Lara. It might be a while if there were injuries in the nursery."

Judd had forgotten the alarm in the emotional chaos of the attack on Brenna. "Are you capable of guarding him? I know he was your friend."

"I want to tear him to pieces." His claws were out. "But I

won't let him die—Tim's family deserves the honor of ripping his two-faced heart from his fucking chest."

Accepting that, Judd left to return to Brenna. He found the apartment full. Surprisingly, Lara herself was looking at Brenna's cuts, while Hawke asked her questions and her brothers swore in low, continuous bursts. Outside, someone was already trying to repair the door he'd busted. He heard Sing-Liu's cool voice giving the orders.

"Judd." Brenna's face lit up the second she saw him. She went to hold out a hand but dropped it halfway.

He grabbed it anyway. Damn the consequences. "The nursery?" he asked Lara.

"Looked worse than it was," she said. "No kids hurt but that was by sheer luck. If a pup had crawled into the doorway when it came down—" She shook her head.

"A diversion," Judd said. "He had to get D'Arn away from Brenna."

"D'Arn's already beating himself up about it." Riley blew out a breath. "But Dieter knew what he was doing—I would've taken off for the nursery, too. Bren can look after herself, pups can't."

Brenna shot her big brother a smile at the vote of confidence, before returning her attention to Judd. "I was telling Hawke how it happened. I left to grab my comm equipment from my room and when I came out, he was standing here." Her voice shook, not with fear but anger. "He smirked at me, said no one's here to protect you now, little girl. He had that injector in his hand." She pointed to the small cylindrical object lying in a corner.

A wall hanging crashed to the floor, the tough plasglass cover splintering.

As everyone else turned toward the sound, Brenna squeezed his hand. The warning worked. He pulled his rage under control, but it was an uncertain control at best. "When did you remember about the van?"

"That smirk." She almost spit out the words. "It made me want to kill and then I knew why."

Hawke kicked aside a piece of debris on the floor—a large

splinter from the door. "No wonder you blocked it out. One of us served you up to die." His eyes had gone pure wolf.

"Yes." Her tone softened, grew sad. "He killed Tim, tried to kill Drew, gave me up . . . and for what? Money."

"I'll find out what he knows." Hawke glanced at Judd. "Can you help?"

He thought of how Dieter's heart had felt in his hands, so slick, so crushable. "Give me a week. I'd kill him right now."

"It'll take him longer than that to heal the damage Brenna tells me she did." Lara's tone was without its normal gentleness. "I've got to go stitch him up now."

Hawke went with Lara. Judd looked at Drew and Riley. "Give us a few minutes."

Both men left after a short, tense silence. Judd took Brenna into her room and closed the door. She stood with her back to it as he leaned over her, palms braced on either side of her head. "You're okay." Not a question, because even bruised, she was standing strong.

"You're not." She took a handkerchief from her pocket and dabbed at his jaw and he realized he was bleeding from his ear canal again. Worry laid another bruise in her eyes, turning the areola of blue almost indigo. "You can't wait much longer."

Taking it from her, he finished the task and shoved the cloth into his jeans pocket. "You didn't need my help."

She smiled, teeth sharp. "I knew you'd come. That's why I fought so hard. I knew that by the time I got tired, you'd be there." Her smile faded. "Go, calm down. I'm okay."

He left her and it was the hardest thing he'd ever done. The urge to crush out Dieter's life beat in him with every pulse of his own heart, a pounding echo that knew nothing of logic or sense. It just wanted justice. In his current state, he couldn't even act on his decision to break Silence. He was too unbalanced.

Walking out into the snowy spread of the inner perimeter, he attempted to work off some of his energy by going through a number of strictly choreographed hand-to-hand combat moves. He had to wipe more blood from his nose before he began. The color was close to black—the countdown was reaching the final stages.

When Tai materialized out of the forest an hour into his session, he had to force himself not to react with unwarranted aggression. His control was still fragmented, his rage to kill a trapped beast inside him. "What are you doing here?"

"I was heading back to the den after a run. Been out since this morning." He thrust a hand through his hair. "I don't suppose you could teach me some of what you were doing."

"It requires discipline," he replied, realizing Tai had no awareness of the chaos that had ruled the den less than an hour ago. For some reason, that knowledge broke through his anger. "You can't fight instinctively—you need to think before you react."

Tai put his hands into his pockets, bunching up his shoulders. "You think I can't do it?"

"I think you'd be going against your nature, but that's not a bad thing. It'll teach you to focus and channel the abilities you already have."

Tai's grin was young, cocky. "Yeah, I'm not too bad, huh? I got in a few shots with you and you're a lieutenant."

"True."

The smile faded and Tai took his hands out of his pockets. "Thanks for not ratting me out to anyone. About going clawed, I mean."

Judd remembered Lara's advice. He just listened.

"I got frustrated and lost it," Tai admitted. "I apologize."

"Fine." Judd jerked his head. "If you want to learn something, follow me."

Tai came to stand beside him. "What do I do?"

"Think. Stand in place in this position." He showed the position. "And think about what your body is capable of, what will push it to the limit, what won't. To use a tool effectively, you must first know its capabilities."

Tai took a deep breath. "My body as a tool? Okay, I get it. I think."

Oddly, teaching Tai discipline brought Judd's own darkness

under almost total control. By the time Brenna found him a few hours later, as the trailing edges of the day faded into night, he was thinking relatively clearly.

"I'm sorry," she said after Tai left, pulling her thick coat tighter around her body. "I needed to be with you. Stupid after I acted so strong and unaffected by the attack. I should go—our being close will hurt you."

"Never be sorry for coming to me." Picking up his discarded jacket, he shrugged into it. "Do you want to go for a walk?"

She nodded, lower lip trembling for an instant before she got it under control. "I'm such a baby. I was fine as long as I was cleaning up, but as soon as I stopped, I got so *angry*. Almost as if I was picking up everyone else's anger, too."

He matched her smaller strides as they walked, choosing to focus on the lighter aspect of her comment—they'd discuss the other later. "You might be a baby, but you're mine. And I like babysitting."

Her laugh was surprised. "Very funny. Anyone else saying that would be dodging claws right now."

He thought back to D'Arn and Sing-Liu's interaction the day of the war games. Finally, he grasped what had seemed so puzzling then. But the similarity was only on the surface. He and Brenna were different in one crucial respect, a difference they had both gone to great lengths to avoid discussing—the lack of a mating bond between them.

He was a psychic being. He would have seen it had it been present in any form. That it wasn't, was a sign that though they might be drawn to each other, they weren't made to fit. He didn't give a damn. He was keeping her.

"What was Tai doing with you anyway?" she asked when he remained silent.

"Tai makes a good student. But when did I become a teacher?"

"You're a lieutenant, a big brother to the young ones."

"Ah." That made sense. "They trust me."

"Yes."

"I could damage them."

"But you won't."

Such faith for a renegade from the Net. "It's time."

She understood at once. "Here?" They were in a very small clearing between towering redwoods. "It's dark."

"It's as good a place as any. And there's no need for light where I'm going." He took a seat on a fallen log after brushing off the snow and Brenna sat beside him. "I might not respond if you call me. Don't panic."

"I won't." Her voice trembled. She took a deep breath. "I won't." Far stronger this time.

"You also have to be prepared for the possibility that this might not work, that we'll have to separate permanently."

Her skin paled. "It'll work."

"This time stubbornness won't do it," he said, attempting to be gentle but knowing he sounded harsh. "It's lasted so long because of how solid it is. The conditioning reprograms the most fundamental aspects of our brains. To break full Silence is one thing—but to make use of an isolated aspect of it as I intend to, might be another altogether." What he didn't want to tell her was that the attempt could prove fatal. But he would not lie to her. "If I do it wrong, I could trigger the most extreme level of dissonance."

"Are you telling me you could die?"

"Yes."

Her face twisted. "You can't die. You're mine."

"I have no intention of doing anything wrong and every intention of surviving." He was an Arrow, and for the first time, that might be a good thing. "I was trained to circumvent and use pain to my own advantage. Trust me."

Swallowing, she nodded. "I know I can't help, but—"

"You can help." It was something he'd realized during the calm fostered by teaching Tai. "After putting Andrew's heart back together, I recovered far quicker than I should have in terms of physical strength. I think it was because of you."

"How?"

"I don't know." There was no bond, but she reached him in ways no one else ever had. "If you ever find your true mate," he said, "I won't allow you freedom." He didn't have such goodness in him.

She scowled. "I'm a one-Psy woman."

Satisfied with the acceptance, he nodded. "Keep in physical contact with me."

She blanched. "It hurts you when I touch."

"Because I'm conditioned to see it as a danger. It is one—touch anchors me to you, which threatens to break Silence."

Swallowing, she nodded and clasped her hand over his shoulder. "The first thing I'm going to do after you come back is pet you all over for as long as I want. Promise you'll let me."

"Promise." With that sensual goal as his guiding light, he closed his eyes and went deep into his mind. Deeper than he'd ever before gone. What he saw threatened to shake his confidence in his ability to use the Protocol to his advantage.

CHAPTER 45

He had never realized how far the talons of Silence had dug into his brain. Removing them felt like picking out thorns one at a time. But the strangest thing was that, though he was operating exclusively on the psychic plane, he could feel Brenna beside him, her hand having moved to close over his forearm, an anchor that kept him centered.

Extraordinary.

The outer ring of conditioning was deceptively easy to unravel. Deceptive because midway through, he realized it was linked to the dissonance loop—on a level that would cause unconsciousness. He stopped, retraced his steps, and found the embedded triggers. Disarming them was eerily similar to taking apart a thousand tiny explosive devices. Good thing he'd been trained for just that. Of course, this was a little different. One mistake and he'd cause an implosion in his brain. So he wouldn't make mistakes.

By the time he finished, he had a new respect for the programming process. They'd done a hell of a job on him. There had been not one but six Black Keys built into the initial layer, contingencies upon contingencies. If he hadn't been as skilled as he was, he could have activated any one of them several times over.

It made him wonder about Sascha and Faith. Sascha was easy to explain—Silence had never "taken" with her. Her ability had simply run so counter to it as to make conditioning impossible. But Faith *had* been under and, from what he could understand, had shattered Silence during a major emotional storm. She'd never mentioned aggressive factors such as Black Keys and psychic grenades meant to shut down the body and mind.

Those facts bolstered his earlier theory—that the programming was altered to suit the needs of each individual child. He'd required extremely severe controls because of his Tk-Cell abilities. He couldn't fault his trainers for that. But he had a suspicion that those controls had been further strengthened because of his future as an Arrow. They hadn't wanted to lose their best assassin.

The worst danger appeared on the third level—lines of conditioning tied directly to his ability to kill with a stray thought. After examining them for several minutes, he opened his eyes. Brenna's concerned face was the first thing he saw.

"What is it?" Her hand clenched on his arm.

"This is where I have to choose which parts of Silence to delete and which to leave functional. Too much and the dissonance will keep trying to disable me. Too little and I'll eliminate the safety systems that stop me from killing by accident." As he had killed eight-year-old Paul, a name he'd never forget, a face that would haunt his dreams forever.

"Why don't you take a break?" Brenna stroked his hair off his forehead in that habit she had. "You were under for an hour."

He allowed himself to touch her cheek with his knuckles. "No. It's better if I do it all at once. If I delay, some of the embedded protocols may reinitiate."

She rubbed back against his touch. "All right. Do what you have to do. But remember—if you kill yourself you'll be in big trouble."

Nodding, he closed his eyes and returned to his mind. And

found a hidden reservoir of emotion. The conditioning was anchored in guilt, fear, protectiveness, and a fierce desire to keep people safe. They'd used his own emotions to chain him. Part of him appreciated the efficiency, but another part was so incredibly angry, it was a chill across his soul.

However, he didn't have time for anger. Not today. Calming his mind again, he began to unlace the threads of control. Step by slow step. It felt like hours passed. Then suddenly he was at the center point, where a choice had to be made. Reason clashed with his need to be free. He needed the warning system, but he didn't need it crippling him. He undid the entire structure.

It took as long as it took. But finally, it was done. His Psy powers were now free of any restraint. But it wasn't a freedom that was good. As Tai had to learn discipline over his physical strength, Judd had to maintain it over his psychic abilities. The only difference was that Judd couldn't afford *any* mistakes.

It took him a long time to find a solution and, once again, it was his training as an Arrow that came to his aid. "I'm setting a trip wire," he said out loud, knowing in his bones that Brenna was terrified for him.

"What will activate it?"

"It'll snap my ability shut if I attempt to use it to kill." For anything short of a killing rage, he'd have to rely on his skills at regulating emotion. That, he could do.

A small pause. "Won't that disadvantage you?"

"No. I can reverse the tripped wire in a split second, and my other abilities will continue to function during that time."

"A split second."

He recalled the way she'd kissed him to stop him from ending Dieter's life. "That's all I need." A moment's clarity to make the decision to kill rather than being held hostage to his dark gift.

No, he thought, it wasn't wholly dark. It had helped save Andrew's life—there was a way it could be utilized for good. Pre-Silence Tk-Cells, trapped by their out-of-control emotions, had never learned that. And post-Silence Tk-Cells had never been given the chance to be anything but sanctioned killers. But now he had that chance, that choice. "It'll work."

"Then do it." A statement of loyalty, of togetherness, of such complete trust that he felt it *inside* his mind. Mentally frowning at the impossibility, he finished laying the psychic trip wire. That done, he went even deeper, to the place where the conditioning was a hard shell around his emotional core, segregating that part of him. The shields were fragmented but holding. He put a psychic hand on the first one.

A shock wave of excruciating pain shot through his body.

Then Brenna cried out.

Gritting his teeth, he opened his eyes to see her face gone white. "Brenna?"

"Oh, God, Judd." She squeezed his hand. "I felt the . . . shadow of that, an echo. If what I felt was diluted, how are you still conscious?"

"Why did you feel it?" Protective instincts roared to life. "We aren't mated."

Her shattered eyes went wide. "Are you sure?"

His heart actually stopped for a second, he wanted so much for her to belong to him on the most irrevocable level. "I guess we'll find out." He went back into the minefield of his consciousness, throwing a shield around Brenna at the same time. But he knew that that would only mute the impact, not stop it altogether, not when he didn't know the origin of the link that connected them.

He spent several minutes looking at the emotional blocks. "I have to destroy them. No subtlety. A total wipeout."

"What will it do to you?"

The real question was—what would it do to her? He could weather just about anything except her hurt. "There'll be pain."

The soft brush of lips against his cheek. "Pain I can take."

He didn't question her, didn't doubt her. Brenna had earned his respect the day she'd come out sane from that bloody room where she'd been held. "No matter what happens," he told her, "don't let anyone else interfere."

"But—"

"No one."

"Fine, but not if it gets to the point where you might die."

"Accepted." Arrowing his senses to a fine laser point, he sliced the shields in half.

For a moment, there was nothing. True silence. Pure calm.

Then agony streaked through every nerve ending, every synapse, every sense he possessed. He heard Brenna scream and the protective core of him refused to allow that. He threw up an instinctive block against a connection that shouldn't have existed and had the satisfaction of hearing her shudder in relief. A second later, the pain blanked everything from his mind.

CHAPTER 46

Shoshanna Scott met her husband, Henry, in their living quarters after their operations had been completed. Ashaya Aleine's closest aide, the one who had implanted them in the first place, had done the retraction. It had taken an hour each, the procedures complicated by the way the implants had integrated into their neural cells.

"How do you feel?"

"A slight headache and some weakness in my limbs but that's supposed to pass." Henry answered her question in the spirit in which it had been asked. Concentrating on the physical. They were husband and wife for propaganda purposes only—the humans and changelings seemed to like the idea of a couple in the Council.

"I'm much the same." She took a seat beside him. "It's to our advantage that we were implanted after the others." It had given them plenty of warning of the experimental implants' catastrophic failure. "It's a pity the implants were so degraded they won't be able to reverse engineer them."

"Perhaps we should rethink the idea of storing backup files on the Net."

"No." Shoshanna agreed with the other Councilors on this, shortsighted though many of their decisions were. "We upload it, we chance a leak. Aleine will be able to put it all back together."

"It will take months if not years for her to get back to where she was before the sabotage." Henry shifted. "It's disconcerting to have to return to this ineffectual method of communication."

During the past two months, they had been functioning as a flawless psychic unit, sharing every thought. However, they hadn't quite become one mind—Shoshanna was aware that she'd wielded more power in the unit. It proved the theory that there must always be a controlling mind. For example, the eight below them had been unable to merge into Henry's and Shoshanna's minds but the reverse hadn't held true. "We'll return to it one day. What's the status of the remaining four participants?"

"Alive but agitated."

Shoshanna stood. "Take care of it."

"I already have." Henry mirrored her stance. Their minds were still attuned on a level beyond the norm, but without the implant, that link would eventually fade. "I gave a final order prior to the removal of my implant. They'll end their own lives one after the other during the next eight hours."

"Excellent." What it was to truly wield the power of life and death—the others knew nothing of this. If they had, they would've pushed Protocol I faster instead of insisting on the current snail's pace. "That ties things up nicely." Now they had to ensure the Council didn't backpedal from the idea. It had to go ahead. Shoshanna intended to become a queen in truth, to hold lives in the palm of her hand.

CHAPTER 47

Brenna's wolf was going crazy trapped inside of her. "Baby, please." Judd's head remained unmoving in her lap as she stroked his hair off his forehead over and over. It had been three hours since he'd gone down, taking her share of the pain as well as his own. The only thing keeping her from breaking apart was the certain knowledge that he *was* alive. She knew it in her soul. They were bonded whether anyone could see it or not.

Full dark had fallen long ago, along with the temperature. Judd's lips had begun to turn blue three minutes ago, as if some internal battery had died. Everything in her wanted to run for help, but he had made her promise not to let anyone else interfere. Her hand clenched on her phone as she ran her eyes over his body. His chest moved up and down. His breath came out. But he was so cold, so scarily cold. Colder than the snow.

This wasn't right. He was Pack. What he'd done so many times for the others should be his due now. To lean on Pack was no shame. Except that she knew he was too proud, too used to standing alone. But she couldn't watch him die. "I'm sorry, my darling." She flipped open the phone . . . and found it dead.

Throwing it aside, she began a frantic search of Judd. Nothing. But she knew he always carried a phone. Her mind went back to the image of him pulling on his jacket in the clearing. It had to have fallen out then. "No."

A movement in the forest. Her heart leaped in her throat, followed by predatory calm. *No one will touch him.* Her claws pushed at the edges of her skin as her eyes focused on the source of the sound, every instinct primed to defend her mate.

The wolf that emerged was almost invisible against the snow, his pelt a thick silver-gold that acted like camouflage. Relaxing from her offensive stance, she returned her attention to Judd as Hawke shifted to human form and came to kneel on Judd's other side. "You didn't signal for attention."

She shook her head and met his eyes. "He's exactly like you."

"Hell, I know that. I expected *you* to have better sense." A sharp reproof. "How long?"

"Three hours."

"Can we move him?"

"I think so." But she wasn't going to risk it. "I don't know if there was any . . . damage." Brain damage. He was Psy—they were their minds, and things that erupted from the mind outward had the ability to destroy them. "Moving him might make it worse."

Hawke's eyes flashed to pure danger. "The damn Psy is too stubborn to die. Keep him alive while I get Walker and some heating sheets."

"Go." Brenna kept her hands on Judd's cheeks. "I'll be here."

Hawke left without anything further, disappearing into the woods in a flash of silver-gold. With his speed, help would be on the way in under half an hour. But what could Walker do? He wasn't a Psy medic and even if he had been, what medic could possibly see inside a mind as guarded as her Psy's? She knew his shields to be impenetrable.

Not against you.

Her breath caught. She wondered if the cold was starting to affect her brain. "Judd?"

I'm here. I have to repair some damage before I rise to full consciousness.

That sounded too much like him to be her imagination. "Damage?" she whispered.

Don't worry, baby. I'll be fully functional. A definite sensual emphasis on those last two words.

She wanted to thump him for worrying her so, but what stopped her was the open affection in his mental tones. She'd never heard that in his voice. But now he was speaking to her without any barriers . . . trusting her with everything he was. Swallowing, she wiped the backs of her hands across her eyes. "You idiot. I'll damage you myself if you don't shut up and hurry."

Male laughter in her mind. He sounded just as she'd always thought he'd sound if he laughed—arrogant, a touch bad, and drop-dead gorgeous. *I can hear your thoughts.*

"Then stop listening." But she was too happy to worry. And . . . this was Judd. He had under-the-skin privileges. "How can we talk like this anyway? None of the others can." Not that she'd seen.

I'm a high-level telepath. I could always send, even to very weak receivers, and you're not weak.

A small silence. "What did Enrique do?" She'd been avoiding the issue after no one had seemed to be able to give her any answers, but now Judd was in the one place she had vowed to never allow another being. And it felt right. "Tell me, I'm ready."

I don't know what his intention was, but it looks like he might have opened your mind in a way it was never meant to be opened. That's why you've been picking up fragments of others' thoughts and dreams, why you've been acting out of character. I need to teach you to shield, not like a changeling but like a Psy. Until you can, I'll shield you.

"Well, if we can talk like this, at least some good came out of that." She dropped a kiss on his forehead. Then frowned. *Can I think to you?*

Yes. He sounded delighted. *Brenna, it's not just my telepathy and the changes in you that are allowing us to speak. I can see it—a bond like the one to my familial Net, except this one is . . . it's . . . I'm no poet . . .*

A caress whispered through her mind and she knew he wanted her to close her eyes. So she did. A second later, she felt something travel down the bond. It was an image of the bond itself. A stunning kaleidoscope, twisted through with the martial threads of a soldier and the bright, animal sparks that represented her.

A tear streaked down her face. *I love you.*

You're mine.

She laughed at the possessive tone. "I've always been yours. Now hurry up or the others will find me here talking to myself."

I told you I didn't need any help.

"And I told you you're Pack now." She would beat that into his head even if it took a lifetime.

He went silent, obviously working. She didn't interrupt him and when he lifted those dark lashes twenty minutes later, all she could do was smile. "Hey."

Looking up into her eyes, he raised a hand to close over her nape. "Come here."

Bending down, she touched her lips to his. Warmth flowed from her to him and then back. The bond pulsed before sparking, sending a small electric shock down her spine. Gasping, she broke the kiss. "I don't think that's normal."

"You're mated to a Tk." He smiled and while it was small, it was most definitely a smile. The impact was, to say the least, devastating. "It looks as if I can do all sorts of things to you now that the bond's functioning as it should." As if to prove that, the next pulse traveled directly to the heat between her legs.

Sucking in a breath, she leaned over and bit his lower lip. "My turn." Mate, he was her mate. Hers forever. "Mine."

"Yours." His hand tightened on her nape as he allowed her to take advantage of him.

"Why wasn't the bond working before?" she asked the next time they came up for air. "My wolf couldn't sense it."

"Silence." Shadows in his voice. "It had me wrapped up so

tight, I was blocking it, likely stopping you from feeling it, too. To accept it would probably have led to a fatal strike from the dissonance, so my brain protected itself the only way it could." There was anger now. "Silence tried to destroy us before we could begin."

"But the bond was always there," she whispered. "So take that, Psy Council. Not even your damn Silence can stop what's meant to be."

Judd's eyes widened at her vehemence and then that small smile widened a fraction. "I thought I told you to come here."

"And I thought I told you not to mess with me." But she went. Sometimes, you had to give in to a male. Especially when he was yours and he looked at you with that naked heat in his eyes.

It was amazing what a man could do when he was properly motivated, Judd thought as he straightened Brenna's clothing. Just in time. Four wolves burst out of the forest seconds later. Walker wasn't that far behind, having been brought there on a snowmobile loaded with emergency medical equipment.

The wolves shifted as his brother got off the snowmobile and walked across. "Are you all right?"

Judd nodded. "Yes."

But another conversation was taking place on the Lauren-Net.

You've disabled the Silence Protocol. There was no judgment in his brother's tone. *It's already influencing the familial Net.*

Judd realized Walker was right. *We've been living with emotion since the children started adapting. It won't harm them.*

No. Walker's psychic presence was a star that had an odd twisting motion at the center. He wasn't a martial Psy, and no one had ever been able to figure out what that twisting motion meant. *There's a new mind in the Net.*

Judd blinked and looked again. There she was, linked to the Net through him and protected by his powerful mind. None of the others could touch her, though her strong, affectionate nature was already influencing the flows of the tiny LaurenNet. *Brenna.* She couldn't see this, couldn't see her wild silver star with ricocheting shards of vibrant blue, but it was something that calmed his psychic mind. He could protect her now, no matter where she was. He'd know if she shed a single tear.

She's making the Net stronger.

Of course she was. *She's a wolf.*

You're sure?

Judd knew they were no longer talking about Brenna. *I'm safe.* Reaching back, he took his mate's hand in his. *Have you seen the other changes in the Net?* Faint sparks of color where there had once only been black and white.

I think it represents a formerly suppressed aspect of Toby's abilities. It doesn't fit the parameters of any known designation, but I have my suspicions.

So did Judd. *We'll talk later.*

Hawke narrowed his eyes as Walker stepped back. "I leave you going blue and thinking I'm going to have to dig a grave, and return to find you . . . well *exercised.*" A pause that took in the rucked-up snow. Behind Hawke, Lara did a bad job of hiding a grin. "You want to explain that?"

"No." Judd felt Brenna's blush in his mind and knew she'd realized her packmates could smell the scent of their recent explosive union. He liked the idea of her being covered in his scent. "There's nothing to explain."

Hawke grunted, amusement in his eyes. "Right. Let's head back."

"Give me a minute." It was Riley.

Judd met the other man's eyes as everyone else dispersed. Beside him, Brenna went very quiet. Her brother came forward. "You ever make her cry, I'll break every bone in your body, tear you to pieces, and hold a barbeque for the wild wolves."

"Riley!" Brenna sounded shocked.

Judd wasn't—despite Riley's calm exterior, the male was as ferally protective as Andrew. "I think Brenna is more than capable of doing that herself."

"Judd!"

Riley's face broke out in an uncharacteristic grin. "Yeah, she is." Reaching out, he kissed his gaping sister's cheek before pulling back and shifting. Then he was gone.

"I can't believe you said that." Brenna was scowling when he turned to her. "I would never hurt you."

He wanted to laugh at her outrage. "I adore you." And now he could truly protect her—what he hadn't told her was that Enrique's alterations had put undue pressure on her brain. Because her brain was changeling, not Psy, it hadn't had any way to vent that pressure. Sooner or later, things would've gone to a critical state.

The reason for her present health was that, even dormant, the bond had somehow leached off enough of the overload—dispersing it through his psychic channels—that she didn't collapse. But now he could consciously regulate the pressure, reducing it and shielding her, until she learned to do it herself. It would be hard but not impossible, not with Brenna's strength of will. "You are the most stubborn, most beautiful woman I know."

"Oh . . . how am I supposed to stay mad when you say something like that?" She stamped her foot but her lips were curving up into a smile. "You're pretty, too." She grinned at his scowl. "But you're the most infuriating man I've ever met."

"Too bad. You're stuck with me."

Standing on tiptoe, she spoke against his lips. "I like being stuck to you."

He was about to kiss her when she wrenched away. "You want a kiss? Come and get it." A taunt, an invitation, a lovers' game.

Judd had never played much. He had a feeling that was about to change. "You should know never to dare an Arrow."

"You're all talk, Judd Lauren." A blur of movement and she was gone.

Feeling his heartbeat speed up, he pushed off after her. He'd get his kiss. And more. Using the bond, he sent her explicit images detailing the prize he intended to claim.

Not fair, came the breathy response. *Now I'm all hot and wet.*

He tripped. *You did that on purpose.*

Nuh-uh. If I'd wanted to mess with you, I'd have told you about this fantasy I have of having you at my mercy.

That intrigued him. *What would you do?*

This.

Images cascaded into his mind, affectionate, lush, and so incredibly erotic that he found himself fighting his body's desire to descend into pure sensation.

Let me?

He was used to protecting his back, to never giving anyone control over his body or his mind. *I'm yours.* It was the final surrender.

Sascha couldn't believe the difference in Brenna when she saw her the next day, having come up to the den to talk to Lara about a different situation. "She's happy, healed," she said to Lucas on the trip home, her ears still full of the sound of the SnowDancer's laughter. "And Judd—I wouldn't have believed it if I hadn't felt it with my empathy. He might look unchanged on the surface, but he *loves* her." So deep and true it almost hurt. Sascha knew—she loved Lucas like that.

"Then why do you sound so sad, kitten?" He threw her a concerned look before returning his attention to the rough mountain road.

"She was betrayed by one of her own," Sascha whispered, shaken. "I thought Pack was safe, was family. If you can't trust Pack, who can you trust?"

Lucas brought the car to a halt in the middle of nowhere and reached over to pull her into his lap. "Pack is safe. Pack is the cornerstone of who we are."

"Then why? How?" She nestled her head under his chin. "Dieter was a SnowDancer soldier, but he's so twisted." Even walking past his cell had made her sick to her stomach. Waves of something rotten, putrid, had emanated from his soul.

Lucas stroked his hand down her back. "Having the animal inside protects us against many sins, but even changelings sometimes spawn evil."

She thought about that for long minutes. "For there to be light, there must be darkness." It was what Faith had said after her escape from the Net. But only now did Sascha truly understand. "If you try for perfection, you become exactly like the Psy." A cold, robotic race without the ability to laugh, love, or cherish.

"No race is perfect." He nuzzled at her. "And I kind of like you, flaws and all."

She found her smile again. "Yes. Perfection is vastly overrated—if they measured the Psy race's contentedness index, the results would undoubtedly be in the negatives."

"God, you're sexy when you talk Psy."

CHAPTER 48

"You're walking funny," Lucy said, a shit-eating grin on her face.

Five days of out of this world sex with a starving man could do that to a girl. "You're just jealous." Brenna pushed through the door into DarkRiver's business HQ.

Lucy made a mournful face. "Yes, I am. Goddamn but your man is hot. And he *smiles* at you! I've seen him do it, even if no one believes me."

"I know." She smiled herself and it was so wide, her face felt as if it would crack. "What are you doing here anyway?"

"I have to talk to Mercy about a joint holovision project. CTX thing." Lucy looked over her shoulder after naming the leopard-wolf communications company. "Here comes your beautiful man. Talk to you later."

Judd put a hand on her lower back as they walked down to the basement. He did that a lot—touch her. Her smile stretched impossibly wider. "I think we should play 'who's more patient' again tonight."

"Fine." He sounded oh so Psy but his hand had slipped

down to caress her hip. "You do remember that you always lose?"

Losing had never been so much fun. "We'll see." She walked through the basement door to find Dorian already at the console. "Where are Lucas and Hawke?" The alpha had preceded them here.

"At the building site," Dorian replied, referring to the joint Psy-changeling development being designed and built by DarkRiver for Nikita Duncan.

"I thought the wolves were silent partners in the project," Judd commented as she took her seat beside Dorian and began to check the lines of programming for the last time. "They just supplied the land, correct?"

Dorian nodded. "Lucas and Hawke were talking and decided to give themselves an airtight 'alibi.'" He smirked. "Hard to accuse them of masterminding this when they were in a meeting with Nikita at the time."

Of course, Judd thought, the Council would know exactly who to blame for the technological strike, but that was the point. The alphas were sending a message: You attack us and we'll bite back, and we'll do it where it hurts. The six Psy assassins who had butchered the DawnSky deer had already been dispatched—that op had taken place the same day Judd obtained the names. Now it was time for the second strike.

He glanced at his watch. "The stock exchange opens in ten seconds."

"Give it a few minutes—let them think everything's okay." Dorian leaned back in his chair as they waited. "Okay. Time's up. You want to do the honors, kid?"

"Oh yes." Rubbing her hands, Brenna held her finger over a key. "They should have never come into our territory and taken the lives of those under our care." She pressed down. "We look after our own."

The Psy Council convened an emergency session within minutes of the exchange failure. They had barely gotten a handle on that situation when other systems began to fail in a relentless cascade. Major Psy banks and large Psy businesses were the worst hit.

There was no signature, no way to identify the perpetrators of the rapid-fire assault. But Nikita Duncan had looked into two pairs of alpha-changeling eyes today. She got the message. And she made sure the rest of the Council appreciated it.

For the first time, no one argued with her. The damage was too widespread, the intelligence behind the stealthy attack too finely honed. There was no doubt the animals had won this skirmish.

EPILOGUE

It happened in the middle of a wild outdoor lovemaking session that had gotten more than a little vigorous. Winter had left with languid softness and now spring was a cool breeze on her skin. Judd picked Brenna up and put her flat on the ground. Her breath rushed out—not because he'd used excessive pressure—on the contrary, her landing had been angel soft. No, it was because he hadn't used his hands.

Attuned as he was to the bond, he froze in the act of ripping off his shirt, leaving his ridged abdomen bare. "Brenna."

"I'm okay. It was a surprise, that's all." She meant that. Her mate was a powerful telekinetic and she trusted him never to use that Tk to hurt her.

His eyes darkened, then he smiled. "Do you like surprises?"

That still-rare smile had the ability to send warmth rushing to the juncture of her thighs. Squeezing them together, she nodded. That was when her pants unzipped of their own accord and began being pulled down her body along with her panties.

She couldn't help it. She cried out, especially when he lifted her bottom to help drag the clothing off. They flew to land on the branches of a nearby tree. "Some surprise." Her heart raced. "What's next?"

Not answering, he walked around to stand at her feet, looking down at her body with blatant possessiveness. Her shirt was open and parted to reveal her breasts, her lower body naked, her knees raised. She had never felt more deliciously exposed.

"Spread your thighs." A low, rough order.

She blushed at what he was asking her to do but even as she hesitated, phantom hands began to spread her. Shocked, she didn't fight because those hands *felt* just like those of the man who watched her—watched her as if she were a feast he was waiting to gorge on. Then those invisible hands slid down to her curls and paused.

Dangerous Psy eyes clashed into hers. "I want to open you."

Brenna had known she was getting a dominant male when she chose Judd. His intensity didn't scare her. Rather, it sent erotic need rushing over her body, further tightening the already taut peaks of her breasts and dampening the woman core of her. But what seduced her to complete submission was that, even violently aroused, he had stopped to check how she was handling this escalation of their sexual life, the working of his Tk fully into who they were together.

"Do it," she whispered, the words so thick she had to force them out.

Those phantom fingers spread apart her intimate lips, baring her to the air . . . to his gaze. Blood flooded her cheeks and she could feel herself flushing in other, normally hidden places. An invisible finger dipped into her, pushing in an inch before spreading her cream over the hard bud he'd exposed to the air.

"Judd!" When she could breathe again, she looked up to find he'd undone his pants at last, releasing his erection.

"I want." A bold sexual statement she could only make because this was her mate.

He fisted himself. "This?"

She couldn't believe it. "You're going to tease?" Two could

play at that game, even if Judd was undeniably the more skilled at it. Sliding one hand down her own body, she dipped her fingers into her heat, pleasuring herself with lazy strokes, while she used the fingers of her other hand to caress her breasts, pluck at her nipples.

Judd's eyes followed the movements of her hands, his own moving over rigid flesh in unconscious synchrony. The sight clutched at her stomach, made her want to speed up her strokes, push herself over the edge. But she was determined to seduce him this time.

She withdrew her fingers from her body on a groan . . . and held them out. "How about a taste?"

The tree branches over her shifted in a breeze she couldn't feel, new spring-green leaves flying every which way. *Judd.* He was making it happen, loosening his rigid control. Instead of fear, she felt pure exhilaration. And when he dropped down on his knees between her spread thighs, all she could see were the glowing embers of a very masculine desire in his eyes. Taking her glistening fingers, he tugged them back down to her sex.

"Touch," he ordered, voice harsh. "Show me what you like."

"You know what I like," she said, but followed the command.

Putting his hands on her raised knees, he spread her even farther, as if to better his view. She was so spellbound by the sexual chains of his unashamed hunger that she was barely aware of the crashing movements of the tree branches, the whiplash speed of the leaves circling around them. Her heartbeat was in her mouth, alive and demanding. Her whole body felt flushed to fever pitch. She wanted something thicker and harder than her fingers stroking in and out of the melting warmth of her body.

Without warning, Judd dragged away her hand and took over the task. His strokes were deeper, rougher than her own and they made her cry out in shocking pleasure. She wanted to wrap her legs around him but one of his hands remained on her knee, telling her he wanted her spread open for him. So she kept her feet flat on the earth.

"Good." He slid that hand down the inner face of her thigh

to grip her hip firmly as she twisted under the force of his driving strokes. All thought of taking charge was lost, but it didn't matter, because in this sensual game, surrender was the sweetest of victories.

The edge beckoned, promising hot twisting pleasure/pain that would cut through her body like lightning and turn her mind to pure fever for long pleasure-drenched moments. Anticipation had her holding her breath. One more caress—

Judd withdrew his fingers.

"No," she moaned, so ready to go over she could hardly think.

He shifted his body closer. She felt the tip of his erection nudge at her. Then he gripped her hip tight and pushed in. All the air left her lungs in a harsh exhalation as she felt every thick inch of him scrape past her desire-swollen flesh. Her fingers clawed the earth, but she never took her eyes off his face. What she saw set off the ripples that announced an impending explosion.

He was watching their bodies join, his expression that of a man driven to ecstasy. Red streaked over his cheekbones and his jaw was clenched hard enough to have cracked stone. Beautiful and so sexy she could barely believe he was hers.

He pushed home, going so deep she could feel him in dark unexplored places. Against her spread flesh, the rough material of his jeans, the cold teeth of his zipper, provided an added erotic sensation, a quiet reiteration that Judd was no longer in control.

His eyes finally raised to hers, the gold flecks almost glowing against the bitter chocolate. "I'm going to move now."

That was her only warning before her lover began thrusting into her with hard strokes that bowed her back and tore a scream from her throat. Pure sensation shot through her, eclipsing the anticipation and cascading into her mind . . . a bolt of white lightning that traveled from both ends of the bond to create a sensual inferno.

Male to female. Psy to changeling. Mate to mate.

* * *

She stepped over a broken branch to retrieve her pants. "Baby, I love you, but when we go furniture shopping, I want titanium alloy." In the months since their mating, he'd already destroyed the wooden stuff. Four times. Currently, they had no table, no sofa, and no chairs. "Thank goodness the walls are stone and the bed's got a metal frame."

Her teasing made him stretch out, half-naked and indolently at ease on the forest floor. "If you'd stay still, I'd be fine." Except he didn't sound particularly enthused by the idea of her remaining still.

Turning to face him, she pulled on her pants over bare flesh, shoving her panties into a pocket. She very definitely had his full attention. "Where would be the fun in that?" Grinning, she left her shirt open and walked to kneel beside him. His abdomen was pure hard muscle under her touch. "Aren't you going to get up?"

He put a hand on the curve of her hip, a possessive gesture that had already become familiar. "No. Let's have more sex."

"Insatiable." She kissed him, loving that he trusted her enough to allow her to see him without barriers. As far as the rest of the den was concerned, he was still the Man of Ice. They couldn't understand how she could have mated with him. But he'd earned his stripes as far as being Pack went so they shrugged and accepted the pairing. "Any more sex and we'll expire. Don't you have a meeting with Hawke anyway?"

A grunt and he deigned to get up. Kissing her as she rose to her feet, too, he zipped up his pants. His shirt continued to hang open—from the look in his eye, he was more interested in watching her button up her own. "Shooting practice with Dorian?" he asked after she'd finished.

"He says I'm getting really good." Though that didn't make up for what Enrique had done to her, what he'd stolen, it helped to know she could still defend herself, as well as protect those who mattered to her.

"Hey." Her mate stroked her hair off her face. "No being sad. I can't handle it."

She knew he was speaking literally. He continued to find it

difficult to process certain emotions, but he was learning. "I just"—she gripped his waist with one hand—"I just wish I could go wolf again." But then she smiled and it was real. "I'm happy and strong now, but I'll always miss that part of me. As you miss the Net." He never complained about the loss but she was beginning to understand the depth of what he'd given up to save his family. It must have felt like cutting off a limb.

He kissed her. "You're the sexiest wolf I know." A pulse of love came down the mating bond. It was rich and unashamed and it exploded in her like a bomb.

She was about to reply when her claws sliced out, drawing Judd's blood. She jerked back. "Oh, God, I'm so s—!" Everything disappeared in a familiar burst of searing agony and endless ecstasy, her cells changing on a level that was emphatically changeling.

Judd froze as the world dissolved into a multicolored shimmer around Brenna. Shifting was something he'd witnessed with other wolves, but this was different in the most fundamental way. This was his mate. He could feel what was happening to her as if it were taking place in his own body. Sheer torment and excruciating bliss, an exquisite mix unlike anything he'd ever before experienced.

Seconds later, it was over. In front of him stood a sleek wolf with soft gray fur that beckoned touch. Without thinking, he went to his knees and stroked his hand over her neck, his eyes locked into those so intelligent and unique that they could only belong to Brenna—in spite of the fact that she'd shifted, her irises hadn't lost that flare of arctic blue.

She was the most beautiful thing he had ever seen.

Something came down the bond. Uncertainty. Fear. "What is it?" He thought rapidly. "You're perfect, beautiful," he reassured her. "No errors in the shift."

Laughter in his mind, joy. Pulling out of his hold, she loped across the clearing they had used for their play. He let her go, an odd sensation tightening his chest. He knew she needed her freedom, no matter that he ached to go with her.

She stopped at the edge of the clearing and looked over her

shoulder. His mate might've changed form, but he could read her loud and clear. She was throwing down a challenge. Feeling a smile warm his whole body though only a hint reached his face, he rose. "You're on, Brenna Shane." The meeting could wait. The whole world could wait.

Brenna didn't cut him any slack, taking off through the trees like silver lightning. He ran after her, focusing his Tk into this simple exercise so he could fly alongside the gorgeous woman who was his mate.

The early evening turned to true night and still they ran, playing hide-and-seek with each other, trying to sneak up at times, kicking up fallen leaves just to watch them move. Simple play and the closest he had ever come to feeling like a child.

By the time she'd had enough, they had circled back to their original starting point. They were both breathing hard but energy flickered through the air. When she shifted this time, it was even more beautiful, because he could feel her joy from the start. She appeared from the sparkling motes, a lovely naked woman with a huge smile cracking her face.

"Judd!" She threw open her arms and he bent down to lift her up. Her legs wrapped around his waist as he stood and she laughed. "I can shift!"

Spinning around with her in his arms, he kissed the side of her neck then planted his lips on her mouth. She kissed him back with wild abandon and under his hands, her skin was smooth and hot and welcoming. *Skin privileges*. Breaking the kiss, he drank in the sight of her happiness. "You are too damn gorgeous. In either form."

Her face filled with tenderness. "I was afraid you wouldn't . . . that you'd get freaked out at seeing me as a wolf. Then you told me I was perfect, that I had no 'errors.' " The last word was a tease.

He was incredibly glad his response had reassured her, even though he'd misunderstood the reason for her worry. "You are." He held her with one arm and ran the other over her thigh to curve around her bottom. "And you're naked."

Her eyes went huge. "My clothes!" She looked around as

if expecting them to reappear by magic, though the shift process had disintegrated them. "What am I going to do?"

He felt his lips twitch.

She hit his shoulder with one small fist. "This is not funny!"

"I think you look delectable naked." He kissed her chin. "Of course, I'd have to kill anyone else who dared put their eyes on you."

"I can't walk through the den like this!" she wailed.

He'd noticed that—no matter how blasé they were about nudity otherwise, the wolves followed strict rules in the den about being clothed. The pups were the single exception. "For such a smart wolf," he murmured against her lips, "you're betraying a distinct lack of logic."

"Logic?" She scowled but kissed him back.

"Mmm." He squeezed her bottom. "Shift. Wear your fur." That was acceptable behavior. Soldiers often lost access to clothing and had to return in animal form.

Her mouth fell open. "Oh." A sigh whispered through her whole body. "I'm going to have to get used to this all over again."

"You're welcome to forget the clothing anytime you like."

"Thanks. But you don't get a vote—you lust after my body." Her teeth nipped at his lower lip. "Why do you think it came back now?"

"Maybe it was time—you were ready for it."

She gave him a sweet kiss. "I think you helped with that. Made me understand that my soul hadn't been destroyed by that monster. That I survived in every way."

He didn't agree. She was the one who'd fought to reclaim her life. "Your courage amazes me."

"And your love makes me whole." She made her confession without shame.

He wanted so much to say it back but the words stuck in the fading grip of Silence. He'd never be easy saying love words.

Her lips brushed his. "I know, baby. I can feel you loving me deep inside."

Judd figured he must've done something right along the

way. How else could a rebel Arrow have earned the right to call this amazing woman his own? Even if it was a mistake, too damn bad. He was never giving her up.

In the psychic plane of the LaurenNet, a wave of love traveled in every direction, emanating from a bond that was not Psy but changeling, a bond that tied an assassin to a wolf, a bond that was . . . unbreakable.

ACKNOWLEDGMENTS

Writing is a solitary business but it's not a lonely one, especially not when you're surrounded by as many wonderful people as I am.

At home: My family, the ones who have to put up with my single-minded focus when I'm working and who do it in such style. Thanks for not making me cook or clean . . . or vacuum . . . or do the laundry . . . I love you guys!

On a California beach sipping a margarita (well, she might be if she didn't have obsessive-compulsive clients): Nephele Tempest, my agent and the first person to tell me she loved my Psy/Changeling world. Thanks for being such a great advocate for my work. If we ever manage to meet in person, the margaritas are on me!

At my publisher: Cindy Hwang, my brilliant editor and someone who gives me the freedom to follow my imagination wherever it takes me; Leis Pederson, superefficient editorial assistant (and someone who is probably sick of hearing my voice after those marathon editing session over the phone!); and the *Sensation*al behind-the-scenes team. A huge thank-you for everything you've done since the very first book in the Psy/Changeling series.

In unknown locations: All the booksellers, readers, reviewers, librarians, and bloggers who have supported my books to date. If I tried to list you all, I'd run out of room, which, I think, is an amazing, humbling thing. Thank you.

Acknowledgments

Outside the door demanding I come out or they're going to drag me out: My friends, who put up with my hermitlike tendencies without crossing me off their invitation lists. You know who you are. I feel blessed to have you in my life.

And inside my head: My characters, who let me tell their stories. Thank you.

Turn the page for a sneak peak at the fourth novel in the Psy-Changeling series, *Mine to Possess*

Talin McKade told herself that twenty-eight-year-old women—especially twenty-eight-year-old women who had seen and survived what she had—did not fear anything so simple as walking across the road and into a bar to pick up a man.

Except, of course, this was no ordinary man. And a bar was the last place she'd expected to find Clay given what she had learned about him in the two weeks since she'd first tracked him down. It didn't bode well that it had taken her that long to screw up the courage to come to him. But she had had to be sure.

What she had discovered was that the Clay she'd known, the tall, angry, powerful *boy*, had become some kind of high-ranking enforcer for the dominant leopard pack in San Francisco. DarkRiver was extremely well-respected, so Clay's position spoke of trust and loyalty. The last word stabbed a blade deep into her heart.

Clay had always been loyal to her. Even when she didn't deserve it. Swallowing, she shoved away the memories, knowing she couldn't let them distract her. The old Clay was gone. This Clay . . . She didn't know him. All she knew was that he hadn't had any run-ins with the law after being released from the juvenile facility where he had been incarcerated at the age of fourteen—for the brutal slaying of one Orrin Henderson.

Talin's hands clamped down on the steering wheel with white-knuckled force. She could feel blood rising to flood her cheeks as her heart thudded in remembered fear. Parts of Orrin, soft and wet *things* that should have never been exposed to the air, flecking her as she cowered in the corner while Clay—

No!

She couldn't think about that, couldn't go there. It was enough that the nightmare images—full of the thick, cloying smell of raw meat gone bad—haunted her sleep night after night. She would not surrender her daytime hours, too.

Flashing blue and white lights caught her attention as another enforcement vehicle pulled into the bar's small front parking lot. That made two armored vehicles and four very well-armed cops, but though they had all gotten out, none of the four made any move to enter the bar. Unsure what was going on, she stayed inside her Jeep, parked in the secondary lot on the other side of the wide road.

Sweat trickled down her spine at the sight of the cop cars. She had learned young to associate their presence with violence. Every instinct in her urged her to get the hell out. But she had to wait, to see. If Clay hadn't changed, if he had grown worse . . . Uncurling one hand from the wheel, she fisted it against a stomach filled with roiling, twisting despair. He was her last hope.

The bar door flew open at that second, making her heart jump. Two bodies came flying out. To her surprise, the cops simply got out of the way before folding their arms and leveling disapproving frowns at the ejected pair. The two dazed young men staggered to their feet . . . only to go down again when two more boys landed on top of them.

They were teenagers—eighteen or nineteen from the looks of it. All were obviously drunk as hell. While the four lay there, probably moaning and wishing for death, another male walked out on his own two feet. He was older and even from this distance she could feel his fury as he picked up two of the boys and threw them into the open cab of a parked truck, his blond hair waving in the early evening breeze.

He said something to the cops that made them relax. One laughed. Having gotten rid of the first two, the blond man grabbed the other two boys by the scruffs of their necks and began to drag them back to the truck, uncaring of the gravel that had to be sandpapering skin off the exposed parts of their bodies.

Talin winced.

Those unfortunate—and likely misbehaving—boys would feel the bruises and cuts tomorrow, along with sore heads. Then the door banged open again and she forgot everything and everyone but the man framed by the light inside the bar. He had one boy slung over his shoulder and was dragging another in the same way the blond had.

"Clay." It was a whisper that came out on a dark rush of need, anger, and fear. He'd grown taller, was close to six-four. And his body—he had more than fulfilled the promise of raw power that had always been in him. Over that muscular frame, his skin shone a rich, luscious brown with an undertone of gold.

Isla's blood, Talin thought, the exotic beauty of Clay's Egyptian mother still vivid in her mind even after all these years. Isla's skin had been smooth black coffee, her eyes bitter chocolate, but she had only contributed half of Clay's genes.

Talin couldn't see Clay's own eyes from this distance, but she knew they were a striking green, the eyes of a jungle cat—an unmistakable legacy from his changeling father. Set off by his skin and pitch-black hair, those eyes had dominated the face of the boy he had been. She had a feeling they still did but in a far different way.

His every move screamed tough, male confidence. He didn't even seem to feel the weight of the two boys as he threw them into the pile already in the back of the truck. She imagined the flex of muscle, of power, and shivered . . . in absolute, unquenchable fear.

Logic, intellect, sense, it all broke down under the unadulterated flow of memory. Blood and flesh, screams that wouldn't end, the wet, sucking sounds of death. And she knew she couldn't do this. Because if Clay had scared her as a child, he terrified her now.

Shoving a hand into her mouth she bit back a cry.

That was when he froze, his head jerking up.

Dumping Cory and Jason into the cab, Clay was about to turn to say something to Dorian when he caught an almost sound on the breeze. His beast went hunting still, then pounced out with the incredibly fine senses of a leopard, while the man scanned the area with his eyes.

He knew that sound, that female voice. *It was that of a dead woman.* He didn't care. He had accepted his madness a long time ago. So now he looked, looked and searched.

For Tally.

There were too many cars in the lot across the wide road, too many places where Talin's ghost could hide. Good thing he knew how to hunt. He'd taken one step in that direction when Dorian slapped him on the back and stepped into his line of sight. "Ready to hit the road?"

Clay felt a growl building in his throat and the reaction was irrational enough to snap some sanity into his mind. "Cops?" He shifted to regain his view of the opposing lot. "They gonna give us trouble?"

Dorian shook his head, blond hair gleaming in the glow of the streetlights that had begun flicking on as built-in sensors detected the fading light. "They'll cede authority since it's only changeling kids involved. They don't have the legal right to interfere with internal Pack stuff anyway."

"Who called them?"

"Not Joe." He named the bar owner—a fellow member of DarkRiver. "He called *us*, so it must've been someone else they messed with. Hell, I'm glad Kit and Cory have worked their little pissing contest out but I never thought they'd become best fucking friends and drive us all insane."

"If we weren't having these problems with the Psy Council

trying to hurt the pack," Clay said, "I wouldn't mind dumping them in jail for the night."

Dorian grunted in assent. "Joe'll send through a bill. He knows the pack will cover the damage."

"And take it out of these six's hides." Clay thumped Cory back down when the drunk and confused kid tried to rise. "They'll be working off their debt till they graduate."

Dorian grinned. "I seem to recall raising some hell myself in this bar and getting my ass kicked by you."

Clay scowled at the younger sentinel, though his attention never left the parking area across the road. Nothing moved over there except the dust, but he was a leopard. He knew that sometimes prey hid in plain sight. Playing statue was one way to fool a predator. But Clay was no mindless beast—he was an experienced and blooded DarkRiver sentinel. "You were worse than this lot. Fucking tried to take me out with your ninja shit."

Dorian said something in response, but Clay missed it as a small Jeep peeled rapidly out of the lot that held his attention. "Kids are yours!" With that, he took off after his escaping quarry on foot.

If he had been human, the chase would've been a stupid act. Even for a leopard changeling, it made little sense. He was fast, but not fast enough to keep up with that vehicle if the driver floored it. As she—definitely *she*—now did.

Instead of swearing in defeat, Clay bared his teeth in a ruthless grin, knowing something the driver didn't, something that turned his pursuit from stupid to sensible. The leopard might react on instinct, but the human side of Clay's mind was functioning just fine. As the driver would be discovering right about . . . now!

The Jeep screeched to a halt, probably avoiding the rubble blocking the road by bare inches. The landslide had occurred only forty-five minutes ago. Usually DarkRiver would have already taken care of it, but because another small landslide had occurred in almost the exact same spot two days ago, this one had been left until it—and the affected slope—could be assessed by experts. If the woman he chased had been inside the bar, she would have heard the announcement and known to take a detour.

But she hadn't been in the bar. She'd been hiding outside.

By the time he reached the spot, the driver was trying to back out. But she kept stalling, her panic causing her to overload the computronics that controlled the vehicle. He could smell the sharp, clean bite of her fear, but it was the oddly familiar yet indefinably *wrong* scent under the fear, that had him determined to see her face.

Breathing hard but not truly winded, he came to a halt in the middle of the road behind her, daring her to run him over. Because he wasn't letting her get away. He didn't know who the hell she was, but she smelled disturbingly like Tally and he wanted to know why.

Five minutes later, the driver stopped trying to restart the car. Dust settled, revealing the vehicle's rental plates. The birds started singing again. Still he waited . . . until, at last, the door slid open and back. A slender leg covered in dark blue denim and a black ankle-length boot touched the ground.

His beast went preternaturally quiet as a hand emerged to close over the door and slide it even farther back. Freckled skin, the barest hint of a tan. A quintessentially female form unfolded itself from the Jeep. Once out of the car, she stood with her back to him for several long minutes. He didn't do anything to force her to turn, didn't make any aggressive sounds. Instead, he took the chance to drink in the sight of her.

She was small but not fragile, not easily breakable. There was strength in the straight line of her spine, but also a softness that promised a cushion for a hard male body. The woman had curves. Lush, sweet, curves. Her butt filled out the seat of her jeans perfectly, arousing the deeply sexual instincts of both man and cat. He wanted to bite, to shape, to pet.

Clenching his fists, he stayed in place and forced his gaze upward. It would, he thought, be a simple matter to lift her up by the waist so he could kiss her without getting a crick in his neck. *And he planned to kiss this woman who smelled like Talin.* His beast kept growling that she was his and, right that second, he wasn't feeling civilized enough to argue. That would come later, after he had discovered the truth about this ghost. Until then, he would drown in the rush of wild sexuality, in the familiar yet not scent of her.

Even her hair was the same unusual shade as Talin's—a rich, tawny gold streaked with chocolate brown. A mane, he'd always called it. Akin to the incredible variations of color in a leopard's fur, something outsiders often missed. To a fellow leopard, however, those variations were as obvious as spotlights. As was this woman's hair. Beautiful. Thick. *Unique*.

"Talin," he said softly, surrendering completely to the madness.

Her spine stiffened, but at last, she turned.

And the entire world stopped breathing.

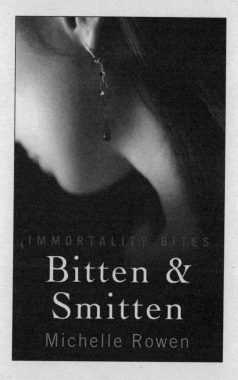

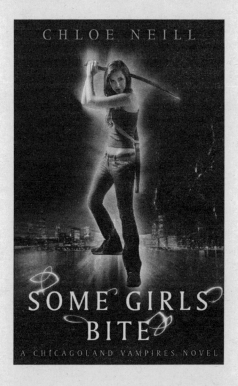

Nalini Singh is passionate about writing. Though she's travelled as far afield as the deserts of China and the temples of Japan, it is the journey of the imagination that fascinates her most. She's beyond delighted to be able to follow her dream as a writer.

Nalini lives and works in beautiful New Zealand. For contact details, and to learn more about her and her novels, please visit her website at www.nalinisingh.com.